A WOMAN BETWEEN TWO WORLDS.
A MAN BETWEEN TWO CODES.
A LAND BETWEEN TWO MASTERS.

Samantha Allyn was an innocent when she was captured by the Apaches. By the time she was returned to the white world, she was a woman, her body brutally used but still enticing, her spirit cruelly wounded but still stubbornly strong as she faced a society that welcomed her with false kindness and masked condemnation.

Lieutenant Tom Royal was the man who was to have married her, and suddenly found he could not. Torn between his vows as an officer and a gentleman and his primal male emotions, he found escape in the spreading conflagration of battle as redman and white man clashed in the great struggle for the west.

Both these people—a fiercely courageous woman and a desperately tormented man—had to find their destinies in a time of testing in an untamed land, and in the uncharted regions of their own innermost hearts . . .

Fawcett Popular Library Books
by Oliver B. Patton

☐ The Hollow Mountains   08462 $2.75
☐ My Heart Turns Back   04241 $2.75
☐ Western Wind   04634 $2.95

The Hollow Mountains

By OLIVER B. PATTON

For the Chiricahua Apache the Mountain Spirits are more important than any other supernaturals except for Child of the Water and White Painted Woman. They live in the Huachuca Mountains, which the Chiricahuas call the Hollow Mountains.

FAWCETT POPULAR LIBRARY • NEW YORK

THE HOLLOW MOUNTAINS

Published by Fawcett Popular Library, a unit of CBS Publications, the Consumer Publishing Division of CBS Inc.

ISBN: 0-445-08462-6

Printed in the United States of America

First Fawcett Popular Library printing: May 1976

11   10   9   8   7   6   5   4   3   2

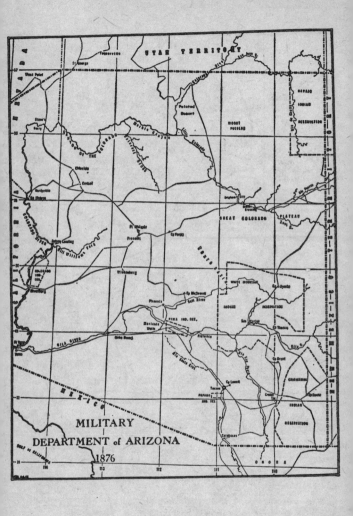

MILITARY
DEPARTMENT of ARIZONA
1876

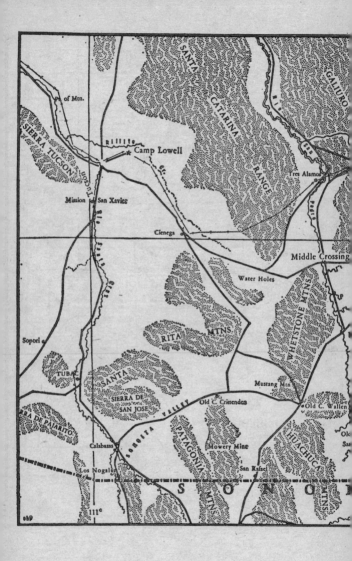

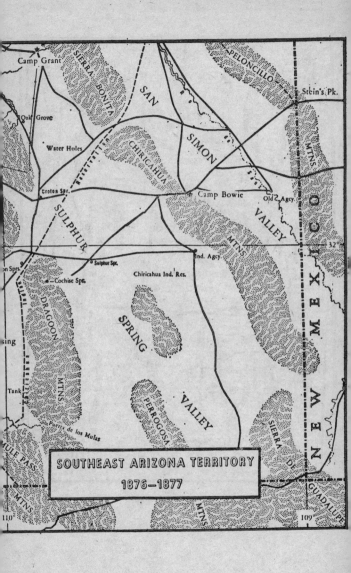

SOUTHEAST ARIZONA TERRITORY
1876–1877

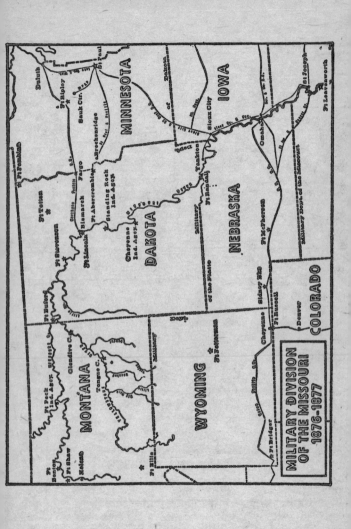

MILITARY DIVISION
OF THE MISSOURI
1876-1877

PREFACE

As the soldier-priests of Spain pressed north through Sonora and Chihuahua they encountered Indians who not only resisted Spanish civilization but struck back at it savagely. Lean brown warriors came out of their mountains like smoke on the wind, raiding and killing until the little villages around the missions were threatened with extinction. By 1700, the Spanish referred to all these incorrigibly hostile Indians as Apaches, a name translated by the peaceable Papago Indians simply as "the Enemy."

By 1876 the Apaches had been at war with the white man for more than two hundred years. The Mexican governors who replaced the Spaniards tried a policy of "extermination" that, of course, only inspired greater Apache fury. Between 1820 and 1840 they slaughtered more than five thousand Mexicans and all but wiped out their northern settlements.

In that same time, the first American trappers and prospectors appeared along the Gila River in Arizona. These mountain men got along tolerably well with the northern Apaches but the end of the war between America and Mexico brought an influx of Americans with the illogical notion that because they had defeated the Mexicans they had somehow become owners of the Apache lands. Since the Mexicans had never conquered or owned

9

the land, it baffled the Apaches how they could have lost it to anyone.

Mistrust and hostility grew until the pattern was interrupted by the American Civil War. The United States Army abandoned Arizona and New Mexico briefly to the Confederates, on whom the Apache practiced his arts until the blue-coated soldiers returned for the next round. With the end of the Civil War came an even greater swarm of American settlers, crowding the Apaches intolerably. By 1871 the uproar forced President Grant to intervene personally. The first head to roll was that of the local Army commander.

Brevet Major General George Stoneman, commanding the Military Department of Arizona, had done his best with small resources and a totally confused government policy toward the Indians. In 1870 he had waged a series of campaigns, claiming more than two hundred Apaches killed, but he had only provoked massive retaliation by the survivors. The Apaches terrorized southern Arizona and even struck at the territorial capital of Tucson. At that point the citizens took matters in their own hands. In April of 1871 they surrounded a village of peaceful Arivaipa Indians near Old Camp Grant and all but exterminated it. Most of the Indian men were absent with their chief, Eskiminzin, but the citizens' score was as repulsive as it was impressive. They killed seven men, at least seventy-five women and children, and they captured twenty-nine children, whom they sold into slavery. Arizona rejoiced but the eastern newspapers called it the Camp Grant Massacre and the President stepped in.

He sent Vincent Colyer, Chairman of the Board of Indian Commissioners, to settle the Apaches on reservations, and Colyer did fairly well. He gathered most of them onto four reservations in Arizona and New Mexico but he left out of this arrangement Cochise and his Chiricahua Apaches, who were deep in the mountains of southeast Arizona. He could find no one brave or foolish enough to go into those mountains in search of Cochise.

The War Department foresaw a steady leakage of Apaches off these reservations; they disliked the locations and they were always the ultimate losers in the war between the Army and the Interior Department over who ruled them. Stoneman retired and the Army sent in Lieutenant Colonel George Crook in his brevet rank of Major General.

Crook was the right man. He affected a shabby dress that dismayed his officers but appealed to soldiers, and he had some radical notions about Indian fighting. He separated his command from its cumbersome wagons, substituting pack mules, and he introduced winter warfare. By April 1873 he had combed central Arizona, killing or rounding up all the Apaches he encountered. He was ready then for the main event, intending, as he put it, to iron all the wrinkles out of Cochise's band, but he was forestalled by the one white man in Arizona who dared talk to Cochise on his own ground: Tom Jeffords. Before Crook could strike, Jeffords and that eccentric old soldier, General Oliver Howard, settled Cochise and his people on a generous reservation in their own mountains.

Crook was promoted to Brigadier General in the Regular Army over the heads of numerous seniors and moved to the Department of the Platte, where the Sioux promised work for a man of his talents. Colonel August Valentine Kautz, already in Arizona as commander of the Eighth Infantry Regiment, replaced him as commander of the Department, resuming his wartime rank of Brevet Major General.

When Kautz took over, Arizona was garrisoned by his own Eighth Infantry and the Fifth Cavalry Regiment. In 1875, the latter was replaced by the Sixth from Kansas, and to save money, instead of moving the regiments by rail and steamer, the War Department simply ordered them to exchange stations by marching overland, carrying with them everything they owned. It took seven months to complete the exchange and when the dust settled, Arizona was guarded by twelve troops of cavalry and twelve companies of infantry, two of the latter borrowed from the neighboring and less turbulent Department of California.

This was a relatively large force but there were signs it might be needed. The Apaches had never liked the reservations assigned them by Mister Colyer and now the Indian Bureau pressed them to move again, to a single large reservation near San Carlos. Some resisted and others simply disappeared. Special Commissioner Dudley and Agent John Clum tried to hurry reconcentration by burning the agency buildings and the huts of the White Mountain Apaches and herding their dispossessed charges toward San Carlos. About two hundred of them broke away, supposed to be headed for Cochise's reservation in southeast Arizona.

The southeastern corner of Arizona Territory was the ancient heart of Apacheria and home of the Chiricahua Apaches. There were three bands of Chiricahuas, with adjoining territories: the Mimbreños, ranging into New Mexico; the Pineria Apaches, who lived in Old Mexico; and a central band, called simply the Chiricahuas or sometimes the Cochise Apaches.

The traditional home of the central band was a broad wedge-shaped valley and the mountains enclosing it. The upper end of the wedge was called the Arivaipa, and the lower, the Sulphur Spring Valley. The whole ran northwest from the intersection of Arizona and New Mexico with Old Mexico for a hundred and thirty miles, traversed midway by the principal stage road across Arizona. This entered from the east through the Chiricahua Mountains via Apache Pass, crossed the valley floor and exited west through a gap between the Galiuro Range and the Dragoon Mountains. The fact that the Americans considered the border with Old Mexico as some sort of boundary to this wedge-shaped territory meant nothing to the Apaches.

In the spring of 1876 there were two principal occupants of the valley: the Chiricahuas and the United States Army. There were a few ranchers in the upper end but in the Sulphur Spring Valley the only white men were the Chiricahua agent, Tom Jeffords, and two men who kept the stage station at Sulphur Spring.

There were two Army posts: Camp Grant near the apex of the wedge and Camp Bowie, guarding the eastern mouth of Apache Pass. Two minor mountain ranges, the Perrogosa and the Sierra Guadalupe, thrust up into the base of the wedge from Sonora and in extension of the former several isolated buttes rose abruptly from the mesa. On these and in the surrounding mountains lived the Chiricahuas. Their famous leader, Cochise, had died in 1874 and since then his people had remained at peace on their reservation under his son, Tahzay.

It was an uneasy peace. In the preceding winter some Mimbreños and Coyoteros uprooted from the White Mountains by the Indian Bureau had moved in with the Chiricahuas and made trouble. Historic bad blood between Coyotero and Chiricahua bred fighting and some killing and by spring the Coyoteros moved on, leaving a suspicion that the white-eyes, as they called the Americans, would soon press Tahzay to move also.

Agent Jeffords shared that suspicion. In February the Indian Bureau cut off the promised supply of beef for his Indians and he had no alternative but to let Tahzay range abroad in search of food. He was nervous about this and so were the two troops of the Sixth Cavalry now garrisoning Camp Bowie. Early in April a hunting party under Tahzay moved to the Dragoon Mountains a dozen miles from the Texas and California Stage Company station at Sulphur Spring. A quarrel broke out and two men and a boy were killed, the latter a grandson of Cochise. Tahzay promptly brought most of his people back to the Agency but two brothers, Eskinyea and Pionsenay, stayed with about a dozen other men and their families. This was trouble, looking for a place to happen.

Three Coyoteros, run away from the San Carlos reservation, persuaded several of Eskinyea's young warriors to join them on a moderately successful raid into Mexico. They brought back several horses and about a hundred dollars' worth of looted gold dust and bar silver. When

13

Rogers, the stage agent, heard of this he made the worst and last mistake of his life. He let it be known he would trade whiskey for the gold or silver.

On the sixth of April he sold Pionsenay some particularly bad whiskey and next morning sold him more. That afternoon, Pionsenay and his nephew, both sullen drunk, returned to the station. Rogers had a belated attack of caution. He doled out a few drinks and said there was no more. Pionsenay did not debate the matter. He shot Rogers and helped himself. When Spence, the cook, appeared, Pionsenay killed him too. He and his nephew then packed all the food, ammunition and whiskey they could find on the station horses and rode merrily back to camp. If Eskinyea had any qualms about what they had done, they were dispelled by Rogers' evil whiskey and the whole band took the warpath joyfully.

On the eighth they killed a man named Lewis on the San Pedro River, wounded another and stole four horses. The whiskey ran out and caution returned. The brothers gathered their little band and headed for Mexico.

When Agent Jeffords learned of the murders he sent a runner to Camp Bowie and went himself to Tahzay. Lieutenant Austin Henely led forty troopers through Apache Pass at a gallop. Tahzay and his people disliked the looks of these cavalrymen and Jeffords had to stay to calm them. When he was sure they would remain at the Agency he rode after the soldiers.

He caught up with them at Sulphur Spring in time to help bury Rogers and Spence, and rode with them on Pionsenay's cold trail. By some accident, the soldiers cornered a part of the fleeing band in the San José Mountains just north of the Mexican border. The Apaches climbed to the highest peak they could find and nothing but a direct assault on foot would have carried their position. Henely rejected that. Since he had brought neither rations nor extra ammunition he could not lay siege so he called it quits, certain the renegades would run for the border as soon as he withdrew.

But as the troopers rode home, sharp eyes watched them from the heights of the Whetstone Mountains.

Pionsenay with half a dozen warriors and their women and children had separated from Eskinyea and holed up while the soldiers chased the remainder. Pionsenay was pleased to see them returning empty-handed and he sent a man to find his brother.

"Say to Eskinyea I will meet him in the Huachuca Mountains and we will stay there for a while. The white-eyes will not look for us. They think we have gone south."

He put his women and children in a deep wooded cleft among the peaks and rode north until he could look down on the stage road from Tucson to Apache Pass. He took three experienced warriors with him though he had no objective other than to see if more soldiers would ride out of their fort near Tucson.

All the next morning he watched the road. No soldiers came but about noon there was a plume of dust by the Cienega de los Pinos, turned up by the wheels of the Texas and California Company celerity wagon. There was no sign of an escort.

The stupidity of the Americans baffled Pionsenay. In the past five days he had killed three of them and wounded another. They sent horse-soldiers after him from one direction and an unguarded stage wagon from the other. He studied it longingly.

Tahzay and his American friend, the Chiricahua agent, had forbidden raiding on the American side of the border but that edict was broken now. Pionsenay was in enough trouble to make a little more insignificant. He lifted his head and grunted and his warriors grinned. That stage wagon would stop at the Middle Crossing of the San Pedro River to water the four horses.

They mounted and rode hard for the river. Even with its double team, Pionsenay knew they would be there before the stage wagon. There would be time enough to set the trap.

ONE

The eastbound stage from Tucson to Mesilla was ordinarily a two-horse, four-passenger celerity wagon but since the preceding Friday, when the Apaches killed the agent at Sulphur Spring, the wagon had been double-teamed. The Texas and California Company was not overwhelmed by the incident. Service was resumed after a one-day suspension and aside from the double team the Company's only concession was to route the stage around Sulphur Spring station for a while. Some of the passengers complained that a Concord coach would be better than the light wagon but the Company was sparing with its coaches.

The celerity wagon with its canvas top and rolled-up side curtains made passengers nervous but that was because a lot of them still thought of Indians in terms of bows and arrows. The Apaches carried the bow and even the lance but they were only substitutes for a rifle when the range was close or silence was required. If they were going to attack the stage, which the Company thought unlikely, a coach was little more protection against bullets than the wagon and the latter was a lot faster.

The morning Samantha Allyn and her aunt Thisbe Ehler boarded the stage was clear and almost chilly. There were April days in Tucson when the mercury

17

topped a hundred but this was not one of them. Thei
escort, Lieutenant Touey, failed to appear but there wer
two cavalry troopers waiting outside Major Lord's doo
when the ladies came out. They doffed their forage cap
and beamed at Samantha.

"Mornin', ma'am," said one. "Welcome to Arizona.

Samantha smiled at him happily. "Thank you. Ar
you going in the stage with us?"

"No, ma'am. We just come to help with the baggage
Mister Touey, he said to tell you he's sorry he can't b
here to see you off but he's gotta be at the commissary'
office."

"Oh, that's too bad! Are you from Camp Grant?"

"Yes'm. We're goin' back day after termorrer witl
Mister Touey. He's bound to be there in time fer th
weddin'."

They put the baggage in a pushcart and followec
Major Lord and the ladies to the stage station. Three mer
were already seated in the light wagon; one young anc
clean-shaven, the others bearded like most Samantha hac
encountered during the five jolting days of coach trave
from the California coast to Arizona. With the ladies
this would make one more passenger than the celerity
wagon was supposed to carry but the double team wa
expensive and the extra fare inclined the company to
carelessness about the rules.

The three had crowded into the front seat, according
the ladies the luxury of riding face-forward in the rear
When they climbed aboard, the young man introducec
himself. He was a whiskey drummer returning to St
Louis and he chattered amiably as if to make up for the
dour silence of his companions. Samantha smoothed her
skirt and did not mind his admiring glances as much as
she should have.

She had donned that morning an outfit made for this
day and never worn before. The skirt was plain, narrow
at the knees with just a hint of flare at the braided hem
which brushed the ground. Even the slight bustle still in
style that year had been omitted, and the severe line of
the suit was kind to her slender figure. The skirt was

topped by a basque of the same material, dark green hard-finished serge, with tailored lapels and lightly padded shoulders. It was boned and fitted very closely at waist and bosom, relieved only by a froth of ruffled blouse at her throat.

Aunt Bee had approved the fit when the tailor in Leavenworth finished the suit but Samantha paid him a surreptitious visit later and directed the reworking of several critical seams. The reappearance of the suit that morning had provoked her aunt's astonishment.

"Land sakes, Sam! What's happened to that basque?"

"Nothing, Aunt Bee. Why do you ask?"

"It didn't fit like that in Kansas! You can't have put on weight, have you?"

Major Lord had winked at her approvingly. He liked Lieutenant Royal's girl. She was slim and straight and very poised. She wore her dark hair drawn back to a smooth bun and beneath the clear line of her brows, wide gray eyes returned his look with a twinkle in their depths. Her features were a trifle thin and finely drawn for his taste but there was strength in the firm chin and wide mouth and when she smiled, her lips curved in a provocative sweetness that made him wish away his years. It was the mouth, he decided, that belied the primness of carriage and the modest eyes; the full lower lip thrusting out a little beneath the long, arching curve of the upper and the faint upturn of both at the corners. Strong, yes, but he detected beneath her composure a keenness and vivacity held deliberately in check, managed with a skill unusual for her youth.

When he handed her into the stage she did not flutter or say meaningless things. Her hand rested on his for a moment and there were dancing motes of gold in the gray eyes.

"I hope I may come back soon, Major Lord. It was very kind of you to take us in."

"My dear, it has been my great pleasure. I shall see you at your wedding if I can get to Camp Grant in time; if not, I will expect you and Tom to call as soon as you return to Tucson."

The stage rolled across the mesa at a fast clip, the lofty, pine-clad peaks of the Santa Catalina Mountains lifting to the north. The drummer pointed out the white walls of the ruined mission of San Xavier del Bac and told them how it was built by the Papago Indians and the Spanish priests who Christianized them.

According to Papago legend the padres made them fill the walls to the top with firmly mounded earth on which the dome was laid in place. To get the earth out afterward, they told their charges they had scattered gold pieces in the fill and the Papagos dug it out in search of these. Fourteen years of hard labor completed, Padre Baltasar Carillo climbed to the dome to put in place the last bricks but in his eagerness he slipped and fell to his death. The Papagos said his ghost still kept watch over the ruined building. Samantha was fascinated by the story but since it had to be shouted, the young man leaning close to tell it, she did not encourage him to go on. She leaned back and learned to hook her heels over the transverse batten on the floor between the seats and thus keep the shattering bumps from pitching her forward onto the men's knees. Her eye was caught by a glistening peak, rising far to the south, and it was not until a long time later that she learned this was Baboquivari, sacred mountain of the same Papago Indians who built and maintained the mission for many years after their Spanish priests had been driven from Arizona.

It was still pleasantly cool and the countryside was beautiful. As far as the eye could see, the mescal was heavy with soft, velvety flowers. Among this rose the white-plumed Spanish bayonet and here and there towered the stately pitahaya cactus, some still bearing ruby-colored buds of fruit not yet gathered by the birds. On their left, between the road and the Santa Caterinas, there were glimpses of the Rillito Creek in its random appearances aboveground.

Their first stop would be the Cienega, a swamp where the Rillito rose in a gap between the Sierra Colorado and the northernmost finger of the Santa Rita Mountains to he south. It was midmorning before they reached the tation, a bleached adobe building in a grove of small ines.

"Cienega Station," drawled the guard. "Change teams eah. Yew ladies want t'git out an' stretch yore laigs?"

Aunt Bee clucked disapprovingly at his language but amantha was delighted to leave the uncomfortable vagon.

"How much farther is it?"

"Tuh Croton Spring, little lady? Lessee . . . eighteen nile tuh Middle Crossin', twenny-five from theah tuh h' Spring. Make it 'bout forty-five in awl. Don't go thet way much nowadays. Jest since them Injuns raised a uckus at Sulphur Spring. Yore soljer gonna meet yuh theah, hey?"

"However did you know that?"

"Shucks! Everybody in Tucson knows 'bout yuh an' h' lootenant fixin' t' git married."

In the ramada of the station the drummer gave her a drink of warm, brackish water from the clay *olla* hanging there on the porch. She made a wry face at its taste.

"You'll get used to it, miss. This is better than most as a matter of fact."

The team was changed with practiced speed and the driver called them back to the wagon. Aunt Bee winced as she settled on the thinly padded seat.

"Mercy!" she panted, fanning herself, "I do hope it isn't too much farther."

"He said it's less than fifty miles. If we go as fast as we did this morning we can be there in four or five hours." She hoped the guard had not shortened the distance just to please her.

Their pace slackened, though, as the heat increased. The driver alternated between a walk and a trot and his passengers dozed uncomfortably. They labored up an interminable slope and after what seemed hours, topped the crest and pulled up to blow the winded horses. Aunt Bee awoke with a start.

"I don't see a soul. Where in the world are we?"

21

Her question startled Samantha from a pleasant day-dream of her own—a dream of Tom Royal and Camp Grant, though she had no idea what the Army post looked like. Her hands flew to her hair, settling the perky chip hat with its falling ribbons. She looked about doubt-fully.

"We can't be there yet, Aunt Bee." Nevertheless she searched for the blue-clad troopers who should be wait-ing for them. She brushed at the dust on her skirt. "Do I look all right?"

Her aunt smiled at her. "You look good enough to eat, Sam."

The whiskered face of the guard appeared beside them and he made a necessary rearrangement of the wad of tobacco in his cheek.

"Yew ladies makin' out awl raht?"

"Oh, yes . . . we're fine. But where are we now?"

He shook his head good-naturedly at Samantha and spat copiously. "Raht down theah a piece is thuh Middle Crossin' o' th' San Pedro Rivah." He pointed to a belt of green traversing the desert. "Croton Spring's 'bout thutty mile more."

Samantha let her breath out in a long sigh. It was taking forever and a day to get there, she thought.

"Well, why are we stopping here?" demanded Aunt Bee crossly.

"Got tuh blow them hosses, ma'am. We bin climbin' raht smart tuh git heah. Soon's they's blowed we'll git on down an' water 'em an' then we'll be gone. Y'awl want out agin?"

Aunt Bee shook her head but Samantha jumped down. Her narrow heels sank in the sand, throwing her off-balance, and the guard steadied her with a hand on her arm. "Keerful, missy! Gotta git yew thar safe an' sound. Don' want no trouble with thet soljer o'yourn."

"Merciful Lord!" gasped Aunt Bee. "Isn't it hot! Sa-mantha, you shouldn't walk in that sun."

Obediently Samantha hugged the wagon and the scrap of shade cast by its canvas top. The horses scented water and stamped restlessly while the driver went to each, lifting hooves to look for stones.

The guard lounged against the dashboard, shotgun cradled in his arm, and pretended to study the green trace of the San Pedro River but Samantha knew he was really watching her. It bothered her no more than the admiring looks of the drummer. She was too full of her own happiness to be bothered by that. She caught his eye and smiled, not flirtatiously but joyously, only wanting to share with him her happiness.

Suddenly and incredibly the iron-strapped top of the dashboard exploded with a shower of splinters that stung her face. The air split with a crack and there was a distant sound as if someone had beaten a carpet.

The guard groaned and tobacco juice sprayed from his lips. He bent over as if searching for something on the ground, kept on bending until he sprawled at Samantha's feet and the shotgun rapped her ankles painfully.

"Hi!" squalled the driver. "Git in! Git in thuh gawdam waggin!"

Kee-rack . . . wump! The sounds were closer together this time. One of the horses screamed and collapsed, threshing in the harness. There was a distant drumming of hooves on hardpan and a lost, terrifying howling. Through the mesquite Samantha caught a glimpse of a running horse, fast-running on a long arc that bent toward the stage. She saw no rider; more horses but no riders.

"Samantha!" wailed her aunt.

The drumming turned to thunder that struck her a stunning blow and spun her around to see the rump of a spotted pony scrambling like a cat in the sand as it plunged in front of the rearing team.

She saw the rider now. He stretched out an elongated arm that spat smoke and a pale orange flash that knocked the driver from his seat.

The maddened team lunged around the downed horse and the stage jerked away from her. She ran after it but the spotted pony came back to block her. Its head struck at her, snakelike with wild, white-rimmed eyes, foam

23

spraying from the nostrils. She fended it off with both hands and almost went under the flying hooves but her hair was caught and jerked her forward in a shower of hairpins. She was jolted along for an agonized moment, then dropped.

On her knees she looked for the stage. It was too far away. She scrambled for the mesquite, hobbled by her skirt, and heard again the rasping breath and thudding hooves of the pony.

But this was a different one, gray and bigger. Through the screen of her flying hair she saw the rider quite clearly. Where there should have been eyes there were only black slits in a band of yellow encircling the face. She knew what he carried in his hand. Beyond the clump of feathers metal glinted in the sun. She had seen these on the wall of the Officers' Mess at Fort Leavenworth. She had no breath left to cry out. She turned, turned again, tried to run and went to her knees in the sand, waiting for the antique barbarity of the lance in her flesh.

It did not strike. The horse blew foam in her face and she was caught by her hair again, hauled to her feet and dragged alongside the walking horse. There were no more shots. No more howling. She could not count the Indians milling about the stage. One of them brought a team horse with the cut harness still trailing behind him and she was hoisted roughly onto his back.

She saw her aunt clinging to the side of the stage wagon. "Aunt Bee!" she cried out and someone struck her a blow on the temple that made her reel. She clutched the horse dizzily, knowing if she fell she would be trampled or they would kill her.

The rump of the gray horse backed into her, crushing her legs, then went away fast and her own horse broke into a lumbering canter, shying around a bearded man face up in the sand. The harness rings gouged her thighs and beside her now rode the nightmare figure with yellow-striped face and black hair bound in a twist of cloth.

"Hai!" he yelled. "Hai-yah!" slashing with a quirt at

her horse. There were horses all around her, dim figures in the choking dust; they went at a pounding run across the desert and into the mouth of a canyon, then up and up until the canyon was a narrow slot floored with sliding gravel in which the stage horse floundered clumsily. The pace slowed but for Samantha everything was motion. She moved and so did everything around her in a blur of men and horses and earth. She understood nothing but the absolute necessity to stay on the horse's plunging back.

They reached a crest and paused. The stage horse hung his head and blew in great racking gasps. His neck was soapy with sweat. She looked for Aunt Bee but saw only the despairing, death-white face of the young drummer before the Indian gave his barking cry and plied the quirt again.

Her horse shambled forward but would not run until the hideously striped face bent toward her, an arm reaching down. She shrank from the knife but it was not for her. With a squeal of agony the stage horse lunged forward.

They went on and up endlessly. If there were a trail she could not see it. Sometimes her legs were crushed against the rocks as the terrified horse leaned away from an abyss. When they rode into stunted pines that slashed her face and tore her hands from their grip she knew she was close to the end of her strength. She put her face on the sweat-slick neck of the horse and sobbed. The trees grew taller, shutting out the sky, and they went silently now on a carpet of pine needles. She heard dogs barking, a high-pitched, excited yapping; then there were children running beside her. A young Indian woman caught the horse's head and yelled something. She stared uncomprehending and was pulled off the staggering horse.

The woman jerked her arm and struck her repeatedly with a switch, pointing at a low hut among the trees. Samantha ran to it, dropped to her knees and crawled inside into an acrid smell of smoke and untanned hides.

25

Aunt Bee was thrust in beside her and they clung to each other, deafened by the bedlam outside.

"Aunt Bee . . . Aunt Bee, what will happen to us? What will they do to us now?"

The older woman did not answer, only rocked to and fro, whimpering. Samantha could not make her speak.

They were left alone. The sun went down and the wickiup, or hut, grew dark inside. Aunt Bee lay face down and shuddered and nothing Samantha could do would comfort her. The shouts and the barking of the dogs outside never seemed to slacken but now, in the night, they grew to a terrifying uproar. The Indian woman came back with a knife instead of the switch and gestured menacingly.

"¡Venga!" she hissed. Aunt Bee wailed and the girl kicked her. "¡Venga pronto!"

"Aunt Bee, come on!" Samantha begged. "Don't make her angry! She wants us to go out!" She urged her aunt before her, flinching from the knife point that pricked her forward. Under the trees a fire burned with Indians crowded about it.

The woman pushed through the people, clearing a way with sharp, peremptory cries. Brown faces hemmed them in; broad faces with glittering eyes and open mouths shouting unintelligible things. Samantha clung to Aunt Bee and the slender brown Apache woman shoved them both.

"¡Mire!" she commanded and Samantha looked where she pointed. Her stomach heaved in revolt.

Suspended by the ankles from a tree branch, the naked white body of the whiskey drummer writhed and jerked. The women prodded him with sticks and giggled when he yelled. Samantha put her hands over her eyes but they pulled them down.

"¡Mire!"

"Oh, Lord!" whimpered Aunt Bee. "Oh, Lord God . . ."

The drummer raved and struggled while the Apache women built a little fire beneath his head. An Indian man squatted by the captive, smiling. Now and again he patted the white man's shoulder and said something to

26

im but he did not hurt him. That was left to the women. They fanned their little fire and blew on it cautiously. There was a smell of burning hair and the drummer screamed. His face was just above the coals and he coughed horribly. Between spasms of coughing he cursed and screamed and Samantha fought back waves of nausea.

"Let me go!" she begged. "Please, let me go! I don't want to see!"

But they would not let her go nor would they allow her to shut her eyes. When she did the Apache girl stung her with the knife. The naked white body jerked like a piked fish and the curses changed to pleas. The women fed their fire with twigs but they did not let it flame up about the blackened face. In that sooty mask the eyes rolled white and mad with agony.

The drummer set his body swinging and the Apaches did not stop him. The longer he did this, the longer he would stay alive. That was what they wanted. In the end his brains would roast in his skull and they were content for him to put this off as long as he could.

Time passed slowly and horribly. The drummer's crazy jackknifing stopped and he hung limp, making a hoarse animal sound. His cheeks popped and hissed. Fat sputtered in the fire and Samantha was violently and helplessly sick. The Indian women drew back and struck her in disgust.

When their victim no longer even groaned the women poked him with their sticks. They consulted in low voices and tried again with knives. The blackened, hairless head lolled unrecognizable and there was no sign of life. The drummer was dead or gone where even the knives could not recall him so the women drove Samantha and her aunt back into the wickiup with blows and laughter.

Samantha wondered hopelessly when their turn would come. There were stars outside, and somewhere a pleasant tinkle of falling water. She craved water, her mouth evil-tasting in the aftermath of nausea, but she was afraid to ask for a drink.

After a while the Apache girl came into the hut and rolled herself into a blanket without a word or look. Samantha pressed close to Aunt Bee and waited, wondering. She slept in brief snatches, overwhelmed by exhaustion. For a while there was a murmur of voices outside and occasionally a coal in the fire snapped but no one came for them.

TWO

Camp Grant in 1876 was the largest Army post in Arizona. Commanded by Major Charles Compton of the Sixth Cavalry, it was garrisoned by three troops of his regiment and a company of the Eighth Infantry: eleven officers and more than two hundred soldiers in all.

Both civilians and military called it New Camp Grant because for twelve years there had been another Camp Grant forty-five miles northwest at the junction of the Arivaipa and San Pedro rivers, abandoned in 1872 when malarial fevers threatened to wipe out the garrison. The new post at the foot of Mount Graham in the upper Arivaipa Valley was healthier and far more pleasant.

Where the camp lay, the valley was about fifteen miles wide. Eighty miles northeast on the Gila River was the San Carlos Indian Agency in charge of a young man named John Clum. Tucson and headquarters of the Sixth Cavalry at nearby Camp Lowell were a hundred and sixteen miles west via a passable wagon road running south down the valley to join the east-west stage route.

The post was laid out around a parade ground sloping rather sharply to the south, on which side stood the soldiers' barracks. On the east and west sides were hospital, guardhouse, warehouses and offices for the adjutant, quartermaster and commissary. Here was the terminus of the military telegraph line from California which had reached Camp Grant in February, but since there was a ninety-mile gap between Grant and the New Mexico border where the line from the east ended, a message to Washington still had to go via California.

The north side of the parade ground was given over to officers' quarters. Several of these were imposing buildings of stone laid in mud mortar with wooden floors and ceilings but the remainder were of the usual frontier pattern with rammed earth floors and no ceilings. In these, muslin stretched from wall to wall at the top of the partitions served as a ceiling and gave a false sense of privacy to the two or more families sharing the structure.

Off the southwest corner of the quadrangle stood the post trader's store and behind it a long, low adobe building divided into two-room accommodations for sixteen married soldiers. Officially the laundresses' quarters, this was always called Suds Row and the soldiers who occupied it did so by virtue of the special status of their wives.

Since 1802 a regulation had specified that every company in the Army could have four laundresses, each entitled to rations, quarters and government transportation when her company moved. There might have been a time in the Army when a company laundress was an unmarried female whose principal concern was washing clothes but in 1876 this ancient regulation provided the only means by which a soldier could marry and keep his family with him.

The Army would not knowingly enlist a married man and no soldier could marry openly without his commander's permission. Particularly on the frontier this was never given unless a vacancy existed among the laundresses of the soldier's company. The system was under

29

perennial attack by the Inspector General of the Army who found it impractical, expensive and often inhumane Government transport for a laundress was rarely more than a place for her and her children in a baggage wagon, and in the West the housing was likely to bear out his views. The Army took care of its own as best it could but officers' ladies and laundresses alike often lived in tents or adobe huts.

In 1876 Inspector General Marcy was inflamed anew by an investigation into the use of tea by the Army. An equally antique regulation authorized a pound and a half of tea for every hundred rations issued and it required little effort to establish that soldiers never drank it. Still it was being drawn regularly. A laundress was entitled to a ration a day and with it went the tea. Marcy's computations showed that laundresses cost the government several hundred thousand dollars a year which he deemed unjustified by their services. He prodded Secretary of War Belknap until the latter recommended to President Grant that half the laundresses in the Army be dropped from the rolls.

Old Soldier Grant delayed and in March of 1876 Belknap resigned his post in haste as Congress began looking into some unusual financial arrangements between his wife and the post trader at Fort Sill in the Indian Territory. Post traders throughout the Army were appointed to their virtual monopolies by the Secretary of War.

But the laundresses of Camp Grant had long since formed an indecent opinion of Mister Belknap and were not surprised by the scandal, which took second place to far more exciting news of the moment. In addition to the sixteen soldiers' wives at Camp Grant there were no less than six officers' ladies and the wife of the post trader and this unusually large feminine contingent was about to receive a new recruit.

In 1874 when the Sixth Cavalry was in western Kansas, Second Lieutenant Thomas Jefferson Royal graduated from West Point and joined Captain Tullius Tupper's G Troop. At Fort Leavenworth Tom Royal met the daughter of an infantry officer who had been killed in the Oregon Indian wars and his subsequent long-distance courtship of Samantha Allyn had been a major concern of the ladies of the regiment. They rejoiced when she accepted him; agonized with him when border troubles canceled his leave at Christmas of 1875 when they were to be married at Leavenworth. At their urging he asked Samantha to come on to Camp Grant and be married there and they held their breath until she agreed.

Samantha's mother had survived her husband only three years and thereafter she had lived with a formidable maiden aunt who would, of course, come with her to the wedding. All Camp Grant followed anxiously the westward progress of Samantha and her aunt Thisbe Ehler.

Camp Grant had never had a wedding and its first would be a grand one. There was neither chapel nor chaplain but the only chaplain in the Department had promised to come all the way from Prescott to marry Tom Royal and his girl. The wedding would be in Major Compton's quarters, which he now doubted were his at all. As the wedding date drew nearer, women and soldiers swarmed over the house, painting and patching and scrubbing.

One of the garrison officers, in San Francisco to attend a court-martial, was charged with procuring champagne and his success was legendary. By some miracle he returned with forty-eight straw-wrapped bottles which survived their journey by steamer, barge and wagon. Before the snow disappeared from the top of Mount Graham a quantity of it was packed into wooden boxes, hauled down and buried under sawdust in a pit. The Good Templars Lodge was borrowed and furbished for a gala reception after the wedding and by the eighth of April all was ready.

Into these happy preparations like a bombshell fell the news of the murders at Sulphur Spring. General Kautz alerted every cavalry troop within reach of the Chiricahua reservation and Colonel Oakes, Sixth Cavalry com-

31

mander, restricted the three troops at Camp Grant to the post under orders to march on three hours' notice.

The ladies raged and their husbands grumbled but Major Compton would make no exception. Lieutenant Royal could not be spared to meet his girl in Tucson. But the trouble did not spread as expected. Camp Bowie reported the Chiricahuas quiet with only a few renegades running for the border and Lieutenant Henely after them. The stage company missed only one day's run from Tucson to Mesilla and when they resumed business they routed the stage through Croton Spring, so close to Camp Grant that Major Compton relented and said Tom could meet his ladies there.

Providentially Lieutenant Touey of C Troop was in Tucson and he could meet Samantha and her aunt. He was given his instructions by telegraph and again the ladies rejoiced. The wedding could take place in spite of the alert, which would only add a dash of excitement.

On the night of April eleventh, Tim Touey telegraphed that Samantha and her aunt had arrived. They would stay that night with Major Lord, the district quartermaster in Tucson, and take the stage east next day. By noon they should be at Croton Spring.

There was an impromptu bachelor dinner in the Officers' Mess that night with the usual songs and jokes but not much to drink. Major Compton attended to see to that. He was only forty, young for his rank in 1876, but he had seen a lot of service and he remembered his orders to put three troops of cavalry in the field on three hours' notice.

Tom Royal needed no drink to sustain his happiness. Both Compton and Tom's troop commander, Tullius Tupper, had always considered him a bit too reserved and intense a young man but this night he surprised them. His sandy hair tousled and damp from some prank involving a cup of water, he responded gaily to the chaffing of his friends. Lean-flanked and long-legged, he was a big, solid man with a driving energy that showed even when he was still. His blue eyes sparkled now and his normally serious mouth relaxed. Now that he was to be married, the other lieutenants told him, he had to grow a mustache. Unlike most of them, Tom Royal remained as clean-shaven as a cadet. They sat upon him and with some vile-smelling substance for adhesive provided him with a flowing beard and mustache of frayed hemp which matched his hair and brows in color and looked astonishingly real.

Major Compton approved. There was no more promising young officer in the regiment, but to his way of thinking Tom Royal needed chaffing. He was overly serious, too ambitious and sometimes humorless. That last flaw, in the major's view, was most serious and needed correcting.

By midmorning next day Tom and an escort of troopers were off for Croton Spring, accompanied by a curtained ambulance for the ladies.

The soldiers had taken unusual pains with their appearance and looked a little solemn in consequence. In honor of the occasion they wore their dark blue flannel fatigue blouse and forage caps instead of the usual field dress of gray wool shirt and black campaign hat. As soon as they had disappeared, Camp Grant began some last-minute preparations.

A Dougherty wagon, top off, was given a last rubdown and trimmed with greens and paper streamers. The rest of G Troop polished its buttons and prepared to meet the returning couple at Riley's ranch, just outside the post. Here the sprightly Dougherty wagon would replace Tom's ambulance and be led home by a makeshift band composed of the cavalry trumpeters with the fifers and drummers of the infantry company.

Camp Grant waited. They waited through the scorching heat of noon and into the afternoon, at first amused, then irritated and finally alarmed. About two o'clock Lieutenant Kerr, the adjutant, came to whisper to Major Compton. The telegraph was dead. It was so often dead this proved nothing but Compton took the news unhappily. When at last a cloud of dust, moving far too rapidly, rolled up the road from Croton Spring, he watched it grimly.

There were only four riders and the ambulance, bouncing emptily behind them. One man rode for the parade ground, where the officers and ladies were gathered, and the rest broke off at the stables. Corporal Tinney came off his lathered horse stiff-legged and his face told them all they needed to know.

"What happened, Tinney?"

He had trouble getting the words out. "Middle Crossin', sir. Driver must of stopped to water th' team. They killed him an' the guard and a couple passengers . . . both men."

"The women?"

"No sign. Some footprints . . . women's shoes. One team horse left. They shot him an' cut him outta th' harness. Took all the rest."

"Where's Mister Royal and the rest of the men?"

"Lookin'," replied Tinney glumly.

"Dammit to hell! With six men?"

"Four, sir. Lootenant Royal he sent Sarn't Lowery and Miller to Reg'ment at Lowell. Them telegraph wires was cut an' he said they'd oughtta know what happened fast. He told me to bring th' ambulance back and tell you about it."

Compton swore again under his breath and pulled out his watch. It was after four o'clock.

"Not one damned thing I can do now!"

It was a double disaster. Four civilians murdered and two women gone. Four soldiers and a grief-crazed lieutenant searching for death. Their own if there were enough Indians, and it would not take many to ambush four troopers with Royal leading them; the lives of the captive women if they pressed a small band too hard. Even the girl couldn't keep up and they would kill her. He did not like to think about the older woman's chances. He shut the watch case with a snap and put it away; struck his hands together in a gesture of frustration. The sound echoed against the barracks where the soldiers stood in groups and eyed him curiously.

"All right. First light tomorrow we'll take a troop and look for them. I want the best two Indian scouts we've

34

got. Mister Kerr, get the orders out and . . ." he looked at the women talking in hushed voices among themselves. "Get this damned post undecorated before daylight."

THREE

The door of the wickiup faced east and caught the first faint light of dawn. Samantha turned on her side and tried to identify what she could see through it. Somewhere a dog barked monotonously. Fool thing, she thought. They must feel quite safe or they would never let him make that noise.

She had slept. Even the hideous death of the drummer could not stay the exhaustion that overcame her.

The wickiup was chilly in the time before dawn but the offensive odors remained. She glanced at the Indian girl who slept soundlessly and thought of crawling nearer the door so she might see more but put the thought from her. It seemed essential that neither she nor Aunt Bee provoke their captors in any way. They had killed the drummer and they might only have waited until today to kill them. But this was a thought she could not entertain. That they were alive at all seemed to her a miracle that must be prolonged by every means. If they could give Tom a little time he would find a way to free them.

Aunt Bee moaned and tossed in her sleep. She lay face down in a sprawl that was shocking to Samantha. Let her sleep, she thought. She will need it. Someone kicked the dog or threw something at him. He ki-yi'd shrilly for a moment and subsided.

She must have dozed again for movement in the hut snapped her fully awake. There was more light and the Apache girl was on her knees, twisting her hair into a knot on the nape of her neck.

She guessed the girl was not much older than herself, though it was hard to tell. She was slender, dressed in a two-piece garment of what Samantha supposed was deerskin, a loose, open-necked blouse and a straight skirt ending just below her knees. She was not unattractive. Her hands and feet were small and her face, though wide across the cheekbones, was handsome, the mouth well-shaped, almost delicate. High on each cheek was a small blue dot, too regular and evenly spaced to be a blemish; obviously a tattoo of some sort. Her hands moved swiftly and she dressed her hair without help of a mirror. When it was knotted she put over the knot a form of stiffened hide in the shape of an hourglass and pulled on high, soft moccasins. This apparently completed her toilet for she gathered some utensils and went outside. Samantha lay motionless. An occasional clink or rattle indicated the Apache girl had not gone far.

The sun climbed until there was a beam of light through the door and now there were many sounds outside. Aunt Bee stirred and Samantha helped her to sit up. She was horrified by the older woman's face. Her skin was tallow-colored; her eyes blank and expressionless.

She tried with her fingers to comb the straw from her aunt's hair. It was hopeless and she gave up. Her own hair was in wild disorder and she had not enough pins left to do anything with it except tie it in a ponytail with a scrap of braid torn from her skirt. The beautiful skirt was ruined, split from knee to hem.

The Indian girl brought a bowl of some sort of mash and put it between them. There were no utensils and Samantha sucked a little from her fingers, finding it as evil-tasting as it smelled. Aunt Bee would neither taste nor smell it.

Nevertheless, Samantha was encouraged. It did not seem to her they would feed their captives if they meant to kill them. This small comfort was short-lived in the face of what happened next.

Aunt Bee stopped mumbling to herself and got to her knees. "Come, Samantha," she said firmly. Samantha stared at her in astonishment. "We are late. Come!"

"Aunt Bee? Where are you going? What's the matter? Aunt Bee . . . wait! Don't go outside!" She was not quick enough. The older woman was out the door before she could stop her. Samantha crawled after her.

"Aunt Bee . . . wait!" she cried. Half in and half out of the hut she crouched, appalled by the older woman's behavior.

Three Indians were squatting around the firepit before the wickiup; the girl, an older woman, very fat, and a man. All three were eating from a communal bowl and all three stared woodenly at Aunt Bee, who walked toward them brushing her clothes vigorously. "Oh, God!" Samantha moaned.

Her fear sickened her. She was afraid to leave the hut but Aunt Bee's trouble was her own and she had to do what she could. The man was on his feet now, watching the white woman closely.

"Samantha, we are late for church," said Aunt Bee in a matter-of-fact way. "If you do not come at once I shall start without you."

It was a thing she had said at least once every Sunday in Samantha's memory, and she had a wild urge to make her ritual response: I am coming, Aunt Bee, there is no earthly need to be early. The insanity of the thing made her head spin. Either her aunt was deranged by the horror of her situation or she had hit on some scheme to try to delude her captors.

Samantha scrambled to her feet and caught her aunt in three running steps. "Aunt Bee!" she said soothingly. "Come back, Aunt Bee . . . please come back!" The older woman gave her a blank look and pushed her hands away.

"I shall not be late," she said. She walked around the firepit straight toward the man and began in a clear, cracked voice to sing:

> "Angel voices, ever singing
> Round Thy throne of light,
> Angel harps for ever ringing,
> Rest not day nor night . . ."

To Samantha's astonishment the Apache got out of the way and let her aunt walk across the clearing into the trees on the other side. Scattered among these were more wickiups and every door held a couple of heads. Some children who had been playing in the open scattered excitedly.

Summoning her courage, Samantha gathered up her ruined skirt and ran. Her flesh crawled for she had no idea what the Indians would do. The man said something quickly and the Apache girl caught her arm.

"Let me go!" she panted. "Please let me go! She's sick . . . she doesn't know what she's doing. Let me go to her!"

The man was gone, walking fast across the clearing. Two others appeared, looking from Aunt Bee to him questioningly. They made no move until he spoke, then one followed the woman and the other ran for a line of horses picketed under the trees.

"Aunt Bee!" Samantha wailed, struggling with the Apache girl. "Come back, Aunt Bee!" She jerked violently, trying to pull free.

My God, she thought, what is the matter with her? "Please . . ." she begged the girl. "Let me go! Don't hurt her!"

If only there were someone who could speak her language. The futility of her pleas was obvious. Wrenching her arm from the girl's hand she started in a stumbling run after her aunt. She did not hear the older Apache woman who was suddenly beside her, moving with startling speed for all her bulk. Deftly she kicked Samantha's ankle, the soft moccasin giving no pain but the blow skillfully directed to tangle the white girl's feet and send her to her knees. Samantha tried to get up and the fat woman struck her with her fist.

"*Dah!*" she hissed.

Whatever she said, the meaning was clear. Tangled in her skirt and restrained by the hand on her shoulder, Samantha could do nothing. She watched her aunt disappear among the pines, the Apache warrior treading cautiously after her.

The older Apache who had sent the young warriors after Samantha's aunt walked to the wickiup of Pionsenay, war chief and captor of the white women. He cleared his throat and waited.

In a moment Pionsenay appeared and greeted him. His visitor spoke, dropping his voice into the deeper register of formal communication which was different from the higher-pitched voice of ordinary conversation.

"Behold!" he pointed with his fist. "The old woman walks away singing." Pionsenay looked and his face was troubled.

"Does she sing her death song or is it magic?"

"I do not know, my brother, but her eyes are bad. She looked at me and my stomach is cold." Pionsenay shot him a concerned look.

"You think she is a witch?"

The other shook his head. "She was not like that at first. It is in my mind that when the white man died she became sick in her eyes and maybe in her head too."

"*Loco,*" Pionsenay murmured and the other nodded.

"This may be. I have told Tudeevia to walk behind and watch where she goes and what she does. If she stops to make magic then he will know she is a witch and what he must do."

". . . and if she does not make magic?"

"Tudeevia will follow her and Schnowin will bring horses. Together they will go where she goes and one will return to tell what she does."

"*Enju!* It is good, my brother. I have seen *Nakaiyi*

39

captives grow sick like that. If the old woman is playing tricks, Tudeevia and Schnowin will know it and bring her back. If she is *loco* she will die soon and that is best."

Faintly the morning breeze brought Aunt Bee's hymn to Samantha:

> ". . . Thousands only live to bless Thee,
> And confess Thee Lord of might."

O Lord, she prayed. Help her. Don't let them kill her. Don't let them kill me either, she wanted to add but it seemed inappropriate. One at a time is enough for any God and we have worked him hard these two days. She remained on her knees until the Apache girl pulled her up.

"*¡Venga!*" she said and Samantha knew what it meant; it was Mexican. She cursed the idleness that kept her from studying the Spanish grammar she took from the library at Leavenworth weeks before she began her journey.

With no words in common both she and her captors were at an impasse, yet the two Apache women tried repeatedly to make her understand something they wanted of her. She could only shake her head in bewilderment. She caught an occasional word of Spanish but they were few and her knowledge of the language was less than superficial. She tried to be attentive, to show she wanted to understand, but she was distracted by thoughts of Aunt Bee and the breathy singsong torrent of sound dismayed and confused her. The fat woman grew irritable and raised her hand as if to strike. Samantha's wandering attention fixed on her at once.

I have to learn how to deal with this, she told herself. There has got to be a way and I have only one chance to learn it. Steeling herself for the blow, she waited. The Apache saw this and held her hand. She expected the white girl to cringe. When she did not, she also waited to see what would happen.

Nothing happened. Samantha gripped shaking hands

before her and faced it out. The woman was impressed. She did not lower herself to test the white girl by feinting blows. She dropped her hand and spoke to the Apache girl, who nodded and went away.

Samantha's nerves screamed. She could face the immediate threat but waiting to know what would come next was worse. After a while the girl returned, accompanied by a boy. His age was indeterminate to Samantha but he was slight of build and he looked very young.

"¿Americana?" he asked. Samantha marshaled her fragmentary Spanish.

"Sí . . . yo soy americana." He looked surprised.

"¡Pero niña, tu comprendes español!" He glanced at the Apache women. "¿Qué pasa?"

"No!" said Samantha. "I don't really. I have only a few words." It was so hopeless. "Isn't there anyone here who speaks American?"

The youth grinned. "Yes. I speak it good."

Her relief was shattering in its intensity. She had an impulse to reach out and touch him in gratitude. There were so many questions crowding to be asked she did not know where to begin.

"My aunt . . ." she pointed toward the trees where Aunt Bee had disappeared. "Where has she gone? What have they done with her?"

The youth shook his head. He was listening to the Apache woman. Samantha was too excited to notice. "Please tell me!" she begged.

"Shoosh!" he said sharply.

"What?"

"Shut the mouth . . . be silent!" She drew back as if he had struck her.

He continued listening respectfully to the fat woman until she had finished, a point she emphasized by walking away and leaving Samantha with the two younger people. The youth frowned at her, increasing her apprehension until she realized he was only gathering rusty English.

"Sheneah," he gestured toward the departing woman,

then at the hut in which Samantha had spent the night, "she say you stay there. You do what Aludin say you do." This time he nodded to the Apache girl. "She is Aludin."

"She is what?" asked Samantha, baffled.

"Ah-lhu-deen! That is her name." It was still not clear, but Samantha waited to see if he would say more. When he did not, she addressed him softly but urgently.

"I don't want to stay here. I want my aunt. I want to find her and we want to go back to our people. We belong to the soldiers . . . the American soldiers."

"Soldiers?" He seemed surprised at that.

"Yes. If you do not take us back to them there will be trouble for you." He listened with a smile on his lips, shaking his head at her words.

"Do you want to start a war?" she demanded bravely. "If you do not free us the soldiers will come." He laughed and spat on the ground rudely. It struck Samantha he was very young indeed. The action had the bravado of a boy.

"Start war? When is no war between Indians and soldiers?"

"Then tell them we are here! They will give you a reward." He frowned.

"What is that?"

"A reward . . ." she explained patiently, "is something good. They will give you money if you take us back. If you do not they will come and fight for us."

"That bad," he told her. "You better hope they don' come fight. My people go away fast . . . very fast. Maybe you don' keep up with them."

His meaning was dreadfully clear. Samantha changed her tack. "But won't you tell them we are here? They will search for us and if they do not know where we are they may come here before you know it."

"We know when they ride out of their forts!" he said proudly. "Let them come." She sighed. This was getting her nowhere.

"What about my aunt? I want my aunt. Do you know where she has gone?"

"What? What you want?"

"My aunt . . ." She tried to find the Spanish word and failed. "The woman with gray hair who went into the forest. Did you see her?" He nodded warily. "Well, where did she go? What did they do to her?" A closed, sullen look settled upon his face.

"I do not know." No matter how she framed the question that was all she got from him.

"What about me? What am I to do?"

"I tol' you! You stay there . . ." pointing at the wickiup, "and do what Aludin say you do."

"How can I do what she says when I don't know what she is saying?" Samantha burst out in exasperation. He shrugged, the vacuous grin fixed on his lips once more.

"She show you. You don' do it, she beat you!" He rubbed his backside suggestively.

"But . . . what then? I must know what will happen!"

"You work. You work for Aludin and for Sheneah until . . ." He shrugged, leaving it unfinished. But Samantha had caught his words.

"Until what?" she demanded eagerly.

"I don' know. Mebbeso Catle he know but he don' tell me."

"Who?" She was trying hard to understand his dislocated English. "Who knows?"

"Him . . . Catle!" He jerked his head angrily toward the older Apache who had walked back from the wickiup of Pionsenay to watch this scene disapprovingly.

To all her questions he only shook his head and frowned. He would tell her nothing more. That was clear. She tried to smile at him, beseechingly.

"Will you help me then . . . please?" He looked doubtful.

"How?"

"Find my aunt and bring her back. She is sick. She must have help. Bring her back to me, please." But any mention of Aunt Bee only returned the sullen look to his face. "Won't you at least find out what happened to her and tell me?" she begged. He shook his head. Nothing.

"Will you come and talk to me again?"

"Maybe."

"How can I ask for you? I don't even know your name."

"I am Severiano."

She repeated it carefully "Say-ver-i-a-no!" He nodded, beaming.

"How they call you, *Americana?*" he asked her.

"I am Samantha . . . Samantha Allyn."

"Sah-mahn-tallen?" he tried it, puzzled.

"No. Sah-man-tha is my first name. That is what I am called. Allyn is my last name . . . family name." He shrugged.

"I call you Sah-mahn-ta. That is hard enough." The Apache girl was growing restless. She spoke to him sharply. He nodded. "You go now, Sah-mahn-ta. You do what she say . . . you know? You don' do it and they beat you, *comprendes?*"

"Yes, I will try. When will you come back?" She was frightened and her loneliness overwhelmed her.

"I don' know. Maybe soon. *Adiós* . . . so long!" He brought out the familiar expression with pride, watching for its effect on her. Aludin was plucking at her arm and she did not notice. She had found someone who spoke her language and he would tell her nothing she needed to know. She was tormented by her fears for Aunt Bee. Miserably she followed the Apache girl to the wickiup.

No time was wasted on the beginning of her education. From a willow basket Aludin spilled what looked like grass seeds into a hollowed rock. Taking another stone, rounded as if it had lain for a long time in a stream, she used this to grind and crush the seeds. Then she gestured for the white girl to begin.

Samantha dropped to her knees obediently and took the grinding stone. When she bent her corset stabbed her and the stiffly boned basque bound her arms. My God, she thought, I cannot work in these clothes and I don't know how to tell her.

She thought of asking for Severiano again but a look at

44

the Apache girl's sullen face dispelled that idea. I have to do something, she decided. She got up and unbuttoned the basque, pointed at the wickiup and made a gesture of taking it off. The Apache nodded.

The hut was nearly seven feet tall at the center and Samantha could stand upright there. While the Apache watched curiously, she stripped off the basque and the flimsy blouse beneath it. She handed the basque to Aludin, who fingered the whalebone stays and looked puzzled. Samantha longed for privacy but she supposed she would never have that. Resignedly she removed her ribboned corset cover and while Aludin looked more and more puzzled, bent forward and struggled with her corset laces.

She got the corset off and dropped it. Aludin picked it up at once. Samantha stood bare-armed in petticoat and skirt. She wrapped her arms about her breasts and looked at the Apache girl helplessly. Aludin only looked blank. Samantha picked up the basque, made a show of examining it, then shook her head and cast it aside. This time, Aludin understood.

From a woven pannier she produced a low-necked, short-sleeved shirt or camisa of heavy unbleached cotton. Samantha pulled it on with a shudder, wondering whose it had been before. She saw no signs that the Apaches made such things for themselves. It was too large but anything was better than her own useless garments. She plucked at her ruined skirt. Even split it was too confining for work.

Aludin considered the problem briefly. Her solution was simple and direct. With a knife she hacked off the garment just below Samantha's knees. She would have cut off the petticoat too, but Samantha protested and removed it. Aludin shrugged and put it and the remnant of braided serge away carefully.

Looking down at her legs, Samantha had a nervous urge to giggle. The ruined lisle stockings and the high, buttoned shoes with their narrow heels were ludicrous. Her ankles were swollen and painful in the tight shoes which had never been meant for much walking.

Suddenly, without warning, tears stung her eyes. The enormity of the injustice which had befallen her was overwhelming. She was to have met Tom in this finery. He was to have been impressed by it. Now it lay in ruins on the floor of an Indian hut and she was a captive without promise of release. Hope there was—she would not stop hoping—but it was hard to feed hope on uncertainty and dread. She fought back her tears and swore aloud.

"Damn . . . damn . . . damn!" she whispered. It was a relief. Aunt Bee would have been indignant, but saying it out loud was a relief. Thought of Aunt Bee brought back her grief. If only she could find out what had happened. She turned in desperation to the Apache girl but the unblinking stare offered no help. Grief was replaced by helpless rage.

Plumping herself on the ground, she tore off the shoes and stockings. The gaily ribboned garters fell to the ground and Aludin snatched them up. Eyeing Samantha's bare feet she had recourse to the pannier once more for a pair of high, deerskin moccasins similar to her own. They were plainer because the toes were not turned up like hers but they fit well enough. She showed the white girl how to fold and tuck the tops to hold them over the swell of the calf. One of them still bore a tiny silver bell but the Apache girl cut this off with her knife and put it back in the pannier.

What a fright I must look, Samantha mourned. If Tom could see me now. Would God he could, she added. O God, she prayed silently, send me help. I will do the best I can but send me help soon. The sun was hot on her shoulders when she knelt again at the grinding stone.

Near midday Aludin gave her meat, strong and unpleasant to the taste, warmed at the fire. She choked it down because she was hungry. Her eyes searched the *ranchería* constantly for a glimpse of Aunt Bee but she saw nothing. In the afternoon there was a stir among the Indians and it was obvious they were making ready to move.

Distracted by worry over her aunt, Samantha was of

little use to Aludin in packing the contents of the wickiup on a runty, evil-tempered pony the Apache girl brought from the picket line in the trees. Her hands hurt her. The brief session with the grinding stone had blistered them and the blisters burst, leaving raw places. When the Indians moved they simply left the stripped wickiups standing. Samantha wanted to search among them for Aunt Bee, but she was afraid. Aludin whacked the packhorse with a stick and motioned for Samantha to walk in front.

She soon had reason to be grateful for the gift of native footwear. The moccasins felt strange and the stones hurt through their thin soles, but she could not have walked half a mile in her own shoes. At dusk they made camp high in a wooded canyon and when Aludin had prepared food for the older man and woman she herself ate and shared her meal with Samantha.

Later she gave the white girl a ragged Army blanket in which to roll herself against the night chill. Samantha hurt in every joint and her fear for Aunt Bee outweighed her apprehension over her own plight, but exhaustion was her ally and she fell asleep quickly.

FOUR

Sergeant Lowery reached Camp Lowell after dark and the post rocked with his report. The word spread to Tucson, six miles away, long before anyone could have ridden that distance to carry it. Within minutes after he heard Lowery's story, Colonel Oakes was on the wire to Department headquarters in Prescott and the civilian telegrapher in Tucson read his message shamelessly. In a case like this he saw no reason to be circumspect and before midnight every saloon in town was talking about it. The Texas and California stage agent was at Governor Safford's house raising hell and everyone predicted a general uprising.

Next morning a detachment from Camp Lowell found and repaired the cut in the telegraph lines and Oakes' first message to Camp Grant authorized a strong patrol to scour the area around the ambushed stage. Lieutenant Kerr filed the message and said nothing. Compton and Captain Madden's C Troop had been gone an hour, with them a pair of Apache scouts, Sergeant Bones and Man-afraid-of-his-shadow—who was known to the soldiers simply as Man.

Compton's relief was boundless when he discovered Royal and two troopers silently gathering the bodies of the four murdered men, guarded by the remaining two men of the escort. He had expected to have to search for them.

Tom Royal's face was tallow-colored beneath fresh sunburn and he was staggering from exhaustion. Compton spoke to him gently.

"You find anything?"

Royal shook his head. "We found a trail . . . couldn't read it but I followed it as far as I could before dark. We lost it then and couldn't pick it up this morning. Thought you'd be here so we came back."

Compton sighed. It must have been a small party then. There was no use giving Royal the hiding he deserved now; that would have to wait. Bones and Man were squatting by the stiff-legged carcass of the team horse, studying the ground, and Captain Madden was watching them doubtfully.

"We were careful not to mess it up," Royal said and Madden nodded. He looked at the celerity wagon and the dead horse sourly. In the mesquite along the river there were buzzards waiting patiently for the men to go away so they could return to the horse. The bodies of

48

the four civilians had been gathered and covered with a tarpaulin. The stage company would send for them.

Major Compton thought the Apaches who hit the stage were probably the same ones who had killed the two men at Sulphur Spring. They might have taken the women to get the soldiers off their trail, which would be sound thinking; any reasoning white man would be cautious about pushing them until he knew what had happened to the women. That much Madden conceded but there was another possibility more likely to him.

Dan Madden had been fighting Indians his entire life in the Army except for the interval when he went East to fight Confederates and he knew them well. There was every indication of a general outbreak by the Chiricahuas and when Indians were about to do that they generally liked to start the festivities with a little show for the young bucks. Tom Royal's girl and her aunt would do nicely. If he were right and there was a trail to follow, somewhere along it they would find what was left of the two women. The old war chiefs would make sure of that just so there wouldn't be any foolishness about calling off the war. He hoped Compton wouldn't let Royal go along because he didn't want to have to watch the boy when they found what he suspected the Apaches had left for them to find.

Bones pointed to something and Madden walked over to him. Seven horses, Bones said. Three shod with iron and four with buckskin. That meant there were only four Apaches. Madden glanced at the tarpaulin. That had to be the stupidest stage driver in Arizona.

The two Apache scouts grunted at each other and then Bones made another pronouncement. All seven horses had carried a rider when they left the stage.

"How th' hell's he know that?" demanded a soldier.

"Shoo! He'll tell you what color them horses was in a minnit!" grunted another.

"Either they took somebody else beside the women or they loaded a horse with baggage. What's left in the stage?" Compton demanded.

"There's some bags in it," said Royal. "Some of them

have women's things in them. No way to tell how much they took, if anything."

"All right. I guess there's nothing more we can do here. Dan, leave four men to guard it until someone gets here from Tucson. If Lowery made it there should be a lot of people here shortly."

"What are we going to do now?" There was an edge of hysteria in Royal's question and Compton looked at him closely. He wanted no explosion here in front of the men.

"Mister Royal, I sent word to John Clum at San Carlos before we left this morning. I think a few sorehead Chiricahuas killed the agent at Sulphur Spring and I think they took your girl and her aunt as hostages. If anybody in Arizona can fix up a deal it'll be Clum. In my opinion, that's the best thing we can do."

"You mean you're not going after them? We've got trackers . . . we can follow the trail now!"

Compton sighed. "We'll follow their trail, Mister, but we're going slow and careful. If there's going to be a real outbreak this could be openers. It might be a trick just to get us to stick our heads in a trap. Look at those mountains, Royal! How much chance have we got to find four Apaches in those?"

Royal put his head in his hands and groaned. The troopers looked away embarrassed and Compton wanted to put his arm around the youngster's shoulder; anything to help him. But he would not. It was bad enough as it was. He ought not to take Royal with him but he knew there was no way to dissuade him from going. Like Madden he had a nagging suspicion the women had not been taken as hostages and that was the sole reason why he intended to follow the renegades' trail. He could not tell Royal that, though.

"Get some scouts out, Dan, and a couple of flankers on each side. Bones, you and Man get going. We'll follow."

In Tucson, Governor Safford was stirring the pot. He sent telegrams to Washington and to General Kautz. He even sent one to General McDowell, commanding the Military Division in San Francisco, which was unusual, for the Division was generally ignored in times of crisis. The *Arizona Citizen* in Tucson filled its front page with bitter comments about the military and McDowell finally telegraphed Kautz he had better do something to soothe his critics.

The War Department began to send petulant queries. In Washington people were talking about the Chiricahua outbreak and this fitted nicely into the plans of the Commissioner of Indian Affairs. The Indian Bureau, its agent John Clum and the civil government of Arizona Territory united in a cry for concentration of the Arizona Indians. Relocate the Cochise Apaches on the San Carlos reservation and put an end to their marauding. To General Kautz's other miseries was added Clum's bombastic announcement that if the Army couldn't do the job he was prepared to do it himself with his San Carlos Indian policemen.

In Kautz's opinion, concentrating all the Apaches on one reservation would be like fencing off a corner of hell and locking all the devils in it. But he was a far-seeing general. If ignorant and greedy men were determined to commit such a folly the Army would pay the price unless it made sure the job was done right. He summoned Colonel Oakes to Prescott and together they laid their plans. Very quietly and without advising the War Department they prepared to round up Tahzay's Chiricahuas and put them where the civilians wanted them.

From the thirteenth to the seventeenth of April, Dan Madden's troop of cavalry and Tom Royal's four men probed carefully into the Whetstone Mountains. A courier from Camp Lowell told them Captain Whitside had taken B Troop of the sixth into the Santa Rita Mountains south of Tucson but that was more to pacify Governor Safford than to search for the lost women. Madden and Royal found nothing. The Apache trail was lost in the flinty ridges of the Whetstones and they could do no more. Supplies gone, they turned back and no man cared to look at Tom Royal's face.

At Camp Grant they found the first indications of General Kautz's planning. The regular monthly wagon train of supplies for the garrison had been received but on its heels came a second—an unprecedented event. Captain Smith, the quartermaster, was jamming stores into every available shelter and no one knew why the buildup. John Clum had sent word he would try to locate Tom Royal's girl and her aunt but Tom discovered that no one had approached the Chiricahua agent Jeffords yet. Major Compton decided it was better to give him something to do and sent him to Camp Bowie with permission to see Jeffords.

Tom Jeffords was a strange man who probably had more friends among the Apaches than among his own people. He was the first white man in Arizona to establish anything even approaching friendship with Cochise, from whom he extracted immunity for the mail riders from Tucson to New Mexico and then an agreement to listen to General Howard when that unusual soldier sought to settle the Chiricahuas before Crook got at them. When this effort succeeded, Cochise insisted that Jeffords become the Chiricahua agent on the new reservation. Unquestionably closer to the Chiricahuas than any man in Arizona, what Jeffords had to say to Tom Royal was hard to take.

"You don't know who's got your girl, Mister Royal," he said. "You don't even know she's alive."

"You have some reason to think she isn't?"

"Of course not! But you got to find out where she is before you can make a trade for her. I know Tucson says half the Chiricahuas have run off but it isn't true. Eskinyea and Pionsenay are gone and they probably killed Rogers and Spence at the Spring. I wouldn't be surprised if they stole your girl, too, but I don't know where they are and I'll lay odds neither does Tahzay. Nobody around here liked that pair."

"How can I find out where they are? How can I get in touch with them?"

"Hell, Mister, the way you soldiers have been flailing around they're probably in Sonora by now. If they took your girl down there they like as not sold her to the Mexicans."

His blunt assessment rocked Tom and he reacted badly. Jeffords understood his anguish and paid him the high courtesy of taking no offense. Nevertheless it was apparent this was getting nowhere and Lieutenant Tate Hulse, who had arranged the meeting, moved in to break it up.

Beverly Tate Hulse had known Tom since 1870 when they entered West Point together as plebes. They had roomed together for four years and on graduation they had entered the same regiment. He knew how to deal with Tom's icy rages. He simply started talking and kept on talking until he drowned out the argument. Tom Royal was a logical man and the noise baffled him. He was too fond of Tate to shut him off and he was incapable of outtalking him. Jeffords watched amused as Tate shunted his friend out of the room.

They made an unlikely pair, Tate Hulse and Tom Royal. Half a head shorter, dark-haired with a square, rugged face, Tate was voluble and easygoing. His wide mouth seemed ever ready to break into an infectious grin; he was rarely serious and never intense. Curwen McClellan, his troop commander, alternately swore and laughed at him. In the field Tate was the equal of any lieutenant at Camp Bowie but in garrison he stayed in trouble. His soldiers took advantage of him but they loved him because he never forgot them. Most of his difficulties with Captain McClellan were on their account. Hence they took care of him and covered for him when they could and McClellan knew that. It was for that reason he had high hopes for Lieutenant Hulse.

By the time they reached Camp Bowie, Tom had cooled off and Tate talked to him plainly. Jeffords was right. Eskinyea and Pionsenay were outcasts from Tahzay's band and if there was a Chiricahua on the reservation who knew where they were he would not admit it. The best bet, Tate urged, was John Clum at San Carlos.

Clum's noisy criticism of the Army raised the hackles of every officer who heard him but he had good contacts among the Apaches. His San Carlos Indian police were loyal. Most important, he had the lasting friendship of old Eskiminzin, chief of the Arivaipas.

When Clum came to Arizona in 1874 he found Skimmy in chains at Old Camp Grant. He persuaded Major Royall of the Fifth Cavalry to let the old man come to San Carlos and Eskiminzin never forgot that act of kindness though there was a good deal about white men he wanted to forget. Now when Clum wanted to know something about Apaches, Eskiminzin could usually ferret it out for him.

"Another thing, Tom; Jeffords is through. He's finished. The Indian Bureau is out to get him and so is the Tucson Ring. He's too smart for the Bureau and too honest for the Ring. He can't protect the Chiricahuas and Tahzay knows it. Clum's your man but you won't get anywhere talking to him like you talked to Jeffords."

"But damn it all, Tate, every day we wait makes it harder to find her! Suppose Jeffords is right and they took her to Mexico; what do I do now?"

"I see Colonel Rivas every month. He's the Mexican commander in Janos and I'll ask him to spread the word in Chihuahua and Sonora. If the Mexicans have her, though, it's going to cost money to get her back."

"I can raise five hundred here and another five back East. Promise him anything he asks. I'll get it!"

Tate sent him back to Camp Grant next day with cheering words but it was hard to do. Sam Allyn was Tom's girl and Tate's grief was a private thing. Together they had met Samantha Allyn at Fort Leavenworth on their way to join the Sixth Cavalry and for a little while Tate had nursed some hopes of his own about the quiet girl who gave them coffee at Major Bell's quarters. In that happy time, two years past, they had chosen her from all the girls at the old Army post and courted her gaily. When she made her choice Tate never grudged his friend the victory but the knowledge that she was gone now, dead or a captive somewhere in Apacheria, tore his heart.

After Tom had gone, he went back to Jeffords to try to smooth things over, hoping to find some clue to her whereabouts. It was a quieter session but no more productive.

Jeffords was bitter. He had seen too much hatred and bloodshed in Arizona, and now he saw the end of the fragile peace he had fashioned with Cochise and General Howard. He knew that men in Washington and Tucson were working against him. He would stay to the end, trying to hold the peace a little longer, but two years of work were going down the drain before his eyes and with it his own reputation. Men called him traitor and Indian-lover and though he cared little for that he saw small hope for peace in Arizona if the Chiricahuas were driven from their ancient home to the reservation at San Carlos. They hated and feared that place and they called it "the caged ground." They would never go there quietly.

FIVE

They came down in the very early dawn from the hasty camp in the mountains and Samantha, racking her brain for anything she had ever heard about escape, recalled a forgotten evening at the Bells' home at Fort Leavenworth. That had been two years past in the summer of 1874 when she first met Tom Royal and Tate Hulse.

Oberleutnant Graf Eber von Alfhen, on leave from a Prussian cavalry regiment, had stopped at the headquarters of the Army Department of the Missouri to pay his respects to General John Pope and dazzle the simple

Army maidens of the post. The count's uniforms were gorgeous, his burnside whiskers enthralling and he never stopped talking in his delightfully fractured English. The ladies were enchanted. He was a welcome change from the aging officers of the departmental staff, for since the Seventh Cavalry had taken the field there was a dearth of young blades at Fort Leavenworth.

Samantha had been more amused than dazzled by the Prussian but his arrival was fortuitous for her. Thunderclouds were gathering among the young ladies of the post because Samantha Allyn monopolized Lieutenants Royal and Hulse and Count von Alfhen postponed the storm.

"Dzhe time to ess-cape," the count told his enthralled audience, "isst vhen dey march. Dzhe Franzosen captived me by Sedan und vhen dzhey tooked me to dzhe city I runned avay. Vhen nobody isst looking I fall down in dzhe ditch by dzhe street und do not moof. I do not efen breeze until dzhey are all gone. Dzhen I esscape!"

"Nothing wrong with his 'breezing' now, is there?" Tom had murmured and she had smothered a giggle.

A sharp stone turned beneath her foot and she almost cried out. For the first hour of the march she had been too busy with her aches and pains to think of escaping but she knew that if she were going to take the Prussian's advice she would have to try very soon.

But she had waited too long. Dawn was flaring in the east and there was already too much light. The trail was not so steep now and the pace increased. Aludin drove her packhorse with a stick. The wall-eyed animal bit viciously at anyone in reach, but when he tried to bite Aludin she dealt him a blow on the head that staggered him. Her temper matched his. She had her hands full with her two charges and she would take no foolishness from either.

Just as the sun flamed above the distant peaks they reached a flat valley floor. Aludin flogged the horse into a trot and gave Samantha a jolting shove. She wanted her captive in front where she could watch her and when either the white girl or the packhorse slowed she used her stick on the laggard.

There were three wagon trails in the valley, radiating from a pile of adobe ruins in the center, but by the time she reached them Samantha was so exhausted she could only fling a longing glance at the deep-rutted tracks.

The valley was at least a mile wide and they crossed it at a jog trot—men, women, children and animals. Samantha's lungs burned and the muscles in her thighs turned to white-hot wires. Her heart threatened to burst into her throat and choke her.

A vedette, or mounted guard, loped beside the column, whipping them on with low cries. From the corner of her eye Samantha saw him, black and menacing against the rising sun, feathered lance jerking to the movement of his horse. Numbing terror flooded back and she ran in a fog of exhaustion and fear. In the end she ran without any thought at all. Aludin whipped her forward until they were in scrub brush with canyon walls lifting again on either side. When they finally stopped, she staggered in a circle until her heart receded from her throat and she could sprawl on the ground without suffocating.

Thereafter she thought of nothing except the necessity of putting one enormous foot before the other. She climbed until she was certain the earth had tilted and she was condemned to climb to the edge of it. When the pony lurched into her she went staggering into the brush and Aludin had to haul her back. It was her baptism in Apache marching and she never forgot it.

Somewhere, high up again, they made another hasty camp. She was totally useless and Aludin did not even try to make her work. The Apache girl thrust bits of scorched meat at her and her outraged stomach rejected them. She wanted only water. When she found a cold, clear rivulet among the rocks she scooped it up with her hands until Aludin pulled her from it. As she fell asleep, numb with exhaustion, she felt a wild, unreal sympathy for the Apache girl who had somehow driven a balky horse and a helpless captive so far and so fast without losing either.

In the dawn they climbed again and Samantha was dumbfounded to find she could move at all. Paradoxically, here in the mountains where there was concealment on every side, she was less inclined to try to escape. The Apaches seemed to know this. Aludin let her walk behind and devoted herself to the balky horse. The animal seemed genuinely lunatic in its determination to cross the Indian girl and she beat him until he squealed and snapped at the passing branches.

There was a flash of bright material beside the trail and a squaw in white camisa and voluminous skirt materialized among the trees, broad face beaming. She exchanged a torrent of meaningless sounds with Aludin, gave Samantha a curious look and joined in beating the packhorse. Children and dogs appeared and they climbed through a rocky cleft into a beautiful basin with thick groves of cedar and mountain oak. A stream brawled down the rocks and threw a fan of glittering spray where it fell into a pool. Scattered among the trees were many wickiups in various stages of construction, some partly thatched with grass, others with still bare poles.

This time she could help a little. She assisted Aludin in unloading the evil-tempered pony and then piled the bags and panniers against a tree while the Apache girl led the animal to a picket line. Realization that she was alone and unguarded for the moment jolted her into wide-eyed alertness. Covertly she studied the inviting thickets and rocky walls of the basin. Then, as if she felt a touch on her shoulder, she knew she was not alone. She turned to see an Apache man and a woman regarding her gravely.

She knew them. The woman was the one who had given orders through the boy, Severiano, at the first camp. The man was the one who had sent the warriors after Aunt Bee. Her heart quailed at sight of him and all her fears for her aunt came back. Because she did not know what else to do she returned their gaze steadily.

The man was squat and looked very strong. His shirt of some coarse, unbleached stuff fell almost to his knees, caught at the waist by a wide leather belt with a sheathed knife on it. Just below his knees, high moccasins ended in a double fold. The face was frightening: broad with deep-set eyes of jet black and the cruelest mouth Samantha had ever seen. Square-cut black hair flecked with gray framed the face, bound from it by a band of cloth about the forehead. He cradled a carbine in his arm and across the deep chest was a homemade bandolier of deerskin with loops for cartridges.

The woman wore the same clothing as the one who had met them by the trail except her skirt was an uneven russet brown, as if badly dyed with some native stain. It was shorter too, falling to just above the ankles to reveal the common, high-topped moccasins beneath. Her hair also was streaked with gray. She wore it loose down her back, not rolled and covered with the hourglass frame like Aludin's.

"Please?" Samantha asked softly. "Can you not tell me where the other white woman has gone?"

It was as if they could not hear her. Not even the expression on their faces changed. "Severiano?" she said pleadingly. *"¿Dónde está Severiano?"* She framed the words haltingly, searching for more. *"Por favor . . . quiero Severiano."*

It seemed to her the man's face hardened a little but she was not sure. Not sure enough to believe there had actually been any communication of her want. She fought back tears of helplessness. But she held her head up and gave them look for look. Aludin reappeared carrying something wet and heavy. She looked at the older couple and dropped her eyes respectfully.

Samantha knew that these two, whose names she could not even pronounce, and the girl, Aludin, were her immediate custodians. She had no way to know that the man, Catle, was Aludin's husband or that Sheneah, who stood now beside him, was his elder wife.

Polygamy was not common among the Chiricahua Apaches but when a man was well-off, a competent fighter and a respected councillor like Catle, they saw no wrong in his taking a second, younger wife. Much depended on the women involved and Catle had chosen well. His women had an easy relationship that made his life more comfortable in many small ways. Aludin had her rights and her privileges; she knew her place and how to hold it. Without resentment she relieved Sheneah of many tiresome chores though that did not mean the older woman was idle. No Apache woman to the day of her death escaped labor a white woman would consider sheer slavery.

Aludin was wondering if a decision had been taken about the white-eyes captive. It would be good to have a servant to share the household tasks but the white girl knew so little about work she would be more burden than help for many moons to come. She did not ask. Catle would speak when he was ready. He turned away now and Sheneah took a hatchet from one of the panniers. She spoke to Aludin, who took a pair of knives.

"¡Venga!" she said to Samantha.

They crossed the noisy stream and climbed through the rocks to a thicket of saplings. Sheneah examined them with care and began to cut those she had chosen, hacking them off close to the ground with her hand ax.

Aludin picked up the first and began trimming away the twigs and leafy branches, Samantha watching closely. The Apache girl did not cut the twigs flush with the sapling but left a short stub of each. When she had trimmed half its length she handed it to Samantha with the knife. By this time Sheneah had cut several more and Aludin began to trim another.

Samantha accepted the task willingly enough but she was clumsy and the knife was dull. She began with care and precision but was soon hacking wildly at the tough oak twigs. In the time she took to clean one sapling Aludin did two and Sheneah continued stolidly hacking down more as if she meant to denude the grove.

It looked easy but it was very hard. Within minutes she had sliced her thumb. She sucked it noisily and Aludin looked disgusted. The raw spots gained by her session with the grinding stone grew painful and in the soft flesh between thumb and forefinger a blister formed and broke despite her efforts to protect it. Left-handed she was clumsier than ever and the only thing that kept her from weeping in frustration was a healthy anger at her own incompetence. It was a reaction that would stand her in good stead in the days to come.

In the oak grove, fighting with the saplings, Samantha did not see the two men who rode into the basin. Had she noticed them she would have given them no more than a frightened glance. To her all Apache men were as alike as so many devils from hell. She could make no distinction among them. It was just as well; these were Tudeevia and Schnowin, whom Catle had sent to follow her Aunt Bee.

Their women came to take the horses and they walked to Pionsenay, who sat upon a rock watching his wives build a wickiup. Eskinyea's band had been first at the rendezvous but the elder chief had not come yet. With a few warriors he was scouting his own trail to make sure no one followed.

"Tell me, my brothers, what of the old white-eyes woman?" Pionsenay demanded and Tudeevia answered.

"We followed her to the bottom of the mountains. She took a long time because she fell down and stopped often to sing her song. We think she spoke to the trees."

"She made magic?" demanded Gil-lee, who was as near a shaman as there was in Eskinyea's band. At least he claimed to have special powers and he always took part in any discussion of strange things like this.

"I do not know," said Schnowin. "Maybe my brother Tudeevia can say. He walked behind her while I came with the horses." Tudeevia gave him a reproachful look.

"I am not a shaman," he said defensively. "I do not know if she made magic but I do not think she did. When she spoke to the trees nothing happened. No spirit came to help her. She did not grow stronger. She fell down more often and it took her a long time to reach the sand below."

"And then?" asked Catle. Tudeevia shrugged.

"The sun struck her head and she lay down. Sometimes she would stand up and sing her song but when night came she lay down and she did not move again. We watched until the sun came up and she was still there. All day we watched. She dug with her hands but nothing came and after that she did no more. When the sun went down we left her and came here. That is all."

"You did not go close to her and see what she did?"

61

demanded Gil-lee. Tudeevia came as near shuddering as a full-grown Apache male could.

"No, my brother. It was clear that the Mountain Spirits would not help her and if there is any Spirit in the desert it did not come. She was old and weak and she was sick in her eyes. You saw her in the *ranchería*. We think she was sick in her head too and since she had no water and can get none where she is we think she is dead now."

It was inconclusive but Pionsenay was satisfied. Catle had seen the woman when she came from his wickiup and he nodded agreement. Only Gil-lee mumbled sarcastically but Gil-lee always muttered and found fault with others.

Meanwhile the three women had cut and trimmed forty or fifty saplings. It seemed an immense number to Samantha, even greater when they were tied in bundles with strips of bark and she had to help carry them to the clearing at the foot of the slope.

Sheneah chose a site and marked with a stick a circle about ten feet in diameter. At intervals of two or three feet around this they dug holes and set in each the butt of a sapling. Since half a score such structures were in progress nearby Samantha knew this would be a hut such as the one in which she and Aunt Bee were put at the first camp. She was taller than either of the Apache women so they gave her yucca leaf strands to tie the sapling tips together while they bent them within her reach. She stood on tiptoe and knotted the sinews awkwardly, adding more when Aludin complained about the job.

Sheneah was making a firepit and Aludin led Samantha to the stream, where they cut tufts of tall, sweet grass to tie on the framework of poles. It made a thin cover and seemed flimsy to Samantha but Sheneah spread hides and scraps of canvas over the grass. Next day they would add more grass and more covering and keep on adding until the wickiup was weatherproof. It took about three days to make a really good hut.

As soon as Sheneah began to spread her skins on the hut they had just set up, Aludin marked off another circle and the whole task was begun again. Before it was thatched, Samantha was trembling with fatigue. Why two of the wretched things, she wondered, until Aludin began to cover the second with material from her own panniers and she understood that the two women did not share a wickiup. Knowing nothing of the relationships in this family group she could not grasp the reason but she was too tired to puzzle over it.

When the second wickiup was lightly covered Aludin called a halt and introduced Samantha to what would become the only real pleasure of her existence. She took her ward to the deep pool below the falls to bathe. It was screened by brush from the camp and whether it was set aside for the women or used alternatively by the men was not apparent. Samantha had no idea whether Apache men bathed or not. Indeed, she would have been surprised to know how clean a folk her captors were.

This was the spring moon—Time of Little Eagles, the Apaches called it—and already there had been a great cleaning of blankets and people. Even the children had been washed. If in the winter moons lice had come to make their heads itch and burn they were gone now. Those who suffered this affliction caked their heads with mud and dried it in the sun before plunging into water to wash mud and lice away.

Aludin took with her a bowl of thick white stuff which Samantha learned in time was pounded yucca root. She viewed it now with the same suspicion she had for all the nameless things in bowls and baskets Aludin kept about her. The Apache girl stripped her slender body quickly and slid into the pool, where she lathered her hair with a handful of the white stuff. It seemed to make elegant suds.

Samantha hung back, glancing about apprehensively. She had never shared her privacy with anyone and was loath to do so now but the clear water was alluring and she surrendered to her more immediate need. She undressed and followed Aludin into the pool, gasping at its chill. It was delightful and she luxuriated in it, soaping and rinsing her hair twice over, taking so long that Aludin

63

was out and clucking at her impatiently before she finished.

On the bank she knelt and shook out her hair until it was partly dry. It reached to her waist when free, dark brown with a reddish tinge that deepened under the sun. She had long complained that it was dull and teased Aunt Bee by saying that when she was married she would buy tints to give it life. Her aunt only sniffed caustically. A little lemon, she would say. A little lemon in the rinse is all a lady ever uses. She plaited her damp hair in two long braids and wondered desolately if she would ever see her aunt again.

Aludin dressed her black hair with a greasy substance that gave it sheen and made it cling together. It did not smell badly but Samantha wanted none of it. She watched astonished as the Apache girl pulled some sprigs of mint and rubbed them between her small breasts. That done, Aludin gathered her soap and motioned to Samantha to follow. Doubtless there was more work to do.

What remained was not onerous, however. She was set to gathering more grass and Aludin showed her how to bundle it to make a pallet, over which she spread the ragged Army blankets. Their familiar gray and faded black letters stabbed Samantha's heart with longing.

The pallets finished, Aludin prepared the evening meal: more of the bitter mush and chunks of fresh meat roasted on sharpened sticks. Samantha guessed this was the dripping bundle she had seen the Apache girl carrying earlier. It was tough and stringy meat, scorched on the outside and raw-red beneath. The taste was repugnant to Samantha but she was hungry and she worried down her portion. Aludin eyed her curiously as she ate.

More in an attempt to communicate than anything else, Samantha held out her piece of meat and raised her brows questioningly. Aludin grunted and patted the pack-saddle on which the cross-grained pony had carried her belongings. Samantha was baffled, wondering if the meat had been all day in the pack, but then a horrid thought struck her. She looked at the picket line among the trees where the Indian horses stamped in the gathering darkness. Aludin shook her head and rubbed her stomach contentedly.

Samantha gagged. At the going-away party given her by the Bells at Fort Leavenworth they had said laughingly, you will have to learn to eat what the Indians eat in Arizona. She lowered her head to hide her distress. The damned horse deserved what he got but she felt no better about eating a piece of him.

Before it was completely dark, Eskinyea arrived and was greeted with pleasure by the Apaches. It was the first time the entire band had been reunited since the killing of the white men at Sulphur Spring. After he had eaten there was a council. He had much to discuss with his younger brother, Pionsenay.

The murder of Rogers and Spence had not been planned. It just happened. Probably the only premeditated act in the whole episode was Rogers' attempt to get his hands on the stolen Mexican silver. When he elected to trade his vile whiskey for the loot he triggered a chain of events beyond control by either side. The first Apache to try to regain some mastery of the situation was Pionsenay. He had no real plan either when he attacked the stage but when he found himself with two captives he began to think of the future. In this he was ahead of his brother.

As far as Eskinyea was concerned, the murder of the two white men at the Spring had simply set in motion a traditional cycle of events. He had hurt the white-eyes and now he would run for the border and stay beyond their reach until their fury cooled or was replaced by another of their ludicrous attempts to make friends with their tormentors. Pionsenay's attack on the stage was simply a part of the pattern. Since they would soon be out of reach of the Americans it did no harm and he approved of it.

He did not approve of the captives, however. He was displeased that Pionsenay had kept one white woman and even angrier about the other. People who seemed crazy sometimes recovered their senses and their tongues. Gruffly he ordered that someone go and keep watch over the woman who had wandered away. As long as she was sick in her head no Apache would touch her but if she had no help she would die soon and that would be best. A guard must be mounted to make sure no one interfered with that.

Then he broached the matter of Samantha and the whiskey drummer. His wife had complained to him about the latter. She felt his people had been unfairly excluded from that sport. Pionsenay had a ready answer.

He had not meant to take the white man alive but when he did he decided to make the best use of him. Uncertain when he would find Eskinyea and the rest of the band, it had seemed best to him to let the women have the white man at once. It was good for the young men too because it made their hearts strong.

Unsaid was the understanding that those who took part or even watched would not soon want to go back to the white-eyes reservation. White men had a strange ritual when they captured an Indian who had killed one of their people. They put iron on his wrists and ankles and held a council that talked for days before they strangled the Indian with a lariat. Blood for blood an Apache understood but that way of killing repelled them.

As for the captive girl, Pionsenay shrugged and turned up his hands. What harm? They were going to Mexico and they were short of cartridges. She was no trouble to take along and there were Mexicans who would give many bullets for a *niña* like this one. They would be in no hurry to return her to her people either.

Eskinyea grunted, satisfied. Thus far his brother's explanation was in accord with the familiar pattern. But Pionsenay did not tell him all his plan. He was as fed up with reservation life as Eskinyea and equally ready for a change but he was in no hurry to go to Mexico. On this side of the border he would have to play second fiddle to his brother but that was tolerable. In Mexico they would both come under the rule of Geronimo and that was not good. He mistrusted and disliked Geronimo intensely and was a little afraid of him.

It seemed to Pionsenay there was a golden opportunity

at hand. If they stayed where they were now, in the most remote peaks of the Huachuca Mountains, they would have a remarkable sanctuary. They could slip into Sonora to raid the *Nakaiyi,* the Mexicans, whenever they wished and neither *rurales* nor Mexican cavalry would pursue them across the border. With the white-eyes girl close-held in the *ranchería* they would be equally safe from American soldiers who would be afraid to attack any Indian camp for fear their women might be in it.

Of course the young men could not raid on the American side of the border, because if they made too much trouble the soldiers would attack in spite of their lost women. This was small price to pay for such safety, not to mention the freedom. Geronimo would be angry because they did not join him and his renegades in Sonora, but they could ride south to raid with him. It seemed to Pionsenay an altogether elegant scheme but he would have to broach it cautiously. Eskinyea's consent was required and Eskinyea was a traditionalist. He had never considered anything except a run for Sonora and it would be difficult to change his mind.

Pionsenay began by advising a brief delay. Maybe the Americans would make a good offer to buy their women. They need not know until the deal was made that one was dead. In the meanwhile they would be quite safe here.

Eskinyea demurred, as Pionsenay had expected him to. There was nothing for them here. The white-eyes soldiers would be swarming all along the border and they would have to hide like rabbits. He wanted to go to Sonora and he wanted to raid. The girl was a burden. Kill her or sell her to the first Mexican they encountered but get rid of her and keep moving.

The band was small, Pionsenay cautioned. What about Tahzay's young men? Not all of them wanted to stay on the reservation. Maybe some of them would come along if they were encouraged. There need be no contact with the white-eyes. As long as they thought their women were still alive they would be very cautious about attacking Apaches. They could wait here in safety until they had talked to Tahzay's people.

About the girl, Eskinyea simply grunted. The idea of a hostage for protection angered him. But recruiting young men from Tahzay appealed to him greatly. They would stay until that had been explored. There was a good deal of discussion as to how this would be accomplished and finally it was agreed that both Eskinyea and Pionsenay would make a quiet visit to the Chiricahua reservation.

In the meanwhile, since he was the leader, Eskinyea's ruling on Samantha was required. She would, he said, live in the house of Catle and serve Catle's wives. She would not be hurt unless she ran away or would not work. Everyone would be warned to say nothing of her or of the older woman to any person who might carry word of her whereabouts to her people. Incidentally, he asked, how was she to be told what to do? Did she speak Mexican?

Hardly at all, Pionsenay replied. But there was the boy, Severiano, who spoke a little of the white-eyes tongue and the girl seemed to understand him. Eskinyea grew as humorous as was possible for him. He said he was glad someone had found a use for Severiano.

This decision made no change at all for Samantha. By the time Catle had told his elder wife, Sheneah, both Aludin and Samantha had retired to their half-finished wickiup. Aludin slept but her captive did not.

She felt the familiar Army blanket beneath her hands and gave thanks she was alive to do so. She mourned for Aunt Bee. The dying fire sent a gleam through the loose thatch and shadows moved before it. Following them, she wondered if somewhere Tom sought her face in firelight as she sought his. If she had been braver and taken the Prussian lieutenant's advice she might be closer to him now.

She remembered something else that happened the day she heard the Prussian boast of his escape from the French. As Tom and Tate walked her home that night under the arching elms of Leavenworth, she had noticed an odd stiffness in her two escorts. It did not affect the courtesy and interest with which they regarded her but entered somehow into the way they spoke to each other.

The walk was long and she had puzzled over it all the way.

Then, at Aunt Bee's porch, illumination came to her; how, she did not know. She was inexperienced but some woman's intuition must have awakened. It was time, she understood, that she make a choice if choose she would.

It was not difficult. She gave her hand to Tate in the usual way but Tom's she took in both her own and smiled at his delight. It was all that was required of her. Tate was still around and no less attentive, but from that night there was a shared happiness and excitement between her and Tom that excluded him.

The Indian girl stirred a little and Samantha watched her with a hatred that was choking in its intensity. Combined with her longing for Tom it was too much emotion and she wept silently.

SIX

Measured against the long history of Apache deviltry in Arizona, the killing of Rogers and Spence and even the capture of two white women were relatively minor incidents. But the Tucson Ring, the merchants who sold and freighted at exorbitant profit the supplies required by the Army, wanted more soldiers to consume more supplies. The representatives of the Indian Bureau wanted all the Indians in Arizona on a single reservation. For different reasons, each had been looking for trouble and all through April they reminded Washington it had been found. The Bureau was the first to move.

On the third of May the Army mail carrier from Camp

Grant, where the telegraph line ended, brought Agent Clum at San Carlos a telegram from the Indian Bureau. "Proceed to the Chiricahua reservation . . ." it said. "Take charge of Indians and agency property . . . suspending Agent Jeffords, for which this dispatch shall be your full authority." Clum read it with glee. "If practical," the writer added, "remove the Chiricahua Indians to San Carlos." Three thousand dollars had been appropriated by Congress for this purpose.

Within the week the War Department followed suit, ordering General Kautz to cooperate with Clum. Kautz swore but he obeyed his orders, offering more than cooperation. He knew the consequences of a token effort at this point. By the seventeenth of May he had the entire Sixth Cavalry in motion. The infantry would stay at home to guard the scattered garrisons. The young lieutenants of the Eighth fumed and connived for a place in the field force. They sniffed the rare chance for a mention in dispatches or perhaps even brevet promotion. So large a concentration of troops with a Department commander in the field held promise of rewards that never came to lonely scouts with half-strength companies.

Between the women of the two regiments there was a chill. Only a very young and foolish bride coveted battlefield promotion for her man and the infantry wives were quietly grateful for the division of labor. The ladies of the Sixth stiffened their backs and hid their fears. Too many of the older ones had seen the world end for one of them when a weary column rode home from a fight with a canvas-sheeted body on a led horse.

Three troops of cavalry assembled at Camp Lowell to form a battalion under Colonel Oakes, the regimental commander, and by the end of May there were seven more troops at Camp Grant. On the third of June the entire regiment was marching toward the Chiricahua reservation. Colonel Oakes went ahead in a buggy to meet Agent Clum and his San Carlos Indian police at Apache Pass.

By dusk on the fourth, Apache lookouts in the Chiricahua Mountains could see dust clouds rolling toward them on every trail and the Chiricahuas stirred restlessly. Wait, Tahzay counseled. Wait and see what the white-eyes want. His own people listened but Geronimo and his band of hard fighters were also on the reservation and they were not so obedient. Tension crackled in the air.

An average troop of frontier cavalry could muster about forty men for field duty. Roster strength was sixty or better but there were no service troops in the Department and all the housekeeping chores had to be met with troopers from the line. Woodcutting, mail carrying, tending the telegraph line and a hundred other odd jobs drained off the combat strength of the cavalry. But the forty men who could be mustered for a fight were not to be taken lightly. They were tough and seasoned; their captain had learned his trade on Civil War battlefields and both he and his lieutenants had ridden hundreds of miles after Indians of one sort or another.

European officers visiting the American frontier shuddered when they first saw these troopers. Nothing, they thought, could look like this and fight. By comparison with the European hussar or light dragoon this American cavalry was poverty-stricken in the way of equipment and looked like ragamuffins.

American officers were equally wrathful about the uniform. The variety of colors and styles issued were a constant irritation and the quality was frequently deplorable. The trooper's hat, for example, was a joke. Since 1872 the quartermaster had been procuring a shoddy gray model which after three weeks, said an angry captain, "became the most uncouth rag ever put upon a man's head." Only this year had the protests taken some effect and the first of a new black issue with a good brim was reaching the frontier. It looked like the beloved black hat of the Army of the Potomac and the officers were a little mollified.

The more experienced European observers were quick to note that most of what this cavalryman carried with him into the field was for his horse. In addition to the regulation nose bag of grain, all western regiments strapped a canvas bag with twelve pounds of oats across

71

the saddlebags on the cantle of their saddles. Up front, on the pommel, was a single poncho-wrapped blanket and a lariat with a steel picket pin snapped to its end. The saddle was a stripped-down copy of a Prussian model brought home by Captain George B. McClellan when he was military attaché in that country. He had persuaded Secretary of War Jefferson Davis of its virtues in 1857 and the U.S. Cavalry had used it ever since.

Personal equipment was very light. In addition to the blanket and poncho there were hung on the near side of the cantle a quart tin cup and a canteen and on the off side a haversack holding the trooper's rations: hardtack crackers and bacon or salt pork packed in a folding meat can which was supposed to serve as a skillet while its lid functioned as a plate.

Only in the matter of weapons was there real uniformity. Despite his complaints that a penny-pinching government denied him a repeating rifle, every trooper still carried the single-shot Springfield carbine; it outranged and outshot every other saddle gun in the West and whatever it lacked in speed of firing it made up for with the priceless ingredient of reliability. Until 1873 it had been of .50 caliber; thereafter it was .45.

The carbine could be carried in a short boot of leather slung on the off side of the saddle or it could be snapped to a sling worn across the trooper's shoulder. Most soldiers scorned the latter. If a man had no immediate need for his carbine he put it in the saddle boot. Otherwise he cradled it in his arm or balanced it across the pommel of the saddle.

His armament was completed by the most highly prized weapon on the frontier: the Colt single-action .45-caliber revolver, commonly called the Peacemaker. There was none better. As far as the soldier was concerned its only drawback was the total eccentricity of the means of carrying it prescribed by the Army.

That eccentricity was the outgrowth of a third weapon issued the cavalryman but never used against Indians. This was the saber, reserved for dress parade. The Ordnance Department reasoned that all cavalrymen fought with the saber and most of them were right-handed. If the trooper needed his pistol he could fire it in his left hand and this odd line of reasoning resulted in a revolver holster designed to carry the pistol on the right hip, butt forward, so it could be drawn with the left hand. To draw it with the right required the flexibility of a snake.

There was not much color showing in a cavalry troop when it rode to fight. Trouser stripes were soon dusted over and though many men bought a neckerchief to keep the dust out of the collarless shirt or to pull up over nose and mouth, these were usually faded checked gingham; nothing fancy. If a whole troop were represented there was a guidon at the head of the column, a swallow-tailed flag in the design of the Stars and Stripes but with the stars in gilt and the troop letter painted or embroidered on one of the white stripes.

The hard-eyed Apache scouts on the Chiricahua peaks could count ten of these guidons moving toward them and their eyes glittered. Horse-soldiers. Plenty horse-soldiers they signaled to the watchers in the valley with their scraps of mirror catching the setting sun.

The Sixth Cavalry spread out and bivouacked around the Chiricahua agency and the assembled Apaches. Colonel Oakes and John Clum sought out Agent Jeffords, who was not surprised at the telegram Clum had received from the Indian Bureau. He told them frankly he did not know how many Apache warriors were still under Tahzay's control. After the murder of Rogers and Spence, a chief named Gordo had taken a large band to the Warm Springs agency in New Mexico. Old Eskinyea and his brother Pionsenay, both ex-war chiefs of Cochise, were missing.

But what bothered him more than the missing Apaches was the presence of Geronimo, Juh and Nolgee with their raffish mixed band from the Sierra Madre of Sonora. Geronimo had long insisted that his band had been included in the treaty made by Cochise and General Howard, and when it suited him he used it to draw rations from Jeffords.

What had been done to restrict the Chiricahuas after

73

their first outbreak, Colonel Oakes wanted to know. Jeffords told him he had warned Tahzay to keep his people east of the Chiricahua Mountains. Any Indian west of there would be treated as a hostile. Clum boasted that he would soon settle matters with his San Carlos police and Jeffords listened sourly. While they talked, all hell broke loose in Tahzay's camp.

Eskinyea and Pionsenay, in search of recruits, had slipped through the cordon of troopers to talk to Tahzay. As night fell on the fourth of June, Eskinyea spoke to the Chiricahua council.

"The white-eyes will take you to San Carlos and lock you up. You know that place. It is hot and flat and the sickness comes out of the ground. There are Coyoteros and Pinal Apaches there. You know what happens when Chiricahuas have to live with people like them."

"We have sworn to keep the peace," answered Tahzay. "My father Cochise made that peace and we have kept it. I do not want to break it now." His younger brother Nachise nodded to show he supported him. Eskinyea grunted.

"What does Geronimo say?"

"Geronimo says nothing here!" Tahzay snapped.

"The white-eyes are lying!" urged Eskinyea. "They always lie! They want the metal in the ground you live on. When they have that ground and they have you caged at San Carlos they will not care what happens to you. Your people will starve! Join us and we will make a fight the soldiers will never forget!"

Tahzay shook his head and Eskinyea gestured in disgust. It was not the kind of gesture you made to a friend.

"Are the children of Cochise all women? Are there no fighters left here in the shadows of the stronghold where Cochise sleeps?"

It was strong talk—too strong for young Nachise. His loyalties were divided, but he could not stomach such insults as these. He rebuked Eskinyea. Several other men began to speak and there was disorder that would never have been tolerated in Cochise's time. Someone cocked a carbine and someone else kicked sand on the fire. The

Chiricahuas split apart in rage, and rifles blasted in the narrow confines of the canyon.

When the smoke cleared six men lay dead and one of them was Eskinyea. Tahzay himself had shot him. Pionsenay was gone, his shoulder broken by a ball from Nachise's carbine. He had taken with him a dozen angry young warriors of Tahzay's band. The authority of the hereditary leader was preserved but the impact on the Chiricahuas was a tragic one.

Next day Tahzay told Clum and Jeffords he would take the remainder of his people to San Carlos if that was what was wanted. There was pride in his face that he had kept his father's peace but sadness too, because the Chiricahuas were badly split. Clum was delighted, but Jeffords pointed out there was still Geronimo to deal with.

Clum scoffed and sent word to Geronimo he wanted to talk to him. Surprisingly Geronimo came. His scouts had inspected the ring of cavalry and urged caution. He seemed very agreeable and Jeffords watched with astonishment and suspicion.

"You will go to San Carlos with Tahzay?" Clum demanded bluntly. Geronimo nodded. He had made peace with the soldiers when Cochise did and his word was as good as any man's. His people were camped nearby and he would go and get them.

"It occurs to me," muttered Colonel Oakes, "that we had damned well better go with him!" but Clum demurred. There was no need for that. He would send a few of his policemen to keep an eye on Geronimo.

They were too few and too late. By the time they reached Geronimo's *ranchería* he was gone with all his people. They had abandoned unneeded baggage, killed the weakest ponies and strangled all the dogs so their barking would not give them away. The trail led south into Mexico.

Clum raged and had small comfort from either Jeffords or Oakes. Their fury was increased when they learned from Tahzay that both Eskinyea and Pionsenay had been on the reservation under their very noses. Eskinyea was dead. They had to believe that because Tahzay

75

said he had killed him and Nachise backed him up. Nachise also said Pionsenay was wounded but no one had any idea where he had gone. It was unfortunate that both Jeffords and the military were so unpleasant to Clum because their criticism may have influenced what happened next.

The day after Geronimo slipped away, an Apache came to the Agency asking for Jeffords. Embittered and fed up with the whole business, Jeffords told him to go find Clum. Clum was the Chiricahua agent now.

Clum listened to the man in astonishment. He had come from Pionsenay and he wanted to make a deal. Pionsenay was hurt and scared. The bullet in his shoulder had been fired by a son of Cochise and the wound would not heal. If he surrendered to the white-eyes would they make his shoulder well?

Clum rubbed his head in bewilderment. The Apaches called him Nantan-betunny-Kahyeh, Chief-with-the-high-forehead, because despite his youth he was bald as an egg. He rubbed hard and tried to puzzle this out.

"Yes. I will bring a doctor and we will do what we can. Maybe it is too late."

"Will the Nantan-betunny-Kahyeh swear to protect Pionsenay from his enemies if he surrenders?"

There was the rub. Clum hedged. Pionsenay had surely been involved in the killings at the stage station and he probably had a hand in the attack on the stage wagon. If the civil authorities in Tucson learned he had come back to the Agency they would demand his arrest.

Clum was honest with the Apache. Pionsenay had been a bad Indian. He had made a lot of trouble for the white men. No one could guarantee to keep him safe from all the people he had made angry. He, Clum, would do what he could but he could not promise much.

The Apache grew sullen and then defiant. If the white-eyes would not honor their word Pionsenay would not come.

"I have given no promise," said Clum. "I will do the best I can to heal Pionsenay's wound but I am not the chief here. Do you think I can give orders to all those soldiers?"

The more he talked, the more suspicious the Indian became. He gathered his weapons and grew very watchful. It was clear that he was about to go.

Clum let him go but not alone. Despite his protests he sent with him Sergeant Tauelclyee and a dozen of the San Carlos Apache policemen.

"You take Tauelclyee to Pionsenay. Tauelclyee will talk. Maybe Pionsenay changes his mind then. You tell him that if his wound smells bad he will die soon. If he comes back with Tauelclyee I will bring the soldier-doctor to heal him. This I swear. No more."

The Apache runner and his unwanted escort disappeared into the mountains and Clum did an unforgivable thing. He said nothing of the visit to anyone. He told Sergeant Tauelclyee to look for the white women if he could get into Pionsenay's *ranchería,* and to make any bargain he could to get them back if they were there. But that was all he did.

Perhaps John Clum felt this was the best way to get Pionsenay back. Perhaps he thought that if he could get his hands on Pionsenay, he could hold him until the women were freed. Or maybe he did not give that much thought to the women, being more interested in showing up Tom Jeffords and the Army all by himself.

He told Tahzay to make ready for the move to San Carlos and he sent word to General Kautz that he would bring the Chiricahuas to the new reservation by himself. He did not need or want help from the military; his Apache police could do the job. Kautz snorted and issued orders for the cavalry to return to their garrisons. As a precaution, he told Colonel Oakes to make sure his troops took their time and were ready for action if the Chiricahuas did not cooperate.

Clum waited for Tahzay to gather his people and for Tauelclyee to return.

SEVEN

Of all the tasks assigned her, Samantha most detested the dressing and curing of deerskin. Catle would bring it, rolled and usually already stinking. If she were not told to begin at once, she would put it by, ostensibly until there was a lull in her other work. In a little while Aludin would look for it and if it were not in view, she would comb the wickiup until she found it. With a grunt of triumph she would bring it out and give it to Samantha, who knew better than to delay any longer. As soon as she finished whatever she was doing at the moment she pegged the skin out to dry in the sun. When dry, it had to be scraped.

Most Apaches used a horn scraper but Aludin had a better tool, an ancient iron hoe blade with teeth filed in its edge. Even with this superior instrument, Samantha found scraping the shreds of fat and flesh from the inside of the hide a tedious and backbreaking job.

Next the skin was immersed in water for two or three days in a hollow scooped in the ground and lined with stiff hide. If it stayed too long it began to rot and the results were painful. Sheneah went into a fury and Aludin sulked. If the timing were right the skin was ready for the next step, which was more difficult than the first. The wet hide was wrapped around a pole and the hair laboriously scraped from it. If it had stayed a little too long in the water it was gelatinous and ripped; if not long enough, all the hair would not come off. When it had finally been cleaned, Samantha would make a pillow of grass and peg the skin over it, inner side up, for another drying. Lumps and hard spots had to be worked out with a stone.

Then came the worst part of all. If the hide passed Aludin's finicky inspection she produced a bowl of deer brains, well-aged. Gagging over this putrid mess, Samantha warmed it carefully at the fire and worked into it with her hands an equal portion of rancid tallow. This was the moment for which every gnat and red ant within yards had been waiting. They came in swarms. Almost weeping with vexation, Samantha fought off this assault and stuffed the hide into a big bowl full of the foul-smelling jelly to be worked endlessly with the fingers until soft and pliant.

Removed from the concoction in which it was softened, the hide was wrung out until almost dry. Samantha then took it to a grassy spot and kneeled on one end while she pulled and stretched the other. If there still were hard spots they had to be kneaded and rubbed with the brain and tallow mixture. If all had gone well this final step took half a day and the end result was soft, well-cured buckskin.

In time this hateful task became less onerous for Samantha, particularly when she had won the right to go as soon as she finished to the pool and wash herself. This was a hard-earned prize. In the beginning she was driven by two devils: fear of provoking the Apaches and the scorn with which they viewed her best efforts. If, as in the curing of hides, her work left her befouled and evil-smelling, she dared not show her revulsion. Intensely particular about her person and its cleanliness, this reduced her to a special misery.

But she persevered, accepting every task given her and doing her best to accomplish it. The work was endless and often disgusting, but she saw that in no way was she singled out for degradation. Every woman in the *ranchería* did exactly the same things.

Aludin was impressed by her charge's determination to master her work, and slowly her attitude toward the white girl changed. Since Samantha seemed incapable of grasping even the simplest phrases in Apache, Aludin could only gauge her feelings by watching her eyes and face. Samantha drilled herself endlessly in obedience and tried to guard her feelings, but inevitably some of them broke through this rigid control. As Aludin's hostility diminished, she became more sensitive to these signs and more responsive to them. If the white-eyes girl were happier and more willing because she had been allowed to bathe, Aludin saw no reason to withhold this simple privilege. Sheneah grumbled but raised no serious objection.

Samantha would come back damp and refreshed and set herself to show her gratitude. The amount of yucca soap she applied to herself in the pool always distressed Aludin but Samantha found that a good way to restore peace was to pound more yucca root without being told to do so.

In this fashion, the days of endless work reeled off in lost succession and one of her particular torments was her inability to keep track of them. She tried notching a twig but to Aludin this smacked of magic and she forbade it angrily. For a while Samantha tried the Apache practice of dropping a pebble each day in a shallow depression behind the wickiup, but Aludin found the little cache and scattered it. But by the waxing and waning of the moon, Samantha knew her captivity was stretching into months.

Until she grasped the harsh realities of Apache life, the Indian women's concentration on the gathering of food seemed obsessive to her. She had come to the *ranchería* in early spring and that was the season when the narrow-leafed yucca plant sent up a succulent stalk which was gathered relentlessly. Aludin cut these in great quantities and Samantha bundled and carried them to the *ranchería,* where they were cut into shorter lengths and roasted over the coals until soft. Much was eaten at once —the burned skin peeled off and the warm stalk devoured eagerly.

But they could not possibly eat all they gathered and Aludin prepared the surplus for storage. Samantha was set to digging a hole in which a fire was built and stones thrown in to heat. When the fire burned down Aludin laid cut and pounded yucca stalks on the hot stones and then covered them with wet grass and earth. Next day, Samantha dug out this trove and spread the steamed yucca to dry in the sun, after which it was packed into the rawhide bags against future need.

When summer came, the yucca bloomed and its white flowers were gathered and boiled; some were eaten at once but a great quantity was dried and stored. Then the century plant, or mescal, came into season and the women ranged far and wide to gather the crowns that formed the bottom of the stalk.

Preparation of mescal was no small task. When a quantity of the crowns had been gathered, a pit was dug and filled with wood and stones. As soon as the wood was burned away, each woman piled her collection of mescal on the stones; wet grass and earth were added and the mescal left to steam for a day and a night. After that the crowns were dried, the soft centers pounded flat, dried again, then covered with a protective glaze of the sticky juice drained from the pounded stuff.

The variety of edible matter derived from all this work astounded Samantha and she learned to tolerate most and even enjoy some of it. She was particularly fond of the bread Aludin made from ground nuts and seeds, baked in a conical loaf in the embers of the fire.

She could not, however, share the Apache fondness for strange meats. It sometimes seemed to her that they would eat any animal that did not eat them first. Wood rats, prairie dogs and rabbits were buried intact in hot ashes, dug up when roasted, then skinned, gutted and eaten. She was familiar with rabbit but all meat roasted with the entrails in it acquired a flavor repellent to her.

Venison she enjoyed but most of what Catle brought Aludin converted to jerky and stored away. Invariably though, when a deer was killed a favorite dish of Catle's was prepared which always gave Samantha the horrors. The paunch of the animal was filled with its blood and to this Aludin added fat and onions and a handful of tiny red peppers. The paunch was then cooked in a pot until the contents thickened almost to the consistency of liver. The only time this task was assigned to Samantha she failed to puncture the membrane as it cooked, resulting in a mild explosion, a terrible mess and three enraged Indians.

Aludin's skill at making jerky was impressive. Whetting her knife to a razor edge, she made slits alternating on either side of a chunk of venison so that when the ends were pulled it opened up accordion-fashion. Sun-dried on racks, the leathery product was pounded fine on a stone, mixed with fat and stuffed into lengths of intestine to make a sort of salami. Samantha's part in this was turning the drying meat on the racks and preparing the intestines, which she loathed.

Her lengthening stay in the *rancheria* wrought many changes in Samantha. As one day succeeded another without the physical violence she anticipated, her fear of death or torture receded though it never disappeared. Daily she saw evidence of the irrational and violent rage that could seize an Apache and she was certain that if she, rather than some horse or dog, provoked that anger, she would suffer the same shocking brutality.

But no healthy young woman could remain constantly panic-stricken. Her willingness to work and her natural curiosity combined to interest her in many of her tasks and distract her from her fears.

Physically she changed also. The reddish tinge in her hair deepened under the sun, but when it was braided she could hardly be distinguished from the young women around her. Where her clothes did not cover her body she burned as brown as any of them. Only her gray eyes set her apart for a close observer. She lost weight and grew tougher, better able to keep up with Aludin on her wide-ranging searches for edible plants and roots. Her hands distressed her to look at but they served her far better than when she first came to the mountains.

In the early days of captivity she had suffered painfully with them. The primitive tools raised blisters that broke and turned to raw sores. The firepit was a special hazard. Everything she touched seemed to burn her and until she learned what to pick up and what to leave alone she approached it with dread.

She paid a penalty for her new proficiency: a job which once required intense concentration became only tedious and gave her time to think. She was nagged by worry over the abrupt and final disappearance of Aunt Bee, whom she could only hope had been lodged with another band of Apaches somewhere. Increasingly she was baffled by the purpose of her captivity.

Since she had neither been killed at once nor handed over to the special mercies of the Apache women, she supposed she was being held as a hostage of some sort. No matter how long they kept her she would never be competent enough to have real value as a servant.

But for what or whom was she a hostage? If the Apaches only wanted to sell her back to her own people there surely had been ample opportunity to do so. Every soldier in Arizona must have been searching for her and word that they would pay the price of her release must have reached the Indians. Had they offered too little?

That thought was impossible. Tom Royal would meet any demand, however outrageous. She was certain of that. But what if Tom and the Army had decided she was dead? That was not impossible and it was terrifying. It reduced her to a desolation so numbing she could scarcely bear it.

As usual, her thoughts were recalled to her immediate situation by inexplicable activity among the Apaches. Any strange actions frightened her, and these were ominous.

She returned to the *ranchería* with Aludin about midmorning after a search for some sort of root, and even before they entered the rock gates she knew something was amiss by the wailing of the women. There were several strange warriors present in the *ranchería* also. She could never keep track of their comings and goings because she still found it impossible to tell one from the other but there were jaded horses on the picket lines and dusty men in war paint in the crowd about one of the wickiups. One of them had been wounded. His shoulder was bound in rags and his arm strapped to his side.

She went into Aludin's wickiup quickly, trying to attract as little attention to herself as possible. With growing wonder and apprehension she watched the Apaches deliberately set fire to a wickiup and let it burn to the ground. The women continued their keening as it burned. Wholly ignorant of the death rites of her captors she wondered if disease had struck the camp and this was their means of checking it. Her only hope of learning the facts of the matter was Severiano, whom she could see among the throng about the burning hut. He could have told her that Eskinyea was dead, shot by Tahzay on the Chiricahua reservation, and that the Apaches always burned a dead warrior's belongings. He might even have explained that the wounded man was Pionsenay, Eskinyea's brother and now by virtue of Eskinyea's death the leader of the band.

Shortly after the strange burning of the hut there was fresh excitement among the Apaches. A dusty runner appeared accompanied by one of the vedettes who always guarded the perimeter of the *ranchería* and the people gathered around him. He was fed by the women and afterward talked at length with the wounded man.

This was Pionsenay's messenger to Jeffords, who had talked to Clum instead and come back with an escort of San Carlos Apache police. They were waiting outside the *ranchería* to hear what Pionsenay would decide. After a little, Pionsenay declared he would talk to Sergeant Tauelclyee in person, but before he did that something would have to be done about Catle's white-eyes girl.

Samantha was still in Aludin's wickiup, halfheartedly boring holes in some tough cowhide to make moccasin soles, when she heard a horse stamp outside and a grunted command in Apache. She looked up nervously to find the door blocked by a squatting warrior. He hooked a finger and beckoned her to come.

She could not have moved if she wanted to. She was paralyzed and could not even draw breath through the scream frozen in her throat. With a grunt of irritation, the Apache caught her arm and hauled her through the door.

Aludin stood silently watching and near her Severiano held the halter of a paint pony. The scream bottled in Samantha's throat burst from her lips in a wordless babble of fear. The warrior shoved her toward the horse and Severiano turned the animal broadside to her.

"Get on!" he told her. She flung a despairing look at Aludin but the Apache girl's face was expressionless. Samantha put her hands on the pony's withers and vaulted onto him. He shifted nervously and the warrior snapped something at Severiano.

"No," said Severiano. "Like this." He spread two fingers and forked them over a thumb. When she did not react the warrior started toward her. In panic haste she hauled up her ragged skirt and swung herself astride the worried pony. With a piece of rawhide thong they tied her ankles beneath his belly. Severiano handed her the braided jaquima bridle twisted in the animal's mouth and pushed her in the small of her back. She wriggled forward, leaving room for him to mount behind her.

Without a word he kicked the pony into a trot toward the opposite end of the *ranchería* from the usual entrance. Samantha had seen the Apaches go out this way but she had never been allowed to use this back door to the rocky basin. It was narrower and far more difficult than the gate she knew but Severiano's heels drummed on the pony's flanks and they scrambled through.

She was too busy and miserable to question him. The thong linking her ankles enforced an awkward and painful seat. She could not grip with her legs and could only push hard on the pony's neck and grit her teeth against the jolting anguish of his trotting.

Severiano pushed the little horse hard along a series of game trails until they were a mile or more from the *ranchería,* then he slowed the pace to the point where fear overcame her discomfort. She squirmed around to find his face inches from her own, white teeth gleaming in his usual grin.

"Wh . . . what are you going to do?" she panted. He patted her shoulder.

"Don' be escared, Sah-mahn-ta."

85

Scarcely assured by his words, she resumed her struggle to cope with the pony's sharp backbone. They rode in silence for another half hour until she could bear it no longer. She begged him to untie her.

"*Sí.* We stop now." He wheeled under a gnarled cedar on a ledge, untied the thong, and helped her to the ground. The pony cropped grass eagerly.

"Sit. We stay here."

Reluctantly she obeyed him. There was a strained silence until her jumping nerves quieted enough for her to grasp that he had told her the truth. He was not going to hurt her. Why, then, had he brought her? She reached the conclusion that something was happening in the *ranchería* that required her absence and when that thought struck her she was dizzy with excitement.

Had the soldiers come? Was it possible at this moment Tom was only a few miles away, trying to make a trade for her with the Apaches? She was shaken by a wild exhilaration. She questioned Severiano eagerly.

"What is happening? Why have you brought me here?"

"I dunno," he shrugged. To every question he gave the same answer, grinning at her frustration. She pounded the moss with a doubled fist in vexation.

"Well, how long will we stay here?"

He looked at the sun. "Not long time. I tol' you, you don' be escared." Again she was quiet. She sat, knees high, chin resting on them, her arms wrapped about her legs. Frustration gave way to despondency and she forgot about Severiano until he put his arm around her waist. Instantly apprehensive, she pushed his hand away and glanced at his face. He was not angry. He only looked wistful and very young.

"Sah-mahn-ta?"

"Yes?"

"You be my woman?"

She was dumbfounded by the question. One of her worst fears when the Apaches took her was her woman's dread of assault by the men. In the east it was commonly assumed that all Indians automatically abused a female captive and her fear of this died slowly when the threat did not materialize. Now, intensely aware of their aloneness on this high ledge, all her apprehensions were revived.

Another of the many things she could not know about her captors was that molestation of a woman in the way she feared almost never occurred among Apaches. They considered such a thing destructive of personal good fortune and no matter what hellish torment they might inflict on a captive they did not rape. Very rarely an Apache might take a female prisoner as his wife and thus absorb her into the band but this happened only after she had long been a captive and then only with her expressed consent. Wholly unaware of this or the constraint it put upon Severiano she watched him alertly, ready for sudden violence.

But he did nothing, only looked gloomy himself. She tried to explain to him how she felt.

"Severiano, when your people stole me I was on my way to be married. Do you know what that means?" He nodded.

"My man was waiting for me. He is still waiting. As soon as I am free he will marry me. I cannot be another man's woman."

He looked a little puzzled and she doubted he had understood, but he had.

"You have *novio,* yes?"

She recognized the Spanish word and nodded. "Yes. The man I have promised to marry. Just as soon as he gets me back I will be his wife . . . his woman."

Severiano looked at her gravely. "But he don' get you back. How you marry with him when he stay in fort and you here?"

"Don't say that!" she burst out. "He will get me back. Maybe right now he is over there trading with your people for me." He looked surprised and a thrill of joy went through her. She had guessed why he brought her away from the *ranchería.*

But she was wrong. Severiano knew what was happening at the *ranchería* and he doubted it included trading for the white girl. On the contrary, Pionsenay needed his American captive now more than ever.

The shaman had told him the bullet in his shoulder, fired by Cochise's younger son, Nachise, would never rest in Apache flesh. Unless it were taken out, Pionsenay's arm would turn black and he would die.

The Apaches sometimes cut a bullet out of a man but the man often died anyway. Pionsenay knew the white-eyes could do it better and that was why he was prepared to make a deal with the Chiricahuas' friend, Tom Jeffords. He had got a quick response to his offer—too quick and too much. Sergeant Tauelclyee and a dozen San Carlos police waiting outside his camp for his answer made the matter pressing.

While Samantha sat beneath the cedar with Severiano, Tauelclyee alone walked into Pionsenay's *ranchería* to make talk. Pionsenay thought less of John Clum than of Jeffords, but the shaman had worried him and the hot ache in his shoulder worried him more. He agreed to go back with Tauelclyee.

Only when that was settled did Tauelclyee ask about the white women.

"We have heard of that," Pionsenay told him. "But we did not have anything to do with it."

Tauelclyee looked around the *ranchería* covertly. There was no sign of white women but he had not expected any. He was certain Pionsenay and Eskinyea had killed the two white men at the stage station and that made it all the more likely they had ambushed the stage and taken the women. The best way to clear that up was to get Pionsenay back to John Clum. If Clum kept the Apache chief long enough, his people would be willing to trade the white women for him. He eyed Catle closely, for Catle would be the leader when Pionsenay was gone and Catle would do the trading when Pionsenay sent him the word.

Meanwhile, Samantha was trying to distract Severiano without making him angry. As her only source of information he was too valuable to lose.

"How is it you speak my language, Severiano?" she asked him.

"I stay with soldiers when I was little kid. I talk good, hey?"

"Oh, yes! But how did you come to be with the soldiers?"

"My mama *Nakaiyi . . . mexicana,* you know? Injuns steal her like you. Keep her long time. Injun man take her for his woman. I don' know that man. When I was little kid soldiers fight Injuns and kill him. Take my mama an' me to fort. She cook an' wash clothes and be woman to soldiers long time."

It was a very long speech, even for Severiano, and he seemed to have lost the thread of his story he was silent so long.

"What happened then?" she asked softly.

"That bad fort. Ground sick and many soldiers die from sick. My mama too."

"Did the soldiers take care of you then?"

He shrugged. "I stay. Soldiers give me thing to eat and I rub boots and sweep soldier house. I stay till soldiers burn down fort and go away."

"Why didn't you go with them?"

"Oh, I like go with 'em but they don' take me. They don' want no greaser kid. Greaser kid with 'Pache daddy no damn good! *Teniente . . .* soldier chief, he say me you daddy goddam Injun an' you mama goddam hoor. We don' want no haffass 'Pache kid like you!"

He did not seem bitter about it. "Is . . . is that all? They just went away and left you?"

"Oh, no! They say lot more. They say me plenty thing." In his labored way he recalled what they had said. One shocking obscenity after another he brought forth with a clinical interest as if he found the words intriguing after being so long unused. It was soldier foulness at its rock-bottom worst and Samantha's face flamed. She clapped her hands to her ears.

"Stop it!" she begged. "Don't say things like that, Severiano. You can't even know what they mean!"

He ceased obediently, interested by her reaction. Obviously he did not really know what he was saying, only bringing out the half-remembered filth of a childhood in the barracks and stables of a cavalry troop. She put her hand impulsively on his.

"I'm so sorry. That was a dreadful thing they did to you."

Her sympathy reminded him of his earlier intentions. He gripped her hand hard.

"You be my woman now?"

"I can't, Severiano! I told you that. Can't you understand?"

He shook his head stubbornly. "No. You don' go back to soldiers. You never go 'way no more. You stay here an' be my woman. I don' let nobody hurt you, Sahmahn-ta."

He rambled on about things she only half understood. If she consented and Catle said yes and Pionsenay did not say no, then there would be no trouble at all. It sounded terribly complicated to her and in no way related to her status as a captive. If they could kill her or torture her any time they chose how could it possibly be so complex and difficult for Severiano to have her if he wanted her? It was wholly baffling but comforting in a way. But that did not help her immediate problem. Somehow she had to put Severiano off without offending him. She had an impulse to giggle. In addition to all her other difficulties there was now the requirement to flirt with Severiano, trying to hold his interest without encouraging him too much. She pulled her hand from his and patted it gently, just as she might have done with a too importunate youth on Aunt Bee's porch in Leavenworth.

"I cannot, Severiano. Not now, anyway. You must give me more time to think about it and I have to talk to my aunt first. Perhaps you can bring me to her so we can talk?"

He shook his head but he smiled happily. "I wait. I got plenty time."

The sun was sliding behind the mountains now in a blaze of crimson glory and he stood up. It was obviously time to go.

He let her ride the pony sidesaddle going back to the *rancheria* and he did not tie her ankles again. There was a rising excitement in her at the thought of what she might find when they reached the Apache camp and she did not mind his arm about her waist.

EIGHT

One of the favorite amusements of Apache men was a card game similar to the Mexican *monte*. They used cards of stiffened horsehide with barbarous and colorful figures painted on them and when a man drew a powerful card he tried to hold it in his hand, to deny it to his opponents until he could use it in his own bid for victory. There were other card games, *conquien*—known to the soldiers as "coon-can" and *tzi-chis,* so complicated none but an Apache understood it. Best of all, though, they liked their own version of *monte* and at it they gambled furiously for high stakes.

When Pionsenay rode out of his *rancheria* in the Huachucas with Sergeant Tauelclyee and his San Carlos police escort he was gambling for very high stakes—his life. He believed that only a white-eyes doctor could cure the Apache bullet that was killing him but he knew better than to put full trust in Tauelclyee's words. A San Carlos Indian policeman might tell the truth but when the white men got their hands on the Chiricahua renegade there would be a new game. Pionsenay the cardplayer held out a powerful card.

This, of course, was the soldiers' girl Severiano took away from the *rancheria* while Tauelclyee dickered for terms. As necessary insurance, Pionsenay dealt into the hands of his opponents some lesser cards: two of the families originally in Eskinyea's band. These women had lost their men in the shooting fray that claimed their leader's life and now they wanted to go back to the reservation.

The women had been absent when Pionsenay's band tortured the whiskey drummer but naturally they knew about it and they had seen the two captive white women. Pionsenay asked no oath of silence from them before he let them leave the *ranchería*. They were Apaches and silence was expected. But Pionsenay knew the power of Clum's Indian police and the way they extracted information from the people on the caged-ground, the reservation. If Tauelclyee betrayed him into the hands of the Americans the question of the women would arise and great pressure would come to bear on the two Apache women and their children. Dependent on Clum's hierarchy of tame Indians for their food, with no man to protect them, the women would sooner or later let slip a little information. Betrayal of their native trust it might be but in this case it would strengthen Pionsenay's hand. It would prove he had held back a powerful card.

At Camp Bowie, Assistant Surgeon Freeman cut the slug from Pionsenay's shoulder, trimmed and cleaned the wound and told Clum there was slight chance the renegade would die from it. The troopers of the Sixth Cavalry were combing Cochise's reservation to make certain all the Chiricahuas were in with Tahzay or had gone across the border and Clum did not send word he had Pionsenay. The renegade's courier had demanded a promise his chief would not be given to the soldiers and Clum kept that promise.

At the same time, though, he betrayed Pionsenay's faith in a far worse way. He had told the messenger he could not guarantee safety and he now told Pionsenay that though the soldiers would not have him, the white man's law in Tucson must. He sent a runner to Camp Grant and the telegraph station to advise Governor Safford he had Pionsenay in custody and would personally deliver his prisoner to Tucson "charged with the murders of Rogers and Spence." It was a message typical of John Clum.

On the twelfth of June, Tahzay and all that remained of Cochise's people under his hand—fifty-nine warriors and two hundred and sixty-five women and children— set out for the San Carlos reservation. Geronimo and his rebellious followers had disappeared into Sonora. Perhaps a hundred and fifty more Apaches had evaded the troops and gone into the Ojo Caliente reservation in New Mexico. High in the Huachuca Mountains waited Pionsenay's little band.

Brusquely, Clum refused any escort by the military and sent Tahzay's people off with fifty-five of his San Carlos police as guards. He planned to deliver Pionsenay to Tucson in custody of himself and Sergeant Tauelclyee. He drove a double-teamed single-seat buckboard with Pionsenay beside him and Tauelclyee riding alongside. No doubt the effect this casual delivery would have in Tucson was calculated.

He never had a chance to find out what the effect would have been, for his bombastic telegram to the governor produced unexpected results. He planned to stay the night of the thirteenth at the Sulphur Spring station, scene of the murders with which he had "charged" his prisoner, but when he reached that place he found waiting Deputy Sheriffs Charlie Shibell and Ad Linn from Tucson. They carried with them a formal warrant for the arrest of Pionsenay, and Clum could either hand him over or come along to watch. The latter role did not appeal to John Clum at all and with ill grace he turned over his prize. Pionsenay did not indicate what he thought of this, only complained about his shoulder.

To Shibell and Linn he looked like a mighty sick Indian and it was a mistake they would not soon forget. They took custody of Pionsenay about two o'clock in the afternoon and at once set out for Tucson, eight hours' drive to the west. For seven of these, Pionsenay appeared to grow sicker, so sick in fact that at the Cienega de los Pinos, an hour from town, Shibell and Linn were a little careless during a halt. An Apache never required more than a little carelessness and Pionsenay faded into the night from beneath their noses.

Governor Safford had a near seizure and for the first time John Clum said things about the civil government he had theretofore said only about the Army. The soldiers never knew Pionsenay had surrendered until after he was gone again. Those who believed Pionsenay held in his camp the two stolen women were particularly incensed; for the rest it was just another example of civilian incompetence. Pionsenay won the hand without even showing his power card.

NINE

When Colonel Oakes ordered the cavalry at Camp Grant held in readiness to march in three hours, one officer was away from the post. Timothy Touey, second lieutenant of Captain Dan Madden's C Troop, was supposed to be in Taylor's Canyon with a detail of troopers and Mexican woodcutters, laying in lumber for Camp Grant. By a stroke of good fortune he had gone into Tucson to get supplies for his camp and was thus able to meet Samantha and her aunt as they arrived from the East.

Restricted to his post by Captain Tupper, Tom telegraphed Tim Touey, asking him to take care of the women and see that they got on the stage for Croton Spring. Tim read between the lines of the message and grinned. He could picture Tom's fury at being held on short rein just as his girl reached Arizona. Fear not, he telegraphed back. I will meet your ladies and see them on their way. Save me a bottle of champagne.

So it was Tim Touey who met Samantha and her aunt and arranged for them to stay with Major Lord. He had supper with them the night they arrived but he was unable to see them off the next day, sending two troopers to take care of their baggage.

He had no inkling that there was trouble until he rode out to regimental headquarters the following day just as the bugler blew boots and saddles and B Troop boiled out of barracks to join the search for the missing women.

Tim wanted to go with them but the wire to Camp Grant was cut and he could not reach his captain. The regimental adjutant was no help.

"Tupper sent you to cut planks in Taylor's Canyon and if you think I'm going to change your orders without telling old Double-Tee, you're crazy!"

"Jim Sands, you're a damned martinet!"

"But a smart one! I want John Kerr's job in your troop and if I get crosswise of Tupper I haven't got a chance. You get his permission and you can do what you want, Tim Touey, but I won't change your orders!"

Touey went back to his woodcutters with hard words. Tom Royal's girl had stolen his Irish heart and the thought of her captive of an Apache buck made him curse in helpless fury.

He did not get back to Camp Grant until late in May, when his troop marched out with Major Compton's battalion for the Chiricahua reservation. Though Royal's troop went with them, Tim had no chance to talk to him.

Compton swung his battalion south in two wings through Railroad Pass, then down the San Simon Valley with the Chiricahua Mountains on their right, the Peloncillos on their left. The endless alkali flats glittered painfully under the hot sun and the troopers measured their progress by Stein's Peak, looming to the east where the stage road entered New Mexico.

For two nervous weeks they scouted the valley, daily expecting to meet hostile Chiricahuas. They met none. Gordo's band had crossed into New Mexico before they could get there and no more followed. Lieutenant Sam Craig's company of Tonto and Coyotero Apache scouts made sure of that. General Crook had said that Indian scouts were the Army's only hope of catching hostile Indians and Tim Touey believed him when he saw the scouts in action.

When the column broke camp in the morning, Sam Craig gave a one-word order, *"U-gash-i! . . . go!"* Without a sound his Apaches fanned out in a shambling, deceptive walk. They kept no formation. To Tim's eyes they looked undersized, short and stumpy, but their chests were broad and deep, their shoulders straight and well-proportioned. Their faces were often clean-cut and handsome.

As a concession to military status the scouts wore an Army shirt of gray flannel, tails reaching to the knee, but beneath this was the native breechclout and thigh-high moccasins. A few wore homemade bandoliers but most had adopted the Army thimble-belt of canvas full of cartridges for their carbines with the addition of a fearsome knife, usually a white man's butcher knife in a leather sheath made by the wearer. Their only authentic mark of government service was a small metal identity tag stamped with a number, worn with amulets, charms and the inevitable Apache bag of *hoddentin,* sacred pollen, about their necks on a thong.

A man had only to march with these *Mansos*—tame Indians as their unreconstructed brethren called them—to know why the latter were so hard to catch. The scouts moved on foot at about four miles an hour; not quite fast enough to make a horse trot to keep up with them but too fast to pace them at a walk. When they broke into a jog they could put a horse out of business in a few hours and they delighted in bedeviling an Army officer who rode with them by setting a pace that forced him to alternate continually between a fast walk and a trot.

General Kautz gave up his search for renegades by mid-June and called the Sixth Cavalry into Camp Bowie for their march home. Here, for the first time, C and G

Troops bivouacked together and Touey had a chance to talk to Tom Royal.

He found Captain Tupper first, and Tupper pointed to another campfire. "Royal's there, Mister. He'll be glad to see you. I guess you were the last one of us to see his girl, weren't you?"

"Yes, sir, I met her and Miss Ehler when they got to Tucson."

Tupper pulled his mustache and sighed. "I suppose I ought to have let him go, but would it have done any good?"

Tim made the tactful assumption that this was a private question and went in search of Tom Royal. He found him sitting on his bedroll alone before a small fire.

"Hello, Tim," Royal greeted him. "I'd been hoping to see you."

"First chance I've had. How are things with you?"

"I'm all right. I'm grateful to you for what you did for Sam in Tucson. Seems you were the last to see her except for the stage people and there aren't any of them left to talk to."

"I'm surprised they didn't ask for an escort."

"If I'd been there they'd have had one."

Tim looked back at Tupper and remembered the unhappy question he had asked himself. No matter what happened there would always be that question between these two.

"I did see Hogan," Tom continued. "He put her bags on the stage. All he could say was she sure looked pretty."

"Tom, I'm sorry I wasn't there when she left."

Royal made a push-away gesture. "Hell, Tim, I don't blame you for that. I don't blame anybody but myself. I should have been there somehow. Tell me what she said. How did she look?"

"She looked wonderful. She looked just like a girl ought to look, going to her wedding: happy, proud . . . pretty isn't the word for it."

"What did she say about the trip? Was it all right?"

"She liked it. She said her aunt got tired but she didn't

97

mind at all. She said the best part was the steamer from Frisco to San Diego."

"Did she say why they didn't stay on it around the Cape and up the river to Yuma?"

It seemed a casual question but Tim understood its meaning. If they had taken the longer way they would not have reached Tucson when they did.

"One day or another, Tom; what difference? You know those Apaches didn't take that stage just because she was on it. It could have happened any day."

"But I might have been there to help."

"Ah, Tom, don't do that to yourself! We'll get her back. Everybody says the Apaches will keep her alive until they can make a good trade for her."

"I know. Clum, Jeffords, they all say that. I don't believe it. I'd rather go after her."

"But where? Have you any idea who took her?"

"I think it was the same bunch that killed those two men at Sulphur Spring: Eskinyea and his brother, Pionsenay. I might have known for sure if that bastard Clum hadn't been so smart!"

"What do you mean?"

"They were back on the reservation right after we got here. They came in to try to get some of Tahzay's bucks to join them. There was a fight and Eskinyea was killed and Pionsenay wounded. He ran off but then he came back and Clum didn't tell us."

"Why not, for God's sake?"

"Because he wanted to take Pionsenay into Tucson all by himself and grab all the credit. Then Governor Safford outsmarted him. He sent a couple of deputies to take Pionsenay away from Clum and within six hours they lost him!"

"But where? How?"

"I don't know. He got away and I never had a chance to talk to him. I might have found out something. Hell, if he took Sam, we might have been able to trade him for her. I never had a chance!"

"What are you going to do now?"

"That stupid bastard Clum sent an Indian scout to get

Pionsenay. I'm going to San Carlos and try to talk to the scout. He may know something. He got into Pionsenay's camp. They'll have moved by now but at least it's a start. If we could pick up their trail . . ."

"But if Clum and Jeffords say stay away from them until you can make a trade what good will that do?"

"Sooner or later we'll stop listening to those two and then we've got to know where to look for her."

Tim stood up and nudged the fire with his toe. "Maybe you're right, Tom, but I wouldn't rush it. They've got to know what they're talking about; they've been with these Apaches a long time. If you jump those renegades they might kill the women and run for Mexico."

Royal put his hands together and pushed until the ridged muscles were visible even in the flickering firelight. "God! I don't know, Tim. That's what they say but I know what I want to do . . . and they won't let me!"

TEN

G Troop of the Sixth Cavalry returned to Camp Grant on the eighteenth of June and next day Tom Royal rode for the San Carlos Indian Agency a hundred miles distant.

He arrived the day after Tahzay and his dispirited Chiricahuas reached the reservation and Agent Clum was not immediately available. The Indian Bureau had realized a good part of a long-cherished dream—concentration of all the Apaches in Arizona on one reservation. Their joyful announcement of this glossed over the rather large number of Apaches who had escaped the net and John Clum was intent on seeing that the remainder stayed concentrated. This task took priority over everything else at the moment and the arrival of Lieutenant Tom Royal was no exception. The lieutenant could wait awhile.

Tom was quite aware of Clum's views on the military and did not look forward to asking favors of him. Nevertheless, everyone who had any experience of Apaches said Clum and his tame policemen were the best hope of finding and trading for his girl. Once upon a time it would have been Tom Jeffords—whose wards were not *Mansos,* tame Apaches—but Jeffords was through now, set aside by the Bureau, and John Clum had the power.

For all his brash and scathing criticism of the military, John Clum was a sympathetic man, hardly older than Royal, and he knew misery when he saw it.

"Mister, I'm sorry about your girl and her aunt," he said and he meant it. "I'll do everything I can to help."

Tom explained that he thought Eskinyea and Pionsenay had taken the women. Eskinyea was beyond anyone's reach now and the matter of Pionsenay had to be approached gently. Clum blustered a little about that. Had he been allowed to bring Pionsenay in as he intended, the old renegade would never have got away.

"When Tauelclyee went after Pionsenay I told him to look for the women. He didn't see them, but naturally they wouldn't let him unless they wanted to. I asked Pionsenay about them myself when he came in and of course he denied everything."

"Could I talk to this Tauelclyee?" Tom asked. "If I'm right about this he's been closer to them than anyone."

"Sure. I'll send for him."

Tauelclyee came and with him the Arivaipa chief, Eskiminzin, Clum's right-hand man among the Indians at San Carlos. Both listened gravely while Clum explained what was wanted. Tauelclyee responded.

Pionsenay had the women. If Pionsenay hadn't got away the white men would have found out. It was a good thing Pionsenay did get away.

"What do you mean by that?" exploded Clum.

Tauelclyee shrugged. When the white man's law got an Indian they might talk for a long time but in the end they put the Indian on a riata and hung him from a tree. He shot a glance at the soldier. Would they stop just because the Indian said he knew where the soldier's women were?

Neither white man could answer that. It hardly seemed necessary to Tauelclyee to explain what Pionsenay's women would do then or to elaborate on why Pionsenay's escape was a pretty good thing. He waited.

"All right," said the soldier. "Now he's back in his camp and Tauelclyee knows where it is. Why don't we go take the women away from him?"

Tauelclyee looked disgusted and Eskiminzin tried to explain. He talked very slowly as if to children. If Pionsenay had the women he was keeping them to prevent just that kind of foolishness. As soon as the soldiers appeared the band would scatter like quail and one of two things would happen. They would cut the women's throats just as they did with dogs and worn-out ponies or they would take the women into Mexico with them.

"What good would hostages be in Mexico?" Clum asked.

None at all. The Indians would sell the women to the first Mexican who could meet their price.

"Well, what's wrong with that?" Tom fumed. "That's what we want to do . . . get them away from Pionsenay. The Mexican government would send them back to us."

The Apaches regarded him in silent wonder. Americans thought they owned this country but they really didn't know much about it, not if they thought a Mexican who bought a pair of women from the Apaches would turn around and hand them over to the government. Mexicans had a loose set of rules about captives bought from Indians. About as loose as those applying to Indian women and children caught by the *rurales*.

When the Americans stopped fighting among themselves a few years back they had passed a law against slaveholding, but it wasn't very carefully observed by Mexican-Americans along the border or across it. On the American side they saw nothing wrong in buying even their own people from the Indians and keeping them in peonage that differed little from slavery. Every Mexican-owned brothel in Santa Fe or down in Texas had a few wretched Indian or half-breed girls to prove that. Neither Apache thought it wise to explain conditions in Chihuahua and Sonora where a woman didn't have to be Indian or half-breed to wind up in the same fix.

There might be a few officials in the Mexican states who would return an American woman to her people for a handsome fee, but Pionsenay would hardly do business with them. A certain amount of this had to be explained to the young soldier, but since the Apaches were understandably delicate about the explanation it was doubtful he was convinced. He kept going back to one point. What made Tauelclyee so sure Pionsenay had the women and just where was he keeping them?

Identifying the location was hopeless. Tauelclyee could find it in the night but he couldn't read a map and how could you tell a man who didn't know one rock from another where something was located in a pile of rocks? Maybe the soldier would talk to the two Apache women who came out of Pionsenay's *rancheria*? By bitter experience Tauelclyee had learned that no American believed just one Indian; he wanted a whole crowd of Indians to confirm any point.

Eskiminzin demurred. Tahzay and his people had just arrived. They were weary and frightened and they had many enemies among the conglomerate bands assembled at San Carlos. If the soldier sent for a couple of women and asked a lot of questions he might set the whole reservation in motion. When Clum got the drift of that he backed Eskiminzin adamantly. The very thought made him shudder.

Naturally the soldier got angry. John Clum's status with the Indian Bureau worried him not at all. He wanted his women. Old Eskiminzin intervened.

"I find out," he said. "I send someone. If Pionsenay got women I find out what he trade for. My word."

It was the final word, too. Neither Indian felt there

was any more to be said on the subject and there was no use pushing. Tom stayed the night at the Agency and next day tried again to make Clum send for the Apache women. Clum would never have achieved as much as he did without listening to the advice of his Apache friends and he was smart enough not to circumvent them.

"Keep your soldiers out of the Huachuca Mountains," were Clum's parting words to Tom. "You can hit 'em if they come out to raid, but don't go in there after 'em. Those are going to be Pionsenay's rules and if you want to see your girl again you'd better live with 'em. Give old Skimmy a chance and he just might make a trade for you."

ELEVEN

Severiano reentered the *ranchería* by the front gate and Samantha slid off the pony by Catle's wickiup. She looked around eagerly. She had no idea what she expected to find but it was impossible to suppress the excitement she felt.

It died hard, that excitement. One day and then another passed and nothing happened. Aludin's manner did not change and the rest of the Apaches treated her with complete disinterest.

A few days later there was a stir in the camp but it did not concern her. The Apache with the bandaged shoulder was back again. He was greeted with pleasure and even Samantha could detect the deference with which he was treated. Obviously he was a man of importance and she knew that the last time he came to the *rancheria* Severiano had taken her away. She could not find Severiano to ask for an explanation, however, and so did not know of Pionsenay's lucky escape from the Tucson deputies.

Now the sumac bushes began to bear their berries in quantity and a spasm of activity overtook the women. All day they ranged the mountainside gathering berries, which were spread on a hide and picked over carefully. The good ones were left in the sun to dry then put into the grinding stone and reduced to a fine powder which Aludin mixed with previously prepared mescal.

Samantha detested the grinding task. It was mindless work, primitive and tedious. She would far rather have wandered the flowering slopes to gather the fruit. Only when there were no more berries to grind was she released from her hated *metate* and allowed to go with Aludin and the others to search for the sumac bushes. They found an unculled thicket surprisingly close to the *rancheria* and as she pulled the berries with stained fingers it suddenly struck Samantha there were no guards about even though they were out of sight of the vedettes above the camp.

The plan—if it could be called a plan—took shape in her mind at that moment. She worked her way down the slope away from the others and no one noticed. The sumac was so dense it was impossible to see more than a few feet even though she could hear the other women all around her.

Reaching the lower edge of the clump she saw the shadows stretching far across the little clearing below. The sun would be down in a few minutes and Aludin would come for her. She would grunt and point or, if angry, might even say, "*¡Venga!*" Samantha sometimes felt that simple command had been assigned her as a name. No Apache ever said more to her. Severiano knew and used her name but no one else even tried.

Once, when her witless inability to communicate with anyone had driven her to despair, she had begged

Severiano to tell her again what she should call the Apache girl who rarely left her side.

"Aludin," he said in mild surprise. She had long tried to sort out of Sheneah's hissing, slithery conversation a name for her custodian but she had never succeeded.

"Ah-loo-deen?" she essayed and he laughed.

"Not like that." He repeated it, making an explosive hissing sound of the last syllable.

She tried again, puckering her lips and blowing through her teeth and did a little better. Severiano nodded and when she tried it on Aludin, the Indian girl was astonished. She seemed pleased, though.

The clearing below the sumac thicket was full of jumbled rocks and one of these was split, the cleft just deep and wide enough to hide a crouching girl. Samantha wedged herself into it. She had trouble with the basket of berries but it seemed better to hide it as well as herself. If they found no trace of her they might think she had simply returned to the *ranchería.*

She had no clear idea of where she would go if they gave her time enough to escape. She remembered the wagon tracks they had crossed coming to the *ranchería* and they were her goal. The Apaches would follow and she never doubted they would find her trail but they hated moving in the night and if she could reach level ground by dawn there might be one slim chance she could find help before they caught her.

She heard movement in the sumac and Aludin calling in a low voice. One of the other women also called out and someone laughed, a happy sound, loud and unrestrained. She was reassured. If they were searching for her seriously they would not be laughing. The voices of the women faded comfortingly but Aludin called again, quite near.

It was puzzling. If Aludin thought her prisoner had run away she would surely have set up an outcry. There was a prolonged silence and she began to shiver though it was not chilly in the sun-warmed rock. She peered out cautiously.

Nothing. No sound and no one in sight. She decided

to go farther down the slope and began carefully to work the basket free. The sudden rumble of a man's voice froze her in place. Aludin made some response and she understood what had happened. The Apache girl had been waiting quietly in the sumac. She jammed herself back into the split rock and wondered frantically what to do.

Aludin was coming now. She could hear the whisper of moccasins on rock. Samantha did the only thing she could. She curled up in her cleft and pretended sleep.

Something jabbed her painfully in the leg. She opened her eyes and stared foolishly at the angry face of the Apache girl. There was something more than anger in the glittering eyes but Samantha was too frightened to read it.

"U-gash-i!" snarled Aludin, using the explosive Apache word for "go!" She emphasized it with another thrust of her stick.

"Ouch!" squeaked Samantha, scrambling from her hiding place. When she was out, Aludin brought the stick down hard on her bare legs and she cried out in pain.

The voice of the man called through the sumac. "Hai!" said Aludin. Catle appeared and eyed the both of them angrily. Without a word he turned and went back into the thicket. Aludin brandished her stick and Samantha hurried after him.

The evening meal and preparations for bed passed as usual with only Aludin's black looks to mark the episode. Samantha began to hope they believed her little farce.

It was a futile hope. Early next morning, Catle's elder wife put her head into their wickiup and said something to Aludin. This was unusual, for Sheneah almost never entered the hut shared by the younger women. Aludin was upset. Her face never betrayed anything but Samantha had learned to tell much from her actions. She left the wickiup at once and Samantha braided her hair with shaking fingers.

It appeared that Catle had already eaten, which meant that Sheneah had prepared his food. Aludin raked the ashes from the firepit and when Samantha tried to help she was pushed aside. As soon as the ashes were removed, Aludin began with great industry to grub up the fire-blackened stones ringing the pit. Samantha was baffled until it dawned on her this was simply make-work, the first she had ever seen any Apache perform. Catle appeared but his young wife kept her head down and her hands busy. When he spoke, Samantha quailed. To her ears all Apache sounded harsh and irritable but there was anger in Catle's voice that needed no knowledge of his tongue to recognize. Aludin left off working at the stones and stood up but still she did not look at her husband. Sheneah waddled into view looking smug and holding a freshly cut willow withe. Samantha shivered.

It was clear someone was going to be punished, but who? If that switch were all her botched attempt to escape would cost she welcomed it. But what if Aludin shared it? It would be her fault and it would cost her all the favor she had managed so laboriously to win from the Apache girl. She wondered if Catle would beat them both in public. Several women and children were already watching curiously.

All her questions were answered at once. Catle stopped speaking and stalked away, Aludin following. Sheneah pointed her fist at Samantha and she jumped to her feet. She thought she was to go into the wickiup but Sheneah blocked the way. Her menacing figure kept the white girl moving around the hut.

Sheneah followed and without warning began to ply her switch. She did not use it on Samantha's back but on her legs and the short skirt was no protection. Samantha pushed both hands into the yielding cover of the wickiup and after a moment put her head down on them and fought for silence.

She had no experience to guide her but she did the one thing that could help. She did not cry out or try to run away. The switch frayed and broke and Sheneah stopped. She examined it with interest and threw it away, then walked back to the firepit. Samantha followed, shaking so uncontrollably she had to steady herself with a hand on the wickiup. It was finished. That was all. As if nothing untoward had happened the daily work was resumed. Sheneah was preparing to make tiswin, a sort of weak corn beer, and she wanted Samantha to help.

Just-sprouted corn kernels had to be ground very fine and simmered in a quantity of water; not a very demanding task. Samantha's only error was to put too much wood on the fire, which made the pot boil and brought Sheneah grumbling back. Apparently it was only supposed to simmer and thereafter Samantha watched it carefully.

A long hour later she was roused from her apathy by the appearance of Severiano. He squatted beside her and poked at the fire with a stick.

"Don't," she warned him. "You'll make it blaze up and the pot will boil."

"*¡Así es la vida!* Make bad *tulepah* an' Sheneah beat you again." Samantha bit her lip and wondered if he had watched.

"What is *tulepah?*"

"*Tulepah* . . . tiswin . . . same thing. Like yellow stuff in bottle your soldiers drink."

Beer, she thought, looking into the pot. How can you make beer from a mess like that? The liquid had thickened and was bubbling through a crust of scum with little popping noises.

"She hurt you, Sah-mahn-ta?" She gave him a sidelong glance. He was grinning as usual and she shrugged.

"You don' try to run away no more, hey?"

"I didn't try to run away!"

"Hoh! You hide in rocks so Aludin think you gone home an' then you gonna run away."

"I didn't! I did no such thing! I was tired and the sun was hot and I went to sleep."

"You don' fool Apaches, Sah-mahn-ta. That damfool thing you do. What you do if you run away, huh? Where you go? Nothin' down there but rock and sand and no water. Apaches ketch you quick an' what you think they do then?"

She felt a thrill of horror. "What? What would they do, Severiano? Would Catle torture me?"

"What you mean?"

"You know . . ." She gestured vaguely, reluctant to be explicit. "Like the white man they took from the stage with my aunt and me."

"Oh, no! Women do that thing an' they don' do it till Pionsenay say them do it. You don' belong Catle, Sahmahn-ta; he jus' keep you for Pionsenay."

This glimpse into her status in the *ranchería* intrigued her but Severiano was not through yet. He cut off her eager question brusquely.

"I tell you, Sah-mahn-ta, you don' do that no more. Nex' time mebbe Pionsenay say to Catle make you never run no more."

She stared at him, round-eyed in apprehension. "How?"

He had been shaving splinters from a twig with his knife. With the back of the blade he traced a line across the tendon just above her heel and she shrank from its touch.

"Why does he keep me here, Severiano? Why doesn't Pionsenay sell me back to my people?"

The familiar closed look settled on his face and she knew the answer before it came. She sighed. "Will Catle do anything more to me now?"

He chuckled. "I don' think so. Mebbe he beat Aludin a little."

"Why, for God's sake?"

"She don' see you hide in rock. She don' watch good and then she scared. She don' call Catle come help look for you. Catle plenty mad." He grinned wickedly. "Catle don' ever beat Aludin before. Now is time he tan her ass a little."

"Stop it, Severiano! You promised not to talk like that any more."

"I forget. But you do good, Sah-mahn-ta. You don' yell when Sheneah beat you. You jus' like 'Pache woman now."

It was high praise but hard-earned. Her legs still burned

from the switch. He touched her foot with his hand and she flinched.

"Sah-mahn-ta?"

"Yes?"

"Mebbe I go now an' ask Catle can you be my woman?"

"Oh, Severiano," she began placatingly, "I told you before I like you. I do. I like you very much but I don't want to belong to you or Catle or anybody else except the man who is waiting for me down there. Can't you see? I want to go back to my own people. That's where I belong."

He jabbed angrily at the fire and she fended off his stick.

"Please! You must know what it's like to be separated from your people."

He seemed very angry and Samantha was afraid. She watched him anxiously.

"I don't know what to do! I don't know what to say to you!"

"Say you be my woman. I be good to you. I don't whip you like Catle."

"But I want to go home! I want to go home to my own people!"

Her stubborn repetition of the words made him even angrier. "Lissen, *Americana!* You ask why Pionsenay don' let you go? *Bueno!* I tell you! Down there white soldiers they ride out of fort an' they ride back to fort but they don' look for no fight. They don' chase 'Paches no more. How come they don' go in mountains no more? Don' burn no wickiup. Don' kill no 'Pache womans . . . steal no 'Pache kids. Huh? You *sabe, Americana?"*

"Because the Apaches have me here." It was not a question. It was a simple fact; the only logical explanation of why they kept her.

"But my people must have tried to buy me back!" She looked at him pleadingly. "They have tried, haven't they?"

He answered her with another question.

"You see 'Paches take their guns and ride away from

here? You see what they bring back? Horses an' cows an' blankets?" She nodded. "*Bueno*. You know where they go?"

"Mexico?" The word came from her in a whisper, forced through the chilling knowledge of what he meant.

"*Sí!* 'Paches don' steal *yanqui* horses. Don' kill no white people no more. Mebbeso your people like that, hey? Mebbeso they say this good. We don' do nuthin', 'Pache he don' do nuthin'. *Bueno! Muy bueno!*"

"No! Oh, no! I don't believe that!"

He shrugged. "How come? You one girl . . ." he held up a thumb ". . . jus' one white girl. 'Paches fight your people again an' plenty white girl dead. Mebbe your people make good trade with you, hey?"

"God help me!" she moaned.

"No. I don' know 'bout your god but I don' think he help you. I help you if you want. You say me, Severiano, I be your woman an' I help you. You *sabe,* Sah-mahn-ta?"

He left her and she pushed her way into the oak thicket to look for more firewood. He is lying, she told herself. He is only trying to make me do what he wants. But the cold logic of what he said was inescapable, numbing. She built up her fire and sat beside it, arms wrapped about her knees, trying not to think at all.

The afternoon wore away with dreadful slowness. Before the sun touched the rim of the surrounding peaks Samantha had plumbed an abyss of hopelessness she had never known before.

Aludin came at last and her blank face was frightening. The usual round of preparation for the evening meal began, Aludin tending her bread while Samantha warmed meat before the coals. The silence was painful and she decided to break it somehow.

"Ah-luh-deen?" she whispered. She could hear Sheneah and Catle talking in the other wickiup and she did not want to attract their attention. Always before, Aludin had been amused by Samantha's attempt to say her name. There was no hint of amusement on her round face now.

"*Bueno,* Ah-lhu-deen?" she pleaded.

111

Astoundingly the set mouth relaxed, curled in an exaggerated grimace of anguish that was genuinely comical. The Apache girl pursed her lips and rubbed her haunches gingerly. It was so funny and so wholly unexpected, Samantha laughed aloud. The voices in the other wickiup ceased instantly and, like any Apache child, she covered her mouth with her hand and looked abashed. For just a moment, Aludin's black eyes twinkled in amusement—the first common emotion Samantha had shared with any of her captors since she had been taken by them.

TWELVE

After Tahzay and his people departed, quiet settled on the abandoned Chiricahua reservation for a little while, but not on Washington. Echoes of the move reverberated there for months.

Clum boasted to the Indian Bureau that he had managed the removal without assistance from the Army and in spite of Tom Jeffords' mismanagement of the Chiricahuas. Jeffords resigned bitterly, advising the Commissioner of Indian Affairs that the killing of Rogers, Spence and Lewis was not an Indian outbreak but the result of the idiocy of the stage company agent who sold whiskey to outcast Apaches. He denounced the removal of Tahzay as a flagrant breach of trust by the United States and disappeared from the scene.

General Kautz deplored the whole affair, naming Clum a troublemaker and Jeffords dishonest. The latter had been padding his headcount of Chiricahuas, said Kautz.

There were indeed some four hundred Apaches unaccounted for after all the returns were in; Jeffords, Clum and the Tucson politicians swore they still lurked on the old reservation but Kautz claimed they were a figment of Jeffords' crooked ration returns.

General Kautz's reports suffered when two prospectors ventured onto the old reservation in mid-July and were promptly murdered by someone. There was a great to-do in Tucson with repercussions in Washington. According to Tucson newspapers, two innocent Americans had been slaughtered by several hundred renegade Apaches still occupying the Sulphur Spring Valley despite Army claims that the area had been cleared of all Indians.

But General Kautz had more pressing problems than this in his Department. With the bulk of the Apaches gathered at San Carlos, he now had Army posts with no Indians to watch and Indians without enough soldiers to watch them. He wanted to concentrate his troops and abandon some posts, but the contractors in Tucson and their politician friends would have none of this. Scattered posts meant fat freight contracts and the illogical result in Arizona was more Army posts. F Troop of the Sixth Cavalry camped on the Gila River to guard Clum's nervous assembly of Apaches around San Carlos and their tents and adobe huts were eventually dignified by the name of Camp Thomas.

En route to the Gila, F Troop stopped for a while at Camp Grant, crowding the barracks there intolerably. The situation was complicated by the fact that though at least one troop of cavalry would normally have been absent scouting, thus making more room, this was not now the case. Major Compton had talked with Clum and then with Colonel Oakes, the cavalry commander, and the latter agreed that until there was some proof that Tom Royal's girl and her aunt were dead or out of Arizona it would be unwise to raid Apache *rancherías* in the mountains. The result was an immediate slowdown of cavalry operations. The reason was not discussed. This was the beginning of the undeclared truce engineered by wily Pionsenay.

There was no holiday for the soldiers, though. "Idle hands are the devil's workshop," said Colonel Oakes and retreat parade in full dress uniform was reinstituted at once. Other occupations were revived. Openmouthed Indians came to watch sweating cavalrymen making *moulinets, pointes,* cuts and parries on the drill ground with long-unused sabers.

"En tierce . . . POINT!" bellowed a red-faced lieutenant. "TWO!" and the troopers lunged, thrusting sabers forward. "THREE!" and they returned to the spread-legged guard position.

"Hai!" murmured the enthralled Apaches.

One morning late in June the fretful bang of the reveille gun brought the swollen garrison of Camp Grant out to a welcome sight. During the night one of Esteban Ochoa's wagon trains had arrived with supplies. Only M Troop of the cavalry groaned. They were detail troop that week and theirs was the task of unloading the wagons.

Through the blazing morning and into the afternoon, M Troop labored under the eye of their commander, Captain Bill Rafferty. About midafternoon the lid was pried off the last packing box and the troopers paused to mop their brows.

"What's in that one?" asked Captain Gil Smith, the quartermaster.

"There's a envelope here, Cap'n," said a trooper, plucking it from the shredded newspaper which seemed to fill the box. Smith opened it and read the contents.

"Good God in the foothills!" he said slowly.

"What's the matter?" demanded Rafferty. Smith passed him the letter.

"No!" Rafferty shook his head, looking up from it. "I don't believe it."

"What'll I do with them?" asked the quartermaster.

"Give 'em to the infantry?"

"Never get away with it!"

"Give 'em to Dan Madden then. Remember when those new fatigue blouses came in last year and C Troop got 'em all? Madden was pretty cute about that. He's got it coming to him."

"It's a dirty trick but you're right." Smith considered for a moment, then grinned. "Captain Rafferty," he said formally, "will you be good enough to have that case nailed up again and delivered to C Troop in half an hour? It should take me about that long to endorse this letter to Captain Madden."

"Very good, Captain Smith." The two officers exchanged elaborate salutes and the troopers eyed them suspiciously.

Exactly thirty minutes later a messenger from the quartermaster bearing a letter and four troopers of M Troop carrying a box arrived simultaneously at the C Troop orderly room. The box was not heavy enough to require four men but there had been some competition for the job. The bearers put it down on the barrack stoop and lingered curiously.

Captain Madden opened the letter and his face went first red then white with rage.

"That skunk! That low-down, conniving . . . !" His exclamation trailed off into obscenity and the two sergeants in the orderly room stared at him in surprise. Dan Madden was a choleric officer who never hesitated to say what he thought but he was rarely foulmouthed.

"Bring that goddam box inside!" he said hoarsely. "Get it off the stoop!"

At four-thirty every afternoon there was no parade, Major Compton left his office and made a circuit of the parade ground that brought him to his quarters just as retreat was sounded and the flag brought down. Anyone who had reason to avoid the eye of the post commander took care to disappear as he made this leisurely stroll. The major understood and accepted that but if a man came out of doors during his circuit of the post he expected a salute and a greeting. Now, as he passed C Troop, two men appeared in the door of the supply room, caught sight of him and ducked back. Compton saw them.

"You men!" he barked. "Come here! Both of you."

He was framing a reprimand when something about their appearance stopped him openmouthed. The two troopers halted and saluted in unison and for the first time in his life, Compton failed to return a salute.

"Wha . . . what have you got on your head, soldier?" They glanced sidelong at each other trying to decide who had to answer. "You!" Compton resolved the dilemma with a shaking finger.

"Sir . . ." the soldier began, then swallowed hard, his face a picture of misery.

"Don't mumble, man! Speak up!"

Every window and door in the barracks was filled with fascinated faces. The soldier took a deep breath and spoke loudly. There could have been few in the garrison who did not hear him.

"Sir, it's a piss helmet!"

Compton's eyes bulged and his mustache twitched violently. At a distance the post commander appeared to be struggling with rage. Only the two troopers before him knew that it was not fury but laughter he was trying to hold back. Silently he saluted and waved them away before he walked to the C Troop supply room.

Unaccountably, no one warned Captain Madden and his two sergeants. They were staring morosely into the open crate when the supply sergeant recognized their visitor.

" 'Shun!" he roared.

"Dan . . ." Compton began, then eyed the sergeants. They faded from the room. "What's going on here, Dan?"

"If this is a joke, Major, it's a damned poor one! We'll be the laughingstock of the Territory! I protest, sir! I'll . . ."

"Now, now . . . easy does it. Take it from the beginning, Dan."

"You saw those filthy things! Look in that box! There's eighteen more of those dung-colored abortions in there!"

Compton peered into the box curiously. "Were there some instructions with them?"

"Here! Right here! Endorsed to me by Captain Acting Assistant Quartermaster Gilbert Smith . . . damn his beady little eyes!"

The major read aloud in a wondering voice, ". . . dur-

116

ing the recent investigation relative to the campaign hat, the Quartermaster General of the Army obtained from Great Britain, through the generous aid of Sir Edward Thornton, samples of the cork helmet worn by British troops in hot climates . . ." He paused to look again into the box. ". . . the purchase of one hundred of these helmets complete with puggarees was authorized by the Secretary of War for trial by troops in Arizona. Forwarded herewith are twenty helmets to be issued for test to selected members of the garrison at Fort Grant . . . appropriate report of their merits or deficiencies will be rendered not more than ninety days after their receipt."

He lowered the letter and looked at the irate commander of C Troop. "You got all of them?"

"Every damned one!"

"Smith should have consulted me on this," said Compton mildly. "How many have you issued?"

"Two. I suppose you saw one?"

"Both. At the same time. Take out three more, Dan, and give them to your people and send the rest back to Smith. I'll have five sent to each company on the post. How does that suit you?"

Madden was so relieved he found it difficult to reply. He nodded.

"And, Dan . . ." Compton turned back, "one other thing . . ."

"Yes, sir?"

"I suspect you'll have less trouble with them if you instruct your men exactly what to call them."

"Call them!" raged Madden. "What in hell should I call 'em? They're pith helmets, aren't they?"

"That's a mite hard to say, Dan. Why don't you just call 'em 'cork helmets' like it says in the letter?"

G Troop of the Sixth, also at Camp Grant, had more serious troubles: it was Tom Royal's troop and he had served in it ever since he graduated from West Point. Call to quarters one hot July evening found the men of G Troop lounging on their bunks, enjoying a smoke and the desultory small talk that filled the interval until taps was sounded.

It was more than a month since George Custer and most of the Seventh Cavalry had met disaster on the Little Big Horn but it seemed the discussion of this event would never end. Since opinion of Custer was sharply divided, discussion generally ended in a quarrel.

This evening, before that point was reached, the first sergeant put his head in at the door and shouted gruffly: "Get them lights out when taps goes! The Officer o' the Day's standin' outside an' I don't want no gig fer lights tonight!"

"Yes, Sarn't," answered the room orderly respectfully. "Who's O.D. tonight?"

"Mister Royal, so watch yer ass!"

"Pore bastid!" murmured someone. "Don't reckon nobody's heard nuthin' 'bout his girl, has they?"

An old soldier called Pop Simmons knocked out his pipe and scratched his bald head with the stem. "Sometimes ye git 'em back but most times ye don't."

Pop was a wispy little man of unknown age who looked as if a high wind would take him off. His looks were deceiving; he could outlast most men on a rough scout and he was one of perhaps a dozen men who had been with the regiment since it was formed in the first year of the war. No one knew how many times he had put on corporal's stripes because no matter how often he did he soon returned to his usual rank of private. Pop's affinity for whiskey kept him in trouble.

"Hell, Pop," put in Corporal Haynie. "We got them little gals back from the Injuns in Kansas . . . German, Jarman . . . I fergit their names now."

"Yeah, but they was just little bitty kids. Mister Royal's gal was growed up an' a looker too, I hear tell."

"What difference's that make?"

"Keerist, man! When them Injuns in Kansas took a growed-up white woman she wuz public propitty fer all th' bucks in th' party till they got back ter camp. After thet she belonged to th' buck what got her an' he cud do just whatever he tuk in mind to with her. She had ter work fer his squaws jest like a slave an' if th' buck
118

showed her any favor them bitches beat th' hell outta her."

"Hell, a gal young as Royal's wuz kin take a sight o' beatin'. She warn't sickly, wuz she?"

"Beatin's jest the half of it. If the squaws make too much fuss, the buck's likely to trade er gamble a captivated woman off. I heard of 'em bein' gambled off two er three times in one day. If she put up a fight they'd jest stake her out an' leave her till she got sense.'"

"They kill her then?"

"Naw! Even Injuns ain't thet wasteful. They keep her till she's plumb wore out er th' troops gits too close to 'em. They git pressed an' the buck what owns her'll cut her throat er if he's feelin' mean, he'll hamstring her and jest leave her lay. I say, by Gawd, young Royal an' his gal're damn lucky if them red bastids kilt her when we run 'em acrost the border into Mexico!"

Outside the long, sweet notes of taps echoed against the slopes of Mount Graham but the men were listening to Pop and the candles went unsnuffed. Pop was delighted with his audience and he leaned forward, emphasizing his words with jabs of his unlit pipe.

"I say Mister Royal never shud o' brought thet pore gal out here like he done! He knew whut cud happen to her. I put some blame on th' ol' man, too. Thet was a dirty trick, ol' Tupper makin' thet boy stay here 'stead o' goin' to Tucson to git them wimmen, but thet don't 'scuse Royal none. I don't wonder he's so miserable knowin' whut done happened to thet gal since them Injuns got they hands on 'er. By Gawd, he—"

The door of the squad room crashed open against the wall and there was a wild scramble for the candles. Before they were out there was time to know the white face of the officer in the door. The soldiers held their breath, waiting for the explosion.

But there was none. Lieutenant Royal said not a word and after a moment they heard his spurs clink on the gallery floor.

"My God! How long was he standin' there?" breathed someone. "Didn't nobody hear him?"

119

"Long enuf to fix our wagon! Oh, man, the first soldier's gonna give us hell termorrer!"

But strangely the first sergeant said nothing. Obviously Royal had not spoken to him.

"Somethin's got to give purty soon!" they told each other. "Never seen a man look as bad as that one!"

THIRTEEN

Late in July, Lieutenant Tony Rucker found an excuse to visit Camp Bowie, which still had its problems despite the removal of the Chiricahuas from their old reservation to San Carlos. He had recently been loaned by Captain Rafferty to command F Troop, which was marking time at Camp Grant until it acquired an officer of its own.

He wanted to show off a little. His onetime West Point classmate, Austin Henely, commanded a troop at Bowie and Tony wanted to show him that he wasn't the only second lieutenant in the regiment with a command. They had entered the Point together but Rucker fell afoul of the Academic Department and dropped out, gaining his commission a month after his former class graduated.

He was greeted by Henely and Tate Hulse, the only other lieutenant at Bowie, and they welcomed him even though he was weighed down by command and full of misinformation about their troubles. The bodies of two murdered prospectors had been found on the old Chiricahua reservation and there had been a furore in the Tucson newspaper.

Henely had sent a patrol under Sergeant Marcus Robbins, who found a cold trail and followed it to the Mexican border, where he stopped. The *Arizona Citizen* castigated the Army for failing to pursue the killers into Mexico and remarked that little more could be expected when no officer was present.

Colonel Oakes had reacted badly. He blasted Henely for sending a sergeant and issued a furious order that American troops "in hot pursuit" of Indian renegades would follow them into Mexico if necessary. Rucker twitted his classmate about this and provoked a wrathful response.

"Mark Robbins won the Medal of Honor fighting Indians! He didn't need me to bird-dog him. Besides, I would have done just what he did. Colonel Oakes says cross the line but has he told Governor Pesquiera? The Sonorans raise unshirted hell when we ride across their border."

Tony Rucker chuckled. "The Old Man has to do something when they ride him like that. It's no problem anyway if we don't push the Apaches any more than we are now."

"I've been wondering about that," Henely said. "What's going on anyway?"

Rucker shrugged. "Tom Royal's women is my guess. Nobody will come out and say it but what else can it be? Clum has told everybody the only way to get them back is stay out of the mountains and trade for them."

"And just give those renegades a license to steal?"

"Have you seen any Apaches down here?"

"No, but what about those prospectors?"

"You said yourself it was probably Mexicans who killed them. Think back, Aussie. Have you had a single report of Apache raiders since those women were taken?"

"Well . . . dammit, no!"

"All right. Think that one over. And while you're at it, how about some supper?"

Coming out of the Officers' Mess after the meal, Tate Hulse sensed a movement in the gloom of the ramada and froze. Rucker did the same. In the bar of lamplight from a window a brown figure materialized, hands held out to show empty palms.

Tate relaxed. "Bubber? You looking for me?" It was one of the Coyotero Apache scouts and Tate addressed him by the name the troopers used because they couldn't pronounce his real one. Tony Rucker peered closely at the Indian.

"Why it's Kad-kha! How, friend!" He knew a surprising number of the Indian scouts with the regiment and remembered them all. He held out his hand and the Apache took it with pleasure. The white man's greeting pleased them and they enjoyed exchanging it.

"You want me, Bubber?" Tate asked. The Apache shook his head. Tony Rucker was more familiar with the problem of communicating with the scouts and he made the proper opening. He took a sack of tobacco from his shirt pocket and rolled himself a cigarette, then passed tobacco and papers to Bubber in an offhand gesture.

The Apache acknowledged the offer with a grunt and made himself a smoke. Then he squatted, disappearing from the shaft of light. Both lieutenants followed suit and Rucker struck a match to light the cigarettes.

In the road there was a startled exclamation and the oily double-cluck of a carbine hammer pulled back in haste.

"All right, sentry! It's all right," Tony called, uncupping the match to show his face. The soldier uncocked his weapon and walked on, light from the window glinting on his spurs. Tate fidgeted while the other two smoked in silence. After an interminable time Rucker made a slight gesture with the glowing end of his cigarette and Bubber grunted again.

"Nantan-betunny-Kahyeh say you look for soljer womans." A surge of keenest joy went through Tate Hulse and Rucker sensed it. He put a restraining hand on the younger officer's knee.

"That's Clum he's talking about. Take it easy now and let him say his piece."

But Bubber waited politely until he was sure the two

officers had nothing more to say to each other. Rucker had to break the silence again.

"You know where is soldier woman, Kad-kha?"

"No."

Tate moved impatiently and again Rucker nudged him. He knew there was no way to hurry this.

"You hear talk about soldier woman?"

Bubber made what could be an affirmative noise. He put a hand into the light, two fingers extended, then gestured behind him. Two days ago.

"Pinaleño man stop here. His woman say she see white woman . . ." A finger held straight up in the light. "Up there . . . way up."

"In mountains?"

"Yah. That way." He used the beam of light as a man would use a blackboard to draw on, pointing to the west through the soft lamp glow. It would take an hour to pinpoint the location if it could be done at all by talk. Rucker postponed that effort.

"Soldier woman in 'Pache camp . . . in *ranchería?*"

"No. Pinaleño woman hunt something to eat. She alone. White woman alone. No 'Paches. White woman speak. Say thing make Pinaleño woman scared. Much scared. Pinaleño woman . . ." he blew out his breath and made a shooing gesture. The Indian woman had run away.

It made no sense to Tate. How could Sam or her aunt have spoken Apache to a squaw?

"You know what white woman say? How she speak?"

Bubber's face was in the light now and he looked both puzzled and reluctant. He had already said more than he would ever have said to Tate Hulse or Henely. But Tony Rucker was different. He had been on two long patrols into the White Mountains with Rucker, who never missed a chance to hold these fantastic conversations with his Apache scouts. This was putting a strain on his limited English but he continued.

"You know that time Nah-deh-gah say you 'bout 'Pache Ghost Peoples?"

"*Anh!* Yes, I remember good." Nah-deh-gah was a

Chiricahua scout and one memorable night he had made a valiant effort to explain to Tony Rucker about the Chiricahua supernaturals. "I remember Life Giver and White Painted Woman and Child of the Water. I remember Coyote stories and House of Mountain Spirits . . ." He pointed to the west. "Way up in mountains. Nah-deh-gah tell good story."

"Yah. *Enju* . . . good! White woman speak Pinaleño woman. Say 'Pache Ghost Peoples bad. Say bad peoples live in mountain. Pinaleño woman run away fast. She scared they . . ." his hand moved toward Tony then snapped shut like a trap. Tony Rucker sighed and Tate could contain himself no longer.

"I don't understand it but can't we talk to the woman? Does he know where she is now?"

Bubber understood the question. He even answered it. "Pinaleño man go reservation. Go speak Nantan-betunny-Kahyeh. Maybe get tobacco for good story."

"Then she's at San Carlos! We can—" Rucker shook his head.

"I doubt you'd get anything out of her Bubber hasn't told you." He turned back to the scout.

"Bubber, what kind of clothes did white woman in mountain have?"

" 'Close'? What mean 'close'?"

Tony plucked at his shirt. "What she got on her . . . like this?"

"Hai!" Bubber thought a moment. "Pinaleño woman say she got . . ." He touched his own coarse, smock-like garment. "Long." He touched his neck and his moccasined ankles.

"What color? Red? White like you got?"

"Nah." Bubber thought a moment. Unable to find what he wanted in English, he shifted to Mexican: "*Azul.*"

"I thought so," Rucker muttered. He pushed his tobacco and the packet of thin American papers, so prized by the Apaches, into Bubber's hand.

"Kad-kha, you tell good story. Good as Nah-deh-gah. I thank you." He stood up and held out his hand.

Bubber shook it heartily. *"Schi-cho . . .* friend!" he said, then he faded into the darkness.

Tate Hulse blew out a long breath. "If I listened to much more of that I'd be as crazy as the both of you. Did that woman see Sam Allyn or didn't she?"

"I don't think so."

"Then either she was eating *peyote* or she's got one hell of an imagination!"

"Not necessarily. When that happens to a white woman we call it a miracle."

"Ah, come on, Tony!"

"I'm sorry, Tate. I know how much it means to you. I thought we had a break too but . . ." He shook his head. "I don't think this has anything to do with Tom's girl or her aunt."

"Then you know what he was talking about? It makes sense to you?"

Rucker shrugged. "I've heard something like this before."

"Then will you for God's sake explain it to me?"

"All right, sport, but let's see if Henely will give us a drink and then I'll tell you."

Henely met them at the door of his adobe quarters. "Where the devil have you two been? What . . . ?" he broke off, seeing Tate's face. "What's happened?"

"Give us a drink and we'll tell you."

In honor of the occasion, Henely produced loaf sugar to kill the taste of the alkaline water and made a whiskey toddy. Rucker recounted Bubber's story and Henely looked as puzzled as Tate.

"Explain, professor!" he demanded.

"She could have been eating *peyote,* like Tate says. Doesn't matter really. She saw something. Since she's Apache it was probably her idea of White Painted Woman and that would be like a good Catholic girl saying she had a vision of the Virgin Mother. If you could equate Apache divinities with ours I'd say they both have about the same relative status."

Neither Henely nor Tate could argue that. It made sense in a way. Then Tony Rucker grinned.

"There's another possibility, though . . ."

"What?"

"Bubber says the white woman was wearing a long blue shirt. Have you ever heard of *La Señorita Azul* . . . the Blue Lady?" Both his listeners shook their heads.

"A long time ago when the Spanish first got here their priests found something very strange: Indians who had a vague notion of God; not an Indian god but something like our Christian one." He paused to roll a cigarette and the others waited.

"Brother Alonso de Benavides wrote about it and so did Father Kino. They got here in the 1600s. When those padres found what looked like traces of Christianity in these mountains they were dumbfounded. They asked the Indians where they learned these things and the Indians said the Blue Lady told them. A beautiful young woman in a long blue robe. She would come to them sometimes and then disappear again."

"Did the priests believe that?" Henely asked quietly.

"Why not? Stranger things happened to those men. They believed in God and they saw no reason why he couldn't do something like that."

"That's a lot to take on faith alone."

"But they didn't! About the middle of the seventeenth century in Spain there was a religious order of women who wore blue robes. Their mother superior was named Marie Coronel and during her lifetime she told her nuns about miraculous trips she had made to New Spain to convert the savages. She described the Indians and the places she had seen. After she died her women wrote down everything she had said and when the priests came back from New Spain they read these reports. They were accurate. She had described Indian tribes and places they knew no white man had visited until twenty years after she died."

"Maybe she got to Mexico for a visit and just made up these stories?"

"The record says Marie Coronel never left Spain."

Tate shuddered. "Dammit, Tony, you're worse than

Bubber. Where in the world did you get all this . . . this . . ."

"Hogwash? Call it what you want, youngster. I've listened to every Apache who'd talk to me. If I've got to fight 'em, I want to know how they think. That's sacred country down there for the Chiricahuas—those mountains Bubber was talking about. Those are the Hollow Mountains where the Mountain Spirits live. The Chiricahuas say a stranger may get in there but if he gets out, he won't be the same man who went in. Might even apply to Pinaleños, particularly a squaw who ate a few cactus buds when she was supposed to be hunting grub for her man."

FOURTEEN

The end of the summer drew near. It was the time called by the Apaches Large Fruit and the harvesting and storing of foodstuffs by the women absorbed Samantha in a never-ending round of work.

In a way she welcomed this. The more she knew of her captors the more clearly she understood she might get away but inevitably they would catch her. Or she would die in the harsh deserts surrounding their mountain fortress. Work was a narcotic for the despair born of understanding.

Pionsenay's women were as concerned for the future as their captive, though Samantha could not know this. If any of the men had asked them they would have elected to return to the reservation, an unhappy place but a safe one. For a second choice they would prefer to stay where they were, though when Ghost Face, the winter, closed on these mountains the living would be very hard. The long-talked-of and always impending trek into the Sierra Madre of Sonora dismayed them most of all. No amount of plunder or freedom could outweigh their dislike for life with Geronimo and his uncouth band.

So they gathered food industriously. They knew a return to the reservation was impossible for Pionsenay and they never dreamed of deserting him. They only wanted to make certain that if staying in the Huachuca Mountains depended on a store of food it would be ready. If they gathered enough to make this possible they would have done well. If they gathered so much it would be difficult to move they would have done very well indeed.

Their nervous energy infected the men and meat-hunting was intensified though some of this could be simply a result of idleness. Both men and women understood that Pionsenay had engineered a standoff with the white-eyes soldiers. From Severiano they knew their captive girl was the promised woman of a soldier *nan-tan*, a leader of the horsemen with the yellow-striped breeches, and that her presence kept the soldiers away. The women approved of this but the young men chafed under Pionsenay's enforcement of his part of the unspoken truce. They wanted to raid on the American side of the border but he would not let them.

So there were more raids into Mexico and more hunting by the men. The raids into Mexico began to bring back Mexican corn, which was welcomed joyfully. From this was made the weak beer: tiswin or *tulepah*, as it was variously called. Samantha's hours in the *ranchería* were divided between tending the boiling mash for beer and preserving "hoosh" from cactus fruit. The latter had to be dried, mashed and pressed into cakes over which was poured the sticky juice from the pulp to seal the cake against spoilage.

Out of their shared punishment by Catle there grew between Samantha and Aludin an increasingly easy relationship. It was at best a sort of accommodation but Samantha drew pride from it. Aludin never struck her any more; she was allowed to bathe whenever this did not conflict with assigned work and there was a more even sharing of the hard and repulsive tasks. Obedience, responsiveness and a growing competence were Samantha's weapons in this campaign but these were rooted in a courage she did not know she possessed.

Recognizing the hopelessness of escape without help, Samantha searched for a way to send some sign of her existence to the world beyond the *ranchería*. It was a slim hope. Even if she managed to leave a message somewhere it might be found, she could not say where she was held. She simply did not know.

The location of the *ranchería* thus became a goal which she pursued whenever she saw Severiano. She gave up badgering him with questions about Aunt Bee or her own prospects and tried to prize out of him some identification of the locality of the *ranchería*.

"What is that? What do you call it?" she would ask innocently, pointing at a nearby peak.

"Montaña . . . mountain."

"I know that! Doesn't it have a name?"

"I dunno."

"Oh, Severiano!"

He enjoyed her frustration and that made her furious so she turned to questions about the Apaches which he would answer. She had many of these, particularly about Aludin and Catle's household. She knew now that Aludin was the younger of Catle's two wives and she could see that her presence in Aludin's wickiup had created some delicate problems.

Inborn Apache reserve forbade Catle to pay a nocturnal visit to his younger wife while the white girl was in the wickiup and for some reason he would not simply order Samantha out. It was thus necessary for him to summon Aludin elsewhere and this coming and going in the night first alarmed and then amused Samantha.

If there were children of Catle's first marriage with Sheneah they had died or moved away; Samantha never saw any younger Apaches at their firepit. She guessed that the addition of Aludin to his household was so recent

129

there had not yet been time for children of that union. She queried Severiano persistently about these arrangements and found him willing to answer but hard put to translate Apache relationships into English.

Sheneah he identified as "She-who-sits-first," which seemed logical enough, but Aludin's title came out as "She-who-sits-on-her," which was baffling.

"Sits on who?" she demanded.

"Sheneah!" replied Severiano irritably. She had to give up in the end. That title indicated Aludin was dependent on Sheneah but obviously this was incorrect. Aludin was always doing little things for the older woman and more than her share of the household drudgery. The semantic confusion of this paled into insignificance, however, when Samantha encountered other family relationships.

Once a middle-aged woman stayed for some days in the wickiup with Aludin and Samantha and there was obviously great affection between the two Indian women. Samantha could not know that the visit was unusual by Apache standards and would not have occurred in normal times but she could see Catle's reaction and was astounded by it.

As soon as the stranger appeared Catle made himself scarce. His hunting trips became more frequent and of greater duration and Samantha saw him at his own wickiup only rarely. She had been a member of this little group long enough now to detect some signs of emotion on their faces and throughout the older woman's visit Catle looked irritated and bedeviled. During one of his rare evenings at the firepit the woman appeared unexpectedly and Catle faded into the darkness with a grunt of surprise. Had he not brought Aludin so much meat they could scarcely cope with it Samantha would have thought him rude and inhospitable. She took up the matter with Severiano and he groaned.

"What for you wanta know that, *Americana?*"

"Am I not supposed to know? Is it bad to tell me?"

"No. Not bad. But it goddam hard to tell!"

She had tried to stop his swearing. His language could be so vile and obscene it sickened her and she had managed to convince him that if he swore when he talked to her she would avoid his company. He accepted this and thereafter tried not to swear but from time to time he forgot. She tolerated that in her need to talk to him.

"That woman she is mother of Aludin. Her man gone to Mexico and she stay till he come back." That meant another raid and Samantha shuddered.

"All right. She is Catle's mother-in-law. Why does he go away as soon as she comes? Why doesn't he talk to her?" Severiano knit his brows and studied the question.

"What you call her?"

"She is Catle's mother-in-law."

"Nah!" he shook his head. "I dunno 'bout that. 'Pache say Catle 'carries a load' for that woman. He got to get her something to eat an' he got to give her place to sleep, but when she here he got to vamoose."

Samantha looked at him in disbelief and he swore under his breath. "Look . . . when Catle take Aludin for his woman he can't look at her mother no more. He can't be in same place with her. He can't talk with her an' she don' talk with him. She want something she tell Aludin and Aludin tell Catle. He gotta get it but he can't talk with her."

"That's the strangest thing I ever heard! Why must he do that?"

"I dunno. All 'Paches do that. He can't talk to sisters of that woman. He can't look at 'em. Mebbe sometime one of them women she say he talk to her but they gotta talk different. Not like he talk to Aludin an' Sheneah."

"What does that mean . . . 'talk different'? You mean they use a different language?"

"I dunno, dammit! You don' know till you speak 'Pache. Catle gotta talk one way to me an' Aludin and Sheneah an' different way to them women. Jus' like he talk different to Pionsenay an' other old men when they sit and smoke an' talk about what they gonna do pretty soon."

His tangled and frustrated explanations were confusing but they gave her some clues to what was going on. She concluded there was a tribal taboo on association with a wife's mother that extended to all her female relatives but the business of "talking different" baffled her.

Bored by her questions Severiano put her at once on the defensive by returning to his favorite subject: when would she become his woman? She countered by asking how this could be accomplished and he launched on an endless, rambling discourse that was as confused as it was confusing. She extracted one comforting thought from it. His intentions, at least by his own standards, had to be proper, for nothing so complex and formalized could possibly be dishonorable.

She turned and twisted as best she could. She told him that since she was already promised to another man she could do nothing until released by him. To do otherwise would bring bad luck to everyone. That impressed him but he insisted there were ways to make it all right and that he could arrange everything with a white-haired old man whom he pointed out to her.

"That man he know all 'bout them things. He got ways to fix it good. I gotta give him couple horses an' then he fix it."

"I'm afraid, Severiano. Something terrible will happen."

She doubted that he believed this but something seemed to make him cautious. Perhaps there was some tribal law that forbade him to force her. Brought up on whispered tales of Indian brutality to captive women she found that hard to believe and when she was with him she was always apprehensive. But there were other weapons than force. She knew what he was doing. In a dozen transparent ways he would harass and frighten her; hold back much and invent more, hoping in the end she would turn to him as the only escape from virtual slavery.

FIFTEEN

Lieutenant Henely kicked his horse into a hard-breathing scramble up the last few yards of the slope. At the crest he reined in. The horse hung his head and blew painfully, raising puffs of dust beneath his nostrils. He was sweat-slick and winded.

The scorching sun directly overhead seemed to push waves of heat down through the heavy, motionless air that pressed hard on man and horse. Henely's uniform was soaked and he stood in his stirrups to get air between the wet saddle and the seat of his pants. Sweat trickled from under his campaign hat into the sodden kerchief bound over nose and mouth against the dust. He hooked it down with a finger to breathe deep of the searing air.

In front of him the ground tilted up toward the first peaks of a mountain range five or six miles away. Countless dry washes, more like gullies actually, traced their way down from the peaks in sweeping parallel curves. It was mean country to scout. If a man rode the ridges he could be seen for miles. In a wash he could see nothing himself because his head was below the neighboring crest.

Perhaps a mile behind him was the unmarked Mexican border. He had been deep into Chihuahua, all the way to Janos, but there had been no fighting. General Kautz had sent word to the governor-general of the province before Henely went in. Now he studied the dun-colored peaks northwest of him, noting traces of green in the draws on the higher shoulders. These ought to be the

133

Mule Pass Mountains. From his saddlebag he pulled the map that Lieutenant Thomas, the acting Department engineer, had made. It was a good map, clear and beautifully hachured, much prized by the Army in Arizona. He spread it on his pommel and put his compass on it. Turning the horse with his knees, he oriented the map and grunted with pleasure. They had crossed the border just where he planned.

Half a mile to his front a black hat bobbed into sight from a wash, marking the line of scouts preceding the patrol. He had departed Camp Bowie on the last day of August with twenty men of his own troop and ten more from Camp Grant under Lieutenant Royal. Four of the Tonto Apache scouts from Bowie had been assigned to him for the long patrol into Mexico.

They had not encountered a single hostile Indian but of the thirty-four men who started he had brought back only twenty-nine. The tequila and the señoritas of Janos had proved too alluring for five of his troopers and they had deserted. Worse, they had taken horses, weapons and equipment with them. He swore bitterly under his breath, thinking of what Captain McClellan would have to say when they got back to Bowie.

He pursed his lips and blew sweat from the tip of his sun-blistered nose. A little to his right another rider climbed into view and threw up his hand in signal to the men behind him. That was Tom Royal. It was unusual to have two officers on a scout like this but Royal had persuaded Major Compton to let him go.

The Apaches had taken Royal's girl and her aunt in April and now it was almost September. A long time without any word to go on. Royal went out on every scout he could and Henely had seen him often during the summer, more silent and tight-jawed each time. It must be hard to keep on hoping against hope but no one had ever heard Royal say a doubting word. When he wasn't on scout he was badgering the Indian agents, still trying to make contact with the Apaches whom he believed had taken his women. Henely refolded his map, put it away and kicked his tired horse into motion.

134

Royal met him halfway, nothing visible of his face except slitted eyes between hat brim and kerchief. Henely pointed toward a gap in the peaks ahead.

"That's Mule Pass. We'll bivouac there tonight. Send a man to the scouts and tell 'em to hold up when they get there. Where'd the Tontos get to?"

Royal pulled down his neckerchief and licked cracked lips gingerly. "That one with the corporal's stripes said they were going to make a sweep around the head of Sulphur Spring Valley. He went north."

That must have been Happy. No need to worry about him; he would find the patrol before dark.

"What about water?" Royal asked.

"There was a spring in the pass the last time I came through here. We'll find it if it hasn't dried up. How do we stand in case there isn't any?"

"Short. Not much on the pack mules and I doubt there's enough to wet a cup among the men."

Henely nodded. There were five more days' rations on the mules, enough to take them back to Bowie, but they had to find water by morning at the latest.

"All right. Let's move out." The troopers had closed up behind them, slumped and bone-weary in their saddles. Most of them had put their carbines in the saddle boot and Henely snapped at the younger officer.

"Wake those people up, Tom! Make 'em look alive. If there's water up there we could have company tonight."

"Have you seen any fresh trails?" Royal's eyes glittered.

"No, but that doesn't mean a thing. Lots of ways to get into Mule Pass besides this one."

Royal nodded, turning back toward the file of dusty troopers. Henely could hear him chewing at the sergeant in a low, harsh voice. Man, he thought, if he doesn't get his girl back he's going to go hard. Pity. He was a damn fine lieutenant but if he turned hard and bitter he was going to be a mean one. No use worrying about that now, though. The immediate problem was Royal's consuming desire to tangle with hostile Apaches. If they got into a fight he would have to be watched carefully. He swung

135

his hand forward in the signal to move and the clink of unholstered carbines was comforting behind him.

The sun was sitting on the peaks by the time they climbed out of the maddening washes and cut the faint wagon track leading through the pass. He turned west into the setting sun and began studying the shoulders of the broad gap. He could see a couple of his scouts dismounted under the scrub mesquite near the divide and he hoped some of them had at least gone over it a little way. Should have got here earlier, he told himself. Should have put somebody through the pass and scouted the other side before bedding down.

The wagon track made an S-turn around a couple of low hills blocking the mouth of the pass and Henely thought the second and higher of the two might make a good place to bivouac. He climbed it and grunted in satisfaction. It was crowned with a shallow depression ringed by runty cedars, deep enough to give cover to the animals but not too big to defend with his few men. There was movement in the cedars and his hand jumped to his Colt. It was Happy, the Tonto scout. Either he had got there before the soldiers on point rode past or he had slipped in behind them.

"One of these days, Happy, you're going to pull that trick and somebody's going to nail you."

The flat brown features split in what was probably a grin. The reason the soldiers called him Happy was because he so seldom expressed any emotion at all.

"You find any trail?"

A shake of the head.

"How about water?"

"I find."

Henely heaved a sigh of relief. Behind him, Royal was guiding the column into the depression, the men dismounted and wary, leading their horses. Henely watched satisfied as he posted a dozen men around the rim of the cup on their bellies, carbines ready. The rest of the detachment unsaddled, cursing the thirsty and fretful animals. Royal came up, beating dust from his trousers with his hat.

"Water?"

"Happy found it. Take five men with three horses each, all the water bags and half the canteens. Better take four more men to outpost the spring. Soon's they're finished come back and get five more with the rest of the horses and canteens. I want the rest of the men to get started cooking before dark. Ryan!"

Sergeant Ryan jogtrotted to Henely. "Let 'em brew coffee and fry some bacon, but not too many fires and keep 'em small. At least ten men on guard all night. You can relieve 'em as often as you want but I want 'em awake. Spread 'em around this bowl and make sure each one knows where he can find you or me or Mister Royal."

Ryan shifted the tobacco in his jaw smoothly and saluted. He had been fighting Indians a lot longer than Austin Henely but he couldn't have done any better himself. It was a relief to be out with a lieutenant who learned fast and took advice. Nevertheless a man couldn't let these youngsters get above themselves.

"Yessir. Uh . . . Lootenant?"

Henely grinned. "What'd I forget?"

"Kin we fill canteens agin soon's we've et?"

"Sure, so long as you get everybody back in here before dark." Ryan was right. It was never smart to bed down with half-empty canteens when water wasn't handy. The sergeant's eyes twinkled but his seamed and leathery face betrayed nothing. He returned to his men and nudged a squatting trooper ungently with the toe of his boot.

"Chrissakes, Runt! You tryin' to wake up ever' Injun in ten miles?"

The soldier addressed as Runt sighed. He had been pounding a canvas sack on a rock with the butt of his carbine. "You want coffee, don't you, Sarge? Howinhell else I'm gonna make it?"

"Jest scrooch th' butt aroun' on it, stupid! You don't gotta pound it."

Coffee rations for a trooper in the field were issued in the bean, unroasted and unground. Before he could make a cup of coffee he had to roast the beans in a Dutch oven

137

if he had one; in a skillet if he did not. Then he had to "grind" them somehow, the usual procedure being what Sergeant Ryan had interrupted. Runt was the bugler and had the extra duty of cooking for his sergeant. He had already roasted, partially burned to be exact, enough coffee beans for the both of them and was trying to break them up in his canvas bag.

"Ain't got no crackers left, Sarge," Runt complained.

"Comin' up."

Where the packsaddles had been pulled off the mules a trooper prized the lid from a wooden box of hardtack and swore feelingly. "Will ye looka that!" He waved a stained slip of paper plucked from the top layer of brownish-white crackers. "May, 1864!"

"The bloody angle . . . !" muttered Ryan, remembering a nightmare fight with John Gordon's ragged Confederates in the jungles around Spotsylvania Courthouse one May night twelve years past.

"Huh?"

"Nuthin'!" He shook his shoulders as if throwing off something. "Twelve years, aged in th' wood. Ought t' be 'bout prime, men. Let's git it out!"

Canteens and bellies full, fires out and guards posted, Henely's troopers slept. The single gray blanket and rubber poncho were enough for this climate. Sometimes a man would add his saddle blanket to his bed but it was dark blue with an orange stripe, easily detectable by a sergeant who generally raised hell because unless all the sand was beaten from it in the morning the horse would suffer.

When dawn painted the Chiricahua peaks orange, the corporal of the guard shook each man awake. Along the makeshift picket line a horse stamped and blew but there was no other sound. The men crawled at once to the rim of the hollow, carbines ready in the routine stand-to with which experienced troops met the dawn in Indian country. A detail of troopers gathered horses to be watered at first light.

Nothing stirred beyond the perimeter and Ryan dispatched half a dozen grumbling men to outpost the bivouac. Coffee-less and chewing unhappily on hardtack, they hoped they would be relieved before the fires were all out. Henely rubbed whiskered cheeks and rinsed his mouth with coffee. Ryan prodded the men through their morning chores and there was nothing for the officers to do now.

"Aw right! Saddle up! Check yer weapons an' don't nobody tell me at noon he ain't got no water. You ain't got a full canteen now, go git it!" There was not much to pack; in minutes the horses were saddled and the pack mules loaded. Tom Royal dashed a half-finished cup of coffee to the ground and pointed excitedly.

"Look at Happy!"

The Tonto scout crouched just below the crest of the lower hill, a hundred yards away, his carbine held over his head parallel to the ground. He pumped the weapon rapidly up and down, swung it vertical for a second; then repeated the up and down movement.

". . . two . . . three . . . four . . . five!" Henely counted. He lifted a hand in acknowledgment. Happy was pointing east, back down the pass.

"Tom, take some men and get over there! I'll mount the rest and follow."

Royal was already scrambling down the slope, followed by four or five of the men who had flung themselves prone by the officers. Before he could reach Happy a shot set the pass to echoing.

"Damnation!" Henely swore. "Who did that?"

"One o' them outposts, I reckon!" Ryan answered. Both men flinched as the air above them cracked sharply. "That's comin' our way!"

Troopers wrestled with excited horses and Henely took them scrambling down to the wagon track, led horses bucking wildly. At least three carbines were booming now from the lower hill and several more bullets cracked over their heads.

Tom Royal and Happy came down to Henely in sliding leaps. "I didn't see 'em!" Royal panted. "Some damn fool spooked 'em before I got up there."

"How many?" Henely demanded of the Apache scout. Happy spread the fingers of one hand.

"Come on ponies. Damn bad soldier shoot! Got 'em all!"

"I know that, dammit! Where'd they go?"

"No go!" The Tonto cocked his head and grinned as a ricocheting bullet snarled over their heads. The distant thump of the rifle followed plainly. "Got women. Stay an' fight till women gone."

"All right! Let's go get 'em! Tom, you—" He did not finish the order. All along the crest of the lower hill dismounted troopers were standing up, firing as fast as they could load.

"Gawd a'mighty, look at 'em! Look at 'em go!" bawled a sweating soldier. He threw up his carbine and fired, the recoil almost pitching him backward from the crest. A cloud of evil-smelling smoke drifted back from the firing line.

Henely and Royal climbed to see. What looked like a crowd of gypsies was spread out and moving fast across a little flat southeast of their hill. The leaders were already disappearing into the rough terrain beyond.

The Indians had apparently come up the track making for the pass when the outpost fired at them and now, instead of turning back into Mexico, they were trying to get around the soldiers and on into Arizona. Royal caught a glimpse of a woman's bright skirt as she flogged a pack horse into the stunted brush beyond the flat. A few men, lagging behind the women and horses, turned to fire at the troopers lining the hill. The distance was six or seven hundred yards and the soldiers' wild shooting was doing no damage.

"Mount up!" Henely shouted. "Get 'em mounted, Ryan!"

"Won't they come back into the pass higher up?" Royal demanded.

"Not if we're in it. All we can do now is try to catch up with them. Let's go!"

He fanned out a thin line of soldiers and they rode hard across the flat in pursuit. It was hopeless from the beginning. The Indians were already well into the mountains, scattered and climbing hard. Again there was a scattering of shots from the warriors covering their women and trying to slow the soldiers. They hit no one and since the troopers were using their pistols now, they did no harm either.

Henely threw up his hand to signal halt. There was no use riding into the brush-choked draws; it would be like going into a briar patch after a rabbit. Far up one of the draws, two Indians suddenly broke cover, bent over and whipped their ponies. There was a burst of fire from the few men who were still using their carbines and to everyone's astonishment the rearmost Indian pitched off his horse.

"Give us some covering fire, Ryan! Come on, let's try to get that one anyhow!"

Henely led Tom Royal and a dozen men up the draw while the rest of the detachment banged away to discourage the Indians from coming back. Whether they tried to pick up their comrade or not no one knew. A bullet or two sang down the draw toward the galloping troopers.

They found the Indian where he had dropped. The .45-caliber slug had taken him squarely between the shoulders. Henely turned him over with his foot and clucked in disgust.

It was a boy. Fifteen at most, maybe younger. He didn't even have a rifle. His pony had disappeared and no one wanted to go look for it in the brush. This was the total outcome of the fight: a slim boy on the blood-stained gravel. His eyes were open, staring through a film of dust, and a smear of blood spread across his cheek from his nostrils.

"Poor little bastid," muttered one of the soldiers.

"Don't waste no pity on him," said another. "Jes' like th' man said: nits make lice an' that's one we ain't gotta hunt down sommers else!"

Tom Royal stared grimly at the dead boy. If only he had lived a little while. Young or old, an Apache could seldom be persuaded to answer questions if he didn't want to but they might have been able to get something out of him. He looked up at the silent, motionless peaks above and was shaken by a spasm of helpless rage. Someone of that fleet band knew where Samantha was. He was certain of it and he had lost the chance to find out what he wanted more than life now.

"Who was it, Happy? Whose Indians?" Henely asked.

The Apache shrugged. "*¿Quíen sabe?* Geronimo maybe."

Henely shook his head. Doubtful. Geronimo would have had more warriors and no women if he were coming back into Arizona. Maybe they were trying to get back to a reservation. But how could you find out? Wild and wary as animals they were. There was just no way to make talk and find out what they wanted. When they saw soldiers they bolted.

"Is there anything on him that could tell us who he is? Who he belongs to?" It might help a little if he could bring back that much information. One dead boy was not going to balance five deserters, though.

SIXTEEN

Other than the strain of constant, low-key skirmishing with Severiano, Samantha found herself in the first days of fall under no great duress. Physically she was now capable of any task set her. Her body had toughened and she had learned to bear hardship with the stolid acceptance of the Apache women. What all this had done to her appearance she was not quite certain. Aludin had a piece of mirror and on rare occasions she was able to steal a glimpse of herself in it. Generally she had to be content with peering at the wavering image of her face in the bathing pool.

The watery reflection told her that her face was thinner. Like her body, there remained not an ounce of superfluous flesh on it. Her cheekbones seemed more prominent and in consequence her mouth and eyes were larger than she remembered them. The finer details, revealed by Aludin's mirror, were more startling. There were new lines about her mouth and at the corners of her eyes. The eyes had become the dominant feature of her face. They seemed to her sunken in the spare lines and curves of brow and nostrils, fiercely alert and watchful. When I get out of here, she wondered—if I get out—will Tom accept these changes? Can I learn to be soft and feminine again just as I have learned to be hard and watchful?

The almost frantic gathering of foodstuffs which drove the Apache women through the last of the summer days slackened and the pace of life in the *ranchería* slowed. Now the only excitement was furnished by the periodic return of a few young warriors from pinprick raids over the border into Mexico. The Apaches made much of these returning heroes, greeting them with ritualistic fervor which seemed exaggerated to Samantha when she saw how small were the fruits of their raiding.

Generally they brought back a few horses or steers, sometimes a few pieces of clothing or shoddy tinware. Though she watched always for captives, there were none.

When the young men rode in through the cleft in the rocks they were greeted by shrieks of delight from the women. Severiano had explained to her the meaning of the burning of Eskinyea's wickiup and since no more were burned, she supposed no one had been lost on these raids.

The welcoming celebration began with a feast and the consumption of a great quantity of tiswin. Samantha worked with Aludin at the preparation of food for the feasts, a common enough task for her except for the time when the raiders brought a mare heavy with foal and she was introduced to another repellent Apache delicacy. The mare was slaughtered and her flesh served as a main course, followed by the special treat: her unborn foal stewed in a great kettle with herbs and seasoning.

Before the meal ended the drummers began. A camp kettle partly filled with water and tightly covered with a wet cloth gave a deep, booming beat when pounded with a looped willow sapling. The tempo of this kettledrum was slow and menacing. In a little while smaller drums joined in, filling the intervals between the booming of the larger with a quick, nervous thumping. Then one of the raiders would run into the firelight, stamping and singing a harsh and repetitious song.

One by one, each member of the war party took his turn and Samantha supposed they were boasting of their exploits. No one ever interrupted these unrhythmical sagas and each was greeted with applause. When the young men had exhausted themselves or were too full of tiswin to go on dancing, another part began.

Men and women formed in two lines facing each other and to the accompaniment of drumming and chanting one line advanced as the other retreated. It all seemed pointless and confused to Samantha. Old Gil-lee watched the stars and about midnight would bring an end to the dancing in lines. Then the elder Apaches and the very young dropped back and seated themselves in a wide circle.

It was the turn now of the maidens and young men and the drums quickened their beat. The young men knelt solemnly around the fire and the girls danced around them, their faces alive and mischievous. At a signal, they broke their circle and stole forward shyly, selecting a partner by touching him on the shoulder. Now the couples circled the fire side by side, the young men unchosen still kneeling in the center.

This puzzled Samantha, for among the circling couples there were pairs of young women dancing together. It was a complete reversal of the white man's custom and though she supposed there were Apache males with whom the girls did not want to dance, this neglect of a few men seemed also a sort of teasing or coquettishness on the part

144

of the maidens. Perhaps it was a way of bringing an errant suitor into line by exposing him to the social disgrace of kneeling unchosen through the dance.

It was decorous enough at first but after a while, when the drumming and singing grew faster, the girls' dancing became sinuous and a little abandoned. Not all the couples who left the circle to rest returned to their former places. Some slipped away into the darkness.

Since no one objected to her presence, Samantha knelt behind the outermost circle of watchers and saw it all. The first time was interesting but after that the monotonous pounding of the drums was oppressive and the endless repetition of the dance bored her. Every Apache in the *ranchería* attended these functions but the shadows of the vedettes on the rocks above warned her there was no chance of slipping away under cover of the celebration.

But the routine into which the camp had settled was shattered one day by a visitation of another sort. One of the vedettes came from his post at a run about noon and then a stream of Indians poured through the rock gate. These were strangers and Samantha was alarmed. They were an ill-kempt lot, the women raggedly dressed and the men in full fighting kit with faded paint on their faces.

There were so many it was obvious they could not all be absorbed by the *ranchería*. The women prepared food in the firepits of Pionsenay's people but unpacked little other than their utensils and Samantha took this as a welcome sign their stay would be short. They brought with them half a dozen skinny and exhausted cattle and one of these they killed and butchered at once.

A husky young brave walked to within five or six feet of the animal, lance balanced casually in his hand. Without visible preparation he drove the weapon into the steer just behind the left foreshoulder and with a prolonged bellow of fear and agony, it staggered forward and pitched on its knees. The women closed in, their knives stripping off hide and flesh before the wretched beast was dead.

Two of them fell to arguing about their shares but were

ignored by the others, who thrust them aside to get at the steer. In a second they were fighting like furies. Their shrieks rang from the rocks. The other women paused to watch and children appeared magically to stare open-mouthed at the spectacle. Two men stepped in cautiously to relieve them of their knives but beyond that no one interfered.

Samantha hugged a tree and wished she were else-where. She had become accustomed to running with Aludin to the scene of any excitement just like any other Indian, but now she regretted her curiosity bitterly. She had never seen Pionsenay's women behave like this.

Snarling like cats the two squaws bit and tore at each other. One was older and heavier and her weight told. She pinned the younger to the ground, knelt on her breast, and plucked handfuls of hair from her head. The recumbent one squalled in pain and fury.

Satisfied, the victor stalked away while the loser shrieked imprecations at her back, careful however to re-main prone as she did so. The watchers laughed and joked and in a few minutes both contestants, bloody and disheveled, were back at the rapidly disappearing beef. Samantha took advantage of the lull to slip through the throng toward the safety of the wickiup. She had not gone a dozen yards before she encountered something far more terrifying than the fight.

A young woman leaned spread-legged in utter weari-ness against a pony, her forehead resting on the animal's flank. Long black hair, matted with dirt and twigs, hid her face. Samantha thought she was an Indian girl worn out by the last march of this wild band. But the longer she stared the more chilling the doubt that assailed her. The body revealed by the ragged camisa was too ful-some, the skin too light for an Indian.

The pony moved, stamping hide-shod hooves, and the woman pushed herself erect. Samantha's heart lurched. This was no Indian girl and she had ample reason to be exhausted. God alone knew how many days and miles she had been dragged behind the pony by the rawhide riata about her wrists.

Backing away, Samantha collided with an Apache drawn by this fresh diversion. The captive lifted her head. Black eyes, dulled by misery, focused on the white girl. An expression of incredulous hope tightened the slack mouth.

"*¿Americana? Ay . . . ¡Madre de Dios! ¡Ayúdeme . . . ayúdeme!*"

"Oh, my God!" Samantha moaned.

Another Apache peered over the pony's rump, green and vermilion paint banding his eyes and mouth. The free end of the riata lay across the pony's withers and he jerked it, hauling his captive against the nervous animal.

"*¡Madre mía! ¡Ayúdeme!*" wailed the Mexican woman. The Apache struck her with the heel of his hand.

"Let me go! Oh, let me go!" begged Samantha, thrusting at the gathering Indians. Aludin's face, dark and angry, appeared. She gave Samantha a jolting push.

"*¡Vaya!*" she hissed. "*¡Pronto!*"

Fear drowned Samantha's pity for the captive and she took to her heels, the exasperated Aludin belting her on with blows of her open hand.

In Pionsenay's wickiup, neither the squalling fight among his women nor the lesser disturbance of Samantha's encounter with the captive distracted the leader of the strange band from his talk with Pionsenay. Nolgee, the visitor, was pressing his wily host hard.

"Geronimo sends greetings," he rumbled in the stiff, formal tongue. "He asks when his brother will keep his word and come to the Sierra Madre."

Pionsenay doubted this was Nolgee's mission but he accorded the question a proper period of consideration.

"Soon," he said at last.

Nolgee did an unforgivable thing. He spit in the fire where his expression of disgust hissed on the coals. It was a thing that could have cost him his life.

Pionsenay regarded him with mild disbelief. There were two ways to handle this. He could turn the wickiup into a slaughter pen by an angry retort or he could treat this vulgar Indian with the disdain his ugly gesture merited. He chose the latter and his subchiefs and Nolgee's

147

wolfish followers relaxed slowly in astonishment. Pionsenay knew what was itching Nolgee and he meant to use it to his own advantage.

Geronimo's lieutenant, Nolgee, had been raiding in Chihuahua—too successfully for his own good. Greedy Nolgee had stolen so many cows and horses he could not drive them away before the Mexican *rurales* caught up with him. Still too greedy to abandon his loot and run, he had fought a two-day running battle that cost him three fighting bucks and most of the horses and cattle and other plunder except a few pieces of silver from a village church and one Mexican woman.

Running hard for home, his party had overtaken a band of Apache women and children led by two old men. They were drifting south from the Mimbreño reservation at Ojo Caliente in search of relatives supposed to be with Geronimo. Nolgee could neither abandon them to the Mexicans nor push them fast enough to escape his pursuers. He did what Apaches had been doing for years: dodged across the border into Arizona and headed for the nearest friendly *ranchería*.

That had got the *rurales* off his back but not his bad luck. With sanctuary almost in sight he had run head on into a detachment of white-eyes soldiers in the Puerta de los Mulas, the Mule Pass, and the yellow-legs got off one lucky shot that dropped a fifteen-year-old boy dead from his pony. It was a minor loss compared with three warriors dead in Chihuahua but the boy was a nephew of Geronimo's and they were not even able to recover the body.

It was enough to put a well-mannered Apache in a temper and for a savage like Nolgee it was insupportable. He saw only one thing he might salvage from this disaster. If he could bring back with him Pionsenay and the latter's band, Geronimo would be a little mollified.

Pionsenay understood this. There were young men in his band who itched to go south and raid with Geronimo and he would have to handle this carefully. He was not ready to go but he wanted to stay without the taint of cowardice.

"Soon!" grunted Nolgee sarcastically. "How soon, my brother?"

Pionsenay smoked awhile in silence. "We lack cartridges for the American rifles," he said mildly.

"Oh? You have burned much powder then?"

There was a strained silence but Pionsenay had one thing going for him. Almost as much as a fight the Apaches liked to watch a clever man in council and everyone wanted to see how he would get out of this.

"Only *Nakaiyi* bullets. My young men have brought back enough of those from their raids."

Nolgee's nostrils flared dangerously. Matching raids into Mexico would get him nowhere but he had nothing else to offer.

"You have strong young men. If they ride with me to Sonora there will be more than *Nakaiyi* bullets for the taking."

"Perhaps. But they are learning how to raid without being caught and this is a good place to learn. Maybe a few of them will want to go with Nolgee to help fight the *Nakaiyi* soldiers or . . ." he eyed Nolgee innocently, "my brother is welcome to stay here until the soldiers have gone back to their fort."

Nolgee was learning the hard way that few men traded insults with Pionsenay and came off unhurt. The watchers were amused. Any rude man can spit in a fire but it took a smart one to put him in his place as Pionsenay was doing.

Nolgee's eyes glittered. The implication that he needed help to get home maddened him. Like every other Apache, north or south of the border, he knew how Pionsenay stayed unmolested in his *ranchería* and he growled out something about Pionsenay's white girl captive that was a bit confused except for the obscene parts.

In essence he said there were already so many Apaches hiding behind her skirts there was no room for him even if he needed protection. Having failed to provoke Pionsenay by spitting in his fire, he was now trying to insult the entire band. Pionsenay's face reflected mildly the scorn

149

and amusement that just about summed up the general view of Nolgee at this point.

Nolgee was not too stupid to see this and he stood up abruptly. Abandoning all pretense of formal language he demanded bluntly, "What will you do with this white-eyes girl?"

"When we have enough American cartridges I will take her to Mexico and sell her to the *Nakaiyi* for more bullets. What else?"

"Do you think the *Nakaiyi* will trade with an Apache after what I have done to them?"

It was an unfortunate and foolish piece of boasting. Pionsenay waited for its import to reach the listeners and then waited a bit longer so each could speculate on the variety of cutting replies he could make. Shrewdly, he made none at all. Instead he asked Nolgee a question in the way old men question a novice warrior they are teaching to think.

"What would you do, Nolgee?"

"Kill her!"

Pionsenay did not have to spell out the usefulness of his captive; it was understood. Nolgee's response was thus as stupid as his manner of giving it was rude.

"Ah! I see," said Pionsenay, looking thoughtful. He did not even look out of the wickiup but everyone knew he was thinking of Nolgee's captive.

"That filth!" snapped Nolgee, jerking his head over his shoulder. "Men do not burden themselves with things like that. Tonight my women will finish her!"

This did not explain why he had dragged his wretched Mexican captive all the way from Chihuahua into Arizona but he did not have to. Pionsenay understood that too. By a quirk of fate the woman was still in Nolgee's hands after he had lost almost everything else he had stolen from the Mexicans. She was just about all he had to show for his raid and that had kept her alive thus far. Now, stung by Pionsenay's scorn, he condemned her. Pionsenay shrugged.

"I wish there were room in this place for Nolgee and his people to stay here tonight. Maybe some of my young men will want to watch though it is less than four moons since we did this thing ourselves."

The casual reference to the death of the whiskey drummer completed Nolgee's defeat. He had set out to ridicule Pionsenay and lost at every turn.

"That is four moons too many! *U-gash-i!* . . . go!" he snarled at his followers. "Go and make ready. We sleep by the running water below this place."

While this was going on, Samantha crouched in Catle's wickiup. Aludin's full parfleches at her back were comforting and she breathed the familiar odors of the hut gratefully. There was danger outside but, childlike, she took comfort from familiar surroundings.

Aludin was puzzling. She had been angry but now she seemed worried. She did not go outside yet she had nothing to do in the wickiup. She looked out from time to time and worked haphazardly at a pair of moccasins she had started some days before.

Aludin's concern for her ward had never extended visibly beyond mild curiosity about physical injury, perhaps the proffer of a simple remedy for a cut or burn. This was something else and a cold hand closed on Samantha's heart.

If Aludin were concerned, it meant there was a threat over which she had no control. The visiting band of Indians must pose that threat and Samantha explored a waking nightmare of possibilities.

The shadows marched eastward across the *ranchería* and she sat frozen. Only her head turned stiffly from side to side as she tried to catch each whisper of sound outside. When Nolgee broke up the council and hustled his people away there was much to hear and identify but the noise subsided without untoward event and Samantha began to breathe a little deeper.

Aludin's watchful attitude did not change, however, and as a wire is twisted, Samantha's nerves tightened again. When dusk fell the Apache girl left her and Samantha heard her blow up the coals. Automatically she crawled out to help.

"*¡Ponte en marcha!*" snapped Aludin, pointing at the

151

wickiup, and Samantha rejoined her demons in the hut. She heard Catle come to eat, grunt something at Aludin and go away again. Sheneah came later and the two Indian women spoke for a little while in low voices. Then even that ceased. There was a strange silence throughout the *ranchería* as if everyone waited for something.

Aludin returned with food, a thing she had not done since the first morning when she brought a bowl of bitter gruel. Samantha quailed at this kindness and could not touch it.

Night came and the interior of the wickiup was no blacker than the abyss of fear in which Samantha waited. Then the screams began.

In the beginning they were ululating, gorged with pain and terror beyond human knowing. They stopped and the thick silence lengthened. When they recommenced they were different—a crescendo of choking shrieks that made a woman's hair move on her head.

Nolgee had not gone far. The tokens of his rage came easily on the night wind to anyone who listened. At intervals the inhuman screams were choked off but always they began again. The endurance of the crazed Mexican woman was unbelievable.

Strained too taut, too long, Samantha's courage snapped. She began to moan and it was as if something beyond her will made these sounds. Aludin gripped her shoulders, struck her, even tried awkwardly to soothe her. Nothing checked the rising tide of hysteria.

"O God!" she begged. "Let her die! Why don't you let her die?"

She rocked to and fro, eyes shut, hands clamped over her ears to shut out the dreadful cries. Long after they were inaudible they still rang in her head.

About that time, Pionsenay walked heavily to the wickiup of Schnowin. "When the sun comes, my brother," he said, "Nolgee will be gone. He will leave something."

Schnowin nodded. It was not a thing he cared to look for but he understood what Pionsenay wanted. It was also not a thing that should be left for anyone to find.

SEVENTEEN

Tate Hulse had an idea but he needed help to carry it out. He needed a great deal of help that was not available at Camp Bowie. He needed an old head and the best he could think of was Carp Van Sciver at Camp Lowell.

Polycarp Van Sciver was a senior first lieutenant on general service with Department headquarters staff. An all but fatal wound had almost ended his military career during the war but his record was so good the Army kept him on after the reorganization of 1869. He had the promise of the first vacancy in the Quartermaster Corps and while he waited he did odd jobs like the one he had now in Arizona.

Tate had known him since 1870 when he entered West Point. Carp was then an instructor of mathematics at the Military Academy and when Tate had come near to failure in the tough first-year math course, he had come to Van Sciver for help.

Carp could not give personal coaching but he found a senior who would. Under the first classman's tutelage, Tate squeaked by the midyear exams and clung to a passing grade until spring. He brought an enormous bouquet of primroses from Constitution Island to Carp Van Sciver's wife as an indirect token of thanks and there began a lasting friendship. He and his room-mate, Tom Royal, became regular visitors at Ellen Van Sciver's cheerful home. Cocoa and cake tempered the bleak existence of a plebe in cadet barracks and Carp's pretty young wife with her Southern drawl enchanted them both.

153

She had married Carp just after the war when he was on occupation duty in the defeated South. On occasion she referred lightly to herself as the captive of Carp's spear but the war was not a topic of discussion in her house and how she came to marry a Yankee lieutenant was not known.

So it was that when Tate conceived a risky plan to recover Samantha Allyn from the Apaches he turned to Carp Van Sciver.

His first opportunity to go to Camp Lowell was provided by a visit from Major Biddle, Department inspector general, whose regular circuit took him through Camp Bowie to Lowell and back to his office at Department headquarters at Fort Whipple. Tate procured the job of escorting Major Biddle from Bowie to Lowell.

In September 1876, Tucson was the capital of Arizona Territory and Camp Lowell was seven miles northeast of town. This was New Camp Lowell, built by its first occupants, the Fifth Cavalry. The Fifth built ambitiously. They set out cottonwood trees along the roads and around the parade ground and laid out commodious quarters of adobe brick, so commodious that some were still unfinished when the Sixth Cavalry took over in 1875.

The parade ground was large and set around it were two company-size barracks, a band barracks, post headquarters, the hospital and seven sets of officer's quarters. Behind these were stables, guardhouse, bakery, warehouses and the post trader's store and, surprisingly, nine sets of two-room quarters for married enlisted men.

When Colonel Oakes arrived, he brought with him one troop, his regimental band and a small staff. He ran a lean headquarters—a dozen sergeants and clerks and two indispensable staff lieutenants: Adjutant Jim Sands and Quartermaster Charlie Gordon. He inherited, already ensconced, a mixed bag of departmental staff officers and sergeants, including Lieutenant Van Sciver, the post quartermaster.

Dusk was falling as Major Biddle's party arrived from Camp Bowie. Tate stabled his horses, arranged to bed his troopers down in the cavalry barracks, then headed across the parade ground for Officers' Row. The Van Scivers occupied the next to last quarters at the western end of the line of adobe houses, separated from the parade ground by a plank walk and a row of young cotton-woods.

He had to walk the length of the row to reach his destination and midway he overtook two small figures pulling a homemade wagon whose ungreased wheels squealed so atrociously they did not hear him coming. A small boy with a ragged forage cap on the back of his head greeted him cheerfully. His companion was a girl perhaps a little older. The wagon gave off a pleasant odor of fresh-cut pine.

"Evening, sport," Tate responded. "What have you got there?"

"Lightwood. Best there is for startin' fires. You want to buy some?"

Tate laughed. "What would I do with it? I'm just passing through." The girl plucked her companion's sleeve and whispered to him.

"We already delivered to ever one that takes from us. This here is left over. You can have it extra cheap." He eyed Tate hopefully.

"How much is extra cheap?" Tate asked the girl, who had obviously suggested the bargain, but she would not answer him. Instead she whispered again to the boy.

"Two bits?" offered the latter doubtfully. Tate whistled in mock dismay. "Ever thin' in the waggin and delivered to boot!" There was another consultation with the silent partner. "A dime?"

Tate clapped him on the shoulder. "I wasn't trying to beat you down, old man! I just wanted to see what the manager would say." He grinned at the girl, who ducked her head.

"She ain't the manager! She just helps out. I take care o' the kindlin' and Katy does the watercress . . . when there is any."

"By George, it's a regular contractor's firm! Tell you what . . . have you already left some at the Van Scivers'?"

"Naw! That Dutch dog-robber o' ther'n cuts all their

155

wood. He won't give us a chanct." His scornful epithet for Carp Van Sciver's soldier orderly indicated a good deal of bitterness.

"All right," said Tate, lowering his voice confidentially. "Here's a quarter and you come on with me."

Both children eyed the coin doubtfully.

"We said a dime."

"And I said I was only joshing. That's too much wood for a dime."

"Gee, thanks, mister! Where you want us to put it?"

"We'll ask the Van Scivers. Come on."

He knocked on the door, which was opened by Ellen, ducking her head so the lamplight would show the face of the caller.

"Tate Hulse!" she exclaimed delightedly. "Where in the world did you spring from? Carp!" she called over her shoulder. "Look who's here!"

The wagon squeaked minutely and she squinted past Tate.

"Who's that . . . Timmy Hennessey? For goodness' sake! And Katy too. What's this all about?"

"We brought you some fat pine. Best there is for startin' fires."

"Tate, you goose! Come on in. Timmy, if you'll just bring that around back I'll show you where to put it." Carp appeared in the door beaming with pleasure.

"It's the mathematical genius himself! Come in, Tate, and welcome."

The hall seemed full of Van Sciver children though there were only two. Everyone talked at once and Tate swung small Annie shoulder-high until she squealed in delight.

"How about something to cut the dust?" Carp asked.

"Have you had any supper?" Ellen demanded. Tate shook his head. "Oh, Lord! I think there's some cold steak pie. I'll warm it for you."

She led the way through the hall and into the gallery connecting the main house with a separate adobe building containing kitchen, dining room and pantry. Here she pushed Tate down at a table and bustled around, shaking up the stove and setting out silverware. There was a familiar squeak outside and she clapped her hand over her mouth.

"I completely forgot them!" She threw open the door. "Timmy, just pile it right here and Wentz will get it in the morning. Aren't you chilly, Katy? Where's your jacket, child?"

Katy scuffed a shoe and said nothing. "Come inside, missy, while your brother stacks the wood."

"No'm, thank you, ma'am. He's 'bout done."

"All right, but don't go yet." Ellen opened a tin pie safe and took out a plate of dark brown cookies. She offered them to the Hennesseys and each took one. "Go on, Timmy! You'll hurt my feelings. Take some more." Each took another. Ellen swept the remainder into a scrap of paper, made a twist of it and put it in the wagon. "There! Thank you for the lovely kindling and don't stay out, Katy, without a jacket . . . you'll take cold."

"Wait till Wentz sees that," chuckled Carp. "He'll think you spent hard money for kindling and he'll have a fit."

"The devil with him! Is that why they don't come to us any more? Poor little kids; I'll have a word with friend Wentz tomorrow!"

"Who are they?" asked Tate, peering into the pie safe.

"Their father's a private in the infantry company," replied Ellen. "A no-good Irish bum! He drinks his pay and beats his wife and if it weren't for those two children I don't know what she'd do."

Tate found a cookie that had escaped from the plate. "Didn't know we were enlisting married men. Something new in the infantry?"

"No," replied Carp. "Same old story. He was a sergeant when he married Big Kate . . . just can't keep his stripes. John Andrews says he'd make first sergeant if he could stay off the bottle."

"Tate Hulse, sit down and stop eating cookies!" exclaimed Ellen. "You haven't changed since you were a cadet."

"Mamacita at Ochoa's doesn't make anything like this,"

157

he told her, grinning. With Annie on one knee and Robert on the other he attacked the steak pie.

"What about Tom?" asked Carp. "Has he heard anything?" Ellen rapped the back of his chair with her spoon.

"Not now! Wait till I get little big ears in bed. Come on, you two, let poor Tate finish his supper in peace. It's way past your bedtime."

The children were escorted out in a flurry of protests and when Tate had finished, Carp led the way to the room he used for a study. Few Army quarters for lieutenants provided this luxury. The inhabitants of Camp Lowell often blessed the ambitious plans of the Fifth Cavalry, for the smallest house in Officers' Row boasted three large rooms and two small ones, not to mention the detached kitchen and dining room. Being a senior first lieutenant, Carp had the further amenity of wooden floors in contrast with the rammed earth in some of the quarters. He offered cigars and whiskey and they smoked in silence until Ellen called from the sitting room.

"Come out! I want to talk and you've been in there long enough."

She gave them coffee in her prized Meissen and Tate saw that he was honored.

"Now tell us!" she demanded. "Have you heard anything new . . . anything at all?" He shook his head.

"I haven't seen Tom in a month but I don't think he's heard a thing. He'd have got word to me if he had."

"You mean he's just waiting? It's been five months now!"

"I know. That's what everyone says to do. He went up to San Carlos and talked to Clum and old Eskiminzin and they think the two renegades who murdered the stage agents last spring took Sam and her aunt up in the Huachucas somewhere."

"Well, for goodness' sake, why don't you just go up there and take them out?" burst out Ellen.

"It isn't that simple. Clum, Jeffords, Eskiminzin . . . they all say if we try it the renegades will murder the women and run for the border. They think Pionsenay kept them at first to protect himself when he came in to have his wound doctored. Now he's holding them because it keeps the troops off his back. If that's true there's a chance he can be traded out of them when he gets tired of sitting in the Huachucas."

"Has anyone tried? Has he been offered something for them?"

"Oh, Lord, yes! Money, cattle, horses, safe-conduct to San Carlos . . . everything he doesn't need and doesn't want!"

"That's a strange thing to say, Tate. What does he want?"

"I'll tell you what I think . . . rifles and cartridges!"

"We can't give him those! He'd just use them against us."

"I know, but he isn't going to give up those women for what we're offering. Look at it from his side. While he's got Sam and her aunt the troops will leave him alone. When he wants horses or cattle his bucks go raiding in Sonora or Chihuahua for them. The Americans aren't bothering him where he is and the Mexicans can't get at him. It's a perfect arrangement."

"Those poor women! How awful!" murmured Ellen.

"Something's got to give pretty soon," said Carp grimly. "I know there's a sort of truce now but it can't last forever. Sooner or later they'll raid on our side of the line and then Governor Safford and his wolves will start baying at us."

"I know. You're right and we've got to do something before it happens. That's why I'm here." Ellen and Carp looked at him sharply.

"What are you thinking?"

"Whiskey!" There was a long moment's silence.

"It's against the law, isn't it?" Ellen asked. Her husband nodded.

"It is, and if the Army knew you were even thinking of it, you'd be cashiered."

"I know that too. Have you got a better idea?"

"What does Tom say?"

"I haven't asked him. I wanted to talk to you first." Carp bit the end from a cigar and lit it.

"They'd trade for whiskey, I think."

"But . . . what a risk, Tate!" put in Ellen. "You could never do it without being found out."

"I wouldn't go through Clum or any of the Bureau people. I'd get Tony Rucker to make the deal with one of his Apache scouts. Tony would keep his mouth shut and those scouts would do anything for him."

"You've got to buy the whiskey . . . quite a lot, I should think. Everybody would know."

"No . . ." drawled Carp. "That's what you want me to do, isn't it?"

Ellen looked from one to the other of them and caught her breath. "You're stark, raving mad . . . the both of you!"

"Is there any other way?" Tate demanded of Carp. The latter shook his head.

"Will you do it?" Tate persisted.

"I'll give it a try. How much do you need?"

"A barrel at least. I'd want it in four ten-gallon kegs. That way it can be packed in on muleback."

"That's smart. I've got to go to Fort Stanton next week or the week after. I can buy it in Mesilla and have it consigned to you at Ochoa's in Bowie. I'll have the kegs packed in boxes so they won't be so obvious and they'll come in from New Mexico with a freighter. It'll look like something you ordered from the States."

Ellen drew a long, ragged breath and they both looked at her. "You think it won't work? You object, my dear?" Carp asked softly.

"Of course I object! You'll both be broken for it." There was an uncomfortable silence, then without any change of expression she turned to Tate. "Have you enough money?"

Both men grinned in relief and Ellen stood up, shaking out her skirt with a rustle. "Where do you plan to sleep, Tate Hulse?"

"I was going to ask Bob Hanna if I could bunk in with him."

"It's too late for that now. Come on, I'll put you in the

back room. Carp, haven't I asked you not to smoke in here?"

They went into the hall and Tate brushed against a tuft of long, black hair hanging from a wooden plaque on the wall. He fingered it curiously.

"What is this? A scalp?" Carp chuckled.

"That's Ellen's trophy. They gave it to her at Camp Verde."

"I didn't even know you were at Verde. Tell me about it."

"We were there for a few months before we came to Lowell. Ellen kept chickens in a little shack out back. I was away for a couple of days and while I was gone one of the Tontos off the reservation tried to get himself a hen. Ellen heard the noise and saw his backside sticking out of the shed. She put a full load of number sevens in him with the shotgun."

Tate glanced at Ellen, who looked smug. "Why didn't you call the guard?"

"Hmpf! By the time he got there I wouldn't have had a chicken left."

"What did he do?"

"The Indian? He said something outrageous to the chickens and took himself off."

Both men laughed. "The guard saw him going, Tate, and he said that Indian hit the ground once every twenty feet. Adna Chaffee made that thing out of horsehair and gave it to Ellen at a party."

"My!" said Tate. "I was planning a raid on the pie safe tonight but I don't think I will."

EIGHTEEN

The fall days in the high places were alive and golden, the nights crisp with an edge of chill heralding the dawn. But Samantha paid no heed to the changing seasons. The nightmare conclusion of Nolgee's visit had stunned her.

As the days stretched to weeks and months and no great violence was done her, she had convinced herself there was a design in her captivity, that the Apaches held her for some special purpose and as soon as Tom Royal learned this he would find a way to free her. This conviction kept her sane, hopeful and industrious, the latter because she saw the need to draw as little attention to herself as possible. The screams of the Mexican girl put an abrupt end to all that.

Her original terror recaptured her. These people took prisoners simply to provide an object for their mindless ferocity. If they kept them alive, it was only until the mood or season or some obscure ritual invited the atrocious orgy of torture. This outlook bred in her a numb indifference.

Sheneah grew irritable but Aludin knew what ailed the white girl. She suspected her captive would soon go *loco* like the old white-eyes woman. Whether out of fondness for her charge or simply because she had come to prize the extra pair of hands for work, Aludin did what she could to prevent this. She found work for Samantha as far from Sheneah's angry eyes as possible and she was unusually patient with her.

Aludin's concern and a reawakening sense of overwhelming injustice drew Samantha out of her depression. She had traveled thousands of miles to marry Tom Royal and had fallen into a hell worse than any she had ever imagined. Where was he? Why had he not found her? She pounded her fists in helpless fury on the hide she was scraping. I will get out of here, she swore. I will get out of here in spite of all of them and I will do it myself.

Once again she considered escape by her own means and that required the indifference of her captors if not their favor. That night, when Catle grunted for his tiswin it was Samantha who jumped to fill his bowl and bring it. Aludin, whose task this had always been, watched in astonishment.

The onset of fall offered a desperate chance. Dry leaves and pine needles now carpeted the grove surrounding the *rancheria* and it seemed to Samantha that if she could start a fire upwind of the wickiups, she might create sufficient uproar to cover her escape. She dared not save food against such a possibility but she had learned a good deal about edible plants and roots in the mountains and that did not worry her. What did nag at her was the absolute necessity for water and something to carry it in if she managed to get down to the desert below.

As always, even the simplest idea was impossible to implement. How could she start a fire? Catle wore at his belt a pouch with flint and steel. She had several times helped Aludin make tinder for him from the dried and pulverized pith of elderberry stalks. But none except Catle ever touched these tools. Aludin no longer preserved fire by nursing embers in a bowl but her new method was scarcely better. She had made a long fuse of shredded juniper bark rolled and netted in yucca strings. When rain threatened, this was lit and brought into the wickiup, which it filled with a noisome smoke. Afterward it was nursed into flame with pinches of dried horse manure and delicate puffs of air. Clearly Samantha could not hope to walk away from the wickiup with the smoking juniper punk; everyone would want to know where she was going.

There remained one possibility. When they were away from the *rancheria* and a fire was required, Aludin produced it with a primitive apparatus of her own making. Shaving a juniper stick to the thickness of her little finger, she gave it a dull point which was put in a notch on a piece of dried yucca wood. Shreds of juniper bark and grass were heaped about the notch and Aludin then twirled the juniper between her palms until a wisp of smoke appeared. Blown upon carefully this spark could be nursed into a flame.

It looked ridiculously easy but for Samantha it remained a sometime thing. Success depended upon too many variables, all just right: yucca and tinder very dry, juniper dry and hard, speed of twirling precisely correct. Even when a spark appeared in the crumbly yucca, one puff too hard could blow it away. The Apaches were amused by her attempts to master the fire tools and after a while paid no attention to the fact she kept them in her waistband.

Her chance was not long in coming. Aludin was away somewhere and Sheneah wanted oak spits to grill her meat. There was no oak nearer than the grove screening the back entrance to the *ranchería* and Samantha held out her hand for a knife with a pounding heart. Sheneah gave her a dull one, naturally. She never gave a good one but that was no problem for Samantha now. She knew how to give even a bad blade a razor edge on a smooth fieldstone. She stole a pinch of the horse manure tinder Aludin kept in a bowl in the wickiup and set off for the grove.

Everything worked. Within minutes she had a spark and the tinder was perfectly dry. A curl of smoke filtered through her little tepee of pine needles; a bright, breathless flicker of flame followed, its passage marked by crisped needles rather than fire. Samantha blew cautiously and a narrow crescent of black edged by flame spread in the layer of pine needles.

Simultaneously she heard footsteps behind her; a hand rested on her shoulder and a moccasined foot stamped out the spreading fire.

"Sah-mahn-ta! What you do, girl? You *loco?*" It was Severiano. He squatted beside her, patting out the sparks with his hands. When they were out he picked up the fire drill and examined it curiously. "Why you come way up here an' make fire, *Americana?*"

She said nothing. She was too frightened to speak and it must have shown in her face. Had she been quick and glib enough she might have spun an explanation that would have satisfied the half-breed youngster. Perhaps not. Maybe like the Apaches he could smell fear.

He tested the wind with his face, looked down at the wickiups below them and then back at her fire drill. *"Mire,* Sah-mahn-ta," he told her, pointing up at the rimrock with his chin. "You see Indians there?"

She shook her head.

"They there. They see you every time. You think you start fire an' those men come down here?"

"I . . . I don't know."

"No, *Americana!* You don't fool those Indians. They don' come down here. They stay in rocks and watch. When you walk out, they know. How far you think you walk, Sah-mahn-ta?"

She dropped her eyes. He was right. She should have known all that.

"You see, Sah-mahn-ta? You no can run away. Your people don' come here and you no can run away from 'Paches. Why don' you be my woman, Sah-mahn-ta?"

Frustration and helplessness drove her to madness. On her knees, fists clenched and trembling, she faced him furiously.

"You lie!" she hissed. "You always lie to me! I've tried not to make you angry because you're the only person here I can talk to, but you know that as well as I do and you've treated me shamefully. Well, I've had enough, you hear? You disgust me! Do you understand what I say?"

His face was a study in bewilderment and dawning anger but she was beyond reason now. She rubbed it in.

"I will never be your woman, Severiano! Americans don't abandon their people. They will come for me and when they do I hope they kill every man, woman and child in this village!" She leaned forward to thrust her face at his. "Do you understand me?"

He understood. His face was frozen and it was all Apache now. Whatever her reasons for disliking him, he saw only in her white face the same loathing he had seen in the soldiers who cursed him and kicked him out of their barracks years before. With great dignity he stood.

"You be sorry for that, *Americana!*" he said stiffly.

She got up and stumbled past him down the steep trail. Aludin waited at the wickiup for her and one look at the Indian girl's face made her forget Severiano. She was hustled into the wickiup but as she went she saw the *ranchería* was swarming with strange Apaches.

It was obviously a war party and without the hangdog look of Nolgee's band. The warriors looked to Samantha like so many lean and vicious hunting dogs. They came in with yelps of greeting and at their head rode the most frightening Apache she had ever seen.

Thick-chested and heavy-shouldered, he sat his pony with an animal grace. The blunt, thrust-forward head wore a cap of black hair falling thickly on either side of a face that was a study in cruelty. He looked neither to the right nor the left, and Pionsenay's people made a path for him as he rode.

Samantha saw only a particularly ugly and menacing Indian. Apache dignity frequently seemed merely pompous to her so she did not recognize a leader of some degree in this visitor. It would have meant nothing more to her to know that his Chiricahua name—never used, of course—was Go-klee-yeh.

About twenty years before Pionsenay took Samantha Allyn from the Texas and California stage, the Mexicans, so the story went, ambushed and killed some Apache women and children, including the first wife of Go-klee-yeh. Three Apache chiefs took up his cause and the following year formed a war party to take revenge. It was quite a war party, led by three famous Apaches—Mangas Colorado, Cochise and Juh—but the man who won most fame was the young Apache in whose behalf they rode.

Forever after he was known by the name the Mexicans gave him in battle: Geronimo.

The friendship of the older chiefs soon cooled. Mangas denounced Geronimo as a troublemaker and Cochise subsequently forbade him to enter the Chiricahua strongholds. But Mangas was murdered in 1863 by California volunteer troops and eleven years later, Cochise died of natural causes on his reservation. Only Juh remained and he joined Geronimo in the Sierra Madres along with Nolgee and the outcasts of half a dozen Apache bands. Few Apaches other than those of his immediate band liked or respected Geronimo, but almost all feared him.

Typical of Geronimo was his return to the Chiricahua reservation to claim a share in the treaty General Howard had made with Cochise. This was the reason for his presence he gave to both the soldiers and Cochise's son Tahzay, yet all the time he urged Tahzay's young men to break the treaty and come south into Sonora with him. He had not been successful and had been keeping an eye on Pionsenay's little band ever since. He knew the white-eyes suspected Pionsenay of helping to murder the stage agent but not until Nolgee's chapfallen return did he understand why Pionsenay had not crossed the border for safety. Now he intended to do something about this.

Unlike Nolgee, he came prepared to play a strong hand. He brought enough fighting men with him to give any detachment of Sonoran *rurales* a panic seizure and he brought also a redoubtable shaman, an old man named Nochalo. Displaying his affinity for renegades of any kind, he had also picked up en route a young Mexican-American rascal, O'Brien, whom he encountered in Cocospera.

Rafael O'Brien was a colorful figure who had managed in his short span of twenty-nine years to fall afoul of almost every law officer on the border between San Diego and Brownsville. In the process he had developed a number of warm friends among the Apaches with whom he traded whiskey or cartridges for stolen American and Mexican goods. One of the things that endeared him to the Indians was the impartiality with which he changed

167

sides, playing off Americans against Mexicans or vice versa as the occasion permitted. They had not yet caught him fighting against Apaches though they suspected him of this.

Samantha did not see O'Brien enter the *ranchería* because Aludin drove her into the wickiup and would not let her out again. The memory of Nolgee's visit lay heavy on both young women.

Geronimo's first move was to ensure that when he spoke to Pionsenay it would not be in a small council of Pionsenay's choosing. This was easy enough for he had brought with him so many warriors they could not all fit in a wickiup. The older men might think him an upstart but the younger ones were awed by his battle record and he wanted them to hear him. A large gathering about the council fire would ensure they did so.

That night, Geronimo spoke first. He pointed out that Pionsenay had promised to come to the Sierra Madre and he, Geronimo, could not understand why there had been so much delay. He had been so distressed by the failure of his brother, Pionsenay, to come south that he had traveled all the way from Sonora to find out what was wrong. He suspected, he said, that the only reason why there had not been a union of the two bands was Pionsenay's natural reluctance to impose on another chief's hospitality, and this gave him even more pain. He was impressed by Pionsenay's good manners, but he was deeply puzzled by them.

There was hardly a word of truth in the whole oration. The notion of identifying either Geronimo or Pionsenay as leaders of great refinement was enough to make the older Apache chuckle. Neither was hereditary chief of anything; both were simple war leaders whose rank and influence depended solely on their success in battle. But he spoke persuasively and there were many young warriors who cared nothing about such fine points of tribal etiquette. These were impressed and Pionsenay saw he was in for a bad time.

When Geronimo relinquished the speaker's role to his host, Pionsenay did the best he could. His words were flowery and circumspect, for he could not state his position too clearly. Nolgee, in his boorish way, had made clear the implication of cowardice in using a white captive to protect the band against the white-eyes soldiers. Pionsenay temporized and renewed his promise to go south as soon as his band was fully equipped, but Geronimo attacked the weak point at once. He had been waiting for the opportunity.

In grave tones that caught the attention of every Apache there, he said that something very serious about Pionsenay's captive had come to his notice. With this introduction, he called up Nochalo.

The old man was impressive. Despite his white hair, he was alert and erect and he spoke in solemn words that sent chills through his hearers. Not twelve suns past, said Nochalo, I had a great dream. My Power came to me and told me why Nolgee suffered so many losses on his raid against the *Nakaiyi*. My brothers, he said, there is a witch among us.

He then told them the story of the old white-eyes woman who had escaped from Pionsenay. It was not clear from whom he had gotten this story but that only increased its effect. She was dead; there was no doubt of that. Singing her magic songs, she had wandered into the desert and died and both Schnowin and Tudeevia would attest to that fact. They nodded uncomfortably. But when she died, said Nochalo, her Power did not die with her; it simply transferred itself to the young white-eyes woman. It was there now. As long as it stayed among the Chiricahuas it would make trouble for them and any other Apaches who associated with them.

With that, Nochalo sat down and everyone looked at Pionsenay, who knew he was trapped. Next to incest, witchcraft was the most abhorrent crime known to Apaches. No more serious charge than one of these could be brought against man or woman.

"How can we be sure this white-eyes girl is doing all these bad things?" Pionsenay asked. He addressed the question to Gil-lee, who was the nearest to a shaman in his own band. Gil-lee claimed to know all about Powers, good and bad, but he was such a querulous old woman of a man that no one put much faith in his abilities. Gil-lee grunted.

"What did he say?" demanded Geronimo contemptuously.

"Elk meat," repeated Gil-lee. "If you make a witch eat elk meat he will be sick and you will know he is a witch." Elk meat made a lot of Indians sick because it was so strong, but no one wanted to raise that point at a time like this. Besides, there were no elk in the Huachuca Mountains at this time of year.

That point gave Pionsenay hope. He at once proposed a hunt for elk which would obviously require more time, but Geronimo blocked that move easily. Once again he called on Nochalo.

The old man spilled a little brown powder from a twisted leaf into his hand. It was made from a special root which his Power had shown him and it was guaranteed witch-bane. Put a little in a bowl of tiswin and give it to the suspected witch. If he became sick, his evil Power was exposed. Just as good as elk meat and no hunting party needed.

Pionsenay had to admire the trick. If a bowlful of tiswin by itself did not make the white girl sick he had no doubt Nochalo's emetic root would do the job.

"This is a serious thing," he said, shaking his head. "I think there should be more preparation." There was a groan from his listeners and Geronimo regarded him sourly. Pionsenay sighed and nodded at Catle.

The latter brought Samantha, careful not to touch her. He had a pretty clear idea of what Geronimo was doing but he was just as superstitious as the rest of them and Nochalo had worried him. Samantha walked stiffly, stumbling a little because it was hard to make her legs obey her.

The solemn faces in the shifting firelight watched her curiously. Old Nochalo stood alone in the circle and when he pointed his fist at her she dropped to her knees, not in awe of him but simply because her legs refused to support her any longer.

Rafael O'Brien in the second rank of watchers was so close he could have reached out and touched the trembling girl. He studied her slim brown legs with interest.

"How can I question this woman, my brother?" Nochalo asked Pionsenay. "Does she speak the *Nakaiyi* tongue?"

Pionsenay shook his head. "Neither our tongue nor *Nakaiyi*. There is a boy here who speaks a little of her own."

O'Brien had heard of the abduction of the two white women. He knew that the younger of them was promised to an American officer. Obviously this was she and he was delighted. He had an abiding hatred for the American Army and anything connected with it and what was about to happen to this girl filled him with anticipation. He decided it would be even more fun if he could take a part in it.

"There is no need for the boy, my brothers," he said in acceptably formal Apache. "If my friend, Geronimo, and our host . . ." he indicated Pionsenay with a slight nod, refraining in best Apache custom from using his name ". . . will permit, I can speak to the woman in her own tongue."

The Indians looked at him with interest. They knew he had much to do with Americans and it did not surprise them he could speak their tongue. His offer could have been offensive in a more formal council, but none of them thought much of Severiano and they were willing to overlook the point. It was significant that they looked to Geronimo rather than Pionsenay for a response.

Geronimo was delighted with this sudden turn of events. He had known O'Brien for a long time and considered him a more sympathetic interpreter than any Pionsenay could produce. He went through the motions of consulting with Pionsenay before nodding acceptance of the offer.

Someone handed Nochalo a *tus* of woven willow withes, a little bowl coated inside and out with clear pitch and holding perhaps a pint of liquid. The old man sprinkled his powder into the tiswin and stirred it with a twig,

171

muttering as he did so. The Apaches watched respectfully. Nochalo held out the bowl to Samantha.

"Take it, girl," O'Brien said.

"Oh!" The sound burst from her in a breathy gasp.
She twisted around to see who had spoken.

O'Brien was leaning forward, watching her intently.
The olive complexion of his Mexican mother did not dim
his Irish legacy: puckish eyes, snub nose and a wide
mouth beneath the carefully trimmed mustache. Had the
devil himself sprung from the ground at her side Samantha could have been no more startled.

"You . . . you're American?" she gasped.

"God and all his saints forbid! Take the bowl."

Obediently she took the *tus* from Nochalo's hand, holding it as if she expected it to explode. "What is it for?
What am I supposed to do with it?"

Then the inanity of the situation struck her. Not an
arm's length away sat a white man who, though he denied
being American, might be able to save her and all she
had done was ask him what to do with a bowl of greasy
liquor the old Indian had given her.

"My God! Who are you? Tell me what to do . . . what
are they going to do to me?"

The questions burst from her in a torrent and she
stared at him round-eyed, begging for answers. O'Brien
sighed.

It was neither in pity nor sympathy. He was enjoying
this and he meant to enjoy it even more. He answered her
in a low, even voice and the Indians listened carefully
though they could not understand.

"He . . ." O'Brien gestured at Nochalo ". . . says you
are a witch. You inherited the evil eye from an old
woman and you have been killing Indians with it."

Samantha almost dropped the *tus* in horror. "Wh . . .
what are you saying? Are you mad?"

"Hush and listen to me, girl. It's a test to prove you're
a witch." He indicated the bowl in her trembling hands.
"You drink it. If nothing happens, you're not a witch. If
it makes you sick . . ." He flicked a finger across his
throat and Samantha swayed.

172

"You mean . . . they will cut my throat?"

"Ah, no!" he shrugged. "They burn witches."

A moan escaped her. She crouched a little, her eyes trapped and frantic.

"You have seen them do it?" he asked curiously. She nodded, gulping. "An Indian?" he persisted.

"No . . . an American they took from the stage. Merciful God! Can't you help me? Isn't there anything you can do to stop them?"

"Ah, that wasn't a witch," he said, ignoring her plea. "The women did that and they hung him by his feet, didn't they?"

Samantha could only stare at him, speechless in horror. "They do it differently with a witch," he continued casually. "They hang them by the hands and it takes much longer."

She looked as though she were going to be sick before she could drink the tiswin and that would spoil the ritual. "Go on. Drink it. If it doesn't make you sick, you'll be all right." He grinned at her.

Once more her eyes scurried around the circle, searching for hope against the knowledge there was none. O'Brien nudged her with his foot. "Hurry! Drink up, girl!"

The habit of obedience was strong in her. She lowered her head and took a sip of the tiswin. She knew what it was. She had cooked the mash many times for Catle's beer. She had even tasted it and found it repellent. This was even more so; penetratingly bitter on her tongue.

In a spasm of revolt she spat out what was in her mouth and flung the bowl from her. It fell in the fire with a hiss, scattering embers before it. Nochalo skipped away and there was a growl from the watchers. Samantha buried her face in her hands and waited for their violence to strike.

O'Brien had been watching the glint of red in her dark hair. It fell in two braids down her back and at the nape of her neck, where the braids pulled the hair away, the skin was very white. He had thought her too slender when he first saw her but now he could see the compact strength of her body. The small curves and angles of her haunches molded over the heels of her moccasins intrigued him.

There would be violence in a moment, he saw. Geronimo and Nochalo had done their work well and these Apaches were in no mood for delay. He was mildly regretful, but not because he was sorry for the white girl. Then he noticed that Pionsenay was looking hopeful and he had an idea. Once again he addressed the two chiefs.

He chose his words with care and he was very polite. If they would give him a little time, he could talk some sense into this girl. He spoke with gestures Samantha could not see behind her back and the Apaches' anger was tinged with amusement. When Geronimo began to smirk he knew he had succeeded. Pionsenay was strong for any delay so he was no problem. Only old Nochalo was angry. Geronimo grunted.

"Hey, girl . . ." O'Brien nudged her again with his foot. She lifted her face a little from her hands but she did not look at him.

"How would you like to put this off until tomorrow?"

She still did not turn. She made no sign she had heard him but O'Brien knew she was listening.

"Well . . . how does that strike you, girl?"

It struck her quite clearly. She knew exactly what he offered and with the same clarity she knew that any attempt to make herself believe she was in doubt about her choice would be utterly foolish. She got to her feet and faced him.

Some part of her mind said, you don't know he's telling the truth; you don't know what these Indians mean to do. But the faces of the Apaches about the fire spoke louder than that small voice. There was an imperative need to escape those faces and what they promised, and however brief the respite it did not matter. Nothing in this man's power could match what the Apaches would do to her. O'Brien did not have to ask again. Her answer was in her eyes and if there was loathing too that made no difference to Rafael O'Brien.

He said nothing more—simply got up and walked away

without looking back at her. She followed, knowing this was what she was meant to do because the Indians let her pass.

O'Brien went to a wickiup at the edge of the *ranchería* and pulled aside the flap over the door. Light from inside reached for her feet. She dropped to her knees and crawled in. There was a bed of spruce tips with new blankets on it, some packs and an Indian girl who watched silently. O'Brien followed her and the wickiup seemed crowded. He was not tall but in the hut he seemed bigger than outside, stooped over with his hands on his knees. Avoiding the eyes of the Indian girl, she studied his hands curiously. There was a little tuft of black hair on each finger just above the knuckle. She tried to remember if she had ever seen a Mexican with hair on his hands like that.

"Don't mind Suzy," he said. "She's just a Cocopah. They never hurt anybody." The Indian girl's eyes belied that remark. "I'm going to look at my horses."

"All right."

He hesitated and stirred the blankets with his hand. "You could fix this better. Suzy's a bad housekeeper." Samantha shook herself, trying to dispel an acute feeling of unreality.

"Is she going to stay here?"

O'Brien laughed. "She won't bother you. Besides . . . she hasn't got anyplace else to go."

"I see," Samantha said dully. She was seized by an uncontrollable shivering and wrapped her arms around herself tightly. O'Brien watched this with interest.

"All right." He pulled the top blanket off the bed and threw it at Suzy. "Vamoose!" he told her. "Out!" He moved aside to clear the door. Suzy did not look at him. Her eyes remained fixed on Samantha but she gathered the blanket into her arms and scrambled outside. O'Brien slapped her narrow behind affectionately as it disappeared beneath the hide curtain.

"I'll be right back. Don't go out again." She shook her head, still refusing to look at him. "You aren't going to try something damfool, are you?"

Again she shook her head. The thought had not even occurred to her. No matter how repugnant O'Brien and his Cocopah doxy and his new blankets, they were insignificant in comparison with what waited by the fire outside.

He understood this and chuckled. "Fix the bed. I'll be back in a minute."

She submitted gladly to the feeling of unreality, preferring it to anything else. She stroked the blankets, admiring their newness. It had been so long since she had seen anything so new and clean. They were not wide enough to cover the pile of sweet-smelling evergreens. Suzy might not make a good bed, she thought, but she makes a big one. Automatically, she gathered the bed and tucked the blankets under the edges. It made her think of Aludin and the lost security of Catle's wickiup. She wondered if he had gone back to his own bed or was still at the fire. She listened intently and the rumble of voices carried through the trees to her ears. Some of them were still there. She shuddered.

She supposed O'Brien would come back as he said he would. Unless everything that had happened since she threw down the cup of tiswin was a part of some monstrous joke, he would return. She was incapable of exploring that possibility and decided simply to do what was expected of her. It would be better, though, she thought, to get out of her clothes and into the bed before he came back.

Hurriedly she pulled off the skirt and camisa, stripped off her moccasins and slid into the bed. As soon as she did she wished she had put out the tallow dip, but if he wanted light he would only start it again. He probably even has matches, she thought bitterly, as she pulled the blanket to her chin. She was prepared to find nothing surprising about him.

He did in fact return in a few minutes and quite casually sat on the edge of the bed to pull off his boots. She studied his back and wondered if Suzy had made the soft buckskin shirt he wore. It was well-made, she observed critically. Even Aludin would have been pleased with the neat stitching and even fringes. He began to pull it off over his head and she fixed her eyes desperately on the woven dome of the wickiup. The shadows leaped and danced as he pulled the light toward him, to blow it out she supposed, but he did not and she waited tensely.

"Aren't you going to undo your hair?" he asked, turning to look at her.

The inconsequential nature of the question staggered her. She could think of no reply for a moment and finally mumbled indistinctly, "If you want."

He waited, holding up the light, and she understood he expected her to sit up to do it. I will not, she decided grimly, squirming deeper under the blanket.

She pulled out the braids with shaking fingers and curled her body away from him, hands cupped beneath her thighs, gripping hard. When he lifted the blanket there was a rush of cold air on her back and she was suddenly and acutely conscious of her nakedness.

O'Brien was not offended at all. He was delighted by her shyness. He settled himself happily and blew out the light with a loud puff.

NINETEEN

Southern Arizona remained peaceful throughout August of 1876, though there was minor trouble in the north. A band of Indians slipped away from Clum's seething reservation at San Carlos and headed for the remote fastness of the Red Rock country. They were hunted down by Captain Porter and his Indian scouts from Camp Verde; seven Indians were killed and seven captured.

But if there were no hostile Indians loose in southern Arizona, Governor Safford and the Tucson Ring seemed determined to invent them. The contractors in Tucson wanted another Army post in the southeast corner of the Territory, and to justify it there had to be Indians. The Tucson newspapers peopled the Dragoon and Chiricahua mountains with hostile Apaches and though the Army suspected only Pionsenay's little band was in those mountains, its patrols of late had been so diffident that it could not be sure. Not a few officers were growing uneasy about the undeclared truce.

On the twenty-ninth of August, General Kautz's junior aide, Lieutenant Anderson, delivered the morning mail to the general in his office at Fort Whipple and before he could close the door behind him, heard Kautz snort furiously.

The general was an impressive-looking man when in good humor, corpulent but very erect with a full face and plump jowls under a luxuriant mustache, the ends of which drooped sharply. Beneath his lower lip he cultivated a small, neatly trimmed goatee but his jaws were always clean-shaven. The most noticeable feature of his otherwise pleasant and distinguished countenance were his eyes: small and very piercing. When he was angry, Kautz was even more impressive and when George Anderson glanced back in surprise he found his general very angry indeed.

"What is this rot?" Kautz rumbled. " 'The most refractory and desperate Chiricahua Indians are still roaming over the old reserve and harassing the neighboring settlements . . . a number of prospectors and travelers have been murdered and a still larger number are missing who are supposed to have fallen at the hands of these savages . . .' "

Anderson thought he was reading from the newspaper but it was still folded where he had placed it on the table. Kautz scaled a manuscript document onto the pile of letters.

"Just how damned many people have been killed or

lost down there since we moved those Chiricahuas out, George?"

Anderson counted hastily on his fingers. "Two Americans and five or six Mexicans killed, sir, since May. Only Americans missing I know of are Royal's two women and a stage passenger, and that happened before you cleaned out the reservation."

"Colonel Oakes said all the killings after that were done by Sonoran bandits!"

"Yes, sir, he did but . . ."

"But what?"

Anderson looked unhappy and Kautz nodded. "We're not sure because we've been tippy-toeing around those mountains ever since Royal's girl was taken in there." The lieutenant said nothing.

"How long has it been, George, since anything was heard of those women?"

"Sir, I don't think there's ever been anything definite. One of Clum's tame Apaches got into Pionsenay's camp once and he says he's sure the women are there. But he didn't see them."

"Well, what are we doing? What's Royal doing about it?"

"Sir, he and Mister Hulse and everyone else have done just about everything we can. We've sent friendly Indians into the mountains with offers to trade, we've sent the word over to New Mexico and into Sonora . . . we've done everything except move in and sweep those mountains clean."

"I know that, George. I know what's been going on. It couldn't have unless I did. But I think we've about reached the end of our rope with this hands-off policy."

He slapped the papers on the table with his hand. "They're beginning to nip at me, George! I'm going to have to do something pretty soon." He fixed his aide with a grim look.

"You think you can pass that word, son?"

"Oh, yes, sir! I can do that."

"Good. What's it going to do to Royal?"

"He'll be delighted, General."

Kautz looked mildly surprised. "I thought he was dead set on making a trade for his girl?"

"Not any more, sir. I don't think he was ever too happy about that. Clum's the one who keeps saying stay out of the mountains; so did Jeffords, but Royal's been fretting to go in after them with strength enough to do it right."

"Well . . . if no one can make a trade damn fast he's going to get his fight. I'll give 'em as much more time as I can but it isn't going to be a lot." He snapped a finger against the document he had flung on the desk.

"What is that, sir?"

"It's a petition," Kautz said dryly. "A petition from His Excellency, Governor Safford, and the most influential citizens of Tucson urging me to get troops onto the old Chiricahua reserve and stamp out the renegades."

"But . . . don't you have to do something about it?"

"No hurry. I'll give Safford a sharp answer and wait for the War Department to move before I do."

"You'll send a copy to Washington?"

"Hell, George, I won't have to! I'll bet you a good cigar the governor of Arizona has a copy in the mail already."

Lieutenant Anderson scribbled a hasty note to Tom Royal and another to Tate Hulse. The latter was the more important. He knew that Tate strongly advocated patience and a deal with the Apaches and had been moving heaven and earth to arrange one. If he had any plans afoot, he would have to hurry. That night he rode into nearby Prescott with a friend. The town had little to offer but it would be better than the decorous silence of the Officers' Mess.

They left their horses at the quartermaster corral and walked to Prescott's best saloon, the Nugget of Gold, whose owner prized the trade of the Army folk at Fort Whipple and always welcomed a soldier.

The saloon consisted of a single, long room with a bar on the left just inside the door. Opposite that was a roulette table, then a big cast-iron stove, a couple of card tables and at the far end, an ancient piano. Over the bar a big coal-oil lamp hanging from the ceiling provided the main source of light. A smaller lamp on the piano relieved a little of the darkness in the rear of the room.

There were a couple of bedraggled girls, referred to obstinately by the owner as "hostesses," and when there was a crowd, someone would pound away at the piano and one of the girls would try to sing. The clientele arrived armed and spurred, but in deference to Prescott law that required a man to remove his pistol within thirty minutes after reaching town they handed over their guns to the bartender. If there was music, most tried a dance or two with the hostesses—a hazardous effort because they would not take off their spurs.

There were always a few quiet customers who eschewed dancing and gambling in favor of whiskey. The experienced drummers, agents for out-of-state commercial firms, settled down peaceably to drink just enough to get comfortably lit in a sociable way, taking enough thereafter only to maintain that mellow state. The owner and his cronies generally joined this group. George Anderson arrived just as the former was reprimanding one of his girls about her skirts.

"You'd best git them things let out, Mandy, 'fore you take th' air in Prescott agin! Sher'f sees you showin' thet much laig on th' street an' he's gonna run you in!"

The drummers nodded sagely. Mandy's skirts were a full five inches off the floor.

Simon Bellinger, cashier of the Prescott Mercantile Bank, nodded at Anderson and hooked a chair forward for him.

"How's things at the fort, George?"

"Nothing new, Mister Bellinger. So quiet we came in to see what's doing in town."

Bellinger grunted. "Seen the *Citizen?*" He pushed forward a copy of the Tucson paper.

"Yep. Saw it this morning. Looks like the governor's on the warpath again, doesn't it?"

"Sure does. He's hell-bent to get you fellers into some kinda scrap down on the border." The banker laid a finger alongside his nose and eyed the lieutenant confidentially. "I purely admire the way Gennul Kautz has held the lid on Safford's kettle these three months past. Dunno just what kinda deal he made with them 'Paches but I wisht to Gawd Safford an' that pack o' contractors downstate would leave him be with it. Sure has been peaceful this summer."

"Deal?" Anderson frowned at him. "What are you talking about, Mister Bellinger?"

"Aw, come on, Lootenant! I'm a businessman. I know what's good for me. An' for the Territory too. If there's any 'Paches loose down south they ain't botherin' us and you soljers ain't botherin' them. Seems like one damn fine way to do business if you ask me."

George Anderson put down his beer with a thump. He wondered if General Kautz had heard this point of view yet.

Some version of Bellinger's story about a deal between the Army and the Apaches may have reached General Kautz's ears, but before it could have any effect events in the southeast took a serious turn. On the thirteenth of September the bodies of two Americans were found near the San Pedro River and Captain Tupper took a detachment from Camp Grant to investigate. His report was inconclusive; from papers on the bodies the men were identified as prospectors named Johnson and Mowery but there was simply no way to prove who had killed them. Tupper's Apache scouts found tracks of both shod and unshod horses at the scene of the murders and Tupper could only point out the obvious. The men could have been killed by Indians, by Mexicans or by Americans.

Governor Safford denounced the report as an Army cover-up. Having peopled the San Pedro Valley with renegade Apaches, he expected them to kill Americans and here was proof. He was particularly incensed when the *Citizen* so far forgot its allegiance as to publish a long article speculating that Mowery was actually a legendary Arizonian who had entered the Territory before the war, made quite a fortune and name for himself and then disappeared. This was Lieutenant Sylvester Mowery, West Point class of 1852, who while stationed at old Camp Crittenden in 1855 had purchased a mine nearby, then resigned from the service and taken about one and a half million dollars' worth of lead and silver ore from his purchase. He became a delegate to the Congress from the Territory of Arizona and late during the war was locked up at Fort Yuma by the Army on a charge of selling lead to the Confederates. The charge was unprovable and Mowery took himself off to England where everyone supposed he had finally died of high living.

Now, to the governor's disgust, the *Citizen* had him back in the Territory trying to recover his mine but gunned down by old enemies before he could succeed. Safford fired off a telegram to Washington denouncing both Kautz's report and the newspaper and demanding action.

As Kautz had predicted, the War Department had received a copy of the August petition from the citizens of Tucson and promptly sent it on to him for response; he also knew that more demands for action would be forthcoming when the War Department learned of the murder of the two prospectors. They could have been killed by Pionsenay's men and he wanted to scotch the rumors of a deal with that band before Washington took note of them. He summoned Colonel Oakes, commander of the Sixth Cavalry, to Fort Whipple and when Oakes returned to Camp Lowell he had peremptory orders to move.

Tate Hulse went to Camp Grant to see if any more delay was possible. His urgency got him as far as Major Compton before he was stopped in his tracks.

"I've read Captain Tupper's report, Mister. I believe it is quite accurate. I know just as well as you do there is no shred of evidence those men were killed by Pionsenay's bucks but Pionsenay's time has run out! Of course, I'd like to know for certain where those women are before we strike but it's too late now."

"But, sir . . ." Tate protested. Compton cut him off.

"That's all, Mister Hulse! Sooner or later you have to find out that this man's Army reacts violently to the baying of politicians. I've had my orders and now you've got yours. If I hear any more out of you about it I will consider you insubordinate. Is that clear?"

It was quite clear. Tom Royal was back from his scout into Mexico with Lieutenant Henely and Tate went to see him.

"We've got one ace in the hole," Tate told him. "Carp Van Sciver is going to get me a barrel of whiskey. If it gets to Bowie in time it might do the trick."

"What trick? What are you going to do with a barrel of whiskey?"

"Get it to Pionsenay before we go after him. Trade it to him for Sam and her aunt. He doesn't give a tinker's damn for what we've been offering; he's got all the food he needs, he can't use money and he knows our promise of a safe-conduct to San Carlos is worthless. He doesn't want to go there, and even if we could get him there alive those wolves in Tucson would lynch him as soon as they found out about it."

Royal shook his head in astonishment. "You're sunstruck, Tate! You'd be cashiered out of the Army and they'd kill the women anyway. You know Apaches go crazy when they're drunk."

"Eskiminzin can work it. We'll get the women out before we give 'em enough whiskey to get drunk on. Sure it's against the law but what can we do? Those Indians won't trade for anything except guns or ammunition or whiskey!"

"Maybe so but it won't work, Tate. There isn't time enough. You're laying your shoulder straps on the line and you'll be busted just as soon as anyone finds out what you've done."

"So what? What's more important? Your commission or your girl?"

"You don't make sense! I'd lose them both. The minute those Indians get their hands on the whiskey they'll go wild. They'll butcher the women and run for the border just like they did when they killed Rogers and Spence."

"Well, dammit, have you got a better idea?"

"Yes! Just exactly what's finally going to happen. I've been trying to tell you people this for months. We should have gone after those renegades a long time ago!"

"But that's murder, Tom! How can you attack a bunch of Apaches forted up on a peak somewhere and even hope to get Sam away from them alive?"

"What makes you so sure she's alive?"

Tate stared at him in dismay. "I don't know. Nobody knows. That's why we need more time. You're exaggerating about what would happen. If we got Sam and her aunt back alive, Colonel Oakes would shut his eyes. So would Kautz!"

"Possibly. But what about the people in Tucson?"

"What the hell difference does it make? What do you care if it works?"

"I don't believe it will work."

Tate's jaws stiffened, ridging the muscles of his face. "You don't believe it will work or you're afraid of what will happen to you if you try it. Which is it?"

Royal gave him a cold look.

"All right . . . I apologize for that! But if the whiskey gets here before we go, I'm going to try it. You do whatever you damn please but I'm going to try!"

There was a long silence and then Royal spoke softly. "Don't, Tate. Compton's right and I won't let you cross him up. If you try I'll have to stop you and I don't want to do that."

TWENTY

A puff of dawn air invaded the wickiup, stirring Samantha's hair. She burrowed deeper into the bed but the breeze nagged at her until she opened one eye resentfully. There was a strangeness all about her but she clung to the protective warmth of the blankets and denied it. Aludin's familiar hide parfleches were not where they should be. The blanket on her shoulder was red, not gray. Remembrance leaped upon her and drove her to her knees.

O'Brien was gone. In the half-light of the wickiup there was only the Cocopah girl, watching her with hating eyes. She would not think of the night. She willed it from her. But she could not stay here. O'Brien would return or, worse, Catle would come for her. With shaking hands she pulled on her skirt, gathered the camisa and moccasins to her breasts.

"Quiero lavarme," she muttered to the girl.

The eastern sky flamed but under the canopy of trees the dawn light was deceptive and she ran awkwardly. There was stiffness and hurt but she thought only of the pool and her need for it.

A layer of mist clung to the water, circling where the falls plunged through it. She stepped in quickly and was immobilized, gasping, by the icy water. Overhead in the sycamore a bird awoke and began his morning song sleepily. She shook her head against the distraction.

Who would come first? Catle or O'Brien? It made no difference. O'Brien had offered her one night's stay of the horror Catle would bring and she had taken it. He had nothing more to give her. She had no regret about the bargain or its cost; she only wished she had a little more time to think about it.

She had never slept with a man before so everything that had happened in the night was entirely new. Much of it was incomprehensible. She had steeled herself for imagined indignities, prepared to suffer dramatically in exchange for eight or nine hours of life. Instead, O'Brien had asked her mildly if she would unbraid her hair, then he had put out the light considerably and treated her with a gentleness and skill that robbed her submission of any trace of martyrdom.

But there was no more time to think of that. Instead there was Catle and the old man with the cup and after that the fire. The specter of the death of the whiskey drummer stood beside her but this time it was different.

Always before when that nightmare had forced itself upon her she had relived her role as a spectator. Now she saw herself in his place. It was her body that jackknifed above the fire, her flesh that blackened and split in the flames. Long ago, when she first came to the *ranchería,* she had considered suicide and decided she was incapable of it. Now the imminence of death more horrible than any she could devise for herself overwhelmed her.

Her hair fell loose about her face. Shaking it back she walked out until the water reached her breasts. She crouched experimentally, pushing her face into the water. It was cold and dark and terrifying and she straightened up quickly, spluttering and shaking her head. Her hair flung a fan of droplets across the pool, sparkling as they flashed through the first rays of the sun.

O God, she prayed silently, help me to do this. She edged on toward the falls until the water lapped against her chin and mouth. How do you do it? she wondered. Just go under and breathe as if it were air? She crouched again and took a gulping swallow. Water flooded her throat and nostrils, strangling her, and she threshed backward, choking.

"*¿Qué pasa, Americana?*" a voice chirped above her. Coughing and sputtering she held up her hair to see. A small boy crouched naked on the bank. He must have seen her running in the dawn and followed her out of curiosity.

"Go away!" she gasped. "Vamoose!"

He giggled and flicked a pebble, inviting play. She stood up and splashed water at him until he withdrew. Miserable little thing, she thought. Grimly she faced the falls again and gathered her strength to walk toward them.

"*¡Americana!*" It was not the boy this time. A chill hand touched her heart. It was not Catle but another Indian—a young warrior she did not recognize. Behind him was the wide-eyed Cocopah girl. "*¡Venga!*" said the man.

The habit of obedience was stronger than the impulse to throw herself into the deeper water. He would only pull her out anyway. Numbly, she waded to the bank and drew herself up. He pushed her clothes at her with his foot and she put them on, heedless of the water streaming from her body. Her teeth chattered and she did not know whether from fear or chill.

They took her back to O'Brien's wickiup and pushed her inside. The Indian girl crouched in the doorway and watched her unblinking. She was shaking uncontrollably now. Her clothes clung to her and water dripped from her hair. Halfheartedly she began to braid it but its dampness repelled her and she abandoned the task. What use? she asked herself. There were voices outside. The Cocopah leaned to look and O'Brien entered, pushing her aside.

She met his eyes, finding it not difficult at all. But there were other sounds and her attention fixed on them, dreading what they meant.

"Good morning, *Americana*," he said pleasantly. A spasm of irritation pulled at her mouth.

"Don't play with me, O'Brien," she said dully.

"What makes you think that?"

She shook her head and a lock of wet hair fell across her eyes. She did not bother to put it aside. "O'Brien, have the decency to leave me alone, please. If you can do nothing for me at least don't stare at me." He reached out and brushed away the lock of hair. "Maybe I can do something for you. I did last night, didn't I?"

"Yes. You did. I'm not complaining about that."

"All right. Maybe I can do something more for you."

Her heart beat hard—a single, trip-hammer throb. But she could not speak.

"I had a talk with Geronimo and Pionsenay this morning . . ." It was as if a spring somewhere inside of her had snapped loose. She drew a deep, shuddering breath and waited for him to go on. But O'Brien was admiring her small breasts outlined by the wet camisa and he did not continue until she covered them with her arms. He sighed.

"Your people have been very stupid about this. They

188

are always stupid, but this time I would think they'd have broken their damned rules for you."

"So?"

"The Indians need cartridges. They have American rifles but no cartridges for them. I know where I can get ten cases of Springfield cartridges. In a month . . . maybe sooner."

The air in the wickiup suddenly seemed stifling to Samantha and she panted softly. "What are you talking about? I don't understand you."

"It's simple, *Americana*. If I bring them the cartridges, they will give you to me."

So many people want me, she thought. She leaned forward, frowning, and concentrated on his face. "What are you saying, O'Brien?"

"I can't say it any plainer."

"I don't understand. What was all that last night? I thought they decided I am a witch and you said they burn witches."

"They do. But you have to be tested first. Do you think you can drink that stuff and not be sick?" She shook her head and he grinned amiably.

"So. I didn't cheat you. But one way of getting rid of you is as good as another as far as Geronimo is concerned."

"I still don't understand."

"*Americana,* he doesn't give a damn about you. What he wants is Pionsenay and his bucks and as long as Pionsenay has you he isn't going anywhere. He's safe from your people. But if you're dead he can't stay here and there isn't anyplace for him to go except with Geronimo."

Samantha still looked baffled and he shook his head. "You're a pretty girl, *Americana,* but this morning you're as stupid as the soldiers. Geronimo wants you out of his way. I can do that for him and get him cartridges to boot, or he can just finish what he started last night."

"Have I really got a choice?"

"That's what I'm trying to tell you."

"How flattering!" she murmured. "I'm still a witch but

189

for ten boxes of bullets you can cure me. Am I worth that much to you, O'Brien?"

"Yes."

Without any hesitation at all she nodded her head. "All right, I don't know if you're lying to me. I have no way to know. But I'm in no position to make you prove it, am I?"

"Good!" He seemed relieved and that was a small comfort to her. At least he had been in some doubt about her answer. He put out his hand and she stared at it incredulously. Then she understood he wanted to shake hands, to close their bargain as if it were something real and rational. With an acute feeling of unreality she touched his fingers with her own.

"How do you know I will keep my bargain if you take me away from here?"

"I'll worry about that when the time comes."

"And what will become of me while you are gone looking for cartridges? Do I go with you?"

"Ah, no. You stay here, but they'll keep their word unless you do something crazy. They want the cartridges very much."

She shook her head vigorously. "I told you I'm no fool. I should think that would be obvious by now."

"Good. Do you want to stay here . . . in this wickiup, I mean?"

"With her?" Samantha glanced at the Cocopah girl. "No, thank you!"

O'Brien laughed. "Not with her. I'll take her with me."

"Are you going to keep us both?" she asked plaintively and he laughed again.

"Not if it bothers you."

"I don't suppose I'm in any position to be bothered by it."

"All right. I'll get rid of her."

"I would be grateful for that."

"So what do you want to do . . . while I'm gone?"

She considered for a moment. "Can I go back with Aludin?"

"Why not, if you want to?"

She raised her shoulders wearily. "I don't know. If they thought I was a witch last night won't they still think so? Will they take me back?"

"I will speak to Catle. I don't think there will be any trouble."

"That's what I want then." She seemed suddenly resigned, oppressed by weariness. O'Brien eyed her curiously.

"Are you all right? Are you sick or something?"

She laughed harshly. "Something . . . not sick. What do I do now?"

"You can turn in and get some sleep if you want. I won't leave until tomorrow."

She accepted that without comment. The price of her life no longer astonished her—ten cases of cartridges, another night in his bed. What difference did it make?

"I don't have to work? Nothing at all?"

"*¡Dios!* You've been here a long time, haven't you? No, you won't have to work at all today. Get some rest. I have to talk to them again now."

Yes, she thought bitterly. Get some rest before tonight. Someday, sometime, I will have to think about what I am doing but not now. What if I suddenly begin to enjoy it? she wondered. The thought intrigued her, then she yawned. O'Brien chuckled.

"Go to bed, *Americana*. No one will bother you, I promise."

He departed and she combed out her hair with her fingers, trying to dry it. She had no other clothes and there was no use trying to wheedle any from the Cocopah girl. She wondered if Suzy knew enough English to understand what O'Brien had said. Maybe she will put a knife in me or knock me on the head, she thought. That might be the best thing.

She pulled off her clothes once more and spread them to dry, then rolled herself into the thick red blanket. It was a luxury so strange she allowed herself to savor it delightedly. I will think about this blanket and not about tonight or tomorrow or what Aunt Bee will say, she told herself. I am something I don't even want to think about and I may live for weeks and weeks if I don't. The Cocopah girl watched, unbelieving.

"Good night, friend," Samantha told her cheerfully.

O'Brien's offer to buy Pionsenay's captive was unexpected and could be troublesome, but the Chiricahuas had never before had anything that was worth ten cases of cartridges to anybody. Five thousand rounds of .45-caliber ammunition was an enormous price, enough to make any Apache think twice about the laws for dealing with witches. The enlightened practicality of both Geronimo and Pionsenay would ensure that. O'Brien knew a lot about trading with Apaches and he meant to help them find a way out of their difficulty.

With a great deal of delicacy he suggested to the two chiefs that Nochalo have another dream. That would make it easier for the members of Pionsenay's band with whom Samantha would remain while he went back to Sonora for the cartridges. The question of time was raised and promptly settled by Geronimo: one moon. O'Brien thought he could do better than that but he disliked being tied down. Geronimo shook his head. He had this affair on the move finally and he had no intention of letting it bog down. They agreed O'Brien would be back at the *ranchería* in one month or the trade was off. Catle was called in and proved reasonable about taking the white-eyes girl back into his wickiup.

Long ago, word had come to Pionsenay through John Clum's tame Apaches at San Carlos that the soldiers wanted to buy their women back but nothing they offered outweighed the special value Samantha had as a hostage. The Americans seemed to think their promise of safe-conduct to the San Carlos Reservation for anyone bringing in the women was a great prize, but only the Apache squaws wanted that and Pionsenay had no faith in a white-eyes safe-conduct at all. Ever since the policemen from Tucson took him away from John Clum his opinion of the white man's word was very low.

The trade-goods which could have moved him to give up his captive had never been offered. The law forbade the soldiers to give whiskey, guns or ammunition to Indians and it seemed they valued their law more than their women. O'Brien, untroubled by any laws at all, had outbid them.

Physically and emotionally exhausted, Samantha slept until late afternoon, then she finished her interrupted bath and returned to O'Brien's wickiup. Refreshed, she had serious doubts about O'Brien's assurance the Apaches would accept her continued presence in the *ranchería*. His argument seemed reasonable enough but nothing in her experience indicated the Apaches were reasonable people. She could see no alternative, however, and having accepted that, she found she was ravenously hungry. In Catle's household, as in all Apache families, there were no fixed meal hours. Aludin kept something on the fire all the time and everyone, including Samantha, ate when he wanted to. At the moment, however, she did not dare go back to Aludin's fire so she and Suzy eyed each other warily until O'Brien returned.

He called Suzy and gave her a piece of meat and she stirred up the fire sulkily. Then he got a bolt of cloth from one of his packs and handed it to Samantha. "The outside's pretty dirty but you can wash it. There's enough there to make you a decent dress. Can you sew?"

"Of course. I'm not very good with a bone needle and yucca thread but I can make a dress. This is for me?"

"Sure. Don't you like it?"

She unrolled the material and winced. It was yellow calico printed with big cabbage roses. O'Brien was digging in the pack again and did not see her face. He gave her a twist of thread and a paper with two steel needles in it. "No buttons but you can make those out of piñon nuts. Catle's women will show you how."

"They're going to take me back?"

"Sure! That's what you wanted, isn't it?"

"Oh, yes! But . . . it's all settled? I mean, they're going to trade with you for . . . for me?" Her face flamed suddenly and she stumbled over the words. O'Brien was amused.

"I told you they would. Didn't you believe me?"

Samantha shrugged without looking at him. Whatever

193

Suzy was cooking was beginning to give off a pleasant aroma and she swallowed hungrily.

"I traded Catle out of a piece of meat and some mesquite bread. I haven't got any of my own grub left."

"I can eat anything except wood rat," she told him grimly. "Shall I help her?"

"If you want."

Suzy accepted help with ill grace. She had put the chunk of meat directly on the coals and it was charring noisily. Samantha levered it up with a stick.

"Haven't you got a skillet?" she asked O'Brien and when he produced one she was so pleased she overlooked the years of grease and dirt that coated it. Transferring the meat to the pan, she set it to brown and crumbled in a little bread with water to make a gravy. Suzy watched in wonder and when O'Brien sat to eat he crowed delightedly.

"*¡Dios mío!* I am an Irish fool for luck!" Both women regarded him sourly.

After they had eaten, Samantha dumped a handful of sand in the skillet and scoured it clean to the astonishment of both Suzy and O'Brien. Before she finished, he gave Suzy some direction that sent her grumbling off into the darkness with her blanket. Samantha settled herself across the fire from him and watched him circumspectly while he stuffed a pipe with tobacco and lit it with a coal. The smell of real tobacco was a pleasant change from the stinking substitute Catle used.

"Who are you, O'Brien?" she broke the silence finally. "Am I allowed to ask that?"

"Sure, *Americana*. It's no secret. I'm a businessman. I trade with Yankees and Mexicans and sometimes Indians. I buy anything I can sell."

"Including women?"

He smiled. "I never bought a woman before. You're thinking of Suzy? I didn't have to buy her."

"You said you aren't American but you talk like one."

"I told you I'm a trader. I do a lot of business with Yankees."

"You are Mexican, then?"

"I don't have a country, *Americana*. My father was a mick and my mother was a greaser."

She was baffled by the derogatory reference to his parents until she saw he was teasing her, perhaps venting some old grudge against Americans. From Severiano she had some idea of the bitterness felt by the border mixed breed. Seeing she would not respond, he continued with equal bluntness.

"My father was a soldier in your Army and my mother was a Mexican camp follower."

"Your father was in the war . . . in the Union Army?"

"Not that war, *Americana,* the one before that. Did you ever hear of the San Patricio Battalion?" She shook her head.

"The St. Patrick Battalion. The Irish who fought for the Mexicans when the Yankees invaded Mexico."

"Oh! Yes, I've heard of them. My father was in that war too."

"Ah! I can guess what he said about us. Irish deserters and worse, I'll bet. Most of them came from the Yankee Army. My father served with Sergeant Riley in your Army and went with him when he joined the Mexicans. Riley commanded the St. Patricks and my dad was captured along with him after the battle of Contreras. You've heard of that, I'll wager."

She had heard much about Contreras from the veterans at Fort Leavenworth but she suspected O'Brien's views were different from theirs. She saw he expected no answer.

"The Yankees put every prisoner, wounded and all, before a court-martial. Half of them deserted before the war began and they got Yankee mercy . . . two hundred lashes, branded with a 'D' on the cheek and an eight-pound iron yoke around their necks. The rest were traitors because they deserted after the war started and they got the rope. My dad was one of them."

"That's horrible!" she murmured. She found his way of speaking odd and alarming. All this had happened thirty years before but he spoke of it as if it were a recent thing.

"Do you know how they killed them, *Americana?* There was a Colonel Harney of the Yankee Dragoons who was good at killing prisoners. He learned in Florida, hanging Indians your people captured there. He put all the St. Patricks in wagons, even one who had no legs at all and was dying, and he drove them out to a gallows on a hill where they could see the castle in Chapultepec."

He broke off, staring into the fire, and she waited, frightened yet curious for him to go on.

"Harney told them that as soon as the Yankees had killed General Bravo and his cadets they would run up the Stars and Stripes on the castle. As soon as it showed, they were dead men. They waited half a day before the flag went up and then Harney gave the order. Away went the wagons and thirty brave Irishmen choked on the rope!"

She had never heard any of this before and she did not believe it, but she knew better than to contradict him. He took a leather wallet from his jacket and opened it to show her a creased and faded pamphlet inside. "Even some of your own people were ashamed of Harney and his breed. A Yankee named Thoreau had guts enough to write about his shame, but you put him in jail for it."

The bitterness in his voice disturbed her. He hates Americans, she thought, and for something that must have happened before he was old enough to know anything of it.

"What of your mother? Does she live in Mexico now?"

"She died when I was twelve. When my father deserted from the Yankees she followed him and they let her stand on that hill and watch him die. That was September '47 and I was born a month later." The firelight glittered on his eyes. "Are you surprised I don't like Yankees, girl?"

She could say nothing, only shake her head. He was not satisfied with that.

"What kind of people do a thing like that? They say you came out here to marry a soldier. Is that the kind of man you want?"

She caught her breath noisily. "He's not like that! I don't know any who are!"

"*¡Quiá!* You are stupid! They're all like that. They were then and they still are. You think these Indians are just animals, don't you? Well, that's how your people treat them . . . murdering, raping, stealing, herding them into pens and starving them . . . and all the time yapping about the treacherous Indians! *Hola, Americana* . . . don't you know what's happening in Arizona? Don't you know what your soldier is doing?"

"It's not true!" she burst out. "I don't believe a word of it! How would you know, anyway? You couldn't show your face in Arizona!" No sooner were the words out than she wished them back again. Anger at him was a luxury she could not afford. She bit her lip and waited for his reaction.

But he was not angry; he was amused by her sputtering response. "The Army doesn't run the Territory. I go where I please when I want to." He pulled a branch from the fire and she watched it nervously. "You know, after what you've been through, I'd think you'd understand more. I'm not going to hurt you. I think you're a little simpleminded but you've got guts and I like a girl with spunk." He stood up and kicked sand on the coals, a folly that appalled Samantha.

"Don't do that! You'll never get it started again!"

"You talk like an Indian. I've got matches. Come on, let's go."

"Go where?"

"To bed. Where else?"

She walked stiffly before him, her face flaming. At the wickiup, when she stooped to enter, he slapped her bottom casually just as he had slapped Suzy. She whirled, furious, but he caught her elbows and pulled her to him. He meant to kiss her and he expected a fight. She could see he meant to enjoy that too.

She denied him his pleasure, waiting until surprise replaced his anticipation. Her voice shook but she tried to hide her panic. "Let me go, O'Brien, please. I want to say something."

He loosened his grip but he did not release her. "All right. Say it."

"I know how things are with me. I don't want to make you angry."

"That's good. Is that all?"

"No. I have to do what you want. I have no choice. But for pity's sake, O'Brien, be decent to me. You can give me that much, can't you?"

"What do you mean, 'decent'?"

"I'm neither your wife nor a prostitute. Don't treat me like that."

It took him a moment to digest this; then he laughed. "So how am I supposed to treat you? You think I'm doing this for charity?"

"I know better than that. Maybe decency is the wrong word. Can't you just give me a little more time?"

Now she had made him angry. His eyes were hard and his hands hurt again. "Sure. All the time it takes to get into that wickiup." He pushed her roughly. Frightened and indignant, she groped for the door.

Inside he lit the lamp and began pulling off his clothes. "What are you waiting for?" he demanded. She made a vague gesture toward the tallow dip and he grinned.

"No."

"Please?"

"I said no. You want me to help you take them off?"

"Oh . . . no!"

Hating him and loathing herself, she obeyed with shaking hands. Until the night before she had never known a man. She had no real basis for judgment but it seemed to her she could scarcely have been much of a prize for him, yet he appeared determined to repeat the performance. Maybe he just didn't care about that. She wished distractedly she could share his indifference if that was what it was.

She reached defiantly for the lamp but his hand guarded it. She had to stand and bear his amused scrutiny. Deliberately his eyes ranged over her body, measuring every curve and angle with an intensity that took her breath. She was more angle than curve now, not an ounce of spare flesh on her, but the taut leanness of her body made her small breasts more prominent. The hand that shielded the lamp moved to fondle one and she was doubly shamed by her reaction to his gentle touch.

"*¡Dios!*" he murmured and snuffed the guttering wick. Shivering uncontrollably she crept into the bed. His hands met her, turned her to him, and she moaned.

"Please don't pull them . . . they're so sore!"

"All right. But take it easy, *Americana;* don't be so frightened. You're no good that way." His hands searched her body, she trying to meet and block them. It was futile. Gently, insistently, he reduced her to breathlessness.

"Wait . . . Oh, wait! Just give me a minute, please!" she begged. His lips smothered her plea, forcing her own, searching and demanding. He granted her no relief, ceded no advantage. She was doubly invaded and she could only whimper helplessly. Braced again for violence, she was betrayed by his gentleness and skill.

She did not want to put her hands on him and she did not know what to do with them. Each time she tried to evade his insistent lips she bruised her head on a rib of the wickiup. She reached for it with both hands, gripped and clung to it as her willful body defied her. This girl who groaned and shouted and heaved beneath him could not be Samantha Allyn. It was some girl who knew no better.

TWENTY-ONE

Just before it passes out of the United States into Mexico on its way to the Gulf of California, the Colorado River in 1876 made a sharp bend to the west through a rocky defile barely two hundred yards wide. On the California side of this bend was Fort Yuma; across the river in Arizona was Yuma City and the largest Army quartermaster depot in the Territory. This complex was the principal gateway to Arizona and the majority of people bound for the Territory entered here, either by riverboat from the mouth of the Colorado or by stagecoach from San Diego.

Visitors from the East, like Samantha and her aunt, traveled to San Francisco via the Union Pacific and Central Pacific railroads, then south to San Diego by coastal steamer. There they had a choice: continue by steamer around the peninsula of Lower California to the mouth of the Colorado or go directly east to Yuma by stagecoach. The stage took two days, the steamer thirteen, which explained why Samantha chose the stage.

The land route was hair-raising. It was usually made in two days and two nights with stops only to change teams and feed the passengers. The Texas and California Company used big Concord coaches for this trip and packed them full. The overflow clung to the top, reserved for men only because both strength and stamina were required. Four horses snatched the coach across the desolate California desert at record speed, the relays short and stations well-stocked with fresh teams. Then the road pitched abruptly down the escarpment to the Colorado River.

This last stretch of road was famous. It was narrow and its hairpin turns overhung awesome gorges, so frightening that the stage company usually traversed it at night. It took a skilled driver to bring his lumbering coach down the escarpment and keep it on its wheels in the dark but that was better than allowing the passengers to see what was happening. They reached bottom at dawn and could look back in wonder at what they had just accomplished.

From the foot of the bluffs, the coach followed the old emigrant road to the river, past Fort Yuma on its rocky height, through groves of cottonwood and mesquite, and an impenetrable growth of cane and willow. Yuma City, on the east bank, was reached by ferry.

Fort Yuma's small garrison had no difficulty with the peaceful river Indians: Cocopahs, Yumas and Mojaves; but there was a surfeit of guard duty. Horses, mules, wagons, weapons, ammunition and supplies of every kind accumulated in the depot awaiting distribution all over the Territory and they all had to be guarded.

The high rate of desertion among troops in Arizona created another kind of guard duty. Deserters caught and convicted in the Territory were collected at Yuma until they could be transferred to the Army prison at Fort Leavenworth. In addition, since the coastal cities of California were the first goal of most deserters still at large, Fort Yuma tried to keep an eye on everyone taking the stage or a riverboat from the city. Few deserters had money enough to buy a complete civilian wardrobe and most hung onto salable items of their equipment, so the provost guard questioned any man departing Yuma with anything identifiable as Army gear.

Near the end of September in 1876, this surveillance increased the prison population of Fort Yuma by one and started a train of events that would culminate badly in Camp Lowell a month later.

Among the men waiting to board the stage for San Diego, the provost sergeant spotted one whose civilian trousers did not conceal the Army boots beneath them. He engaged the traveler in conversation that led to an examination of the Colt revolver thrust into the man's belt. There was a "U.S." on its barrel and more damning, an "H/6" burned into the wooden grip.

The traveler swore he had won the pistol in a poker game but the provost sergeant detained him until he had sent for a cavalry sergeant to have a look.

Sergeant Peaslack had been sent to Yuma to select from the quartermaster corral a dozen remounts for L Troop of the Sixth Cavalry at Camp Bowie. When he walked into the provost's office, the would-be traveler put his head in his hands and groaned. Peaslack eyed him sourly.

"What's the matter, Gannon? You like the Army so much you can't stay gone?"

Peaslack was disgusted. He had accompanied Austin Henely on the long scout into Mexico from which Gannon and four others deserted so he felt personally involved with them though none were from his own troop. Gannon raised his head and studied the angry sergeant calculatingly.

"That's right, Sarge. I never meant to stay gone."

"What in hell you mean by that?"

"Jest whut I said. I ain't no deserter. I an' my buddies tuk off frum that scout t' keep frum gettin' kilt by that hard-ass Henely. 'Twixt him an' that spook, Royal, somebody was bound t' git it, an' I was bound it warn't goin' t' be me."

"So?"

"So I cum back. I jest turned myself in an' that proves I ain't no deserter. I want outta Henely's troop an' when I git a court fer bein' absent without no leave, I'll git a transfer—an' some time to boot, but it'll be worth it."

The provost sergeant winked knowingly at Peaslack. He could see an old trick shaping up. If Peaslack would swear the man had turned himself in voluntarily, Gannon could escape trial for desertion and the inevitable dishonorable discharge and time at Leavenworth that followed conviction. When a regiment had too many deserters, its courts-martial were quick to accept a guilty plea to absence without leave if there were any support for it at all.

"I'll be going, Sarge," he told Peaslack. "He's all yours but before you take off, you better tell me how much I got to remember about him."

Peaslack nodded, accepting the offer of friendly collusion without comment, but as soon as the provost sergeant was gone, he glared at Gannon.

"You got one good reason why I should save your worthless hide?"

"I got a couple, Sarge. First off, with five deserters frum one scout, even Henely'd be glad t' git one of 'em back."

"Yeah, sure! And what if one of them other four gets caught an' spills his guts?"

Gannon shrugged. "I split off frum them an' turned myself in. Don't matter whut they say. They ain't gonna git caught nohow."

"What makes you so sure of that?"

"You ever hear of a breed named O'Brien?"

"Sure. Everybody in the Territory knows about that renegade. What's he got to do with it?"

"When we headed east frum Janos, we run inta O'Brien an' he treated us good. He said him an' Díaz is personal buddies an' he c'ld git us all made lootenants in th' rebel army. He said Juárez is whipped an' there ain't gonna be no more fightin', jest easy livin' after Díaz takes over. Them other four they tuk him up on it, an' they went south to Durango."

"How come you don't wanta be no lootenant in Díaz's army?"

"I ain't lost nuthin' in Mexico, Sarge. Come on, all you gotta do is say I give myself up to you here in Yuma. Thet doughboy sergeant he ain't gonna tell. He knows when th' cav'ry has provost duty he kin git th' same break fer one o' his people."

Peaslack considered for a moment. "What about that O'Brien? He's in an' outta here all the time. Nuthin' to keep him from shootin' off his mouth."

"Whut kin he say? He seen me in Mexico. So what?"

"I don't like it. We got in a fight with hos-tiles after you bastards took off. They can throw the book at you, Gannon, for desertin' in the face of the enemy an' I hope they do. You got it comin'."

Gannon bared his teeth in a snarl of anger. "Awright, you don't buy my first reason, you wanta hear th' other?"

"What is it?"

"When we met up with O'Brien he wuz comin' frum a 'Pache camp on the U.S. side. There's a white woman in thet camp an' th' minnit O'Brien got there she jumped in bed with him an' said she'd stay there if he'd take her with him. He's gotta buy her off them 'Paches an' when we saw him he wuz goin' t' git th' trade goods."

"Gannon, you been drinkin' too much rotgut tequila! How would a white woman . . ." He broke off abruptly and Gannon smirked.

"That's right, you got it, Sarge! Lootenant hard-ass Royal's girl, thet's who it is! Hustlin' her butt fer a half-breed bummer like O'Brien."

Sergeant Peaslack's face was ugly. "Gannon," he rasped, "you're a lyin' sunnuvabitch!"

"You git me court-martialed fer desertin', Sarge, an' I'm gonna tell it under oath. Maybe they'll believe me an' maybe they won't but it'll be all over th' Territory in a week. How would ya like that?"

The sergeant didn't like it at all. He was sorry for Tom Royal but that was not his main concern. He could already hear every civilian and infantryman in Arizona sniggering and cracking dirty jokes about the cavalry and its women. That could be worse than standing up for Gannon. It did not take him long to make up his mind.

"Gannon, you're a revolvin' sunnuvabitch but I'll back you on one condition."

"That I don't never say nuthin' about Royal's gal? Hell, Sarge, I got more smarts than that! You git me off with nuthin' worse'n absent without leave an' I'll never tell nobody whut I jest told you. I'll swear to that!"

"I wouldn't believe you on a stack of Bibles but you

remember one thing—you mouth off about that girl an' I'll kill you before Royal can. You got that?"

"Sure, Sarge. Anything you say."

TWENTY-TWO

General Kautz having said he wanted Pionsenay, Colonel Oakes prepared to go and get him. He summoned his best officers to discuss the method. There was some talk of sending a large force to surround Pionsenay's *ranchería,* if and when they could find it, while someone tried to talk the Apaches into giving up the captive women. The officers were against this unanimously. They favored a surprise attack.

"How in the name of Sam Hill're you going to surprise a pack of renegade Apaches in a mountain stronghold?" John Clum wanted to know. The Army had not invited him to the council to discuss tactics. Colonel Oakes called him in because he could provide a guide who probably could locate the *ranchería.* But Clum simply could not resist the opportunity to criticize the military. "They'll know what you're up to the minute you ride out of here!" Clum insisted.

Oakes grinned at him. "How do we usually go out of here, Clum?"

"In a column of twos with flags and bugles and wagons and a cloud of dust you can see in Sonora! Don't tell me you're going to try to slip out at night, either." The colonel who had survived two wars and won four brevet promotions in them regarded the young Indian agent with all the tolerance he could muster.

"I won't, Mister Clum. We'll go just as always . . . guidons, trumpets and dust. At least two troops will march out of here and down to the Huachuca Mountains as usual. They'll sashay around those mountains just like we've been doing for the past six months until Pionsenay and his bucks are thoroughly bored with us."

"And then . . . ?" asked Clum.

"That's why I asked you here, Mister Clum. I'd be grateful if you'd find me a couple of your tame Apaches who can lead Captain Tupper to the *ranchería* . . . from the south."

"You mean out of Mexico? What will Governor Pesquiera have to say about that?"

"You should read the elegant letter of apology I have prepared for the governor of Sonora, Mister Clum."

On September 28 Oakes set his plan in motion. Captain Whitside departed Camp Lowell with his troop and marched openly south into the Santa Cruz Valley. When he reached Sonoita Creek he turned east and went into bivouac on the site of old Camp Crittenden. From there he scouted industriously farther east. A few days later Captain Tupper with Tom Royal and half of G Troop left Camp Grant for Dragoon Springs. They too marched in daylight with no attempt to evade observation. At the Springs they were joined by Austin Henely, Tate Hulse and thirty men from Camp Bowie and some unexpected reinforcements.

A Lieutenant Sandlin with nineteen Negro troopers of the Ninth Cavalry and one white civilian scout had trailed some cattle thieves all the way from Mesilla in New Mexico through the Sierra de Guadalupe into Arizona. At the Sonora border they had lost the trail and turned back, stopping at Dragoon Springs to water. When he learned what was afoot, Sandlin asked to join.

Captain Tupper explained his plan. If Clum's guides were correct, Pionsenay's *ranchería* lay somewhere in the Huachuca Mountains between his own force and Whitside's troop to the west. While Whitside scouted the Sonoita Valley and the foothills of the Santa Rita, Patagonia and Whetstone mountains in a routine manner, Tupper and his men would work slowly south. By the end of a week they would be on the Sonora border, which they would cross cautiously as if following a trail. Tupper guessed that by then Pionsenay's vedettes would be sure Whitside was up to nothing dangerous and when he crossed into Sonora, they would lose interest in him, too. On the eighth of October, both forces would converge suddenly, Whitside driving east along the border and Tupper turning back out of Mexico to penetrate the Huachucas from the south. Sandlin's detachment of black troopers were a godsend. The Buffalo Soldiers, as the Indians called them, were tough and experienced. They would accompany Tupper into the Mule Pass Mountains but stop there. On the morning of the eighth, Sandlin could lead them fast across the San Pedro Valley and spread a screen along Babacomba Creek through which Pionsenay would have to break if he tried to run north deeper into Arizona. Sometime during the morning Sandlin's people should make contact with Whitside's troopers as they moved east from San Rafael.

Sandlin wanted to know about the two white women who might still be captives of Pionsenay's band. Tupper only shook his head. If Pionsenay broke north and the women had not been found before then there was small likelihood Sandlin would have to worry about them.

The week passed for Tom Royal with agonizing slowness. Tupper poked his way down the Dragoons and into the Mule Pass Mountains as if he had all the time in the world. He had two good reasons for this. He wanted Pionsenay's scouts to see nothing unusual in his movement and he wanted to spend as little time in Sonora as possible. The venture into Mexico was a weak link. If successful it would give him surprise but if he ran into Sonoran troops he was in trouble. He would have to pull back and there would be no time to tell Whitside what had happened.

Sandlin and his black troopers dropped off at the mouth of the Puerta de los Mulas pass on the night of the sixth, and Tupper rode on into Mexico. On the seventh he struck Cook's emigrant trail, the oldest Amer-

ican road through Apacheria. Turning west, he followed
the trail, skirting the San José Mountains until he reached
the headwaters of the San Pedro River, eight miles inside Mexico. Here he bivouacked. Clum's guides thought
Pionsenay's *ranchería* lay about twelve miles north and
west and Tupper meant to be there by daylight the following morning.

Twenty miles west of Tupper's bivouac lay the straggling Sonoran village of Santa Cruz and about the same
time his troopers settled down for the night a small train
of pack mules arrived in the village. They were unsaddled and their loads put into a grain shed forming
one wall of a log corral behind a *pulquería*. Posting his
helper as a guard, the packmaster went into the dingy
little saloon and seated himself.

"*Buenos días,* Señor O'Brien," said the patron.
"Tequila?"

While O'Brien was still eating his supper there was a
small disturbance at the back of the *pulquería*. A man
appeared from the night and knocked persistently at the
door.

"Señor O'Brien?" he demanded.

The patron gave him a blank look. "I have never
heard of him."

"Then you have stolen his mules."

"The sun has disturbed your head, my friend."

"And O'Brien will take yours off your shoulders and
hand it to you, *cabrón!* Go! Say to him that Julio is here
to tell him of the soldiers on the old *americano* road."

"Soldiers! That lunatic *coronel* in Janos has marched
his rapists out again?"

The man in the shadow beyond the door shifted his
feet impatiently.

"Go, fat one! You are wasting my time which is not
likely to hurt you but when O'Brien knows he will kill
you!"

The patron considered. He was very much afraid of
O'Brien. Almost everyone in Sonora who did business
with O'Brien was afraid of him, which was good for

O'Brien's business. He shuffled away to whisper that there was a bandit outside with some story of soldiers to the east and O'Brien told him to bring the man in.

Julio's story was brief. O'Brien thanked him politely and offered him a drink which was all he offered. When Julio disappeared into the night from which he had come O'Brien lit a cigar and frowned thoughtfully.

The Americans occasionally crossed into Mexico but as far as he knew they only did it when they were chasing Indians. He knew all about the "hot pursuit" policy. But if Julio were telling the truth they were certainly not in hot pursuit of anything now. It sounded more as if they were setting up an ambush for someone.

Himself? How could they know he planned to cross the border tomorrow? Had he been betrayed by Pionsenay or Geronimo? That made no sense. He had what both of those Indians wanted and it was unlikely the Americans had outbid him.

Geronimo. That was something else. Just possibly the Americans had learned he was in the *ranchería* and were either trying to trap him as he came south or were going to make a surprise attack from Sonora. The latter was most likely. They wanted Geronimo bad enough to violate the border but unless they had made a deal with the Mexican governor they would not tarry long. He shook his head, puzzled, and then shrugged. It didn't matter whom the *Americanos* were after. They were there and he had no intention of joining them. He would wait. One of two things would happen. The Yankees would go back across the border or they would set up an ambush. They would wait a long time for Rafael O'Brien to walk into their trap.

But then another thought occurred to him. If they were after O'Brien and O'Brien didn't show up they might go looking for him. They might come so far as Santa Cruz. He asked the patron to send in the man whom he had left to guard the packs.

"By first light, Carlos, I want the mules packed and ten miles south of here."

Carlos studied the glass in front of his boss but there was no expression on his face. O'Brien chuckled.

"No, I am not drunk. Julio was here and he tells me there is a reception waiting for us near the border. I do not care to attend."

Carlos nodded. *"Sí, señor."*

"Go back to the *rancho* of Don Tomás. Put the packs in the usual place and then scatter the mules. I want nothing that even looks like a packtrain if anyone comes."

"Sí, señor."

"I will remain here for a day or two. If nothing happens I will send Julio to tell you to pack the mules and bring them back. If there is trouble I may go away somewhere. I will send you word what to do. Is that all understood, my friend?"

"Sí, Señor O'Brien."

It was good to do business with a man of so few words. There were plenty of good mule skinners in Sonora but few so closemouthed as Carlos.

He was sorry about the American girl. Very sorry. He had been looking forward to that with much anticipation. He wondered if there were some way he could warn Pionsenay but clearly there was not. He would not go himself and he doubted if the Apaches would believe anyone else even if he could get one of the villagers to go. At best they would kill the messenger and the girl before they ran.

But maybe they would get away and bring the girl with them. He would take a trip into the Sierra Madre in a while. They would still want the cartridges. Too bad. A fine girl, he thought. Those two nights were all too short.

TWENTY-THREE

The happening which Samantha had so long waited, hoped and prayed for—and in the end despaired of—came on a morning so cold it was painful to leave her blanket. There had been heavy frost in the night. She left the wickiup to find Aludin blowing up her fire furiously and she hugged her bare arms, wondering how to ask for something more to wear against the cold.

She fingered the knots in the drawstring of her camisa and added another. There were nineteen now and O'Brien had said he would be back in twenty or thirty days. How many had the Apaches allowed him? she wondered. The unwelcome throb of excitement that had stirred her when she thought of him was gone now and that was a small comfort.

Crouching beside Aludin she relished the warmth of the glowing coals. Together they worked to warm meat and mesquite gruel for Catle's breakfast. Sheneah appeared grumbling—about the cold probably. After she and Catle were served the two younger women ate. The day was gray and forbidding, clouds so low over the *ranchería* that Samantha wondered if they brought snow. She shuddered. Life in the wickiup was bad enough without that.

No matter, she told herself grimly. If O'Brien did not return before the snow came, something far worse would have happened. She watched Catle with disgust as he ate his gruel. Habitually he spooned the porridge into his mouth faster than he could dispose of what was already

211

there and in consequence he leaked. But nothing was allowed to get away. With the fingers of his other hand he put back whatever escaped and this minor feat of dexterity always repelled Samantha.

Then the surrounding peaks echoed what could only have been a distant rifle shot. Catle cocked his head to listen and the gruel ran down his chin unchecked. When it was not repeated, Samantha guessed it was someone hunting deer though she had never before heard a shot so close to the *ranchería*. Catle's expression indicated it was out of the ordinary. There was no alarm on his broad features but he was curiously alert.

The echoes died away and she was sure she was right in her first guess, but then in quick succession there were more. Three, four, five, six, she counted in mounting excitement. Catle swiped at his chin with the back of his hand and stood up, the porridge bowl spinning away from him. Pebbles clicked on the slope and there was the slap of hurrying moccasins. A young Apache, carbine in hand, came out of the trees in a loose-hipped, shuffling run.

"*¡Soldados!*" he grunted.

Samantha shut her eyes and hugged herself in wild delight. They had come. At last they had come. The surge of joy gave way at once to alarm. What would the Apaches do? She waited apprehensively.

Sheneah darted into her wickiup and out again, thrusting rifle and cartridge belt at Catle. He snatched them and ran for Pionsenay's hut where the vedette was crouched.

Like an ant nest turned up with a kick, the *ranchería* boiled with activity. Some of the men went out on foot, running. Others scrambled onto ponies and galloped for the rock gate. Women scuttled about gathering children with shrill cries and some were packing their belongings in haste. Aludin jerked at the canvas lashed over the packsaddle and shot Samantha a distracted look. Obviously she too expected an order to move and she wanted her packhorse. More than that she wanted to start loading what she could take with her if she had to go in a hurry. Feminine concern for her possessions triumphed.

"*¡Caballo!*" she snapped. "*¡Pronto! ¡Pronto!*"

Samantha ran for the picket line, her heart pounding. The jostling women paid her no attention as she snatched at the halter of Aludin's pony. She hauled him free but once away from the other animals he spread his forefeet and refused to budge.

The Apaches had taught her how to deal with an Indian pony. She doubled her fist and hit him on the head as hard as she could but he was wild with excitement and reared, snorting. Remembering an eccentricity of cavalry horses who balked if you faced them and pulled on the halter, she turned her back and tugged. It worked. The jittery pony came down, snorting, and followed her.

The confusion was chaotic. The firing was much closer; bullets snapped overhead with the sound of slapping boards punctuated by the howl of an occasional ricochet. Head down and pulling hard, Samantha towed the packhorse toward the wickiup.

A thunder of hide-shod hooves enveloped her. She was overtaken by a knot of riders galloping for the gate and they buffeted her violently, first one way and then another. Fighting to keep her feet, she lost hold of the halter. One of the Apaches slashed her across the shoulders with his quirt and yelled something unintelligible. She clasped her hands over her head and crouched defensively. A hand caught her arm and hauled her against the horse; she cried out in fear.

"*¡Americana!*" The rider bent, yelling at her. It was Severiano, mouthing words lost in the uproar. Grabbing his leg, she hung on until they spun out of the press.

"You know other gate?" he pointed, fighting his pony. She nodded breathlessly.

"Go! Run! Wait for me. I will come!"

She stared up at him, frightened and confused, and he slapped her, jolting her into resentful attention. "They kill you! Soldiers come an' 'Paches kill you! Go!"

She understood that. She had thought of it ever since she came. There had been a time when she catalogued every hiding place in the *ranchería,* every cranny that

213

offered refuge if the soldiers came for her. In the suddenness of the event she had done none of the things so carefully planned. Instead she had run obediently for Aludin's packhorse. Severiano's slap jarred her into realization of this.

He pushed her away, toed his pony into a run after the others, and she turned toward the hidden entrance. He had said run but she was afraid to. She went at a fast walk, her heart in her mouth.

She need not have worried. In their frenzy of packing the Apache women did not even look at her. She went through the wickiups and was scrambling up the rocky slope beyond when a fresh pounding of hooves sent her searching in panic for shelter. A riderless horse was zigzagging crazily between the wickiups.

There was something strange about this one. He was bigger than an Indian pony and he was tripping on a broken rein trailing from a bridle. Brass glinted on the headstall and then she saw the saddle; blanket roll spilling from the straps and a carbine butt thrusting out of the saddle boot. She flung herself down the slope, holding out her hands.

"Hoh, boy! Whoa-up, horse!" The familiar words caught his attention and the flattened ears pricked forward. He whinnied, nostrils flaring. "Easy, boy . . . walk now!" she urged.

The animal swerved toward her but when she reached for the rein he dodged away. Maddeningly he stayed just out of reach but she kept up her crooning entreaties and edged closer, got a hand on his shoulder and stroked his neck. Her other hand found and closed on the rein. There was blood on the unraveling blanket roll and on the horse's neck. Her hand was wet and sticky with it.

"*¡Americana!*" The familiar command made her jump violently. Aludin stood a dozen feet away, her eyes hard and glittering. They shifted from Samantha to the cavalry horse and back again. She jerked her head.

A wave of rebellious fury assailed Samantha and she backed against the horse. "No."

The knife blade in Aludin's hand was dull and wicked

in the gray light. In her other hand was a coiled riata. Samantha's breath locked in her throat. The threat of the knife was real enough but it was the riata that pushed her over the edge of revolt. Aludin would tie her with it. The horse shifted nervously behind her and the butt of the carbine nudged her shoulder. She snatched it from the boot and leveled it at Aludin.

She might as well have pointed her finger. The Apache girl advanced, her knife thrust forward.

Jamming the butt against her stomach, Samantha used both hands to haul back the hammer. Only a fool would stick a loaded carbine in his saddle boot but she had no time to throw open the block and look. She clamped the stock under her arm and the muzzle made small, wavering circles before her.

"Aludin . . . *por favor!* For God's sake . . . stop!"

The black eyes were unblinking. Arms spread, the Indian girl continued her cautious advance.

"Oh . . . God!" moaned Samantha. She jerked hard on the trigger.

The carbine roared, kicking out of her hands with a lunatic force that stunned her and drove the butt into the horse. He fled, whickering in panic.

At that distance the heavy slug knocked Aludin flat on her back. For a moment she lay stunned, propped on her elbows, then her face convulsed in a rictus of agony and she writhed over onto her stomach.

Frozen with horror, Samantha watched her struggle to get on her knees. Her back arched and a torrent of blood burst from her mouth. With a choking groan, she collapsed, shuddered a little, then went flat and boneless.

Samantha circled the body and flung herself at the slope, heedless of the branches that tore at her. Beyond the narrow cleft she found a scrub cedar and crawled into the shelter of its branches.

If the wait had been longer she would have been sick with the horror of what she had done but within minutes she heard rocks sliding and rolling downhill and Severiano was there, looking worried. She put her foot on his instep and swung up behind him. Before she could settle herself he kicked the pony into a scrambling run downhill.

After a little they slid into a narrow corridor leading downward and though the pace did not slow the pony was not gyrating so violently. Samantha raised her head from Severiano's back and peered over his shoulder.

"What happened? Where are they?"

"Black soljers come up big trail. Not many."

"Where did they go?"

"Go back. 'Paches drive 'em off. Plenty more other way. White soljers over there."

She thrust herself away from his back excitedly. "Well, why are we going this way? Go back! Go toward the white soldiers . . . they're looking for me!"

Severiano shook his head. "No good! 'Paches go that way. Go fight. Ever'body go fight white soljers so women can run away."

That made sense. There was nothing to be gained by riding into a last-ditch fight between soldiers and desperate Apaches. The Negro troopers would not have pulled back very far and they might be easier to join. Except Severiano looked an awful lot like a fighting Apache buck. He was not painted but in every other way there was no telling him from the others. That worried her, for even if they were not being shot at these soldiers would be touchy. At least one of them had been killed or hurt unless there was a wound on the horse she had not noticed. Shuddering, she let go of Severiano with her right hand and scrubbed it violently against her thigh. He twisted around to look at her curiously.

"I'm all right. If you see soldiers . . . stop! Hold up your hands and let me call to them. They might shoot at us."

He grunted and for half an hour or more they continued down the corridor before he turned the tiring pony out of it into a grove of tall pines. Beyond it a valley opened downward through the forest, a thick belt of green in its center marking a stream, she guessed.

"Why are we stopping?"

He did not reply. He slid off the pony and walked

cautiously to the edge of the grove, the pony following to snatch hungrily at the grass invading the carpet of pine needles.

Far away and above them Samantha heard firing in long, rolling bursts. The sound sent shivers of anticipation through her. She wanted to hold and savor each moment that passed now. All the months of fear and frustration were slipping behind. Ahead, perhaps in minutes, the first glimpse of blue uniforms, familiar faces, protection and love. She gripped the pony's withers and almost cried out in delight.

Tom. Tom would be there somewhere. It was too much to hope he would be among the first she met, but they had come looking for her. Every man would know her and be eager to find Tom for her.

Severiano came back, behaving rather oddly. He seemed indecisive and his delaying, fiddling with the jaquima bridle and the oddments tied to his buckskin saddlebags, infuriated her.

"Come on! Get on and let's go!" she urged, pointing down the valley. "If we just ride straight down there we'll come out on the flat and we can see everything. They can see us, too, and we won't surprise them. There'll be less chance they'll shoot at us."

"No," he said sullenly.

"What?"

"We go that way." He pointed west, away from the valley.

"For God's sake, why? If you go sneaking through those trees you'll get us both killed! We've got to stay in the open so they can see us first. There aren't any Apaches down here. Listen to that!" The firing on the high slopes continued unabated. If Tom is up there, she prayed silently, God keep him safe for me.

"What in the world are you doing, Severiano?" she demanded of him. He had taken his lariat from the saddle and for a moment she thought he meant to picket the horse. He put his hand on her ankle and looked up at her.

"I leave my people. I run off when they got plenty

217

trouble. Got big fight." He shook his head. "Bad. Can't never go back to 'Paches now."

"Is that what's worrying you? For heaven's sake, don't you know the Americans will be glad to see you? You saved my life! They'll take care of you."

"Mebbeso . . . mebbe not. Sure, I bring you back but they forget that quick. Pretty soon they say me, haffass 'Pache-greaser kid what you hang aroun' for?"

Oh, God, she thought, give me patience. After everything else I've got to try to talk sense into him now. It was too much. Too unfair.

"Severiano . . ." she began, leaning toward him, "listen to me . . ."

"No!" he interrupted. "I ask you many times be my woman. You say me no. Soljers don' know where you are. To hell with soljers! We go to Mexico an' you be my woman all goddam time. I don' care what you want, *Americana*. You do what I say now."

A strangled and furious cry burst from her. She tried to throw herself from the pony but his grip on her ankle tightened, twisted until she gasped in pain. Half off the pony, she fought for balance; felt him noose the lariat about her ankle. He hauled her upright, tied her other foot and then threw the lariat across the saddle pommel. Numbly she saw him pick up the rein and start out of the grove. She grabbed the lariat and jerked violently, almost unseating herself. It was no use. He had knotted it well.

"Severiano!" she wailed, "listen to me! Please, listen!" He only shook his head.

The ground was very soft. The center of the valley was almost a bog. He hesitated, swung east a little, the pony's hooves squelching in the soft muck between ledges of rock poking through the lush grass. Samantha slumped hopelessly. The animal's lunges when he stepped in a pothole jerked painfully at her bound ankles. She pushed down hard on his withers and felt the tears spatter on her wrists.

The shots came from the edge of the clearing, so close they deafened her. She felt and heard the bullet strike the horse beneath her before he gave a groaning bellow and lurched crazily. Kicking wildly in a last attempt to get free of the falling animal, she had a tilted glimpse of Severiano diving for cover with blood staining his shoulder. She screamed once as the enormous weight crushed her leg into the soft ground, then slammed her body onto it. Her head struck an outcrop of rock and there was an instant of explosive pain before she fell endlessly through a black and humming void.

TWENTY-FOUR

Lieutenant Sandlin's detachment of Negro troopers moved faster than they were supposed to; they crossed the San Pedro River below the ruins of the old presidio and were into the foothills of the Huachucas early in the morning. There was no sun. It was hard to tell the time. Sandlin knew he was supposed to spread his men along the line of Babacomba Creek to cut off any Indians who tried to break north when the rest of the force hit them in the peaks, but before he reached the creek he found a fresh and heavy trail leading into the mountains.

He wanted to follow the trail and he wanted to follow his orders, too, so he made the usual mistake of trying to do both. He took ten men and followed the trail, sending the rest of his detachment and the white scout, Wilson, to picket the creek line.

By a freak of luck he made it up the main corridor almost to Pionsenay's stronghold before the vedettes saw him and opened fire. The Apaches were above his troopers in the rocky heights where no mounted man could get at them. The soldiers were boxed in the corridor and the fire was too hot for them. Sandlin tried once to rush the trail but the Apaches knocked a man off his horse with a bullet in his hip before they could even get started.

The troopers pulled the wounded man to cover but his horse panicked and went straight up through the Apache vedettes. Sandlin pulled them back fast. Coming down, they flushed a single Indian. He was on foot and he disappeared among the rocks like a puff of smoke before anyone had a shot at him. A little later they heard a single shot below them and Sandlin hoped his thin line of pickets had scored.

By the time he got his men to the creek and the wounded man bedded down in the adobe ruins of old Camp Wallen, they could plainly hear heavy firing in the mountains. Sandlin thickened his line as best he could and hoped that if the Apaches decided to come his way they would not come all at once. The waiting was tense but nothing came.

About midmorning the white scout from Mesilla asked if he could take a couple of troopers to help him search the head of the valley reaching into the mountains from the site of the abandoned Army post.

"Ah seen thet buck runnin' thew them pines up thar this mornin', Lootenant, an' Ah had me one shot at him. Reckon Ah moughta winged th' bastid an' ef'n Ah did he's like as not holed up thar yet. Ah'd shorely admire to finish him off."

"He's a damn sight more likely to finish you off, Wilson. If he's lying up there wounded he'll just let you walk up on him till he can't miss. Somebody might get him, but not before he gets one of you."

"Aw, Lootenant, Ah ain't thet stoopid! Lemme take a couple troopers to holp me an' Ah'll drive thet buck right down heah in yore lap. Yuh kin git him like shootin' fish in a bar'l ef'n Ah don't git 'im fust."

"I still think he'll get one of you before you even see him."

Wilson sighed. "Lootenant, Ah was huntin' Injuns afore you put thet soljer suit on. Ah kin make thet buck so jumpy he cain't set still nohow. You got nuthin' tew show fer this heah fight 'cep'n one nigger wif a hole in his butt and one lost hoss. Lemme go git thet Injun fer yew, Lootenant."

Sandlin eyed him coldly. He didn't like Wilson on principle and he particularly disliked people who called his troopers niggers. But the idea of going home empty-handed after the abortive try to rush the corridor galled him even more. Wilson could see this going through the officer's mind and he began to grin slyly.

"Corporal Potts!" Sandlin shouted. An enormous Negro, a mountain of a man six feet plus and over two hundred pounds in weight, got out of a shallow rifle pit and trotted to the officer.

"Potts, pick a man and take a walk up that draw with Wilson here. He wants to look for that Indian he shot at this morning and I want you to cover him."

The big corporal rolled his eyes at Wilson. "You skeered to go, soljer?" the scout asked. Potts made no reply, only looked at his lieutenant. Sandlin hesitated a second, then nodded.

"Yessuh," said Potts. "Looshus! Come arunnin'!"

Lucius was half the size of the corporal and a good deal younger, but he looked mean. He looked that way because he had heard Wilson's crack about the wounded trooper and he was hoping that if there were an Apache in the draw he would put a hole in Wilson, too. The three men spread out, Wilson leading, and disappeared into the trees along the east side of the valley.

It took them a long time to work their way up to where the valley was narrow enough that they could see into the pines on the other side. Even then they couldn't see much because the growth was so dense. By the time they got there, both troopers could see that even if he had a bad mouth Wilson knew his business as a scout. He went through the pines like a wraith and they had to press to keep up with him.

All three closed in when they reached the head of the draw and sprawled flat on the thick carpet of pine needles, studying the other side. Wilson said nothing, but pointed

221

to where he had seen the Indian earlier that morning. The soldiers nodded. They were about ready to move around the swampy patch ahead when somewhere above them, not very far, there was a cry. Not a loud cry but very distinct. They froze in place.

It was puzzling. No Indian, no matter how bad he hurt, would cry out like that. They waited curiously.

They did not have to wait long. A young Indian walked out of the pines into the clearing leading a pony with a sick-looking squaw on its back. The way he was parading down the valley like he owned it bothered Potts a little. It occurred to him this was no hostile but just some fool kid who didn't know any better than to take his girl into the mountains in the middle of a small war. He was headed generally west and Potts thought he might be a tame Indian working for one of the farmers around San Rafael.

He was carrying a rifle, though, and he didn't look tame. Wilson was nearest the edge of the trees, Lucius behind him and Potts behind both of them. The white scout seemed to be settling himself for a shot at the squaw, which angered Potts, but there was nothing he could do about it now. Wilson waggled a finger toward the buck and when Lucius looked back cautiously, Potts nodded.

The white scout's shot blasted the silence and they heard the pony bellow. Lucius fired a fraction of a second after and knocked the Indian down but Potts saw him gliding off through the grass like a snake.

"Damn youah soul, Looshus! You done missed him!" He was on his knees, trying to get the wriggling Indian in his sights but it was too late.

"Whut in hell you shoot that hoss fer, Mistuh?" He demanded furiously of Wilson. The scout could have hit the Indian man just as easily. Instead he had killed the horse, which had fallen on the squaw and apparently knocked her senseless.

Wilson grinned wolfishly. "Din't want hit ter run off, Corp."

"Humphf!" grunted Potts. "Come on, Looshus! Now we gots us two o' thuh bastuhds in heah somewheahs."

222

They fanned out across the soft ground gingerly, Potts and Lucius making for the trees on the other side, Wilson heading straight for the downed pony. Potts was worried. He knew Lucius had hit the Indian but he did not know how badly. That would determine how far the Indian would go before he stopped running and waited to ambush his pursuers. When he saw the big smear of blood on the grass he was more nervous than ever.

"Ah'll be go-ter-hell!" exclaimed Wilson. "Thet warn't his squaw atall. He done stole this gal somewheres."

"How come?" Potts grunted, keeping his eyes on the trees.

"He got her feets tied unduh the hoss, thet's how come."

"Thievin' bastuhd! Was Ah you, Mistuh, Ah wouldn't mess aroun' th' middle this heah swamp no longer. That Injun is bad hit. They's blood all ovah heah. He ain' gone fah an' he mought not be gone fah enuf!"

"Don' worry none 'bout me, Corp. Yew an' yore buddy jest take yoreselfs a looksee in them trees an' Ah'll be along direck'ly." He slashed the riata linking the woman's ankles and returned his knife to its sheath. Lucius watched him interestedly.

"Hows 'bout yew gimme a hand heah, soljer, afore yew goes?"

"Whuffo?"

"Jest holp me roll th' gawdam hoss off'n her, will yew?"

Potts snorted. "Mistuh, that Injun bitch is likely broke in three pieces. Thet hoss done fall plumb on her."

"Don' make no nevermind," grunted Wilson, straining at the dead pony. Lucius joined him and they managed with a good deal of puffing and swearing to shift the limp animal enough for Wilson to drag the squaw free.

"She daid, ain't she?" asked Lucius.

Wilson fumbled at her body and shook his head. "Naw! Jest had th' wind knocked outta her. She ain't broke up atall. Groun's too soft." He grinned at the soldier. "Yew want ter hang aroun' tell Ah'm done, Bubber?"

"You, Looshus . . ." snarled Potts. "Cunnel Hatch heah

you bin rapin', he skin you alive! Git fum theah an' move youah ass in them woods!"

The woman groaned and all three men jumped nervously. "You heah me, Looshus?" Potts demanded. Lucius eyed the squaw regretfully but he sidled away from her.

"Sho is uh pritty thang!" he muttered.

"Pritty youah ass, trooper! Come on, now!"

They slipped into the pines and Potts led warily, trying to follow the blood trail and watch the forest ahead at the same time. Lucius glanced back.

"You reckon he kill her when he done wif her, Corp?"

"T'ain't no skin off'n youah butt eff'n he do! Jest you don't hang aroun' that no'count white trash nohow."

"Lissen, Corp . . ."

Potts whirled on him savagely. "Ah heahs one mo' word outta you 'bout that squaw an' you in trouble, soljer! You unnerstan' me?"

"Ah heah you talkin', Corp! Ah jest tryin' t' say that's the onliest squaw Ah evah did see wif blue eyes. Shore seem funny to me."

Potts was intent on the ground and the diminishing blood trail and it took a moment for Lucius' words to sink in. When they did, he stopped abruptly.

"Whut that you say?"

"Now, Corp'ral . . ." whined Lucius. "Git off'n mah back! Ah'm raht behin' you, ain't Ah?"

"Whut you say 'bout that squaw?"

Lucius shrank in alarm from the towering corporal. "Ah say she th' onliest squaw Ah evah seed wif blue eyes. That's all Ah say. Whuffo you . . ."

Potts was moving faster than a man his size had a right to move. He was halfway back to the clearing before Lucius caught up with him.

"Whut ail you now, Corp? How come you run off like that?"

"You dumb nigger! Why'n hell you don' say right off she got blue eyes?"

He came out of the pines fast and before Wilson even saw him he was beside the white scout. Wilson had taken off his pistol belt. His rifle was in easy reach, leaning against the dead pony, but before he could pick it up he was looking into the muzzle of the big soldier's carbine.

"Don' reach for that, Mistuh!" Potts cautioned him gently.

"What in hell's goin' on heah, soljer? Don't pint thet gun at me!"

"Ah jest wants to take me one quick look at youah squaw, Mistuh Wilson. Ef'n she's whut you thinks she is me an' Looshus we be gone sooner. Whilst Ah take my look, you jest be quiet like, huh? Looshus watch youah gun foh you."

"Whut in thunderin' hell yew talkin' 'bout, soljer? Ain't yew got eyes? Kain't yew see she's Injun?"

"Yeah . . . yeah, but Ah jest gotta take me a good look, Mistuh Wilson." Dropping on his knee beside the woman, Potts cupped her head in his hand. She moaned but her eyes remained closed. Very delicately, Potts inserted a sausage-like finger in the neck of her camisa, lifted it and peered inside. Wilson swore obscenely.

"Goddammit, soljer . . git yore black paws off'n thet squaw!"

Potts whistled softly. "Take youahself a look, white man . . . an' be glad Ah done showed you."

Wilson was so dumbfounded he did as he was told. Before he could recover from his shock the woman stirred and looked up at them.

"Tom?" she said quite distinctly.

Wilson jumped as if she had bitten him. "Gret Gawd in thuh foothills! She's white as Ah am! Who is she?"

"She somebody wouldn't spit on you, Wilson! You is th' luckiest man alive this minnit . . . you know that? Them soljers in th' Sixth Calvary bin huntin' this gal sence las' spring. Had you done whut you wuz aimin' to do, they'd a' pulled youah laig off an' beat you plumb to death wif it!"

He gathered Samantha into his arms as if picking up a baby and set off down the valley crooning to her softly.

"Don' you fret, little miss. Ol' Potts done got you now an' he gwine tek good care o' you. Looshus . . . you let that Injun shoot me an Ah'm gonna wring youah neck! You watch now, heah me?"

TWENTY-FIVE

"Where is that damned ambulance?" someone demanded and Samantha opened her eyes cautiously. She was lying on her back looking directly into the sun and its brassy glare exploded painfully in her head.

"Oooh!" she moaned. The thick grayness came back swiftly.

"Shade her face, man! What are you thinking of? Is she hurt badly?"

"Naw, suh." A hand cradled her head gently. "They's a lump back heah big as a aig but she ain' hurt bad. Didn't break nuffin' when that hoss fall on her. That theah groun' real sof'."

"How in hell did the horse fall on her? What happened?"

"Injun come walkin' outta them trees leadin' a pony wif her on it. Looshus he shot thuh Injun but he ain' kill him. He done slip off somewheres. Mistuh Wilson he shot thuh hoss an' hit done fall on her."

"Why'd he shoot the horse?"

There was a barely perceptible pause. "Din't want hit tuh run off, Ah reckon. She all right, Lootenant; jest shook up some. Gimme thet canteen, Looshus."

Samantha felt tepid water on her face and searched with her tongue between cracked lips for drops of it. "Sho, lil' Miss. You kin have all you wants. Jest set up a

226

lil'." The arm beneath her shoulders lifted her and she drank eagerly.

"Thet there ambulance be till dark gittin' heah, Lootenant. How's 'bout we gits us a waggin off'n one o' them farms down to San Raffel? We kin start Purdey an' th' lady fer Camp Lowell an' they kin change to th' ambulance when they meets up wif it."

Samantha dozed fitfully until she was roused again by the anxious face of the lieutenant bending over her.

"Do you think you could stand to ride now, ma'am? We've got a wagon and I've got to get a wounded man started for the hospital. If you're up to it, you ought to go with him."

She nodded. "Of course. I'm all right. Just let me . . . oooh!" She tried to sit up and her head whirled, the lieutenant's face sliding out of focus.

"Don't do that!" he said urgently. "Just lie still."

"Tom?" she whimpered. "Where is Mister Royal? Is he here?"

"No, ma'am. I'm Sandlin of the Ninth Cavalry. Royal's still across the mountain. I'll get word to him just as soon as I can. I promise."

She lifted a hand in weak protest. "Don't let anyone get hurt just for that, please."

"Don't you worry about that, ma'am. Do you think it's all right for us to put you in the wagon now?"

"Surely." She tried to reassure him with a smile but it was a poor attempt. He eyed her doubtfully.

"Just one question, ma'am . . . I'm sorry to plague you now but we heard there were three of you. Two ladies and a man. Have you any idea where the others are?"

Samantha shut her eyes. "The man is dead. I don't know what became of my aunt." Tears spilled down her cheeks. "I haven't seen her in months and I don't know . . ."

"That's all right. Don't talk any more now." He was alarmed by the tears. "I'm sorry to ask but there might have been a chance . . ."

"I understand. Don't apologize, please!" A fresh wave

of dizziness attacked her and she looked up at him a little wildly. "What in the world is the matter with my head?"

"You hit a rock when you fell off your horse. Maybe you have a little concussion and that's why I'd like to get you to Lowell as fast as possible." The concern in his serious young face touched her.

"I'll be all right, Lieutenant, don't worry. My head's too hard to crack."

But the pain and giddiness persisted, making her weak and indifferent to her surroundings. The ranch wagon was old and springless and after a while she could not tell if the groans she heard were the wounded trooper's or her own. A long time later, after she had given up watching the stars because their wheeling made her dizzier than ever, she heard cheerful voices and lantern light invaded the wagon bed. Gentle hands lifted her and put her carefully on a litter in the canvas-sheeted body of an Army ambulance. There were six mules in harness and it swayed sickeningly on high springs but it was better than the bone-jarring wagon. A medical corpsman crouched between the two litters and after another aeon of time she heard him say, "There's Tucson. Won't be long now."

There were golden fringes on the lifting curtain of night when the ambulance stopped before the Camp Lowell hospital. Samantha shivered in the dawn chill when the side curtains were raised. Low-voiced men moved about and only when the wounded soldier groaned was a voice raised warningly. They put her stretcher down on a plank walk in a pool of lantern light.

"All right. Inside and careful now!" Narrow feminine heels rapped on the planks and a soft voice asked anxiously, "How bad?"

"Nothing serious, Mrs. Van Sciver. I think she just needs rest."

"Then why not bring her to our quarters? Let me take care of her."

"That would be better than the hospital. I'll look in later today."

The stretcher swayed off smoothly to the practiced stride of the corpsmen. She moved in her own circle of lantern light that touched the trunks of young cottonwoods in a row, beyond them silent adobe houses, until they came to one where the door stood open and light shone out.

Her head no longer ached so savagely and she told herself she should sit up, get up and walk. They ought not to have to carry me, she thought. But the hushed voices and careful hands of the men and the anxious directions of the woman someone had called Mrs. Van Sciver were soothing. She surrendered to weakness. To be cared for like this was luxury beyond imagining.

They lifted her from the stretcher to a bed that was infinitely soft and inviting. A bed with linen sheets, cool and fragrant with a faint scent that was almost intoxicating. The men tiptoed away and she opened her eyes to another anxious face—a sweet face, framed in russet braids with warm blue eyes full of concern. Gentle hands stripped away her clothes, drew a voluminous nightgown over her head.

"I'm so dirty!" she protested. "I ought to wash . . ." But the hands tucked her firmly beneath the wonderful sheet.

"Not now. Tomorrow. Now you must rest. I'm Ellen Van Sciver and we've been waiting for you for so long. There's all the time in the world to wash, my dear."

"Tom?"

"He's coming. Try to sleep now. I'll leave a lamp burning and if you want anything, call."

Samantha nodded, searching for one of the hands that smoothed the covers. When she found it, Ellen Van Sciver repressed a start. Looking at the grimy, calloused fingers clutching her own, she blinked back tears of pity.

Her husband, Polycarp, waited in the hall and she put a finger to her lips.

"Is she all right?"

Ellen nodded. "I think so. The doctor will come later. Ah, Carp . . . the poor, pretty thing! What cruelty!"

He looked at the clothes in her hands and his face

229

wrinkled in disgust. "Indian!" he sniffed. "What a stench! Give them to me."

"There may be something she wants."

"All right." He bundled the skirt, camisa and limp moccasins together. "I'll put them outside and you ask her tomorrow . . . before I tell Wentz to burn them."

A little while after the sun rose a second ambulance clattered up to the hospital and the escort walked their lathered horses, the troopers stiff-legged and sniffing hungrily at the smells of bacon and coffee as Camp Lowell went to breakfast. Their officer went across the parade ground at a stumbling run toward the Van Scivers' porch. His hand was raised to knock when the door swung open and Ellen shook her head at him warningly.

"Don't you make a noise, Tate Hulse! She's sound asleep."

Dust filled every crease and fold of his uniform, caked and dark where he had sweated through the flannel shirt. His face was deeply tanned beneath the film of dust and the acrid smell of horse from his boots and breeches stung her nostrils.

"Is she all right, Ellen? Is she hurt?"

"I don't think so." She looked past him, shading her eyes against the blazing glory of the sunrise. "Where's Tom?"

"Still in the mountains. Sandlin of the Ninth found her and he sent for him."

She gave him a worried glance. "He's all right? Nothing happened to him?"

"No! My God, no . . . at least I hope not. He was all right yesterday. He should be here shortly. Can I see her?"

"I told you she's sleeping."

"Let me just look."

"All right, but not a word, mind you! Don't you want some breakfast?"

"I can't. I'll get some coffee at one of the kitchens but I've got to get another team for that ambulance and get back to the troop."

"Hello, Tate," said Carp Van Sciver over his wife's head, stuffing his shirt into his trousers and peering at the troopers on the parade ground. "Come in, man. Ellen will give you coffee and I'll look after your detail. How many mules do you want for that ambulance?"

"Six, if you can get them. The faster I get back the better. They may have more wounded."

Ellen would let him go no farther than the door to Samantha's room, from where he could see nothing but the dark fan of her hair on the pillow. She pushed him toward the kitchen.

"Go and wash yourself. There's a basin by the water barrel outside. The coffee's already made."

When he returned she gave him coffee and fresh-made biscuits and he wolfed them hungrily.

"What about Miss Ehler? Did they find her?"

Tate looked up in surprise, his mouth full of biscuit. He swallowed convulsively. "She's dead! Doesn't Sam know?"

"Oh, Lord . . . no! The sergeant who brought her said she didn't know what happened to her aunt . . . hadn't seen her for months! How did you find out?"

"Sandlin found the kid who brought Sam out of the Apache camp. He told them Miss Ehler died months ago. Didn't Sam tell you how she got away?"

Ellen shook her head. "She didn't tell us anything, poor child! I put her straight to bed."

"Well . . ." Tate said, "it seems a kid—some kind of half-breed—was in the Indian camp with Sam. When we jumped them this morning he slipped her away and brought her down toward old Camp Wallen. He ran into Sandlin's outposts and they shot him before he could sing out."

"Oh . . . that's awful!" gasped Ellen.

"He's all right. Got a hole in his shoulder but it takes more than that to kill a breed. Sam's horse was killed at the same time and it fell on her. That's how she hurt her head."

"It seems to me," said Ellen, "we owe a great deal to this 'half-breed kid' as you call him. Where is he now? Who's taking care of him?"

"They took him to Calabasas. Left him with old Ser-

231

geant Rooney there. I don't know more than that, Ellen. I didn't see the kid; I just talked to Sandlin. I'm sure Tom will get in touch with him as soon as he can."

"I should certainly think so! Do you want more coffee?"

"I can't, thanks, Ellen." He stood up and pecked her on the cheek. "God bless you for taking her in like this. I'll be back as soon as I can and I'm sure Tom will be here before that."

TWENTY-SIX

The setting sun thrust a ray of gold through the curtains to warm the colors of the faded Navajo rug. Samantha studied its pattern drowsily and rubbed her cheek against the fragrant pillowcase. Somewhere a man's voice lifted itself in song:

> Muss i denn, muss i den, zum Städtele 'naus
> Städtele 'naus und du, mein Schatz, bleibst hier?
> Kann ich gleich nit allweil . . .

"Wentz!" called a despairing voice. "Wentz . . . please!"

"Mommy! Annie's in the sugar!"

"If you children don't hush, I shall lose my mind! Will you go outside, please!" Ellen Van Sciver sounded distracted.

"When's she gonna wake up, Mommy? When can we see her?"

Samantha's heart moved with joy. She sat up and put her hand to the back of her head. "Ouch!" she gasped.

"Hush! All of you! Did she call?" There were soft footsteps in the hall.

"Mrs. Van Sciver?" Samantha asked. The door opened at once and Ellen peered in.

"Are you all right?"

"I'm fine! What time is it, for goodness' sake?"

Ellen seemed to be wrestling with something or someone unseen. It was a hopeless struggle. On either side of her skirt a small head appeared, bright eyes fixed on Samantha.

"Oh, let them come in! It's perfectly all right."

"Lord knows I tried to keep them quiet!" Ellen sighed. "I don't know who is worse . . . the children or that soldier. This is Robert . . ." she indicated the small boy who appeared to be about six. "This is Annie . . ." The girl was younger. Not more than four at most—a startlingly exact miniature of her mother with russet hair, snub nose, big blue eyes in a round, sweet face. "And I am Ellen. Not Mrs. Van Sciver."

The children flowed toward Samantha, Robert hanging back a little but small Annie squirming onto the bed with total confidence. "We've gallons of hot water ready for you," said their mother. "You must be dying for a bath. Wentz will bring the tub."

At her call a big, rawboned soldier clumped in with a zinc hip bath, bobbing his head respectfully to Samantha.

"Goot evening, madam!" he rumbled and Samantha knew who had sung the German song that woke her.

"Good evening, Wentz," she responded. "Thank you very much."

"I bring hot vater now." It took him three trips with an enormous kettle to fill the tub. Ellen piled towels and soap on the foot of the bed with a bundle of clothing.

"I hope these will fit. If they don't we'll just have to alter them. There is simply nothing to be had in Tucson."

"I must have a trunk somewhere," said Samantha. "I left one here to be sent on to Camp Grant and it should still be in Tucson unless they sent it back East."

"Of course! Why didn't I think of that? I'm certain

233

they wouldn't have sent it back. I'll have Carp look for it tomorrow. Now, children . . . out!"

They protested but she was adamant. "No. Out! Is there anything I can do, Samantha? Would you like me to help you with your hair?"

"Oh, no! Thank you. I can manage quite well." Ellen shooed the children before her and shut the door while Samantha eyed the bath with mounting delight.

The hot water was a shock; a happy shock. She eased herself into it an inch at a time. Once in, she luxuriated in the steamy water and Ellen's scented soap. It was a far cry from yucca root and the icy pool in the mountains. She was humming to herself when she finally and reluctantly abandoned the tub.

Ellen's dress was a bit tight in places but it did well enough and the lisle stockings felt indecently elegant on her legs. The shoes were small but she was so pleased with the dress and stockings it did not matter. She toweled her hair gingerly, avoiding the tender lump on her head and trying, under her breath, to recall Wentz's plaintive tune. Ellen tapped softly on the door.

"Come!" Samantha called cheerfully and again there was the silent struggle in the doorway. "Do let them come in. Truly, I don't mind."

Ellen saw the happiness in her face and beamed. "Does anything fit? Can you wear the shoes?"

Samantha revolved before the mirror admiring the swing of the skirt. "Everything is simply lovely!"

The children climbed on the bed and watched her, round-eyed. Annie was intrigued by the clothes and the women's discussion of their fit but Robert's eyes were fixed on Samantha's hair. While Ellen brushed it out this seemed natural enough but when that was done and his unwavering stare did not shift his mother grew nervous.

He had a propensity for startling questions and she feared what was coming. She was right. When Samantha finally noticed his intent gaze she put her hands to her hair and asked worriedly, "Is something wrong?"

"Is it real?" Robert demanded in a hushed voice.

"Oh, Robert!" wailed his mother. "Do hush!"

"Whatever do you mean?" Samantha asked him curiously.

"Didn't the Injuns sculp you?"

"What?" She looked startled.

"Robert Van Sciver . . ." Ellen began but Samantha interrupted her.

"What is it, Robert? What do you mean?"

"Sculp you!" he repeated stubbornly, making a circular motion about his head with a stubby forefinger. Samantha burst into delighted laughter.

"No, Robert! They didn't sculp me. It's really mine . . . see?" She held up her hair and tugged gently to show him, wincing a little as she did so. Ellen looked anxious.

"How is your head? Dr. Girard was here but he said sleep was better for you than anything he could do. He'll come right over if we send for him."

"There's no need for that," Samantha assured her. "My head's perfectly all right. I've got a bump and it's sore, but that's all. Please don't bother the doctor."

"I'll be delighted not to. All right, you children . . . out you go, and I mean it!" She put them out firmly. "Enough is enough! Who knows what he'll ask next? That boy picks up things from the soldiers that make my hair stand on end." She shut the door and turned back to Samantha.

"Now, let me see what I can do for those poor hands."

Samantha put them behind her back. "I'm so ashamed of them."

"You must not say that!" Ellen's eyes snapped. "You must not be ashamed of anything that has happened. Remember that!"

Samantha stared at her, stricken with panic. This was something she had not contemplated. How much was known of what had happened to her in the Apache *ranchería?* Ellen saw her dismay and thought she had spoken too strongly about the hands. She was conscience-stricken and tried to make amends with a burst of chatter.

For a time they sat head-to-head, while Ellen rubbed

235

sweet-smelling lotion into the cracked and calloused palms. Then she looked up unhappily at Samantha.

"I don't know how to say this, and I know I shall say it badly. Your aunt . . . Miss Ehler . . ."

Samantha drew a ragged breath. "She's dead, isn't she?"

Ellen nodded miserably and Samantha dropped her eyes. "I'm not as shocked as I should be, Ellen. I suppose I've been sure of it for a long time. Poor thing . . . do you know how it happened?"

"Only that she died months ago. When Tom comes perhaps he will know more."

"When will he come?" Samantha whispered, and the anguish in her words was too much for Ellen. She caught the girl in her arms and held her tightly.

"Oh, my dear . . . he'll be here tomorrow! Nothing could stop him, don't you know that?"

In the living room, Carp Van Sciver took her by her shoulders and kissed her cheeks with grave delight. The children, bursting with forbidden questions, led her through the house to show her everything.

Dinner was confused and happy; the concerted efforts of the Van Scivers to please her, to draw her into the close-knit warmth of the family brought tears of happiness to her eyes more than once. Afterward, she insisted on staying in the kitchen until the dishes were done and since no one else would leave it was crowded and boisterous. The children would not go to bed until Wentz brought his concertina and sang for them.

> Fuchs, du hast die Gans gestohlen,
> gib sie wieder her! Gib sie wieder her!
>   sonst wird dich der Jäger holen
> mit dem Schiessgewehr . . .

To the children's unsure voices she added her own clear soprano as she caught the words, and when Wentz, as he rumbled the last line, ". . . with the shotgun," brought down his booted foot in a mighty stamp, she clapped with the children in delight. Robert and Annie went to bed with a round of wet and happy kisses.

"You too, miss!" Carp ordered, smiling. "Your lieutenant will be here tomorrow and we want you bright-eyed."

TWENTY-SEVEN

The dress was silk. Gray with a touch of white at throat and wrist. Samantha put it on with childish delight. She was taller than Ellen and a little larger despite the weight she had lost.

"Oooh!" she murmured, catching sight of herself in the mirror. She put her hand over her mouth in the Indian way. "Isn't it . . .?"

Ellen laughed. "He won't mind that!"

"I wish we could find the trunk. I'm sure there was a corset in it."

"Lord above us, girl!" Ellen exclaimed. "What do you want with a corset? You're as lean as a rake!"

Samantha blushed. "Oh, Ellen, it's so beautiful! I feel such a tramp wearing your beautiful things. Is it really all right?"

"If you mean is it all right for you to wear it, don't be silly. If you mean does it look all right . . ." She raised her brows and made an admiring moue of her lips. They both giggled helplessly.

"Now! I must do something completely wicked with your hair. Sit down!"

Samantha submitted gratefully and when Ellen had

finished, gazed at her reflection in the mirror with astonishment.

"Oh . . . my!" Ellen had piled her hair high and pinned it artfully with a gleaming fall of curls behind.

"They won't last long, but they look so elegant now, don't they? Here . . . put these on." She was holding out a pair of slender garnet eardrops and Samantha remembered Aludin's fascination with the tiny jade pendants she was wearing when the Apaches took her. Wanting nothing about her person to arouse the Indian girl's cupidity, she had offered them at once.

"Oh, Ellen . . . I cannot!" Small acts of kindness such as this were treacherous. They took her unprepared for the swift surge of emotion they brought and she fought back the tears that stung her eyelids.

"Hush!" said Ellen gently. "Can't you see how much fun I'm having?" She darted a glance at the clock on the mantel and groaned. "I've got to go and see what Wentz is doing with the dinner! If he spoils it, I'll kill him!"

"When . . . ?"

"At least an hour, you goose!" She snatched a tiny bottle of perfume from the dresser and put it in Samantha's hands.

"Ooooh!" she said, breathing in the fragrance. "If I don't swoon, I'm sure Tom will!"

"I doubt that very much. Take your time and I'll call you before they come . . . unless you'd rather make a grand entrance after they're here."

"Oh, no! I'd rather not. They? Who else . . ."

"Tate, of course. We couldn't drive him away with fire!" She eyed the younger girl a little anxiously. "You don't mind, do you? I know it's going to be a little difficult, but it would anyway. You know that, don't you?"

Samantha nodded. "I do indeed, but don't worry. I won't come unglued . . . I promise."

Despite good intentions she was in the living room far too soon and the waiting was agonizing. The rumble of voices and eager knocking at the door brought a surge of panic.

Carp whistled boots and saddles tunelessly under his breath and Ellen jabbed him with her elbow. It was just what Samantha needed and when Tom appeared in the doorway she was dissolved in helpless laughter, Carp and Ellen watching her delightedly.

"Sam!" he said hoarsely.

"You . . . you're late," she managed idiotically. "I've been waiting ever so long . . ."

In the burst of laughter that followed he was across the room before she knew it. She lifted her face to him and his confused reaction was pure comedy. She ached for him to take her in his arms and kiss her but he fumbled at her shoulders, touched her hair and finally cupped her elbows awkwardly. His lips struck her forehead a glancing blow and slid down her cheek.

"Tom . . . oh, Tom!" She laughed hysterically. Catching his head in her hands, she pulled it down and kissed him firmly on the lips.

"Hooray!" cheered a voice at the door and Tate Hulse was shouldering Tom aside.

"Excuse me, Mister Royal . . . you've had your turn!" He planted a noisy smack on both her cheeks and then held her away, beaming.

"Samantha Allyn . . . you look like a million dollars in gold! Great God, Sam . . . it's good to have you back!"

His eyes searched her face eagerly, noted the eyes tired beyond tiredness but glowing happily. The rest was just as he remembered—straight nose and firm chin, forehead clear and smooth-sloping, the mouth curving in a warm and generous smile.

"Tom . . . Tom!" he said softly. "You're the luckiest man alive!"

Ellen's dress fitted closely at throat and waist, very narrow at the knees. She managed it with caution, learning again the art of walking in a skirt like this. She seated herself gingerly, Tom standing first on one side and then the other, holding her hand and getting in the way until Ellen pushed him firmly into a chair.

Everyone talked at once and Carp came with glasses

of whiskey toddy. They all drank standing to Samantha and when Tate made as if to shatter his glass in the fireplace, Ellen threatened him with her own. "You break my Belgian glass, Tate Hulse, and I'll break this one on your head!"

Samantha squeezed Tom's hand. "Why did you take so long? Where were you?"

"I was on the other side of that damned mountain. I didn't even know they had found you until I ran into Sandlin."

"Don't believe it, Sam!" put in Tate. "He's been down in Sonora flirting with three señoritas. I got here first, you know. I rode all night just to see you."

"I didn't know that!" exclaimed Samantha.

"Oh, I saw you. Ellen wouldn't let me say anything, but I saw you."

"How awful! I must have looked like something out of a jackdaw's nest."

Tom rumbled protest and they all laughed. Carp was gathering up the glasses but Ellen objected.

"One is enough. You won't know what you're eating and Wentz has surpassed himself with dinner. Let's go in now, shall we?"

She took Tate's arm firmly and led the way down the hall through the gallery to the dining room. She and Wentz had wrought miracles with the dingy, whitewashed cubicle. There were bunches of greens with clumps of crimson berries; a linen tablecloth with silver winking in the soft candlelight.

"Oh!" said Samantha and even the irrepressible Tate was silent in admiration. The dinner was spectacular. From long-hoarded tins Ellen had produced an oyster patty for everyone followed by what she called mock turtle soup, though no amount of gay chaffing would make her tell what it really was. After that there was a saddle of venison with mushroom sauce and even a salad of tired-looking greens.

Wentz circled the table silently, keeping their glasses brimming with a delicious Cucamonga wine that made up for its scant chill with a tart and delightful dryness.

Under its spell, Tom left off staring at his girl long enough to tell the story of the arrival of the British helmets at Camp Grant—with certain emendations in deference to the ladies—and the whole table rocked with laughter.

Then, when the plates were cleared away, Ellen's soldier cook put before her with a flourish a real pie. Samantha's eyes widened in anticipation.

It was not a large pie. Indeed, by comparison with the pies of her dreams it was a poor thing but it was real and it was there on the table. It was brown and crusty and from the latticed top there came a scent of hot cinnamon and lemon and all-pervading sweetness that made her swallow desperately.

Carp was pouring champagne for everyone. The men laughed and their voices rumbled comfortingly, but Samantha could concentrate on nothing except the heavenly aroma of the pie.

"I hope we aren't distressing you with so much drink, Sam," Carp said. "I'm afraid you're coming off the wagon with a mighty thump tonight."

"I may be tipsy," Samantha murmured, "but it isn't from the wine." She was hoping no one noticed how the pie affected her.

Ellen cut it in small, neat wedges and Wentz passed them. It seemed to Samantha he was intolerably slow. She was served first and she did not know how she could wait to begin until the others had their portions. At last, Ellen picked up her fork.

As decorously as she could, Samantha lifted to her lips the first bite. She closed her eyes and tried not to weep. It was hot and sweet and spicy and if the Lord let her live to fourscore and ten she would never again taste anything so good.

"What is it?" Tate demanded, smacking his lips. "How do you do it, Ellen?"

"If I tell, you won't like it."

"Impossible, my dear," said Carp. "Tell us what's in it. I know for a fact there isn't an apple nearer than San Diego."

"All right. It's just soda crackers. You soak them in water and you warm them until they're soft and then you put in lemon essence and cinnamon and sugar and nutmeg. Then you bake them in a crust. Mrs. Biddle taught me and she calls it mockapple, though for the life of me, I don't know why."

Long before she had finished her description Samantha had finished her pie. She tried hard to go slowly but it was no use. Now she pursued the crumbs on her plate and when she realized she was staring hungrily at the remainder before her hostess, her face flamed in embarrassment. Tom eyed her with concern.

"Sam, you look flushed. Are you all right?"

"She is tipsy!" said Tate with mock concern and everyone laughed. Samantha was grateful for the excuse to lower her head and press her hands to her glowing cheeks. As the laughter subsided she heard Tate clear his throat ostentatiously and she saw that he too was eyeing the remaining wedge of pie. Pig, she thought. Greedy pig.

"Mister Hulse!" Ellen chided. "Don't they feed you at Bowie?"

"Madam," he declared, rolling his eyes. "Nothing like that ever appeared at Camp Bowie. I declare, I thought I was in love with Tom's girl but I have made a mistake. Ellen, elope with me and I will buy you a ton of soda crackers!"

Carp and Tom shouted and Ellen's eyes sparkled. "I am not flattered, Mister Hulse. That's insufficient reason for an elopement."

Not only is he a pig, thought Samantha resentfully, but a clever one as well. Now she'll give it to him and he doesn't want it nearly as much as I do. Ellen was indeed cutting a generous piece from the slim remainder. Her knife hesitated.

"There's hardly enough left to divide. Perhaps . . ." Samantha's heart sank.

"I'll settle this!" interrupted Carp. Rising, he swept the pie from before his wife, circled the table and put the plate gently before Samantha.

Then her face flamed indeed and she kept her head

down, feeling his hand lightly on her shoulder. He knew. She had not been able to hide her greediness from him. Embarrassment and delight warred within her and to their joy, delight won. She lifted a glowing face to Carp.

"Let them elope, Carp! I'll take you if you'll have me."

"What about me?" Tom demanded. "I seem to be losing out all around."

After dinner there was coffee in the living room and after coffee an awkward silence, broken at last by Carp with a kind and transparent stratagem.

"I've just gotten the third sheet of Thomas' map of Arizona, Tate. I wish you'd take a look at it for me. I think he's put the Apache Mountains in the wrong place." Obediently Tate followed him to the small room called a study and Ellen gathered up the cups.

"You two deserve a little privacy," she told Tom and Samantha. She departed with her tray and Tom came out of his chair with a bound. Samantha met him joyfully.

He came to her, arms outstretched, and gathered her close. She offered her lips and he took them eagerly. The faint scent of Ellen's perfume intoxicated him and his kiss was gentle at first, then demanding.

Her response was equally hesitant but her mouth softened beneath his and she clung to him, sharing his excitement in a burst of delight.

"Sam . . . my lovely Sam!" he murmured, his eyes searching hers. "You're thinner, Sam, but you feel . . . Oh, I don't know! When I thought I might never hold you like this again, I died a little. I died a little every night since you've been gone."

"I know . . . Oh, Tom . . . I know!"

He kissed her again, searching for her response, and she knew this with intense pleasure. When he released her he slipped his arm about her waist and swung her under the big lamp.

"Let me look at you, Sam!"

"You've done nothing else all evening!" He laughed and put his hands on her hips, holding her away from him. He had never done this before and she saw he was surprised at his own boldness. He was inexperienced with women and he was trying tentatively to establish his possession of her.

"Sam? Did you ever have trouble remembering me?" He shook his head as he said it. "I don't mean it that way . . . I mean . . . did you ever have trouble remembering how I look?"

She stared at him in astonishment and then she understood. With a gasp she buried her face in his shoulder and locked her hands behind him.

"What is it, Sam? What's the matter?"

"Nothing!" Her voice was muffled against his blouse. "Oh, Tom! I'm so glad!"

"About what?"

"That it happened to you too! At first I could see you . . . just as if you were there . . . then you got all stiff and horrible and posed and I couldn't make your face come clear any more. I tried and I tried and I nearly went mad! I didn't know what was the matter."

"Ah, poor Sam! I'm so sorry . . . God! I'm so sorry all this happened to you. Someday, Sam, when you're ready, I want you to tell me everything that happened. When I think about it now, I just want to kill someone . . . anyone! Kill him with my hands!"

For a fraction of a second, she stiffened in alarm, stung again by the question of how much he already knew. She disguised her panic by moving, rubbing her chin against his chest. I won't think of that now, she told herself rebelliously. Not yet. It's not fair.

"You sound dangerous, Tom. We've got to get you over that."

"That won't be hard." He kissed her ear and blew into it softly. "All you have to do is marry me . . . quick!"

Once again there was the chill touch of fear on her heart but it was dissolved by his love. "When, Sam?" he was whispering. "Can't it be right away?"

"Of course. Just let me find my trunk . . . get some clothes." She looked up at him anxiously. "I guess I just need a little time to breathe, Tom . . . to know I'm really free and you're here and everything's all right now."

"If you want, Sam. I love you and I want you and I'll do whatever you want to do, but don't make me wait too long . . . please!"

"Ah, Tom . . . I won't! I love you very much." She turned up her mouth, eyes shut, and her response this time surprised and delighted them both. "Oooh!" she gasped, pushing him away. He chuckled and swung her in a circle, his eyes sparkling.

"I'm just learning, Sam. Can I try again?"

"Not yet! I told you I need time to breathe. Come on, let's go find the others. We shouldn't keep them in the kitchen all night."

He swept her into his arm and they went through the gallery together. Ellen heard them coming and looked out of the kitchen. At the sight of their faces she clapped her hands.

"Carp!" she called. "Oh, Carp! Is there any more champagne?"

TWENTY-EIGHT

Next morning Ellen Van Sciver presided over a gay assembly in her kitchen while a picnic lunch was made and packed. October was a grand month for picnics at Lowell. The thermometer hovered around seventy and there was a good breeze. As the hamper was closed she caught Tate Hulse's eye and he grimaced.

He stood in the gallery with her and watched Tom

and Samantha waving from the buggy. Ellen patted his shoulder.

"Aren't you supposed to be on a court-martial or something?"

"That's not until tomorrow." He grinned down at her ruefully. "You're right, though. If she were my girl and he came with us I'd kill him."

"They aren't gone forever, goose! Come back for supper."

It was a happy meal. They laughed and sang and got in Ellen's way as she prepared it. Carp insisted that Wentz, the orderly, stand Sunday inspection with the rest of his troop and on Saturday night Ellen always dismissed him early to go and get ready. Wentz loathed the weekly confrontation with his first sergeant, who called all officers' orderlies "dog-robbers" and inspected them with special severity and Ellen knew that. She wanted no opportunity for Sergeant Egbert to get at Wentz for dirty equipment.

After supper Tom looked worried. "I may be in trouble with old Double-Tee Tupper, you know. He said I could come see Sam but he didn't say how long I could stay. Maybe I better go back to Grant and make my peace. See if I can get some leave anyway."

"Not to worry," said Tate. "I fixed that."

"How?" they all demanded at once.

"Had a talk with Major Chandler. He's President of the Court and he's having Tom assigned to it."

"What does that mean?" Samantha asked.

"That Tom will have to stay here at least a week. General courts keep banker's hours, too. You'll see so much of him you'll get bored . . . I hope. I'll be waiting."

"That's great, Tate! Bless you. But what'll I do for a uniform? All my dress stuff is at Grant."

"We can find enough here. I've already got you a jacket and you can use Carp's sword and belt. Only trouble is the helmet. Sears has an old one but the chipmunks ate part of the plume and it's pretty small."

Army regulations of 1876 provided for four different

kinds of courts-martial but on the frontier only two were ever used: the garrison court and the general court. The former dealt with minor offenses and the latter with more serious ones which could lead to dishonorable discharge or imprisonment in a penitentiary. Major Chandler's court at Camp Lowell was a general court, assembled like most in this year to deal primarily with deserters. The 25,000-man Army habitually lost upwards of 2,000 men a year by desertion, and in the fall of 1876 the cavalry was leading the race. After the Custer debacle the Congress had authorized a hasty increase in strength in all the mounted regiments and the men recruited in equal haste to meet the increase were deserting in swarms. The Sixth Cavalry had been doing well until this month but now there was trouble.

A general court-martial was impressive. There had to be at least five officer members, including the president, and they all attended in full-dress uniform. Indoors they doffed their plumed helmets but the sword was retained at all times. Witnesses appeared similarly garbed and only the judge advocate and the defendant, if he were a private, wore undress uniform.

The judge advocate was the busiest man in the court. Basically the prosecutor for the government, he had also to ensure that the accused had a defense counsel, see that the courtroom was fully equipped and ready, keep all the members notified of changes in schedules and finally make sure that an adequate record of the proceedings was kept. When the court assembled he administered an oath to each member and was in turn sworn in by the president.

His first order of business before each case was to find out if the defendant objected to the presence on the court of any of its members. If the accused believed a court member was prejudiced against him he could challenge that officer, and if the challenge was sustained the president had to dismiss the member. When such a challenge reduced the court to less than five members everything stopped until a demonstrably unprejudiced officer could be found.

The first case to be heard before Major Chandler's court was a charge of desertion against Private Marcellus Gannon, H Troop, Sixth Cavalry. Lieutenant Henely had made the charge: desertion from a patrol into the state of Chihuahua, Mexico, in the presence of hostile Indians. Lieutenant William Harkens of the Quartermaster Corps had been detailed as defense counsel for Gannon and he had one witness for the accused, Sergeant Horace Peaslack of L Troop, same regiment.

Gannon's case was first because it was expected to be short. A reliable sergeant was prepared to swear that Gannon had surrendered himself at Fort Yuma, never having intended to desert but only to evade harsh treatment by Lieutenant Henely. There appeared to be no evidence to the contrary and Gannon would doubtless lose some pay, garner a few months' "bad time" in the guardhouse, but not much worse. The regiment would not have a desertion on its books and this clearly would influence a court made up largely of its own officers. Harkens was confident he could have the charge reduced from desertion to absent without leave for less than thirty days in short order, but he had overlooked one thing.

Everyone on the court except Gannon had been informed of Tom Royal's late assignment as a member and it was not until Gannon marched in and saluted Major Chandler that he discovered this.

He instantly went pale. Before he could even be asked if he objected to any member of the court he spun around to Harkens, croaking hoarsely.

"Sir! Sir . . . I gotta talk to th' lootenant! Right now!"

"Is something wrong?" Chandler demanded irritably.

Gannon ignored him, plucking at Harkens' sleeve and whispering urgently.

Harkens' face went beet-red under Major Chandler's furious glare. "Sir . . ." he stammered, "I respectfully request permission to withdraw with the accused for a minute before the court is convened."

It was certainly irregular but Chandler gave his consent. Whatever it was, he hoped Harkens could straighten it out. The lieutenant jerked his head at Gannon and pushed him out the door before him.

On a row of chairs in the hall sat the witnesses who would appear before the court that morning and first in line was Sergeant Peaslack. Sword in one hand and dress helmet in the other, he sat stiffly, sweating. When Gannon appeared in the hall he sprang to his feet.

"You lying sunnuvabitch!" Gannon panted. "What're you tryin' to do to me?"

"What in hell you talkin' about? What's goin' on in there?"

"Both of you shut up!" exploded Lieutenant Harkens. From the very beginning he had suspected Peaslack's offer to testify for Gannon but he was familiar with this sort of thing and willing to go through with it as long as Peaslack and Gannon stuck together on their stories. Now something was happening he did not understand and he was worried. He stabbed a finger at the adjutant's office.

"Get in there! Both of you . . . move!"

He dismissed the orderly and shut the door. "All right, let's have it! What's the matter with you, Gannon?"

"Yeah! What's eatin'—" Peaslack began but Harkens shut him off.

"Sergeant, I don't want a word out of you till I ask for it! Shut up!"

"Yessir!" Peaslack had a growing certainty this was going to cost him his stripes if not worse. He glared at Gannon.

"Now!" Harkens turned on Gannon. "What's wrong with you, soldier?"

"It's that Lootenant Royal! You never tol' me he wuz gonna be here! Keerist, sir, I can't stand no court with him on it!"

Harkens looked baffled. "I don't get it. What's wrong with Mister Royal? He isn't in your troop. Not even the same post. What is all this?"

"Sir, if thet bastid there . . ." he pointed at Peaslack, "if he tol' Mister Royal what I tol' him, I ain't got a whore's prayer! I'm done!"

"You mean Mister Royal is prejudiced against you? Is that it?"

"I hope to spit in yer mess kit he is if Peaslack has been talkin' to him!"

"Don't talk to me like that, soldier! If there's something more to this than I know about, spit it out now before we go back in there!"

"I gotta know if thet lyin' bastid has talked to Mister Royal! If he has I'm gonna get hung!"

"I'm not going to warn you about your language again, Gannon! You act like a crazy man! I explained to you that if you think any of the officers on the court are prejudiced against you, you'll get a chance to say so. If you think Mister Royal won't give you a fair trial all you have to do is challenge him. The court will hear your reasons and if they believe you, Major Chandler will put Lieutenant Royal off your case."

Peaslack groaned.

"What's the matter with you, Sergeant?"

"Sir, let me talk to him! Gannon, you crazy crut, ain't nobody told that Lootenant nuthin! For Crissake shut yer mouth an' get on with it. You challenge Mister Royal an' you'll have to tell 'em why, an' then we're all in it up to our necks!"

"Inna pig's ass I'll shut up! I know a rigged deal when I see one! He says tell 'em the truth an' I'm gonna do it. You ain't gonna screw me like this, Peaslack!"

"Oh, Jeezus!" the sergeant groaned. "Sir, you gotta stop him . . ."

But Harkens' patience had run out. Both soldiers were too scared to suit him and he was suddenly afraid himself.

"I wash my hands of the both of you! If you think I'm going to try to defend this man with the two of you carrying on like this, you're crazy! I won't do it and I'm ready to tell Major Chandler why."

"Aw, sir . . . wait a minnit! Gannon, goddammit, tell him! He's your defense counsel. Tell him before you go back in there!"

"I ain't gonna do it! If I gotta say it I'll say it in there jest like the lootenant tol' me to."

"Oh, shit! I'll tell him then!" and he did so.

"You two stay here!" he told them, grimly. When he returned to the courtroom and asked for a private interview with Chandler the major went turkey-red. He was baffled and enraged. He had sat on many courts but he had never encountered anything like this before. He glared at the judge advocate helplessly. The latter was as nonplussed as Chandler but Harkens' face worried him.

"Sir, the court isn't convened yet. If you think it proper, I see no reason why you shouldn't grant Mister Harkens' request."

Harkens did his best to bring some order to what he had to say and when Chandler had heard him out there was no doubt in his mind about what to do. Legal or not, he would not have this told to his court by a soldier.

He called in Tom Royal and spoke to him privately and then he summoned the remainder of the court. They listened in amazement as Royal arose, white-faced, and formally asked to be excused on the grounds that he could not fairly judge Gannon's case. Such a self-indictment would normally have been examined in detail and voted upon by the entire court but Chandler abruptly dismissed Royal the moment he finished speaking. When the lieutenant had saluted and gone he glared at the judge advocate.

"I am quite aware that a member of the court who challenges himself can only be excused by the convening authority. I am also convinced that what I have done is in the best interest of the service and that the commanding general of the Department will agree with me. Have you any questions, sir?"

The judge advocate shook his head. Chandler's eye raked the rest of the court and Tate Hulse had the feeling he had been looking into the muzzle of a loaded gun. No one said anything and the court was convened. Private Gannon reappeared and went through the motions of reporting to the president with glazed eyes. Lieutenant

Harkens stuttered through his plea for reduction of the charge and was supported by Peaslack, gray-faced and shaking. The court accepted the evidence and since there was nothing else to consider, found Gannon guilty of the lesser charge of absent without leave and sentenced him to two months' hard labor without confinement.

Leaving the courtroom, Royal went straight to the Van Scivers' quarters, the too small dress helmet bobbing absurdly on his head. His knock was answered by Wentz, who looked a little surprised at the full-dress uniform but said nothing.

"Will you ask Miss Allyn if I may see her, please," the lieutenant demanded.

"Missus Van Sciver und the young lady haff gone into the town, sir. Missus say they looking for a trunk und they be back for supper. You vant to leaf a card, sir?" He nodded at the card tray on the hall table. Ellen had taught him that he must not hold it out to a visitor.

"What? Oh, hell, man!" Tom exploded. "Tell Miss Allyn I'll be back after supper!" He stamped off the porch and in his rage, forgot about the helmet. He had to grab for it as it slid over his eyes.

TWENTY-NINE

Polycarp and Ellen were reading by the big lamp in the front room when the thud of running feet on the plank walk brought Carp out of his chair with a lunge. It was a sound that got instant attention anywhere in Arizona. The front door burst open before he could reach it and Samantha came in with a rush. Her face told him there was trouble, but not the sort he feared.

"Sam?" Ellen called. She was answered by the thump of Samantha's door and Carp's resigned grunt. He picked up his forage cap from the table.

"I'm going down to have a look at the stables, my dear."

"What's the matter? Was that Sam?"

"Yes, and I don't know what the matter is. Maybe you'd better inquire."

"You are a coward, Carp Van Sciver!"

"I admit it. Shall I look for Tom?"

"I don't think so. She was walking with him." He departed and Ellen busied herself at the sideboard before knocking at Samantha's door.

"Sam? May I come in?"

If there was a response it was inaudible. The room was dark and Ellen felt her way to the mantel, found the candlestick and struck a match. Samantha was sitting on the bed.

"Try this." Ellen held out a squat glass.

"What is it?"

"A toddy. Carp's favorite prescription in time of trouble." Samantha sipped at it.

"Thank you. It's very good."

Ellen settled herself on the edge of the big steamer trunk and waited.

"Drink your toddy, Sam," she said after a moment. The younger girl drank the sweetened whiskey as a child takes its medicine.

"Do you want to talk about it or would you rather I go?"

"It doesn't matter!" Samantha said bitterly, adding at once, "I don't mean that! I'm sorry; please stay."

"All right. Would you like me just to sit with you for a little?"

"No. I mean . . . Oh, Ellen, I need help!"

"I'll try, my dear."

There was another pause before Samantha spoke in a small, tight voice. "I suppose everyone knows what that soldier said this morning." It was more a statement than a question—flat, matter-of-fact, with an edge of panic in the words.

"You mean at the court? I don't think so. No one knows except Major Chandler and Mister Harkens . . . and Tom, I suppose, since Major Chandler spoke to him privately."

"Why? Why did he do that?"

"Speak to Tom?"

"Yes."

"My dear, I don't know. It seems that after he heard what the soldier had to say, Tom felt he couldn't judge the man fairly. Major Chandler let Tom disqualify himself without any discussion of the matter and he could get in trouble for that. I'm sure he did it because he thought it best for everyone. Tom has told no one why he disqualified himself . . . except you, I gather."

Samantha gripped the glass until her knuckles were white and Ellen took it from her.

"I wouldn't let it distress me so if I were you, Sam. Soldiers say terrible things when they're in trouble. No one believes them."

"Tom did!"

"Maybe. I think Major Chandler just didn't want to give the man a chance to air another wild story like the one he told about Aussie Henely trying to get him killed. If that's true he was simply doing Tom a favor."

"It isn't Tom he's protecting. It's me!"

"Sam, I have no idea what the soldier said, but Tom knows better than to believe a cock-and-bull story cooked up for a court-martial. The truth will come out and Tom will know it when he hears it."

"I expect he will . . . God help me!"

The meaning of that despairing cry did not at once dawn on Ellen. When it did, she quailed.

"Do you want to tell me, Sam?" she managed after a moment.

"I have to talk to someone!" The toddy was working now. She was unaccustomed to liquor and the strong, sweet drink had unlocked her tongue. She continued abruptly and without preamble.

"I never knew what would happen to me. I cannot speak Spanish and if I live to be a thousand I shall never understand a word of Apache. I didn't know what they were saying and I could never find out what they meant to do with me. I know it sounds foolish but that was the worst torment of all!"

"Didn't they say anything to you?"

"They talked endlessly but I couldn't understand! When they wanted me to do something they pointed or pushed. When it was so complicated I couldn't understand that, they brought Severiano." She rubbed her brow with her fingers. The drink was making her dizzy.

"Who is Severiano?"

"You know. The boy who brought me to the soldiers."

"Oh." Ellen remembered Tate Hulse's mention of a "half-breed kid." "Was he there all the time you were?"

"Yes."

"Tate called him a half-breed. Is he half-white?"

"No. His father was Apache and his mother was Mexican. Another wretched woman they stole somewhere."

"Poor thing!" Ellen murmured.

"Yes. In the end she gave up, though. She lived with an Apache until he was killed and then she followed the soldiers who killed him. She died and the boy was raised by soldiers. At least he hung around the barracks with them. He learned a little English that way."

None of this made sense to Ellen but she supposed it was leading somewhere. "How did he come to be with the Apaches again?"

"You can imagine what happened to him with the soldiers. He had a frightful dose of how we treat mixed blood. The Army abandoned the post and simply kicked him out. He drifted back to his father's people and they took him in."

"Was he kind to you?"

Samantha laughed bitterly. "I suppose you could say so. He was the only living soul I could talk to and I dared not offend him. That wasn't so easy. He wanted me to be his woman, as he put it."

"But if you were a captive . . ." Ellen left the question unfinished.

"No. He couldn't force me. For some strange reason they don't allow that. If I agreed it would be all right, but I had to agree first."

"And you . . . didn't?"

Samantha shook her head. "He never let up. He tormented me. He said the Americans had traded me to the Apaches to keep them from raiding. He wanted to make me so hopeless I would give up."

"How horrible!"

"It was horrible! An endless nightmare. I had to have his help so I could know what they wanted of me. I had to do what they wanted without showing fear. They're like animals about fear. They can smell it and it delights them. I was so alone and I didn't know what to do."

"But what about your aunt? Wasn't she with you then?"

"She disappeared the day after they took us. They tortured a man to death. One of the men who was on the stage with us. They made us watch and Aunt Bee went out of her mind. Next morning she just walked away. They're afraid of insane people. They let her go. I never saw her again and I didn't know what happened to her. I think Severiano knew but he wouldn't tell me. He said they don't torture women but he was lying as usual. Once they caught a Mexican woman and . . ." She buried her face in her hands.

"Don't!" said Ellen sharply. "Don't tell about it! Don't even think about it!"

"I can't tell it. I didn't see it. I only heard her! I can still hear her!"

To distract her, Ellen returned to Severiano. "In the end, you said, it was Severiano who helped you escape, though."

Samantha raised burning eyes. "Yes, but he didn't mean for me to escape from him. He was going to take me to

Mexico. He tied me on the horse. Didn't they tell you that?"

"Good Lord, no! Did you tell Tom?"

"No. What's the use? He saved my life, I suppose. What difference why he did it?"

"Did he mistreat you after he got you away from the Indians? Is that what the trouble is?"

"Oh, no! He didn't have a chance." Ellen's bewilderment was obvious and Samantha tried to bring some order to her chaotic story.

"It's awfully complicated, Ellen. I think part of what Severiano said must have been true. The Indians felt safe from the soldiers because they had me in their camp. But then a man they called Geronimo came and he wanted them to go into Mexico with him. I guess he could see they wouldn't go as long as they had me, so he had to get rid of me."

"Who told you all of this? Severiano?"

"Oh, no! Geronimo brought a white man with him. I didn't know that until they had a council in the night and a priest, or whatever they call them, wanted me to drink something from a cup. I wouldn't drink it and suddenly this white man spoke to me. He said Geronimo told them I was a witch. Drink it, he said; and if it makes you sick that proves it. Then he told me what they do with witches."

Ellen shuddered. "Don't tell me! I don't want to know."

"They burn them," Samantha said matter-of-factly, "but in a special way."

"But who was this white man?"

"This one was half-Mexican and half-Irish. His name is O'Brien and he hates Americans."

"But he kept them from burning you?"

"Yes. He did. When I wouldn't take the drink he talked to the Indians. He made them laugh. Then he said to me, 'Girl, how would you like to live until tomorrow?' "

Ellen stared uncomprehending for a long moment, then she gasped. "My God! My God!"

Samantha's eyes were frightening. "What could I do? What would you do?"

257

Ellen shook her head, wordless.

"You want the rest? All of it?" Still the older woman could not answer.

"The next morning I tried to drown myself. They stopped me. Brought me back. I thought they would burn me then but I guess O'Brien stopped them again. He said he had made a deal with them. If he brought them cartridges they would sell me to him. I could go with him or stay and be burned. He asked me which I wanted."

She put her hands on her throat and stared bleakly at the mantel. "You haven't said anything, Ellen. What are you going to say to me?"

Ellen caught her hands and gripped them tightly. "What can I say? My God, child, no one should bear what you have borne!"

Her kindness shattered Samantha's control and the gray eyes filled with tears. "You said . . ." she whispered, "Tom will know the truth when he hears it. I have told you the truth. Do you think he will have me when he knows it?"

"How much of this have you told him?"

"Nothing. He knows something from the soldier. Something about me and O'Brien. I cannot imagine how the soldier found out. Tom came to me this evening and asked if it were true."

"And you told him . . . ?"

"Nothing! I would not answer."

"Good Lord!" Ellen had a mental picture of Tom Royal faced with that impasse. "Are you going to tell him?"

"I don't know. I don't know what to do. I don't want to tell him. Why should I have to explain to him? What will he do if I tell him?"

"My dear, he's your young man. You must know him better than I."

"But I don't! I thought I did but now I'm not sure at all. He has no right to press me like this!"

My dear, Ellen thought, you have a lot to learn about Tom Royal, but she did not voice that thought.

"What about this O'Brien? How do you feel about him?"

Samantha's mouth twisted. "Sometimes I wish him in the bottommost pits of hell but . . ." she shrugged, "mostly I just don't think about him any more. What he did to me was horrible and I despise him for it, but he did save my life. I suppose in a way you could call us even. The Apaches were the losers. They never got their cartridges and they lost me."

Ellen shook her head, baffled. "I thought he bought you from them?"

"He was going to but he couldn't. He promised them the cartridges and they said they would keep me and not hurt me until he brought them. Before he could do that the soldiers came. He had me for two days and I had my life. The Indians had nothing."

"Do you love Tom?"

"Of course! My God, I've lived for months on that alone! I did unspeakable things. I worked like a slave and I did it all to stay alive for Tom Royal. Now I'm free and he's here and what happens? Some damned soldier tells him a filthy story and he believes it! Why do I have to fight that too?"

"Aren't you asking an awful lot of Tom?"

"I don't know! I told you I don't know what to do. I know what you're thinking. If I really loved Tom could I expect him to take me just as if nothing had happened? I guess the answer is, I do! All those terrible things didn't change me. I loved him when I came out here to marry him and I still do. Haven't I proved that?"

"I . . . I should certainly think so."

"Then has he the right to question me like this? I haven't asked him where he was all those months I was in that stinking Indian camp! I haven't asked him if the Army really traded me to the Indians for a few months' peace!"

"Oh, Sam, don't! That won't help anything!"

"Ellen, if he would not press me I would never ask those questions. I am willing to call it quits just as I am willing to forget O'Brien. O'Brien is just something else

259

that happened to me like being cold and dirty and hungry and frightened. He's just something else I had to submit to if I wanted to live. I did live! I survived for Tom and the least he can do is take me back without a lot of questions!"

"Sam, you know that's going to be very hard for him."

"Yes. I know that. I know why, too. What that soldier knows will eventually come out and if Tom marries me a lot of people will talk about us. They'll talk about him and maybe it will hold him back. Keep him from promotion and all the things he wants."

She had to stop, to catch her breath. Then she went on. "I've thought a lot about this, Ellen. God knows I had a lot of time to think. I thought about myself. You know I was born in the Army but my father was killed and then my mother died and after that I didn't really belong anywhere. Aunt Bee took me and we lived at Leavenworth. Not on the Army post but in the town. We were on the fringe of the Army. Aunt Bee made dresses for officers' wives and I taught their children and they were kind to us. I pretended I belonged but it wasn't true. I wanted so much to belong and there was no way. Then Tom Royal proposed to me and I was crazy with joy. I've asked myself over and over do I really love Tom or do I just want to be Lieutenant Tom Royal's wife and know I belong somewhere."

"And you found the answer?"

Samantha shook her head stubbornly. "I don't know, Ellen. I never had a chance to know him well. We didn't have enough time together. I love him enough to want to marry him and I'm afraid to tell him all this because if I do he might not have me. Right now all I know is that if he loves me enough he ought to take me without tearing this out of me."

"I think he loves you, Sam. I think he loves you very much." There was too much unsaid, though. The unspoken question hung over them both. Ellen shook her head sadly.

"How did you actually escape, Sam? What became of O'Brien?"

"I don't know. He's somewhere in Mexico, I suppose. That's where he said he was going for the cartridges. The soldiers attacked the camp before he came back and Severiano said the Indians would kill me. I believed him. He took me on his horse and we got away. Then he told me he wouldn't take me to the soldiers; he was going to take me with him. I fought him and he tied me on the horse. I guess we walked into an ambush. The horse was shot and I hurt my head and the colored soldiers found me. You know the rest."

She was silent for a moment and then she pounded her knee in anger. "Why did they wait so long? Why didn't they come sooner? If they had come before Geronimo and O'Brien I might have been dead but I wouldn't be in this trap!"

"They were trying to buy you back from the Indians, Sam. Everyone who knows Apaches said it was the right thing to do. They said if the troops went into the mountains and attacked the Indians you would be murdered. Nothing worked and we were all desperate. Tate Hulse risked his commission to offer the Indians something they would take for you . . ."

"You mean . . . nobody else would offer what they wanted? Where was Tom? What was he doing?"

"He raged! He wanted to go and look for you and fight to get you back and they wouldn't let him."

"Then . . . it's true? The Army was willing to let the Indians keep me if they would stop raiding?"

"Of course not! That's absurd. They were only thinking of you and your aunt. I told you everyone said the Apaches would kill you if they were attacked."

"Did Tom know where I was?"

"No one knew. There were rumors, of course, but nothing you could believe."

"I thought they had given up . . . that no one would ever come! I still don't understand why they didn't come sooner. Oh, Ellen, I don't want to tell Tom. I don't know what he will do!"

"My dear, as you said, if he loves you enough it will make no difference to him."

"Won't it? He certainly isn't too eager to have me at the moment!" She jammed her knuckles against her mouth and looked at Ellen beseechingly. "Tell me what to do!"

"I can't do that, Sam. No one can. It's a thing only you and Tom can resolve. All I can say is be patient; give him time. You both need time."

"But what will I do while he's making up his mind? Where can I go?"

"You will go nowhere! This is your home now and Carp and I want you to stay here just as long as you will. You must understand that!"

"Yes, I do, Ellen." Again her eyes filled with tears. "Thank you very much. I didn't know there were people in the world as kind as you and Carp. But please, Ellen, don't tell anyone else what I've just told you."

"I promise," Ellen replied.

THIRTY

The morning after the disastrous court-martial, a puzzled Tate Hulse knocked early on the Van Scivers' door. Ellen let him in with a finger on her lips. He looked for Samantha.

"She's still asleep. No one's up except me and the children."

"Do you know where Tom is?" Ellen shook her head. "What happened? Why did he leave?" She continued shaking her head. Tate sighed. "Can I have a cup of coffee, Ellen?"

She led him to the kitchen, where Robert and Annie

were breakfasting on oatmeal. They greeted him cheerfully. Ellen made coffee and small talk, prodding the children to hurry. She shooed them out with a warning to be quiet.

"Didn't you see Tom last night?" she asked.

"No. I took supper with the Biddles and when I got back to our quarters he wasn't there. I thought he was still with Samantha, but he never came back."

"You think he left the post?"

"I know he did. He borrowed a horse last night but he didn't say where he was going."

"That's not very smart in this country, is it?"

"He's safer at night than in daylight but I wish I knew where he went."

"Won't he get in trouble . . . just riding off like that?"

"I doubt it. Court's recessed until Monday and Major Chandler would shut an eye even if he missed that."

"You've been busy this morning, haven't you? What else did you find out?"

"Nothing. That's why I'm here. I thought you'd know. What's he going to do, Ellen? When are they going to be married?"

"I don't know, Tate. I have no idea what their plans are. I suspect they had a fuss of some sort last night. She came in very upset."

"That damned deserter!"

"What about him?" Ellen asked cautiously.

"I'll bet a month's pay he's at the bottom of this. He told Major Chandler something that made Tom disqualify himself from the court. It had to be something to do with Sam!"

"Why do you say that?"

Tate twisted angrily in his chair. "What else? The man's not in Tom's troop. It can't be anything personal between them. Tom never saw him until he went on that scout with Henely. The soldier deserted while they were out but I don't think Tom had anything to do with that."

She patted his hand absentmindedly, wondering if Tom Royal had gone to look for O'Brien. If he killed him he could get in serious trouble. Tate eyed her curiously.

"What's going on, Ellen? Do you know something you're not telling me?"

"No," she answered quickly. If he were left to pry at this he might make more trouble than if he were told, but the promise to Samantha held her tongue. She would not break it. Sam needed more help than any of them and if silence was what she wanted, Ellen would keep it.

Tate took his leave after a while, no less puzzled and more troubled than when he came. Ellen asked him to join them for dinner that evening and he came eagerly but it was a joyless meal. Samantha said not a dozen words; Carp seemed morose, and even Ellen could not liven them up. Tate excused himself as soon afterward as he decently could and returned to his quarters miserably. Tom was still absent and no one knew where he had gone.

As a matter of fact, Tom did not reappear until Monday afternoon and then he went straight to the Van Scivers'. Samantha was on her knees on the floor of Carp's study cutting a dress pattern from newspaper when Ellen announced that Tom was there. She found him waiting in the hall.

"Will you walk with me, Sam?" he asked quietly. She took a shawl from the rack and wrapped it about her shoulders. The afternoon was as gray and chilly as her mood.

They walked along the row of adobe houses, her heels tapping an obbligato to the heavy beat of his boots on the planks. His uniform was dusty and travel-stained and she had never seen him look so tired.

"Where did you go?" she asked finally.

"Calabasas."

It meant nothing to her but she would not ask for explanation. He told her it was the settlement on the Rio Santa Cruz where the colored soldiers took Severiano after they found him wounded on the mountainside. They had left him with a retired sergeant who kept a farm in the Sonoita Valley.

"How is he?" she asked.

"All right. His shoulder's healing. I didn't go to see him about that."

Samantha set her teeth. She could imagine what he went for. From the distress on his face she could imagine too what he had heard.

"I asked him about O'Brien," Tom continued doggedly. Samantha would neither look at him nor respond. She walked, head lowered, her mouth set stubbornly. "I only wanted to prove that damned deserter is lying, Sam," he added defensively.

Her face was white beneath its tan. He waited for her to speak but when she would not he blundered on.

"He told me that he asked you many times to go away with him. He said he wanted to help you escape but you wouldn't go. Then—when O'Brien came—you went to him."

Samantha stopped as abruptly as if she had run into something. She could picture Severiano's reaction to Tom. He would say just what he thought this big, angry lieutenant wanted to hear and he would embroider it to his own credit when he could. Bullied or trapped in a lie, he would simply change his story to suit the need. She knew she could never guess all he had told Tom but the tenor of the story was plain. When she stopped Tom did also and peered at her curiously. Across the parade ground the wind plucked at the halyards on the flagpole with a monotonous slap, slap, slap.

"Is that all he told you?" she asked in a small, tight voice.

"Oh, no! He had a lot to say . . . most of it hogwash. He's just a kid and a breed kid at that. He thinks he's in love with you and he actually seems to feel you owe him something."

Severiano's nonsense she could understand. He was a pathological liar. But Tom's willingness to listen, to believe even, lacerated her raw nerves.

"Do you believe him?"

"I don't know what to believe, Sam. I guess most of it is just a pack of lies."

"But you rode all the way down there to listen to them?"

"Well, you haven't told me much to help me know what to believe."

A storm of helpless rage shook her. He had every right to demand an explanation of her and he seemed incapable of understanding why she withheld it.

"So now you want me to explain away Severiano, don't you?"

He gestured apologetically, "No! I'm not trying to make you do that."

"But you are!" she cried. "You got some fool story from that deserter and you came straight to me, asking me to deny it! When I wouldn't, you rode off for three days without a word to a soul and listened to that crazy boy. I don't know a thing about the deserter but I know what kind of liar Severiano is. God knows, I ought to!"

It was bitterly unfair and he made the mistake of resenting it. "Sam . . . listen to me . . ." he began.

"No!" she burst out. "You listen to me!" Her voice shocked him. It was hoarse, desperate, furious. "I have been shamed and degraded enough. I waited and waited . . . and you didn't come!" Her eyes were on his now, slick and frantic. "I love you, Tom, but I will not fight for your belief against a deserter and a crazy boy!"

"I didn't . . . I never asked you to!" he protested in bewilderment. "I don't understand you, Sam!"

"Then I will make it quite clear! Do you still want me, Tom?"

He groaned and rubbed his face with dirty hands. "Of course I want you, Sam. More than anything in the world! All I asked was . . ."

"Then stop asking!" she cried. "Take me without excuses or explanations! I thought fire and knives were not to be borne but you're showing me something worse! Tom, I won't beg for your love . . . I can't."

He was genuinely shocked. "My God, Sam! I don't want you to beg! I couldn't do that and call myself a man."

"What are you doing then?"

His shoulders jerked. "Sam, listen to me. Those men slandered you. I wouldn't be a man if I didn't resent it. If I could lay hands on this O'Brien, I'd kill him. I'd kill that Mexican-Indian if he weren't just a kid. How do I wrong you when all I ask is for you to tell me they're lying?"

She tried hard. She fought back her feeling of injustice and self-pity and tried to be reasonable. He deserved an answer and she did not know whether it was pride or shame that stopped her from giving it.

"You're right, Tom," she said shakily. "I know it's unfair of me yet I can't help it. You said when we're both ready I should tell you what happened to me. Well . . . I'm not ready, and I don't think you are either. Can't you give me a little more time?" She was all but pleading now.

He was a baffled and miserable young man but there was a stubborn streak in him that demanded its due. "I swear, Sam, I'd cut off my hand before I'd hurt you. I know what kind of hell you've had . . . at least I think I do. But I can't see why you won't talk to me about it . . . help me to understand this."

"Then God help us both!" she whispered. He looked at her unbelieving, put out his hands toward her.

"No!" she said, evading them.

"I just don't understand, Sam," he said hopelessly. "You tell me I'm right but then you say I have no right to ask . . ."

"I did not! I said I have no more to give. Is that so hard to understand?"

"Frankly, yes. You make me feel like a cad and I haven't done anything wrong. What is it? What am I doing?"

His plaintive righteousness was unbearable and the more painful because there was a part of her that watched this quarrel dispassionately and insisted he had a right to know. It was not pride, as she would have him think, but cowardice that made her deny him. She twisted her hands in the ends of the shawl and tried once more, desperately.

"I can't make it any plainer, Tom. It isn't fair of me . . . I know that. But you're tearing me into little pieces and I have got to stop you. For months I have not been allowed to call my soul my own and now, here with my own people, it's the same thing. Must you strip me like this?"

It was too much. His misery gave way to anger. "Dammit to hell, Sam . . . a deserter and a half-breed kid say you went to bed with a renegade whose name is a curse the length of the border! Can't you even tell me why they'd both take the trouble to lie about you like that?"

There would be grief beyond knowing for her in this. She knew that. But his anger cut through her reason and her love alike to strike sparks from something hard and feminine and unknowable deep within her.

"Don't swear at me, Tom Royal!" she panted. "Don't speak to me like that!" Tears stung her eyes and her bitterness overwhelmed her. The guard was forming for retreat by the flagpole and the soldiers eyed the bristling young couple curiously. Samantha cared nothing for them but Tom was acutely conscious of their attention.

"Sam! Please listen . . ." She shook her head, tears spilling down her cheeks, salt and bitter on her lips.

"Is that all you have to say?" she whispered. His mouth snapped shut. She spun away from him as the first notes of a bugle call rang out and the soldiers' murmur stilled.

Her back as rigid as if she were on parade she marched down the walk to the Van Scivers' house, head high but unseeing. In the veranda she hesitated, hoping against hope that he had followed, but he had not. He stood where she had left him, but facing the parade ground now, waiting for the bugler to sound retreat and for the flag to come down for the night. The clear, urgent call of the bugle followed her into the house.

THIRTY-ONE

Major Chandler was hardly surprised by Lieutenant Royal's request to be relieved permanently from the court-martial. He had expected it, and though there was no legal basis for dismissing the young officer, he felt confident there would be no difficulty.

"Certainly, Mister Royal. I'll have the orders changed and you needn't wait for them. Ah . . . I think you should have some leave, my boy. Why don't you send a telegram to Captain Tupper? I'd be pleased to endorse your request if you wish." He wanted to add that Tom and his girl could find a better place to discuss their problems than the parade ground during guard mount, but the stiff reserve of the young man deterred him.

"I will get in touch with Captain Tupper, sir, as you suggest." It was contrary to custom for a junior to thank a senior officer for an official act, but Major Chandler's handling of Tom's part in the court-martial was something more than formal. "Sir . . . I'd like to thank the major for . . ."

Chandler cut him short with a gesture. "Say no more, my boy. I only wish the whole thing could have been avoided."

He was feeling very pleased with himself until he sat down to lunch with his wife that noon and she asked in a chilly voice what he had done to young Mister Royal.

"Done? I've done everything I could for him. I've arranged for him to be relieved of all duties so he can be

269

with his girl and as soon as he brings it to me I shall endorse his request for leave."

Mrs. Chandler sniffed. "Did you tell him he had to go to Camp Grant to ask for leave?"

The major put down his fork and frowned at her. "What are you talking about, Amanda? He's preparing a telegram to Tullius Tupper and there's nothing wrong with the wire between here and Camp Grant that I know of."

"I'm sure you're correct about that, John, but Mister Royal left an hour ago with Major Roche for Grant."

"He . . . um . . . did, did he? Well. Yes." And that was all John Chandler had to say on the subject despite his wife's obvious curiosity.

There were only two paymasters in the Department of Arizona, Major Maynadier in Prescott and Major Roche in Lowell. Between them they had to visit every Army post in the Territory every two months and Roche's circuit covered Lowell, Grant, Bowie and Apache—six hundred miles requiring twenty-five to thirty days each time. Roche had just departed for Camp Grant and Tom Royal had joined his escort.

His arrival at Grant was hardly noticed in the excitement of payday. This happy occasion found the entire garrison lined up and waiting. Major Roche seated himself at a table and the soldiers filed past him, each man stepping up as his name was called to sign the payroll or make his mark if he could not write. He had stripped off his white glove from his right hand to do this, and his pay was then counted out into the ungloved hand, after which the trooper stepped back to salute with his left.

There were many supervisors of the pay line. Between paydays a soldier lived on credit, "jawbone," he called it, and the troop barber, cobbler, tailor and laundress waited impatiently for a settlement of accounts. For some there was also the troop loan shark, the man who would always lend a buddy a little something when cash grew short at a simple interest rate of one hundred percent. Then there was the post trader's bill to be settled and when a man came in to do this he could be expected to tarry for a drink or two. On payday even beer at a dollar a bottle sold well. Prices were high because the troops were paid in greenbacks which the frontier merchant discounted at anything from fifteen to fifty percent. Only gold and silver coin were worth face value.

Tom made his way through this stir to his quarters, where Tony Rucker greeted him with astonishment.

"What're you doing here? Where's your girl?"

"At Lowell with the Van Scivers."

"But, man! What . . ." his voice trailed off as he studied Tom's face. "What happened?" he asked finally.

"Nothing."

"But the wedding? These women here will burst if they don't find out something about it!"

"They'll just have to burst then." And like Major Chandler, he would say no more.

At dinner that night in the Bachelors' Mess the other officers were as astonished and curious as Rucker, but Tom's stony face and short answers checked them. They shrugged and returned to the fight in Pionsenay's camp which they had been discussing heatedly. Major Compton was incensed that someone had killed a young squaw in the Apache *ranchería* and they pressed Tom to know if he had heard anything of this at regimental headquarters.

He shook his head and his friends respected his silence. It was obvious he had trouble of some sort and they let him alone. The war against the Sioux and Cheyennes in the north was more interesting than family gossip.

During the summer of 1876 the Sioux Confederation had literally fought the United States Army to a standstill, culminating in the loss of Custer and half his regiment. General Sheridan, commanding the Division of the Missouri, was under sharp attack by the Eastern newspapers for the fumbling summer campaign but he had found one ray of hope. An infantryman named Miles was waging winter war on the Yellowstone River that just might break the back of Sioux resistance before summer came again. Sheridan backed Miles to the hilt, pouring in reinforcements and supplies that would normally have been hoarded for better weather.

Sherman, commanding the entire Army, backed his lieutenant general grimly. He scraped officers and men from every corner of the nation to strengthen Sheridan's hand. Captain Abbott, the post adjutant, testified to this.

"We got an order today to send a lieutenant to Dakota for three months' temporary duty."

"Who's going?" a chorus of voices demanded.

"I'll take volunteers tomorrow and I guess Major Compton'll pick the lucky man."

In the din of animated talk that followed no one noticed Tom Royal's quiet departure. He went directly to Captain Tupper's quarters.

His troop commander greeted him warily. The orderly room had told him Royal was back but he had not seen him personally. "How is Miss Allyn?" he asked bluntly.

"Quite well, sir."

"You left her at Camp Lowell?"

"Yes, sir. She's staying with the Van Scivers."

It was obvious to Tupper that this was getting nowhere. He still felt guilty about his refusal to let Royal meet his girl in Tucson when she arrived from the East, but the young officer's reticence now irritated him.

"Well, what about the wedding, Mister? Will you be married here or do you want to go back to Lowell for that?"

"That's not settled, sir."

Tupper's face grew redder and he controlled himself with difficulty. "Then what," he demanded grimly, "can I do for you, Mister Royal?"

"Sir, I want to volunteer for temporary duty in Dakota."

Tullius Tupper blinked owlishly. "That, sir, will take you out of Arizona for at least three months and maybe more. I gather you think it none of my business but I would admire to know just what you're planning to do. Are you taking Miss Allyn with you?"

"No, sir."

"For God's sake, boy, why not?" the captain burst out.

"Personal reasons, sir."

Tupper leaned back and tried to master his surprise and
272

anger. Young Royal wouldn't be the first he'd seen shy from the altar at the last moment, but after what he'd gone through to get his girl back from the Indians this was incredible. It was increasingly apparent, however, that Royal was not going to explain his motives.

"Mister Royal," he said after a moment, "a lot of people beside me are going to think this extremely odd. You know that if I accept your request they're going to swear I shipped you out of Arizona before you could get married. Is that what you want?"

"I'll put the request in writing if you want it, sir."

Tupper's face flamed. "Don't give me that bullshit, Royal! I know you've had a bad time and your girl a worse one. I'll do anything I can to help the both of you, but I'm double-damned if I see how a tour of the Canadian border is what you need right now!"

"Captain Abbott said there is a levy for an officer for Dakota and I'm volunteering for the job, sir."

His commander sighed. "You're putting me in a hell of a box, Royal. Couldn't you explain a little?"

"My reasons are entirely personal, sir. I don't want to discuss them."

"Well, if I'm asked, I'd have to say you volunteered!"

"I know that, sir."

"And you still want to go?"

"Yes, sir."

Tupper was silent for a long moment, then he sighed again. "All right. I don't understand but I guess I owe you something. I'll speak to Major Compton about it tomorrow; it's his decision."

"I hope you'll support my request, sir."

"I told you I'd do what I can, Royal. I don't like it but I'll do it. You got anything else on your mind?"

"No, sir."

"Well, this is enough to say grace over for the moment! All right, you're dismissed."

When he approached the post commander the next morning, Compton was as surprised as Tupper had been.

"I don't know what he's up to," said Tupper, "but his mind is made up. I'm sure of that."

273

"He's a grown man, Tullius. He must know what he's doing. Anybody else ask for the job?"

"All of them, I suppose. There's a crowd in Abbott's office right now."

"But he came to you last night and now you're in here bucking for him?"

"For God's sake, Major, what am I supposed to do? I owe him a favor and I'm paying it!"

"You mean you're passing the buck to me, eh, Tullius?"

"Charlie, you've known me for twenty-two years! Did I ever pass you the buck? Royal volunteered and I'm recommending you send him. You want it in writing?"

"Don't get huffy, Tullius! You say send him and I'll take that at face value. He's going out of channels unless he signs up with the rest of them at the adjutant's office, but that's happened before. Did you ask him to put his request in writing?"

"No. What difference would it make? People are going to say hard things about us anyhow. You know what they're going to say and you can't stop them."

"Is that what he wants?"

"I'm damned if I know! It doesn't make much sense any other way, does it?"

"Have you any idea what happened between him and his girl?"

"Not the foggiest! Maybe someone at Lowell will eventually tell us."

"All right. So be it. I don't owe you any favors that I know of but I'll do you this one. I hope we're both right."

On a post as small as Camp Grant the machinery could move very swiftly. The adjutant handed Tom orders assigning him to the Department of Dakota and the quartermaster gave him a transportation order to get him to St. Paul.

"This is supposed to get you a seat on any railroad going that way, Tom, but I can't guarantee it. Some of them are refusing to honor Army orders now and they'll make you pay for a ticket. Take enough cash for emergencies and you can file a claim against the Army when you get back."

It took little time for him to pack what he would take with him, after which he wrote two letters, one to Samantha and another to Carp Van Sciver. That done, he had a brief, formal visit with Captain Tupper and departed, avoiding everyone else. The letters were delivered by the mail rider to Camp Lowell three days later and Ellen studied them anxiously when Carp dropped them on the hall table.

"What do they mean?"

"How would I know, Ellen? I haven't read them."

"But haven't you heard anything? Where is he?"

"Camp Grant, I suppose. That's where they came from. Where's Sam?"

"Wentz took her into Tucson in the buggy." She fingered Samantha's letter and put it down reluctantly. "Please open yours, Carp!"

He read it in silence and then handed it to her. Her eyes flew over the single page and she groaned.

"How despicable! How could Tullius Tupper have done such a thing to him?"

"Now, Ellen! Tupper didn't make him go. I saw the levy; it asked for a volunteer. Tom couldn't have gone unless he asked to."

"How long will he be away?"

"Three months at the least."

"It isn't fair!" she cried. "Whatever's the matter with him? How can he do this to her?"

"You know more about that than I, my dear. You've talked to her."

"Damn Tom Royal for a stupid man!" Ellen exploded and her husband looked surprised. It took a good deal to bring language like that from Ellen.

Samantha returned from Tucson in midafternoon and took her letter to her room without comment. Her composure at supper was unsettling and afterward, while Ellen read to the children, she sewed in silence. Not until Robert and Annie were settled in bed did she mention the letter.

"Tom writes that he's going to Dakota for three months. He said he wrote you also; did he mention it to you?"

275

"Yes," replied Carp, frowning, "he did. But Sam, there is something you should understand . . ."

There was a crash of breaking china and they both stared at Ellen in astonishment.

"I dropped my coffee," she said flatly.

"Oh, your beautiful cup!" Samantha jumped up from her chair. "I'll get a cloth from the kitchen."

"Never mind. I'd finished the coffee."

Carp stared at his wife suspiciously. For Ellen the loss of a single piece of her precious china was normally a catastrophe. Now she was icily calm and he knew there was something he should understand from that.

"What were you about to say, Carp?" Samantha asked him.

"I was going to say that you must know we want you to stay here with us until Tom returns." Ellen's eyelids flicked down in a signal that told him he had understood.

"That's very kind of you, Carp, but by next week I shall be working in Tucson."

"What?" The question burst from them both at once.

"I spoke today with Miss Harriet Bolton. They have never had a music teacher at her school and they will let me try."

"But Sam!" exclaimed Ellen. "It's such a long drive back and forth every day!"

"I won't be driving, Ellen. I shall take a room in town."

"Oh, no!"

"Of course. If I stayed here I would need the buggy every day and you can't just turn it over to me."

"But we don't want you to leave!"

Samantha smiled at her gratefully. "You're too kind, Ellen, but let's be logical about this. Tom will be gone at least three months and I can't just sit here in your house doing nothing until he returns." After a moment she added, "If he returns."

They regarded her, speechless. She had put into words what both of them feared to voice. Ellen took a deep breath. "You wouldn't be just sitting. You'd help me. I want your company. Carp, tell her she shouldn't live in Tucson!"

"My dear, it's Sam's decision to make. Have you thought this through, Sam? Are you quite sure? We'd much rather have you stay with us and if you want to work in Tucson I can get another buggy and driver for you."

"Thank you, Carp. I have thought about it a great deal and I'm sure this is the best way. I won't be very far from you, Ellen. I can see you every Sunday if you want."

"What a thing to say! This is your home, Sam, and we want you whenever you'll come."

"Thank you both. I know you mean it and it's the nicest thing anyone ever said to me. I'll come, I promise."

"But a room . . . in Tucson!" Ellen sighed. "Tucson is no place for a lady, and the expense . . ."

"Miss Bolton knows a place. A woman named Herscholdt has a bakery and rooms to let upstairs. Miss Bolton says they are respectable and not too dear. Anyway, Tom sent me some money and that will tide me over until I receive my pay."

"He . . . he sent you money?" Ellen gasped.

"Yes. A hundred dollars. I hope Carp will put it in a bank for me and tell me how to manage it. I never had a bank account before."

Ellen sniffed angrily. "Is that all he sent? What is he going—" She stopped abruptly, silenced by Samantha's look. "Oh, Sam, forgive me! I don't mean to pry, it's just that I'm so distressed!"

"You aren't prying, Ellen, and there's nothing to forgive," Samantha told her gently. "I'll tell you what he said."

"No! No, you mustn't do that! I don't know what's come over me!"

Carp got to his feet and began picking up pieces of china. "I think this is enough for tonight," he said gruffly. "Let's go to bed now and tomorrow we can work out the details."

There was not much to work out, though, he thought.

277

It seemed to him that Samantha had already done that quite thoroughly.

THIRTY-TWO

From Camp Grant to the Sulphur Spring stage station was just under forty miles, and Tom Royal covered the distance in eight hours in an open spring wagon—one soldier driving and another in back, carbine on his knees. The driver made a few attempts at conversation with his officer passenger but soon gave it up.

The new agent at Sulphur Spring was a nervous man, plainly glad to see their blue uniforms. His apprehension was contagious and Tom found himself glancing up at the Dragoon Mountains rising gray and purple behind the station in the slanting rays of afternoon sun.

"You had more Indian trouble?" he asked.

"Naw, thank Gawd! Folks says there ain't none of 'em left up there but I wisht I wuz shore o' that. I'm powerful glad t' have you fellers fer comp'ny. Ol' Jesus there, he ain't right much comfort t' me." It wasn't a private form of blasphemy but only a reference to the Mexican cook peering from the station door.

"How long before the stage gets in?"

The agent looked westward. "Oughtta see it directly. You aimin' t' ketch it here?" Tom nodded.

"Pshaw! I wuz hopin' y'all ud stay th' night. This here is one helluva lonesome place. All them dang mountains an' don't nobuddy know fer shore whut's in 'em."

"They're all gone now," Tom told him grimly, but he

shook his head and jerked a thumb at the wooden crosses marking the graves of Rogers and Spence.

"You reckon they'll stay gone, young feller?"

The trooper in the back of the wagon chuckled and threw down Tom's bedroll. "Don't you worry, old-timer. They burn you out, we'll see the smoke. Give you a handsome funeral." The agent muttered something under his breath and both soldiers laughed. He was a little mollified when Tom told him the escort would stay overnight to make an early start back to Camp Grant next morning. A plume of dust blowing off the Dragoon Springs road marked the approach of the stage and the agent left them to ready a fresh team for it.

The driver fidgeted until the change was made. "Come on, Lootenant," he urged. "Git in. I'd as lief make it through the pass afore dark if I kin." Tom swung aboard and the two soldiers watched him solemnly. As the driver gathered his reins one of them spoke.

"Good luck, Lootenant. First beer you come to, drink one for us."

Ashamed of his glum silence, Tom reached down his hand to each in turn and grinned at them. "Thanks, I'll do that. Keep your hair on and stay away from the girls at Tres Alamos." His reference to the squalid shantytown near Camp Grant and its bedraggled "girls" brought an answering grin from both.

Despite the driver's hurry, dusk was falling by the time they reached Apache Pass and he took the approach at a rattling lope whenever the trail permitted. Inside the forbidding canyon it was dark and everyone breathed easier when the pinprick lights of Camp Bowie appeared beyond the crest.

"I'll stay with Mister Hulse if that's all right," Tom told the officer of the day at headquarters, but the latter shook his head.

"Tate's in the Sierra Bonita cutting telegraph poles, but you can stay in his room if you want."

Tom felt a surge of guilty relief. He had been bracing himself all day for the explanations Tate would demand. He went to bed early and before he walked to the stage station next morning penned his classmate a brief note, remarkable only for how little it said.

The air was cleaner and cooler here in the mountains and the quail whistled nervously at the stage as it rattled out of Camp Bowie. Two hours later they climbed into New Mexico up the slopes of the Peloncillo Mountains, Stein's Peak looming on their left. Departing Arizona was no hurtful thing for Tom. In the past months he had perfected an ability to shut off that part of his mind that dealt with Samantha and he used it now. There would be ample opportunity to think of her in the interminable days of travel to come.

At Mesilla he changed to a Concord coach and turned north up the valley of the Rio Grande, passing Fort Selden—where the black troopers who had found Samantha were stationed—Fort McRae, and finally Fort Craig. He stayed a night there with Captain George Shorkley and his single company of the Fifteenth Infantry.

The doughboys guarded the road and helped police the Mescalero Apache reservation stretching east to Fort Stanton. It had been quiet for months but Shorkley was worried about the influx of White Mountain Apaches drifting away from San Carlos since Tahzay's Chiricahuas had been moved there. People said that Geronimo had been seen at the Fort Stanton Agency seventy miles away.

Tom's road led northward, through Albuquerque, Santa Fe and finally into Colorado and the towering slopes of the Rockies. Here he reached the existing fragment of William Palmer's grandiose dream of a railroad from Denver to Mexico City: a narrow-gauge track ending at Trinidad. Palmer had beaten the Atchison, Topeka and Santa Fe company in the race south but at Trinidad his money ran out.

It was a pleasure to abandon the stagecoach after twelve rolling, pitching days aboard it and to Tom's relief the ticket agent of the Denver and Rio Grande Railroad accepted his Army travel warrant without question.

"Why not?" he shrugged. "Quartermaster in Denver pays hard cash for 'em."

It would have been a different story on a land-grant

railway. The Congress thought the Army should ride free on all such lines and though the latter conceded they were obliged to haul troops on demand, they insisted on being paid for it. The courts ruled in favor of the railways but the Congress simply took refuge in an ancient legislative redoubt. They tacked onto the Army Appropriation Act of 1875 a proviso that none of the money could be paid to a land-grant road for Army travel. In consequence no land-grant line would honor an Army travel warrant and if a soldier wanted a seat he had to pay cash for it.

The train Tom took at Trinidad consisted of four small cars coupled to a ludicrous little engine. All its accessories were outsized by comparison with its small body: a towering bell-mouthed stack, an elongated cowcatcher and a brass head lamp as big as a steamer trunk. The sides of the cab were elegantly decorated with a scroll, a big number "13" and the name "Mosca" in flowery script.

Travel was more comfortable than in a stagecoach, but scarcely restful. In haste to beat its competitor from Kansas, the Denver and Rio Grande had wasted little time on its right-of-way. Cut and fill were shallow and the frequent gorges were spanned by trestles that made a man's blood run cold. They soared up from the brawling streams on clusters of spindly wooden legs that swayed freely when the little train hammered across.

Denver provided a comfortable night in a good hotel and then came Cheyenne in Wyoming, where Tom met the main line of the Union Pacific, which would take him east all the way to the Missouri River and Omaha. A bitter prairie wind drove him inside the station to await the eastbound train.

A wooden bench was drawn close to a glowing stove but it was completely occupied by a portly officer sprawled across it with his boots propped on the sandbox in which the stove sat. Tom saw he was a captain, with a shaggy buffalo coat thrown back from his shoulders, and he warmed his hands, admiring the coat. It seemed an admirable garment for this northern cold and he determined to find one for himself at the first opportunity.

The captain grunted and rearranged himself to free a

small space on the bench. He had to reach across to remove his cap, which bore the flaming shell of the Ordnance Corps, and Tom saw that his right arm was missing, the sleeve of his blouse tucked into its buttoned front. He inserted himself carefully into the proffered space.

His neighbor studied him for a long moment and then broke the silence.

"Long way from home, aren't you, Mister?" The question established the accuracy of his silent scrutiny. The worn, well-fitting uniform and tanned face of the lieutenant disposed of the possibility that he had just arrived from the East and the numbered crossed sabers on Tom's cap announced his regiment.

"Yes, sir. I'm on detached service with the Department of Dakota."

The older officer nodded. "How's the Sixth Horse making out these days?"

"Good enough, sir. Not much fight but we spend a lot of time looking for it."

"Adna Chaffee still with you?"

"No, sir, he left in September to be recruiting officer in Philadelphia."

"Good. He deserves a break. I'm glad to hear it."

Tom glanced at him curiously and the captain chuckled. "I served in the old Sixth until Gettysburg, son."

"Gettysburg? I didn't know . . ."

"Well, it was a few miles from there. We took on a couple of Jeb Stuart's brigades at a place called Fairfield."

"Ah," Tom smiled. "I've heard of that one. There's a man in my troop who was there."

"Lucky he isn't still there. The Rebs rode us down that day. Cost us half the regiment. Chaffee took a bullet and I got my transfer to Ordnance." He flicked the empty sleeve. "So you're going north to fight Sioux, eh?"

"I don't know yet. I suppose so."

"You're wearing the wrong color stripes for that war, Mister."

Tom shifted on the bench. He was not sure he understood the remark and the captain grinned affably.

"That's infantry country, my boy. The cavalry had its chance last summer and couldn't cut the mustard."

That was clear enough and Tom stiffened indignantly. His expression gained him a rumbling laugh and a nudge from the captain's knee.

"I can say it, son, because I was a trooper as long as I could swing a saber. You have to face it. The Sioux whipped the whole Third Cavalry and half the Second with one hand and stopped Custer's clock with the other. That's three of the best cavalry regiments in the Army down the sink in one summer's fight. Those Indians are the best goddam light cavalry in the world and they proved it on us."

The hoot of an approaching train forestalled Tom's heated response. Just as well, he told himself, gathering his baggage. Fairfield was the most disastrous fight in his regiment's history, and just because this old fogy was there didn't make him an authority on Indian-fighting. The sardonic grin and casual wave the captain gave him was salt in the wound.

He found a comfortable upholstered chair in a car that boasted a stove at each end and the conductor told him it would be twenty hours to Omaha, five hundred miles east. By noon they had covered a hundred of them and passed the sprawling boomtown of Sidney, Nebraska. There the track swung alongside the South Platte River and across it a belt of low, rolling hills offered occasional glimpses of limitless prairie beyond. The vista reminded Tom of the country around Fort Leavenworth in Kansas and inevitably of Samantha, whom he first met there.

He saw Leavenworth for the first time in the summer of 1874 when he and Tate Hulse passed through after their graduation leave on their way to join the Sixth Cavalry. The frontier had long since passed the old post on the Missouri River but it remained headquarters of a Department that stretched all the way to New Mexico.

In summer its garrison was gone, scattered along the railways and fighting Indians to the west, and the arrival of two brand-new lieutenants did not long escape notice by the young ladies of the post. The day after their arrival a soldier appeared bearing invitations to a tea dance at the quarters of Major Bell, Department commissary.

There were more young women than men at the Bells' comfortable old house that afternoon and the amount of attention paid to the young West Pointers was distracting. They outshone even a glamorous young Prussian cavalryman, Lieutenant Count von Alfhen, who was touring the American frontier. Several of the girls were quite pretty but the two lieutenants, fresh from the sophisticated East, found them unimpressive.

Yet both of them noticed and remembered a tall, quiet girl with amused eyes and a glint of red in her brown hair, perhaps because she did not join in the flirtatious competition for their attention. Tom was moved to seek her out but before he found her both he and Tate were swept away to a supper party assembled by the Misses Galbraith, daughters of the Department paymaster.

Next day, when they paid their thank-you call on the Bells, Tom inquired of Mrs. Bell about her.

"Oh," replied his hostess, "you must mean Sam Allyn." She made a vague gesture. "Poor Samantha. Her father was killed in Oregon ages ago . . . George?" she called to her husband, who was filling his pipe at the mantel. "George, when was Rosy Allyn killed?"

"Rozier Allyn . . ." Major Bell mused. "Yes. It was 1867. Battle of the Infernal Caverns. One of George Crook's more spectacular disasters."

"George!" gasped his wife. The two lieutenants were shocked and fascinated. At West Point, General George Crook was quasi-sacred and this was the first disparaging remark about him they had ever heard.

"My dear," George Bell continued affably, "Cump Sherman may think the world and all of Crook but I think he's a fraud. Pack mules, by God! Wagons aren't good enough for him; he's got to have a legion of pack mules before he'll stir a foot."

"George, that's quite enough! You'll embarrass these boys talking like that about a Department commander and a famous soldier."

"Famous soldier my sainted Aunt Fanny!" muttered the

major. "Famous for what?" His wife hurried into the ensuing silence.

"When Rosy was killed, his wife Melissa came back here with young Samantha, who was only ten or eleven then. Poor Lissa passed away not long after and her sister came on from Pennsylvania to look after Sam."

"Thisbe Ehler," put in Bell. "Can't forget a name like that."

"Thank you, George," said his wife tartly. "Miss Thisbe and Samantha live in the town and do fairly well. Thisbe's the best dressmaker in Leavenworth and the Lord knows that girl is a worker but, you know, she probably feels just a bit out of things on the post. She's a sweet, well-mannered young thing but I think she's very shy."

George Bell, obviously a defender of Rosy Allyn's daughter, snorted scornfully.

"There you go, Georgia, running that girl down again! The reason she doesn't hunt with the rest of the pack, Mister Royal, is because she works for her living. She teaches music at the Post School and she helps her aunt with the dressmaking. I suspect that's precisely why all the idle flibbertigibbets on this post look down their noses at her."

"Now, George! No one's running Sam Allyn down. She's a splendid young woman."

"And a damned pretty one, too!" rumbled the major, pointing his pipe at his wife. "You know as well as I do, Georgia Bell, that's another reason the elegant young ladies of this post would just as soon not have her around when there's game afoot."

Mrs. Bell looked at her callers and blushed furiously. She changed the subject with a wrench, demanding of Tate if he had read Blackmore's latest book, *Lorna Doone.*

Tate tried to look knowing and talk his way out but he only fell deeper into the trap. He had devoted no part of his graduation leave to reading novels, and he had never heard of anyone named Blackmore. Tom saved him from complete disaster by rising to explain they had another engagement and must take their leave. Gratefully Tate followed him into the hall, where they recovered their gloves and shiny new dress helmets, each covertly admiring his own newly engraved calling card as he slid it into the tray on the hall table.

"Well," Tate chuckled as they walked under the arching elms to the Galbraiths' for supper. "Now we know who she is. All we have to do is find her."

Tom's excursion into the past was interrupted by the conductor, who announced to the car at large they were at McPherson Station and a meal could be had in the sod-roofed shanty beside it.

He used the word loosely. On a plank table were bread, pickles, some rock-hard cheese and thick slices of bologna, dark and very antique-looking. Tom settled for bread and cheese and a couple of hard-boiled eggs he wheedled from the cook, washing them down with coffee whose only virtue was that it was hot.

Back in the car the monotonous clacking of the wheels as they jumped the track joints made him sleepy, but as he dozed off they seemed to chant dolefully, "You'll never come back . . . you'll never come back . . . BACK!"

THIRTY-THREE

It was five o'clock on a bitterly cold November morning when the train reached Omaha. Tom Royal found the platform deserted but inside the depot a trio of soldiers hugged the potbellied stove. They eyed the rumpled, unshaven cavalry officer incuriously. One wore sergeant's stripes, and when Tom's eye singled him out he stood at attention and in the harsh, stilted monotone of an old soldier being formal with a strange officer, announced his business:

"Mail-detail-Twenty-third-Infantry-waitin'-fer-th'-mail-car-t'-unload-Sarn't-Thomas-in-charge-SIR!"

"At ease, Sergeant," Tom told him. "I'm looking for Department headquarters; can you tell me how to find Omaha Barracks?"

"Nuthin' at th' barricks, sir, save one comp'ny o' th' Twenty-third. Departmint's in town. Does th' lootenant want I sh'ld show him whur it is?"

"Yes. I want to find out if I can still get upriver by steamer."

"I kin tell th' lootenant th' answer to that, sir. Not a chance. Ginral Crook come downriver in th' *Benton* two days gone an' it tuk thirteen days frum Fort Stevenson. Watter's fallin' an' there's ice clear down t' Bismarck. I reckon th' *Benton*'s th' last boat on th' Missouri this year, sir."

Tom sighed. "I was afraid of that. Guess I'll have to stick to the cars. How about breakfast? Any place open around here at this hour, Sergeant?"

"Sir, th' lootenant c'ld prob'ly git a bite 'crost th' street to th' River House."

Tom rubbed his stubbled jaw. "Shave too?"

"Hour maybe, sir. Doubt th' barber's there yit."

"All right. I'll see what I can do. Will my baggage be safe here?"

"We'll be here till th' train leaves fer Yankton, sir. Couple hours yet. I'll keep an eye on it personal fer th' lootenant."

The sleepy clerk in the River House Hotel proved helpful after Tom gave him twenty-five cents. He opened a washroom, found a towel and even produced a can of hot water. Tom was more grateful when he roused a cook who gave him fried eggs, ham and fresh biscuits in the deserted dining room. By the time he finished his breakfast the barber had opened the hotel shop.

"Horse-soljer, eh?" he commented, eyeing Tom's trouser stripes. "Seventh Cav'ry?"

"Nope. Just passing through. How about a shave?"

"Best in town." Settling Tom in a chair with a towel about his neck, he stropped his razor and studied his customer.

"I hear tell Ginral Crook's back in town. You come with him?"

Tom shook his head. "I just got here from the other direction. On my way north."

The barber clucked. "That's too bad. Pity ye ain't goin' east. 'Nother year like this one an' there ain't gonna be none o' you young'uns left aroun' these parts. Ol' Phil Sheridan, he sets up there in St. Paul givin' out grand stories to th' newspapers but ye know what's really happenin'?"

"Umph?" said Tom through the lather, which was enough; the barber hardly paused.

"We're up to our ass in Injuns, that's what! Crook he got hisself whupped, Terry an' Gibbon played fiddle-denaught all summer an' Custer he paid the bill. Fer my money he was the onliest one of 'em worth a damn. All them others was hell on rebels durin' the war but they're played out now. Too damn old to be fightin' Injuns is what I think."

He paused to eye Tom expectantly but when there was no response he sighed. "What kin ye expect? Them crooks in Washington is so busy stealin' from each other they ain't got time to worry about Injuns." He waved the razor angrily and Tom winced.

"You watch 'em! Sam Tilden got elected fair an' square an' by gollies them crooks is gonna diddle him outta it. Country's goin' to th' dogs when we can't even 'lect a President any more." He toweled off the remaining lather but when Tom moved he pushed him back.

"Hold still, boy, till I put th' bay rum to ye. Town's full o' good-lookin' wimmin these days. Never kin tell what ye might run into." He bent to ask confidentially, "Ye stayin' th' night?"

Tom laughed in spite of his impatience. "No. I'm catching a train north this morning. Thanks anyway."

From Omaha he went up the Missouri to Sioux City

and then eastward to St. Paul. The trip took thirty hours, though over the last eighty miles the conductor boasted they were making forty miles an hour. He was immensely proud of this though it seemed to Tom that the leaping, jolting cars might leave the track at any moment.

In St. Paul he found that General George Terry, like Crook in Omaha, preferred to run his Department from the town itself rather than from the local Army post, Fort Snelling. The latter was one of the oldest on the frontier and resembled a medieval European fort. Perched on a bluff commanding the junction of the Mississippi and Minnesota rivers, it was surrounded by walls with a stone tower at each corner of its diamond shape. Neither its history nor its appearance endeared it to Terry and he set up a modest headquarters of twelve officers and a like number of soldiers in St. Paul to run the exploding Military Department of Dakota, which in November of 1876 controlled almost one fourth of all the combat troops of the Army.

Major Ruggles, adjutant general of the Department, pulled at his luxuriant mustache and grunted when Tom asked for duty with the Seventh Cavalry.

"Not a chance, Mister. War Department has filled it up again and that isn't what we need you people for anyway."

"Well, where do I go from here, sir? My orders say report to you for instructions."

Ruggles eyed him speculatively. "You looking for a staff job?"

"No, sir. Not if I have a choice."

"Good! If you want to smell powder you don't want the Seventh anyway. They're not likely to get out of garrison again this winter. If there's going to be a fight it'll be on the Yellowstone." He stirred the papers on his desk and extracted one.

"Listen to this! This is Sitting Bull's last message to Colonel Otis at Glendive Creek a month ago: 'I want to know what you are doing traveling on this road. You scare all the buffalo away. I want you to turn back from here. If you don't I will fight you again. I want you to

289

leave what you have got here and turn back. I mean all the rations you have got and some powder. I am your friend, Sitting Bull.' "

He dropped the paper and snorted. "Our very good friend, Sitting Bull. Miles has got in between him and the rest of the Sioux with Crazy Horse and if you want action, that's where it's going to be."

"How can I get to Colonel Miles, sir?"

"General Miles, my boy, and don't forget it! The War Department may have busted him back to colonel but he had two stars when the war ended and he hasn't forgotten it. How much do you know about the fighting up here?"

"Not much, Major."

Ruggles turned in his chair to look at the map that covered the wall behind him. "Military Division of the Missouri . . ." His hand swept the breadth of the map. "Mississippi River to the Rockies. Five Departments: Dakota, Platte, Missouri, Texas and the Gulf. Lieutenant General Phil Sheridan commands from Chicago. You came upriver from Omaha?"

"Yes, sir."

"That's the Department of the Platte. Brigadier General George Crook commands from Omaha. Takes in Iowa, Nebraska, Wyoming, Utah and a piece of Idaho. Crook tangled twice last summer with Crazy Horse and . . . ah . . . had a pretty rough time of it." He rose to spread his hand over the junction of the Missouri and Yellowstone rivers.

"Department of Dakota: Minnesota, Dakota and Montana. General George Terry commands from wherever he happens to be." He slapped the map. "The action is here . . . in Montana Territory. Terry pushed out there last summer and we were supposed to operate with Crook. We never made it. The Sioux stopped Crook cold and they caught Custer split from hell to breakfast and you know what happened to him. Fall caught us, and when the Yellowstone fell so low the steamboats couldn't supply us any more everybody hutted up for the winter."

His finger dropped to the junction of the Tongue River and the Yellowstone. "Miles is here with his whole regiment. But I don't think he's going to wait for spring. I think that just as soon as he knows where Crazy Horse has made his winter camp he's going after him. His base is up there at Fort Buford at the mouth of the Yellowstone, and there's a depot halfway between at Glendive Creek. Colonel Hazen is still pushing supplies up the Yellowstone to him by wagon from Buford. He needs officers to command the wagon trains."

Ruggles returned to his desk and sought out Tom's orders. "Captain Sterrett of the Twenty-second Infantry is at Fort Lincoln now with a detachment of recruits for the battalion at Glendive. He'll leave within the week. I'm going to send you with him to Fort Buford. There's always a chance Hazen will use you with the screen along the upper Missouri, but my guess is he'll send you with a wagon train to Miles. I'll suggest that to him." He grinned at Tom, "You ever done much walking, Mister? Infantry officers walk to work up here and there's nothing but infantry on the Yellowstone."

"I can learn, Major."

"Good lad! Frankly, Mister Royal, horse-soldiers aren't much good up here in winter. Too damned delicate. How're you fixed for winter gear?"

His blood thinned by two years in Arizona, Tom needed winter clothing imperatively. He had nothing to protect him against the sub-zero Montana winter.

"I need everything, sir. I hoped to get it here."

"You can. At the depot at Fort Snelling, but have the quartermaster endorse your orders for the equipment before you leave here."

Tom found the quartermaster warehouse at Fort Snelling and gave his orders to a civilian clerk. "You know what I need better than I do," he told him.

The clerk nodded and began piling clothes on the counter. First was a heavy buffalo skin coat, shaggy and malodorous. With it came a sealskin cap with dangling earflaps and fur-lined mittens with long cuffs. The pile grew: woolen underwear, socks, extra-heavy woolen shirts and a pair of clumsy rubberized canvas boots with metal latches instead of laces.

"Snow-excluders," the clerk said defensively.

"I'm a cavalryman but I know better than to walk in those things," Tom said. "You keep 'em."

The clerk sighed. The Quartermaster of the Army was enthusiastic about the new snow-excluders but only the rawest recruit would have them. They reminded Tom, however, that his cavalry boots would be none too satisfactory for a long hike.

"How about a pair of brogans? You got any of them?"

The civilian nodded; horse-soldier or not, the young officer showed sense. "Yup. Might even find you a pair of the old ones if you're lucky."

"What's the matter with the new ones?"

The clerk gestured scornfully at the discarded galoshes. "More of the same! Lootenant, you wouldn't believe what them people in Philadelphia can dream up. Them new brogans got the soles put on with brass screws."

"Sounds like a good idea to me. Keeps 'em from rotting out when they get wet, doesn't it?"

"Oh, sure! The soles stay on fine but them screws come right through. Two days' march an' you're screwed into them brogans for good!"

Tom got his old-issue shoes, but when they topped the pile he eyed it doubtfully. "How'm I going to carry all that?"

"Them folks back East took care o' that too." He produced a canvas bag a foot in diameter but at least a yard long and began stuffing the clothing into it. "Call it a grain bag. God knows what kinda horse they had in mind when they made it, but it's grand fer any amount o' other things." Each item that went into the bag was noted carefully on an inventory and when the bag was full, Tom had to sign it.

"What happens if I don't come back through St. Paul?"

"We'll find you. We never forget, Lootenant. You wouldn't b'lieve what the Army pays fer some o' that stuff so if anythin' happens to it make sure you save the scraps."

Tom found lodging that night in a boardinghouse that seemed to hold only military transients and some bachelors of the departmental staff. The supper table looked like an Officers' Mess.

"Lieutenant Royal, Sixth Cavalry, sir," he introduced himself to a balding captain who seemed to be the senior officer there.

"Well, glad to meet you, Royal. Is the Sixth joining us?"

"No, sir. I'm on temporary duty at Fort Buford."

The captain whistled through his teeth. "Good luck, Mister!"

The food was plentiful and good, brought to the table by a buxom blond girl with sparkling blue eyes. When she had put down the serving dishes she seated herself amid some scuffling and sprightly banter between two lieutenants who jostled each other for a place next to her. Tom guessed she was daughter of the landlady, a tired-looking woman with faded hair that had once been the same hue as the girl's. She came to the table also from the kitchen where she had apparently cooked the meal herself.

After supper the officers gathered about a tiled stove in the sitting room and someone asked, "Where's the port?" There was a burst of laughter when a bottle of whiskey was produced.

"Liddy!" they called. "Oh, Liddy, bring some glasses, please." The blond girl clucked disapprovingly.

"You know Mama don't like you to drink whiskey in here."

"Liddy, that's not whiskey; that's port. All the nabobs back East drink port wine after dinner."

The girl giggled and disappeared, returning shortly with a tray of glasses. The men gathered around, each pouring for himself from the bottle.

"That's port?" Liddy asked innocently. There was a chorus of assent.

"Of course! Here . . . taste it." Liddy sipped and made a wry face.

"Have a drink, Royal?" a young officer asked. Bottle in one hand he extended the other in greeting. "I'm

293

O'Brien, First Infantry. Heard you tell the captain . . . Oh! Something wrong?"

Tom's hand had jerked violently, spilling whiskey from the glass in it. "No. Just clumsy. Did I get it on you?"

"No harm," O'Brien grinned. "Try again; you lost most of that one."

He refilled Tom's glass but then he drifted away and in a minute he had his arm around Liddy's waist, coaxing her to take another sip from his glass. She fended him off, laughing.

"Liddy!" came a voice from the kitchen.

"Coming, Mama!" She slipped from O'Brien's arm and shook her finger at him archly. "No singing tonight, Mister O'Brien! We can't have the neighbors complaining again."

"You sing with us, Liddy," he urged. "We'll sing hymns and they can't complain." He squeezed her waist and Liddy squealed.

"Liddy! You come out here right now!" called her mother.

Liddy departed with a flirtatious whirl of her skirt and the men settled around the stove, laughing and talking. Tom stared at O'Brien.

He was a short, wiry man with a merry face, clean-shaven except for luxuriant black sideburns. They addressed him as "Harp" and when Tom queried his neighbor the latter explained, laughing.

"The Happy Harp! What else could you call that crazy mick?"

The name was apt. The laughing mouth and eyes radiated Irish charm and deviltry and occasionally something more—something bold and hard and confident. These details struck Tom in a series of small shocks that had nothing to do with the man he was watching.

Until the day of the court-martial at Camp Lowell, the name O'Brien had meant nothing more to him than the source of a border legend. Then suddenly, the legend took form. In the weeks since, he had conceded that Samantha might have been so terrorized and misused in captivity she could turn even to a half-breed bandit if he offered help. But in his minds' eye that bandit was a repulsive man whose only attraction was the help he offered.

The handsome, laughing young Irishman across the room shattered that image. What if the O'Brien of the deserter's story was a man like this? There was no reason why he couldn't be, and such a man would require no reinforcement of terror to win a lonely girl's heart. He had scorned and hated the unknown O'Brien, but it had not occurred to him before to be jealous of him. He was having trouble rearranging his emotions.

"Royal!" his neighbor twitched his sleeve. Boots scraped as the younger officers got to their feet.

"Good night, gentlemen," said the captain, gathering his coat and cap. "Try not to make too much noise tonight." There was a murmured chorus of assurance but the door had scarcely closed behind him when someone sang softly:

> "Oh, my name is Samuel Hall,
> Samuel Hall . . ."

O'Brien preempted him in a clear tenor:

> "My name is Samuel Hall,
> and I hate you one and all!"

He gestured and the others joined lustily in the chorus:

> "For you're a gang of muckers all!
> Damn your eyes!"

"Come on!" he called, "let's have another. Royal, join the choir, man! Can ye sing?"

"I'm beat," Tom replied. "I've been on the cars so long my teeth are rattling and I've got to take 'em again tomorrow."

"Have a drink. That'll stop the rattle."

"No thanks, I'm for bed."

"Bigod an' that's a strange 'un, ain't he?" asked O'Brien when Tom had gone.

"Horse-soldier. They're all odd. What's he doing here anyway?"

"Comes from down on the Mex border somewhere. Heard he's tryin' to get into the Seventh Cavalry."

"That proves he's crazy! Have you seen that outfit since the Boy General took it to hell? Man, you wouldn't believe the trash they scraped up to fill it again."

"Ah, they're not for this war anyway. Crook an' Miles know how to fight an' it ain't with horse-soldiers. Too damn elegant for my money. Ridin' out to fight Injuns with a brass band up front!" He sang mockingly:

> "Instead o' spa we'll drink down ale,
> an' pay th' reck'ning on the nail;
> No man fer debt shall go to jail,
> from Garryowen's in glo-ho-ry!"

Their laughter came faintly to Tom in the upstairs hall and a soft voice behind him asked, "Aren't they awful?"

It was Liddy, arms piled high with linen, blue eyes twinkling. "I was hopin' to catch you when you came up, Mister Royal. I'm glad you didn't stay with them."

"Oh? Is anything wrong?"

"Oh, no! I just wanted to ask you about your room. Mama said you was to go in with Mister Burchart but I guess she forgot about the room upstairs. You could have that if you'd rather be to yourself. It won't be needed till next week."

"I'll be gone tomorrow but I'd like a room to myself tonight if it's no trouble."

Liddy pouted prettily. "No trouble at all but I'm sorry you're goin' so quick."

He glanced at her in surprise and she gave him a dimpled smile. "Why do you say that, Liddy?"

"Ah, you know!" She tipped her blond head toward the stairs. "They're just a bunch o' roughs. It's nice to have a real gent in the house."

"Why, thank you, Liddy. That's kind of you."

She dimpled for him again. "Come on, I'll show you the room. I brought sheets for you."

"All right. I'll just get my bag and I'll be right with you."

But Liddy waited for him. The stairway to the third floor was dark and narrow but not too dark to prevent his noticing the display of sturdy ankles in sheer black lisle stockings as she skipped ahead of him.

"My!" she panted, "those steps'll be the death of me yet."

Tom peered down the short hall doubtfully. "How many rooms are up here, Liddy?"

"Just two," she told him over her shoulder. "Mine an' the one you're to have."

He digested that information a little slowly—too slowly for Liddy, who threw him an arch look.

She opened a door, juggled her linen, and struck a match with which she made ineffectual one-handed passes at a coal-oil lamp on a wall bracket. The flaring match revealed that the room offered little beyond privacy. The ceiling sloped to the floor on one side, pierced by a narrow dormer window, and there was a bed, a washstand and nothing more. The match burned Liddy's fingers and she dropped it with a squeal.

"Oooh!" she said breathlessly. But Tom was still slow. He found a match of his own and struck it on his boot-heel, pushed up the lamp chimney and got the wick alight with difficulty. It smoked, obviously long untrimmed, and it occurred to him that the room was not so much used as Liddy had implied. She began to spread sheets on the bed with a good deal of flouncing and stretching.

Tom moved to help and the musty odor of the straw tick confirmed his suspicion of its disuse but Liddy's perfume was distracting. The more energetically she worked the more distracting it became. He worked his way around the bed, tucking in the sheet until he bumped into Liddy, who had reversed her direction. She straightened up, her pink mouth round and questioning. He pulled her to him and she came eagerly, lips parted and moving beneath his.

"Your mother?" he murmured when they came up for air.

"Downstairs. All the way. She sleeps by the kitchen so's nobody can snitch. Don't worry!"

And for the first time in his life he didn't. His fingers worked clumsily at the endless row of buttons down Liddy's back and when he hit bottom she came out of his arms and the dress in a single deft movement, shoulders gleaming in the lamplight. He could have sworn she was corseted at supper but she certainly wasn't now.

The idea that Liddy had been planning this ever since supper should have annoyed him but it didn't. She leaned across his arm, boneless and heavy, only her hips moving a little. But he was still too slow.

"Come on!" she urged breathlessly.

There were still a lot of clothes and she clung so tight he could not get at them. He worked the chemise straps off her shoulders and she freed her arms with the same deft twist as before. The petticoat joined the chemise and dress around her ankles and he cupped her breasts, nipples hard against his palms. Liddy moaned.

It became a real contest then, he trying to pry her loose long enough to find the secret of the ruffled, knee-length drawers and she frustrating him by sheer adhesiveness. He wasted time on some decorative buttons at the side until in exasperation she guided his hands to the drawstring in back. There was more but not much. He wanted to admire the sheen of her pretty legs in the sheer black stockings but she objected violently.

"Mister Royal . . . please! The lamp. What do you think I am?"

He burned his fingers on the lamp chimney and Liddy escaped. Pulling off his clothes with fumbling hands in the dark he heard the bed cords squeak as her weight descended upon them.

Their lovemaking was wild and infinitely exciting for Tom. Liddy was his first woman and she discovered it to her delight. She managed his initiation with skill and generosity, giving him no time to wonder how he found himself in bed with this pretty, moaning girl. Liddy made up for his clumsiness. She led him without pause to the brink of unknown delight, suspended him there for a few splendid moments with her mobile body, then plunged him into a torrent of sensation that brooked neither thought nor question. Her low, shuddering cry of triumph enthralled him.

Sometime before dawn she slipped away, for when he woke there was nothing left of her exciting body except a hint of perfume on the chilly air. He pushed his face into the pillow trying to capture more of it but there was only a musty odor there.

Shivering, he pulled on his clothes and wondered whom he would find in the kitchen if he went looking for hot water to shave with. After a moment's reflection he was mildly surprised, and then pleased, to find this a reflex concern of no moment at all. He grinned and started for the kitchen, pocketing a hairpin he found beside the bed, not for sentiment but for caution.

THIRTY-FOUR

By mid-1876 the Northern Pacific Railroad reached west from Duluth on Lake Superior to the Missouri River in Dakota. It ended there at Bismarck on the east bank, and for a while that little town was the railhead for the whole northwestern frontier. As long as the Missouri was navigable the Army shipped supplies to its Dakota posts upriver from St. Louis because that was the cheapest way, but when the river fell too low for steamers they went by rail to Bismarck and beyond by wagon. When snow stopped the wagons, troops on the upper Missouri simply lived on whatever they had with them.

The St. Paul and Pacific railway had started west toward Bismarck, but on the November morning when Tom Royal paid his landlady for the most memorable night's lodging in his life and took his leave, the only way to get there by rail was still through Duluth and that was how he went. Directly across the Missouri from Bismarck was Fort Lincoln, where the Seventh Cavalry was recovering from July's debacle and Captain Sterrett readied his recruits for their cold march north.

All river traffic stopped, Bismarck and Fort Lincoln were both convulsed by the quartermaster's efforts to push a last wagon train north to Fort Buford. That post was supposed to be supplying Miles and his regiment, but from the tone of Miles' messages there were not enough supplies and ammunition west of the Mississippi to satisfy him. Amid this uproar, Tom found and reported to Captain Sterrett, who viewed this late addition to his detachment philosophically.

Alonzo Sterrett was an old soldier who had spent his entire military life on the frontier. Not even the Rebellion had been enough to demand his transfer East and with that lost opportunity went his last hope for promotion. Most men would have been embittered but not Al Sterrett. He comforted his bleak existence with a little whiskey, but he could hardly be blamed for that.

In fact, two days out of Fort Lincoln it dawned on Tom that by nightfall each day Captain Sterrett was on the outside of most of a quart of bourbon. It appeared to have no effect whatsoever on his competence; he was as capable at dusk as at dawn and the only change in his appearance was a slightly increased ruddiness of countenance.

The next post upriver was Fort Stevenson—eighty-five rutted and frozen road-miles, of which the wagons covered twelve a day. Sterrett's recruits joined the flank guards during the day and took their turn on night outpost and Tom fitted himself into this routine as if he were one of Sterrett's own company officers.

It was apparent that in this frozen wasteland a strong

train would have no trouble with hostile Indians. Keeping pace with the lumbering, sliding wagons was wearisome but hardly demanded close attention, and Tom's slow march up the Missouri produced a growing discontent with himself—the product of unlimited time to think.

He was not a young man ordinarily troubled by decisions. Early in life he had worked out and tested a decision-making process that proved very satisfactory and bred no agonizing postmortems. He prided himself on the thoroughness and precision with which he approached a decision and the promptness with which he carried it out.

When Samantha inexplicably refused to tell him what had happened to her in the Apache *ranchería* she forced him to react. He felt he ought to know, and he felt she— not the deserter or Severiano—ought to tell him. She had to make the decision herself and at the time it seemed best to him simply to leave her alone for a while. Either she would realize he was right or she would call it quits and go home. It was a neat, logical decision except for one thing: he was in love with the girl and that illogical emotion had wrecked better systems than his.

He had been in love with Samantha from the day he met her and his love had grown in every way he understood. It had survived and been strengthened by her captivity; he admired her courage and competence; he wanted to comfort and protect her; he looked forward eagerly to living with her as his wife. In addition to all that he desired her earnestly in the simplest and most direct fashion. No one would call Samantha Allyn either sensual or provocative but she roused in Tom Royal a healthy if inexperienced lust. That he could see its satisfaction only within certain established formalities of his time and place was natural for him, though that imposed a number of obligations on both of them.

When he left Arizona he had been quite ready to accept either decision by Samantha, but the more he thought about that the more appalled he was by the possibility she might quit and go East. If he loved her so much did it matter what happened in the Huachuca Mountains? He was very close to the conclusion that it mattered not at all to him, but he was still troubled by what others would think and say. He might get over that, too, but it required shifting a lot of mental furniture that had been in place for years.

In the meanwhile what would his girl do? He had assumed she would stay with the Van Scivers until she made up her mind, but why he had thought this would take a good deal of time now baffled him. He had made wrong decisions before and learned from them, but if this was a wrong one he was daily less willing to accept the consequences. He sensed he was taking too much time but he needed more.

So he asked for it. He covered three pages of his pocket notebook with a plea to Samantha to give it to him and the measure of his growing uncertainty was the bitter taste that plea left him. Still, it was the best he could do and when he reached Fort Stevenson he begged an envelope and gave the letter to the garrison mail clerk with a silent prayer that it would find Samantha before she acted.

Improving with practice, the convoy covered the next hundred and fifty miles to Fort Buford in ten days. Built to house the better part of an infantry regiment it had become the main base for military operations in the Yellowstone Valley and it had grown rapidly. In 1876 there were even a few Army wives in residence.

It was commanded by Colonel Hazen of the Sixth Infantry, like Miles a wartime general. With his six companies of doughboys he had a twofold job: to support Miles on the Yellowstone and to guard the banks of the Missouri west to Fort Peck. Every time Miles struck the Sioux in the south some of them broke for the Canadian border and Hazen was supposed to turn them back. Each train guard he sent to Miles reduced his ability to do the latter and he welcomed detached service officers like Tom for the convoy duty, preferring naturally to keep his own for the border mission.

The trail south from Buford to the intermediate depot at Glendive Creek followed the bank of the Yellowstone across the countless streams emptying into it. It had never amounted to much and after a hard summer's use it was heartbreaking. Hazen decided it could bear no more wagons, but since Colonel Otis at Glendive was still trying to move supplies forward to Miles he directed Tom to accompany Sterrett to Glendive and make himself useful there.

The phlegmatic captain had no objections. He had been impressed and intrigued by the young cavalryman during the trip upriver. He knew the itch that sent lieutenants looking for action but he sensed something more in Tom Royal and it puzzled him. The youngster had taken to footslogging without a murmur and his competence with the recruits earned Sterrett's respect and affection. The evening of their arrival at Buford brought an invitation to Sterrett from old friends to come to supper and it was expanded without question to include Tom.

The meal was delicious and their hostess obviously delighted to have company. Because it was cut off from re-supply for part of each year, Fort Buford enjoyed some niceties unknown in Arizona and one of these was a double allowance of molasses. At the Halperns' quarters this resulted in a dessert of superb gingerbread and when the meal was over the guests paid it a moment of silent tribute. Tom broke this with a conventional query.

"Don't you find Fort Buford a lonely place, ma'am?"

"Oh, yes, but it's such a notorious place I was thrilled when I learned I would come here. You remember, Alonzo, that dreadful story about Fort Buford that appeared in all the Eastern newspapers in sixty-seven?"

Sterrett, who had been eyeing the sideboard longingly, turned his attention to her. "That was a complete hoax, Martha."

"I know, but we didn't then. Oh, it was frightful! They said the entire garrison had been massacred, the soldiers murdered and scalped, the lieutenants carved and eaten, Captain Raynor burned alive at the stake and his poor young wife . . ." She broke off, laughing.

Tom couldn't help it if Sterrett was longing for his after-dinner drink, he had to ask.

"What happened to his wife?"

"It was all a fraud, Mister Royal, but it was terribly exciting then. They said the Indians stripped her and bound her on the back of a wild stallion that dashed away with her into the forest. I remember when my mother learned I was coming here she became hysterical."

Sterrett sighed. "Martha, I knew it was a hoax as soon as I heard it."

"How could you?"

He fixed her with a twinkling eye. "My dear, did you ever meet Emmaline Raynor?" Martha shook her head.

"Stunning creature! Magnificent figure of a woman!" He leaned back, apparently recalling with pleasure the image of the beautiful Emmaline. His host looked worried.

"But I still don't see . . ."

Sterrett raised his hand as if taking an oath. "Martha, not even an Onkpapa Sioux would be damfool enough to tie Emma Raynor on a horse once he'd got her clothes off, much less let it run off with her. If he had there'd have been no more trouble in these parts. Every Injun in Dakota would have followed her out of the Territory."

"Alonzo!" giggled Martha, "shame on you!" Her husband scraped back his chair noisily.

"Martha, if you'll excuse us we'll just have a seegar and join you shortly."

She nodded, still laughing. "If you won't be too long. I vow I can't miss any of Alonzo's stories."

There was a cigar and a drink and a few more stories and Martha Halpern pounded on the door, demanding they come out. They gathered about the fire in the sitting room and to Tom's astonishment she expertly rolled herself a cigarette in a brown Mexican wrapper, holding it up to him for a light. He had no matches so he brought a blazing splinter from the hearth and she guarded her graying hair from the flame with her hands as he lit her cigarette.

It was a happy evening. Halpern and Sterrett told stories of life on the frontier and Martha Halpern joined in. Tom had little to contribute but he drank in every minute of it. Their shared experiences and funny anecdotes framed the rosy image of Army life in which he saw Samantha and himself and he longed to join it.

The march up the Yellowstone was rough, but unburdened with wagons Sterrett's detachment moved at a good pace. They encountered no hostile Indians and midway they met two companies of the Seventeenth Infantry on their way out for the winter, released by Otis at Glendive as the supplies stored there dwindled.

General Sheridan had not ordered the establishment of Miles' post at the junction of the Yellowstone and the Tongue until late August and when he did, Miles threw a couple of companies into the position and reinforced them as fast as he could. He had a monumental job, even though he enjoyed a great rarity in the frontier Army: a whole regiment in one place under its own commander. His Fifth Infantry was supposed to build a camp, receive and shelter winter supplies and simultaneously comb the Yellowstone Valley for hostile Sioux. It was just barely possible so long as men and supplies could move on the river by steamer.

But in September, the head of navigation withdrew north at an alarming rate. Supplies were off-loaded wherever a steamer stranded and Miles had to guard them and cut roads to collect them. Much was gathered at a temporary camp where Glendive Creek emptied into the Yellowstone and subsequently more was hauled there over the awful trail from Buford. Lieutenant Colonel Otis, with four companies of the Twenty-second and two of the Seventeenth Infantry, hutted up at Glendive and through the fall doggedly fought one convoy after another south to Miles against hostile Indians and worsening weather.

Since the purpose of the garrison at Glendive was to get rid of all its accidental stores they spent little time on housing. Then winter closed in on them and they made practical if unsightly shelters. Barracks and storehouses were constructed of logs driven end on into the ground and roofed with poles and earth. Stoves were nonexistent so they substituted stick and mud chimneys. When a hut was heated enough to be habitable, the dirt floor became

305

a morass and the inhabitants added layer after layer of saplings, brush or straw just to stay on top of the mud.

The last brush with hostiles along the Yellowstone occurred about a month before Sterrett and Tom reached Glendive, but the garrison had not relaxed. As long as Miles was active there were Indians moving north—hungry Indians. They would attack anything weaker than they if it had food for the taking. Miles' scouts reported Crazy Horse and the Oglala Sioux wintering on the upper Tongue River and he itched to get at them. He was convinced the way to whip Indians was to drive them from their winter camps so they must starve or surrender and he was bound to prove that theory.

Colonel Otis welcomed Sterrett and his recruits with joy. All four of his companies were understrength and short of officers and he put Sterrett in command of one of them at once. Lieutenant Royal was equally welcome. If the snow held off a few more days it might be possible to get one last ammunition train south to Miles and here, unexpectedly, was an officer to lead it.

THIRTY-FIVE

In November of 1876 two topics absorbed the English-speaking population of Tucson: the likelihood that the seat of territorial government would be returned to Prescott, and the approach from the California coast of the Southern Pacific Railroad. They were durable topics. Prescott had been trying to win back the capital for most of the nine years since it had moved to Tucson, and the railroad was stalled again. Southern Pacific track reached to the west bank of the Colorado River and the right-of-way was surveyed all the way into New Mexico, but the river crossing lay in the Army's Yuma reservation and the Army suddenly objected to the long-planned bridge. The dispute was acrimonious and while it lasted the wagon train continued to rule supreme in Arizona.

Freight hauling and contracting was the principal business of Tucson, running into hundreds of thousands of dollars a year. Until the railroad reached the city the prairie schooners would continue to stand in long lines before the warehouses of the giants of the trade: Zeckendorf and Ochoa and DeLong.

Before the month was out, news from the East outweighed local problems. Most Arizonans had voted for the Greenback Party which had died at the polls and the Democratic ticket of Tilden and Hendricks seemed to have won a popular victory. But the Republicans refused to concede. Returns from Oregon and three Southern states were in dispute and without their electoral votes Tilden could not win. Rutherford Hayes might yet be President of the United States.

A few amenities were appearing in the old presidio town. Paved streets were still unheard of but plank sidewalks were growing common. There were neither streetlamps nor drainage but the city tried to clean the garbage from the streets. Water still had to be bought from Mexican carriers because the wells, sweet when freshly dug, soon turned so alkaline they were useless.

Ellen was right when she said lodgings for a lady would be hard to find. There were plenty of boardinghouses but none for a young single woman. She and Samantha inspected the accommodation recommended by Miss Bolton and found it adequate, no more. The tiny room and Spartan furnishings were justified solely by the reputation of the proprietress. The widow Herscholdt accepted only roomers of excellent character and if they wished to stay they behaved with decorum.

Meals were less a problem than expected. Breakfast Samantha took with the widow in the latter's kitchen, lunch she carried to school in her string bag, and for the evening meal she went to Mrs. Neugass' Palace Restaurant, another stronghold of propriety. Most of Mrs. Neugass' customers were men of means and position who enjoyed her good food and the decent atmosphere in which it was served.

Here a young woman could dine unescorted without molestation. She could take her meal alone or in company of her choosing and the gentlemen who had risen to the status of their own napkin ring to mark their places saw to it that no one joined Samantha without her invitation.

The fare was good and plentiful. There was no menu and the diners took what was served. There was usually beef and always chicken, mutton and bacon. Potatoes were beginning to appear now that the Apaches had retreated from the regions where they could be grown. Samantha's particular delight was the profusion of fresh foods. Tomatoes and lettuce, crisp and delicious, were served daily and from Sonora by mule train came wonderful fruits: oranges, limes, quinces, juicy apricots and the sweet black Mexican figs.

Fortunately Mrs. Neugass' fare was inexpensive. The average wage for a teacher in Arizona Territory was a hundred dollars a month, but without certificate and only temporarily hired, Samantha received half of that. Not just her own job but the whole school system seemed a temporary thing, threatened with extinction by the lack of funds. There had been no school at all in Tucson until 1871 when John Spring gathered some boys in a crude adobe building for sporadic classes. Two years later Mrs. Hughes opened the first free public school for girls in the old Pioneer Brewery and later that same year Governor Safford managed to combine the two establishments under the first experienced teachers to come to Arizona. Miss Marie Wakefield and Miss Harriet Bolton were persuaded to come from California to take over.

By 1876 this school enrolled sixty boys and half as many girls. Samantha's employment was an experiment in bringing them a little music and it was not notably successful. There was no piano, only an ancient portable organ pumped by foot. It wheezed and hummed alarmingly but she coaxed from it the simple tunes which were all her students could absorb. They equated music with recreation and saw no need for instruction in the appreciation of either. As a result, Samantha's first classes were noisy ones and the experiment might have ended early had she not displayed a surprising ability to dominate a room full of boisterous small boys. She could be teased and plagued to a point, but when she spoke softly and fixed a youngster with her level gray eyes he fell quickly silent.

On Sundays, Carp and Ellen usually brought her to Camp Lowell in the buggy to spend the day. There were often callers at the Van Scivers' in the afternoon, some too curious, and though Samantha was cheerful and responsive in all else, it was clear that Tom Royal and her captivity were not for discussion. Most respected this but others gossiped avidly and out of that grew trouble.

Perhaps a dozen youngsters came daily by Dougherty wagon from Camp Lowell to the school in Tucson and among these were three girls. All three knew Samantha and considered her an outpost of their Army community. They brought her their news and their troubles and gathered about her to eat their lunch. One day not long before Christmas the youngest of the trio failed to appear.

"Where is Lizzie?" Samantha asked. The older of the two remaining girls looked flustered but her younger companion spoke up.

"She's not coming any more."

"Oh?" said Samantha, intent on the apple she was peeling. "Why not? Is her family leaving Camp Lowell?"

"Susie!" hissed the older girl threateningly but Susie was not to be diverted.

"Her mama says there's bad people at the school an' Lizzie's not to 'sociate with bad people." She lifted a small, puzzled face to Samantha. "I don't think you're bad, Miss S'mantha. What does Lizzie's mama mean?"

"Now you've done it, big mouth!" said the other. "I'm sorry, Miss Samantha; she hadn't ought to have said that. Our mamas told us not to."

Susie's eyes brimmed with tears and Samantha hugged

309

her impulsively. "Don't cry, Susie. It's all right." But the remainder of lunch was eaten in a stricken silence broken only now and then by Susie's gulps of remorse. When they had finished, Samantha took her string bag and cup to the little school office. She had been half expecting this but now she knew how poorly prepared for it she was.

She had been evading certain hard facts and she could do so no longer. There had been no word from Tom since his abrupt departure and if she were honest with herself, nothing he had said before he went was a real promise to return to her. Clearly, the longer she remained in Tucson the more difficult her position would become. Intolerable was a better word for it. It could only become worse and she had to face up to it.

That night she counted up her slender resources. There was Tom's hundred dollars, which she had not touched. She had convinced herself it was meant to help her await his return but it could just as well be a contribution toward her fare back East. It wasn't enough for either but perhaps it was all he had. What she had saved from her meager salary added little. It was time to go, she decided, but how?

Stage fare to Yuma would be fifty-five dollars; she was sure of that. From Yuma to San Diego another forty and the steamer up the coast to San Francisco forty or fifty more. Train fare from San Francisco to Leavenworth was a vague but enormous sum; too much to consider now. If she could get as far as San Francisco she would find a way to earn the rest. But to get only that far would cost at least a hundred and thirty-five dollars without considering food or lodging on the way.

Obviously she needed at least two hundred dollars before she could start. She would not borrow from Ellen so she had to find some way to make more money, an additional job of some sort. If she could do that and if she lived very frugally she could save enough in three or four months. As much as she disliked the idea, there was no alternative.

When the Van Scivers appeared the following Sunday she pled a headache and declined their invitation. Before another week forced her to find another excuse, Ellen learned what had happened. Her informant was little Katy Hennessey, who did not go to school but knew everything that happened there.

"What on earth can we do, Carp?" Ellen asked him. "How can we help her?"

"I don't know." He shook his head. "I don't know what she wants to do now but I'll bet it doesn't include coming out here any more."

"Can't you get word to Tom?"

"By letter, of course. Do you honestly think that would help? If he wanted to resolve this thing he would never have gone, and I don't think a letter is going to bring him back. Has it occurred to you that he simply won't come back as long as Samantha is here?"

"I won't believe that! Tom Royal may be a fool but he is a gentleman."

"All right. But even if he wanted to, I'm not sure he could come back now. There's been fighting on the Yellowstone already and there'll be more before spring. Sheridan's got a winter campaign going and if he corners the Sioux they may keep Tom until it's finished."

They argued the matter endlessly and without agreement and when Tate Hulse appeared a week later they were still at odds over it. Ellen was uncommunicative but he soon pried the story out of her.

"Well, I think someone ought to talk to her and I'm going to do it," he announced righteously. Both Carp and Ellen joined in opposition to that.

"You mean just leave her alone?"

"Certainly!"

"Has she heard from Tom at all?"

"If she has she didn't tell me."

"What in the world is the matter with him?"

It was a well-worn question for Ellen and she sighed. "I cannot imagine."

"Well . . . you're probably right. You usually are. But I'm going anyway."

In Tucson he stabled his horse at the quartermaster corral and set out for the widow Herscholdt's house but on the way he encountered John Clum, just back from the States with his new bride. They were accompanied by old Eskiminzin, the Arivaipa Apache chief.

Clum had gone East to marry his girl and he had turned the trip into quite an occasion. He had gathered a group of Apaches at San Carlos and announced they would visit the Centennial Exposition in Philadelphia on their way to Washington. The Indian Bureau objected and refused to finance the trip but Clum surmounted that obstacle easily. He and his Apaches put on an impromptu show at every stop on the way East and the journey paid for itself. Eskiminzin and Tahzay accompanied him and the venture was a howling success until they reached Washington, where Tahzay fell ill and died. Only the elegant funeral provided him by the federal authorities tempered the Apaches' grief. General Howard and Indian Commissioner Smith attended and a Reverend Rankin delivered a mighty eulogy.

Now Clum was back with his bride and bursting with ambitious plans to form a territorial militia company from his San Carlos Indian police. Governor Safford was once more hounding the Army for failure to pacify southeast Arizona and threatening to call out territorial troops if the regulars did not act.

"I hear Royal got his girl back," Clum said smugly. "I told him he would if he'd just be patient."

Tate gave him a sour look. The Indian agent had lost none of his ability to get on a man's nerves. He would have liked to straighten him out on the facts but the presence of the pretty young bride deterred him. No use starting an argument, he decided. He shook hands with Eskiminzin, responding gravely to the Arivaipa's formal greeting. It was rare to see the old man in town. Not five years ago the good citizens of Tucson had all but exterminated his peaceful band and Eskiminzin avoided the town like the plague.

"I expect we'll see them at Camp Grant on our way home," Clum told his wife, "unless they're still honeymooning somewhere. Are they back yet, Hulse?"

Tate hesitated. "They aren't married yet," he said finally. "Royal's in Dakota on temporary duty."

For once Clum looked astonished. "I'll believe almost anything of the Army but that's too much! You mean they sent him off to fight Sioux before he could get married?"

"How awful!" murmured his bride. "John told me about that poor girl. All those months in captivity and now to be separated from her lieutenant. It seems dreadfully unfair."

Tate tried to change the subject. "We never could make a trade for her. In the end we had to fight to get her back. Eskiminzin was right," he nodded to the Apache. "Pionsenay had her in the Huachuca Mountains all the time."

Eskiminzin acknowledged the compliment gravely. *"Enju!* Soldier got his woman again. Good. Where they go?"

"Lieutenant Royal had to go to the north. Far away."

"So? He take his woman?" The old man's persistence was embarrassing and the Clums were listening with interest. John Clum laughed.

"He had to go fight Sitting Bull, Skimmy. The Army's sore because the Indians killed their yellow-hair general."

"He don't take his woman? They don't live in same house?" There was no way around that one. It had connotations for an Indian that made evasion difficult. Tate had no idea what made Eskiminzin suspicious but the old man was ahead of the Clums, who looked a little puzzled.

"No. When he comes back he will."

"Mebbeso." Eskiminzin shook his head solemnly. "Huachuca Mountain bad. Those Hollow Mountain. Belong Chiricahua. Sometime man walk in those mountain an' he get lost. He walk in House of Mountain People. Mebbeso he see something."

"What does he see?" Tate asked curiously.

"I dunno. Something no good. When he come back he not same as man who walk in."

"What does that mean, Skimmy?" Clum demanded. The old man only grunted. He had no more to say on the matter even to his good friend Clum. Tate would have liked to pursue it, but not before the Clums.

He doffed his cap to the bride. "I've got to be going. It's been a pleasure to meet you, ma'am; I hope San Carlos isn't too lonely for you."

"Not for my girl!" boasted Clum.

Tate was conscious of Eskiminzin's eyes on him as he walked away. I wonder what he meant, he asked himself. Then he remembered Tony Rucker's discourse one night at Camp Bowie on Apache supernaturals and the Chiricahuas' sacred mountains. It was no less strange but he knew what the old man was saying.

Samantha seemed glad to see him despite Ellen's fears, but she was reserved and hard to talk to. The remembered promise of her smile was unchanged but there was a new wariness in the gray eyes that troubled him. He thought she might be constrained by the presence of Mrs. Herscholdt so he proposed that they walk into the town to see a play. A wandering company of Mexican actors had come to Tucson and they offered an opportunity to invite her out.

"You bring her back by midnight, young man," the widow warned. "I lock up then."

"Won't the old dragon give you a key?" he asked as they left the bake shop. Her face lit up in the old way.

"I guess I haven't earned my key yet, Tate. She's waiting to see if I behave myself."

The theater was an open courtyard with a rude stage at one end—planks resting on barrels with a row of smoking candles in tin sconces. There were also two great bonfires to illumine the scene and their warmth was welcome, for the night had grown chilly. For Mexicans the price of admission was fifty cents but for the American officer and his girl, a dollar each. Samantha was aghast.

"Tate, that's too much!"

He chuckled. "I can do it with enough left over for a cup of hot chocolate after. No place to spend your money at Camp Bowie."

The high price of admission entitled them to a seat on the benches, the first row of which was filled with excited small boys shrieking and clapping their hands at the antics of the clown who distracted the audience until the play began. The back rows were occupied by elderly ladies wrapped in shawls and gossiping happily.

It was a harrowing drama, its setting the French occupation of Mexico and the chief villain garbed in an approximation of a French officer's uniform. The story was simple enough. Elena, the beautiful young heroine, was about to be bartered for gold to the villainous Frenchman by her rascally uncle and guardian. Her sole defender was Jorge: young, handsome, patriotic and devoted. His every effort to rescue Elena was thwarted by the scheming uncle. He skulked about the stage, popping out now and then to embrace his beloved when he was not plotting ruin for the foreign invader.

The Frenchman alternately threatened or fawned on the repellent uncle, who connived with him to force Elena into the hated union. Her tears of distress were moving and the elderly ladies in the back row sniffed sympathetically. As the dreadful marriage grew nearer, Elena's laments became piteous. Jorge grew distracted. Between fiery patriotic speeches he hissed words of adoration and encouragement to the girl, who sobbed and implored the saints for aid. The Frenchman smirked in anticipation.

"*¡Muera!* Death to him!" shrieked the small boys and the orchestra played a dirge. Composed of drum, flute and guitar, most of its efforts were dirgelike but this was unmistakable. The audience lived every moment of the play. Even Tate shouted and shook his fist at the French poltroon and Samantha laughed at him delightedly.

Of course it all ended well. The despised Frenchman fled and the uncle was clapped in prison. Elena fell into the arms of her beloved to thunderous applause and the clown marched on carrying the red, white and green flag of the Mexican republic. The audience gave him a standing ovation. Everyone congratulated his neighbor on the happy outcome and Tate bought cups of delicious hot chocolate from an old woman tending a brazier in a corner of the yard.

"Oh, that's good!" Samantha murmured. "But it's hot . . . be careful!"

"Would you like an *enchilada* with it?"

She shook her head. Her struggle to save money had made her miserly and she felt guilty about his spending so much. Tate wanted to ask her about Tom but he did not know how to begin. He tried circling the subject.

"Some of your old friends are back again, Sam. They've been raiding along the border."

"Oh?" she was noncommittal.

"Yes. They chased Sam Hughes for ten miles and ran off a bunch of his horses and then they swung up toward Bowie last week and killed a mail carrier not four miles from the post."

She lowered her cup and looked at him intently. "The mail carrier from here to Bowie?"

"No." Her question puzzled him. "He was coming from New Mexico."

"Did you find the letters?"

It was unlike her to think of the mail instead of the soldier but suddenly he understood. Letters from Dakota would come through New Mexico. He shook his head.

"Usually they just take the bag and scatter the mail. They like the bags for some reason." Samantha could have told him why. She remembered Aludin's days of hard work to make saddlebags for Catle and how the Apache girl would have welcomed a ready-made bag.

"We never found anything," he continued. "They must have burned the letters or buried them."

He touched her arm gently. "You think there might have been a letter from Tom?"

"I don't know." Her voice was so low he had to bend to catch her words. He started to speak again but she handed him her cup and turned away. When he returned she asked what time it was.

"We've got to go. I mustn't be late."

They walked back mostly in silence. He knew she would not speak of Tom and he dared not raise the subject of her present difficulty. As they approached the

316

widow's shop she pointed to the lighted window in the upstairs sitting room.

"My guardian awaits."

"Can't you stay just a few more minutes?" he begged. "It isn't midnight yet."

She smiled at him. "She's very strict and I want to win my key. Good night, Tate, and thank you for a lovely evening. It was very kind of you."

He was a big, rugged, happy man whose emotions always seemed to show clearly. Now he looked so forlorn she was conscience-stricken. She stood on tiptoe to kiss him lightly on the cheek.

"Hey! Wait . . ." he said but she was gone, eyes twinkling. He heard her heels tap lightly up the stairs and in a few minutes the heavier tread of the widow Herscholdt coming down to lock the door. He walked away, hands thrust into his pockets.

"What are you going to do about her?" he demanded of Ellen next day.

"Just a minute!" Carp interposed. "What do you think we ought to be doing?"

"I don't know but we've got to do something!"

"Not necessarily. She's a grown woman and she can probably take better care of herself than half the men in Tucson. We're here and there's Major Lord in town. She knows him and if she wants help she can get it."

"But, dammit . . ." Ellen put her finger on his lips and smiled at him.

"What's bothering you, Tate Hulse, is she didn't want to see you very much, did she?"

"No!" he blustered. "She's Tom's girl and I don't expect her to make a fuss over me."

"Maybe she's Tom's girl and maybe she isn't. Does she have to belong to someone?"

He thought about that for a moment. "Well, in that case why shouldn't I look after her if you aren't going to?"

"I didn't say we wouldn't look after her. What I'm trying to get through your thick head is that right now I don't think she wants any of us around. She wants to be let alone."

"But . . ."

"No. It's that simple. She wants to be by herself. If she wants you, she'll let you know." Carp grinned wickedly. "Did you get the idea last night that she's looking forward to seeing you again soon?"

Ellen was smiling at him too and he looked so crest-fallen they both laughed at him. She gave him a comforting pat on the arm.

"I'm going to do my best to get her to spend Christmas with us. If she will, I'll let you know and you can just sort of turn up. How's that?"

THIRTY-SIX

Colonel Otis studied the boxed ammunition stacked under his lean-to shelters and swore feelingly.

"It's going to snow before I can get it to him and if he has to go after Crazy Horse without it he'll skin me alive!" He looked at Tom. "I've got enough teams for fourteen wagons. You think you can handle it, Mister?"

"Yes, sir." Tom pointed at three canvas-hooded field pieces on oddly slender wheels parked in the open. "Do those go with me?"

Otis sighed and flicked a pebble at the humpbacked guns. "Nope. Miles don't want 'em. Nobody does. They're Gatlings and they're worthless. Two of 'em are fifty caliber and there's no ammunition for 'em. The other's a forty-five but the damn thing's as delicate as a hundred-dollar watch. Get maybe twenty rounds out of it before it jams.

Too bad! If they'd shoot, they'd be worth their weight in gold."

"When do I start, sir?"

"Daybreak tomorrow. I know it's Christmas but Miles won't wait."

That night the hut that served as Officers' Mess was trimmed with candles and greens and was as cheerful as a roaring fire on each of its two hearths could make it. Supper was the standard field ration, but afterward there was a wine punch laced with brandy. It was strong to begin with but after a while someone reinforced it with straight corn whiskey and it became lethal.

There were seven officers to celebrate Christmas Eve on Glendive Creek. They sang all the carols they remembered and hummed the ones they didn't. There were toasts to the President, the Army, its generals and its regiments; to Sitting Bull and Crazy Horse and repeatedly to the ladies far away. The excess of sentimentality depressed Tom and he withdrew to the fireplace, where Sterrett joined him in a little while.

The captain's face was a little ruddier and his hand a little slower than usual but he seemed otherwise unaffected by the explosive punch. He blinked at Tom owlishly.

"Y'know, I been wantin' t' ask you somethin' but I kinda didn't like to do it." He blinked again. "Could be none o' my business."

Tom drew a long breath and nudged the big log in the fireplace with his toe. "Go ahead, Cap'n. I'll tell you if it isn't."

"Comin' back from leave this last time I passed through Leavenworth an' a friend o' mine mentioned a feller named Royal."

"Oh?"

"Yep. Told me Rosy Allyn's girl went out t' Arizona to marry a cav'ry lootenant named Royal but th' Apaches got her first."

There was a long silence before Tom spoke. "He was right," he said flatly.

Sterrett nodded. "I kinda thought so."

"Did you know her?" Tom asked.

"Knew her dad. We were in th' same reg'ment when he was killed. Lissa was at Camp Warner with the girl. Just a little thing then—ten, maybe twelve years old. I dunno. I tried t' keep up with her but I guess I haven't seen her since Lissa died." He rubbed his big shoulders against the log mantel. "Indians killed her, I s'pose?"

"No, we got her back."

"You don't say! Man, I'm glad to hear it." He winked genially. "Sure didn't give you much time with your bride, did they?"

Tom looked at him coldly. "We aren't married."

Sterrett had stooped to poke at the fire and he peered up at Tom unbelievingly. "You mean to tell me Gus Kautz sent you up here before you could marry her?"

"No. I volunteered."

"Well, I will be damned!" exploded Sterrett in amazement.

"Now wait a minute, Captain . . ." Tom began. Sterrett's face grew redder and he cleared his throat apologetically.

"No offense, Mister. Y'see, I knew her people right well and I was fond o' that girl . . . here, lemme get us another." He took Tom's glass and refilled it and his own. By the time he returned Tom was embarrassed by his outburst.

"Tell me about her father," he asked. "I never knew much about him."

"Rosy Allyn?" Sterrett rocked on his heels and studied the raw poles of the roof. "He was a strange feller. You're a West Pointer, ain't you, Mister?"

"Yes."

"So was Rosy. I think it made him kinda notional." He smiled at Tom. "Don't get me wrong. I ain't runnin' it down. I wish to God I coulda come up that road. Maybe it wasn't th' Point but somethin' gave Rosy the idea he oughtta got ahead faster than he did."

"I heard he had a fine record in the war."

"Both wars. When he graduated from th' Point in forty-six he went straight to Mexico. Wounded at Churubusco an' got a brevet for it. Married Lissa in fifty-five an' they had the one girl. When the rebellion broke out he got a commission in th' volunteers, and he had a hell of a record. Wounded twice more and a brevet each time. Came outta the war a major but just like all those folks who got fast rank he was busted back afterward. He never got over it."

It was dawning on Tom that Alonzo Sterrett was more than a casual acquaintance of the Allyns. "How do you mean that?"

"It made him bitter. When he was home he was hard on Lissa an' when he got to a fight he was reckless. Tried too hard to get his rank back an' got himself killed instead."

"How was he killed?"

"Bein' a damn fool. Crook cornered some Paiutes an' Modocs on the Pit River in sixty-seven. They got into a bunch o' piled-up rocks an' Crook got the rocks but th' Injuns just crawled down inside an' kept on fightin'. Nobody in his right mind woulda followed 'em into those caves but Rosy Allyn did. I guess he thought if he could push 'em out Crook would promote him, but instead th' Injuns killed him and six men with him. The newspapers said Crook ordered him in, but it ain't so. Crook's a hard man but he never wasted a soldier like that."

Samantha had never spoken of any of this but if she were only ten years old at the time, Tom reflected, she probably never knew about it.

"Funny thing," Sterrett mused. "Crook decided to pull back so he buried Rosy and his men an' put the picket line over the graves so th' horses would tromp out any trace of 'em an' the Injuns couldn't find 'em. He sent a detail out later to bring 'em in for a reg'lar funeral but either they couldn't find the place or th' Injuns already had. Never found a one. That was hard on Lissa. She'd stayed at Warner waitin' for the funeral."

"Is that when Samantha and her mother came back to Fort Leavenworth?"

"Yep. I stopped there every chance I had, but I guess I didn't keep up like I should after Lissa died." He stared into the fire glumly and Tom took their glasses back to the punch bowl.

Sterrett nodded his thanks and took a long swallow. When he spoke he was looking into his glass and Tom heard him with difficulty.

"Looks like Rosy's luck is followin' his girl. I wonder if she was tryin' too hard."

It was a puzzling remark but Tom gave it no thought. Perhaps it was the punch or more likely a reaction to the hard thinking he had given his problem in the past month but he suddenly needed desperately to talk about it. Alonzo Sterrett was a good listener and Tom talked. He poured it all out—all about Samantha at any rate. It was doubtful he would ever be able to explain Liddy to anybody, including himself. How sleeping with Liddy could make him want Samantha more was beyond him, but it was a fact.

He told of Tupper's refusal to let him meet his girl in Tucson; her capture by the Apaches; the long, agonizing wait while action was forbidden by General Kautz; their raid on the *ranchería* and the happy reunion that followed. He recounted the deserter's story and how he had checked it by talking to Severiano, and Samantha's flat refusal to talk about it. His monologue was neither self-pitying nor critical of Samantha, only a little baffled. It was suspended from time to time as they replenished their glasses but the older man never interrupted. He nodded and listened silently.

"I don't understand why she won't talk to me," he concluded at last. "I love her. I want to go back to her but I'm just not sure I ought to."

When he was sure there was no more, Sterrett sighed. "Does she blame you because it took so long to get her out?"

"No . . . well, I don't think so. She doesn't seem to blame anybody."

"So you volunteered for this job and left her in Arizona. What makes you think she's goin' to wait for you?"

"I . . . I don't know."

"She doesn't have much choice, does she?"

"What do you mean?"

"Where's she going? How's she goin' to get there?"

"I sent her all the money I had when I left."

Sterrett made an odd sound and put his glass carefully on the mantel.

"Do you want some more?" Tom asked.

Sterrett faced him, rocking just a little. "No," he said slowly. "I don't. I've had enough."

But he didn't mean the punch. With care he put a thick finger on Tom's chest. "Mister Royal, you make me sick to my stummick! You're afraid somebody's gonna talk about you if you marry your girl, aren't you? 'Stead o' standin' up for her, you cut and ran. You sent her money! Hell, you want her to run too, don't you?"

It took Tom a moment, openmouthed, to take in this outburst, then his face flamed.

"Captain Sterrett, I don't have to listen to this! You have no right whatsoever . . ."

"Maybe not but you're gonna hear it. You disgust me, Mister, an' I'm gonna speak my piece. What does it matter what a lousy deserter says?" He jabbed with the finger. "What if it's true? What if she had to do it to stay alive? Godalmighty, boy . . . would you rather have her dead? You people didn't give her much help, did you? How come you waited all those months before you went after her?"

"That wasn't my fault, dammit!"

The captain's voice dropped to a low growl. "What matter whose fault it was? The longer you waited the harder it was for her. But it was pretty damned good for Gus Kautz an' that pack o' politicians in Tucson, wasn't it?"

Tom stared at him in horror. "Nobody would do that!"

"How do you know? A smart-ass green lootenant! It kept the Injuns off their backs for half a year, didn't it? If Gus Kautz had stirred up a real war on that border they might have busted him back to runnin' his regiment, an' that's quite a bust from livin' high on the hog in Prescott, shinin' those brevet two stars." Sterrett cleared his throat again.

"I ain't sayin' it happened like that but what d'ye s'pose

she thought? If it looked that way to her can you blame her for anything she did?"

The slugging impact of his questions shattered Tom's indignation. They struck him like a series of blows and he backed away from them as much as from the insistent finger on his chest. Sterrett misunderstood the movement and drew himself up with dignity.

"No. I won't fight you, Mister. I'm too old for that. If you push it I'll apologize but I won't fight."

Tom shook his head slowly and Sterrett understood it was not a fight he was looking for.

"I guess I hadn't oughtta talked so hard, son, but you gotta think about what you're doin' to that girl. No matter what she's done or what's been done to her, she deserves better'n she's gettin' from you. Maybe . . ." he turned away, swaying just a little. "Maybe she deserves more'n you can give her, Royal."

Tom sat down and stared into the sinking fire. He sat long, heedless of the horseplay and tuneless singing around the punch bowl, and he thought hard.

He had left Arizona with a matched set of rather fragile notions and on the trip north every one of them had been broken. The universal scorn with which these foot soldiers viewed a cavalryman had infuriated him until native good sense made him see they were right as far as this country was concerned. The resulting damage to his pride had set him up for harder knocks.

They came fast. Lieutenant O'Brien, Liddy and now Sterrett had each hit him hard and the deeper understanding of himself that resulted was painful. Sterrett's outburst in defense of Samantha had been the hardest to swallow, but it made him see clearly that he had been worse than stupid where she was concerned. He set himself doggedly to find a solution and an idea took shape in his mind.

Abandoning the warm mess hall he picked his way over the frozen mud to the hut he shared with two other lieutenants. Neither was there and the dying fire scarcely took the chill from the night air, but he found a candle and before he rolled into his bunk he covered a dozen

pages with another plea to Samantha for understanding
and a little more time. He did not mention Sterrett but he
explained in detail the idea born of Sterrett's brutal sur-
gery on his previous notions.

THIRTY-SEVEN

A few days later Ellen kept her promise and drove into
Tucson in the buggy to invite Samantha for Christmas.
It was a strange and frustrating conversation. Samantha
evaded politely, never giving her reason for evasion, and
Ellen never revealed she knew it.

Ellen grew a little exasperated. "Well then, just dinner?
Christmas dinner? Only the family. Please come, Sam."

Samantha sensed her irritation at once and blushed
furiously. "Oh, Ellen . . . I'm so ashamed!"

"Of what, for heaven's sake?"

"Of myself for being such a little boor. Of course I'll
come. You're much too kind and I don't deserve it."

Having said on impulse there would be no one but the
family, Ellen was concerned about her promise to Tate. In
the end she decided it would be better not to send for
him. Of course, if he appeared uninvited, she could not
help it but at least she would keep her word to Samantha.

Samantha was upset too. She wanted no part of Camp
Lowell and its wagging tongues but she could not offend
Ellen by complete refusal. She brooded over her plight
for a week and the more she brooded the angrier she became. It was healthier than self-pity but it left her in a
dangerous mood and a few days before Christmas it betrayed her.

She was eating her usual solitary supper at the Palace when an officer in uniform entered, glanced about, and came directly to her table. She watched him with pounding heart, certain he brought some message from Tom. He bowed, smiling, and she remembered his face. He had called once at the Van Scivers' when she was there.

"Mister DeBergh, Miss Allyn. Henry DeBergh. We met at the Van Scivers'." She nodded. If he had a message there was no need for all this. Mrs. Neugass' regulars eyed him incuriously. They could see he was Army and it seemed natural for him to speak to her.

"May I join you?" he asked. It was so different from what she expected that she hardly heard him. He seated himself, waving away the white-jacketed Mexican boy who asked if he wanted supper.

She studied him more closely now. He was tall with wavy black hair, thick and carefully trimmed. His features were regular with the exception of an aquiline, questing nose that would have been obtrusive in a face less spectacularly handsome. His uniform fit him elegantly and he was completely at ease. Still obsessed with the idea that he came from Tom she leaned forward to ask breathlessly, "What is it? Have you a message for me?"

"Not exactly. I called at the Van Scivers' hoping to find you there but Ellen told me you had moved into town."

"So?" She was so puzzled she was abrupt with him.

"Why, Miss Allyn, I only came to ask if you would do me the honor of attending the ball with me on Christmas Eve."

"A ball? Here in Tucson?"

"Oh, no. At Camp Lowell. We're having a formal ball. We've found a famous band and it will be a gala affair. I hope you'll consent."

She had been leaning forward, watching his face intently, and as she took in his words she was speechless with surprise. The effrontery of the man first enraged then intrigued her. He could not possibly be unaware of her equivocal situation and she was inclined to consider his invitation an insult. He was not insensitive; he saw that and looked abashed.

"Please don't take offense, Miss Allyn. We have been introduced, you know, and I thought Mrs. Van Sciver seemed concerned about your long absence . . ."

"You discussed me with Mrs. Van Sciver?" Her eyebrows climbed and a less confident man would have quailed at the ice in her voice.

"Oh, no! Not at all. I . . ." he made a deprecating gesture, "I just gathered that, you know. Please, don't be offended. We don't have enough pretty girls to spare one, you see, and it's going to be a grand dance."

She mastered her irritation and regarded him with amusement. Ellen would choke before telling this man what she thought about anyone. Either he was an accomplished rake or a born fool and he did not look like a fool to her. For a long moment she considered the effect her appearance at the ball would have and a feeling of bitter recklessness overcame her.

"I am not at all offended, Mister DeBergh. Indeed, I am honored. I accept your invitation with pleasure."

He had the grace to look surprised and then delighted. As quickly as she had accepted she was beset with misgivings. What would Carp and Ellen think of her? She cared nothing for what the rest of the garrison would say, and in the end that thought gave her courage. It would be worth it just to watch their faces.

"Miss Allyn, I'm deeply honored. I will call for you at eight at Mrs. Herscholdt's, I believe?" She nodded.

"May I see you home, Miss Allyn?"

She was still studying with satisfaction a mental picture of her arrival at the ball and she had to put that away to concentrate on what he said.

"I've just begun my supper."

"It would be a pleasure to wait until you finish."

She smiled at him wickedly. "Thank you very much but I couldn't think of detaining you so long." She extended her hand to him. "Until Christmas Eve at eight then, Mister DeBergh, and thank you again for your kind in-

vitation." To her mild surprise he accepted his dismissal
as gracefully as he had presented his request.

That night she unstrapped her trunk and took out the
ball gown she had never worn since its fitting. She set her
teeth when she remembered the dreams that had been
fashioned with its making, but she shook out the voluminous skirt and tried it on. Even without her corset it no
longer fitted closely enough but that was easily rem-
edied. There were stays in her trunk and her needle
served her well. The ribbon bows looping up the velvet
overskirt to show the taffeta beneath were crushed from
long storage so they would have to be removed and
ironed out. She fell to work with a grim relish.

Christmas Eve was cold and the widow Herscholdt eyed
her bare shoulders with raised brows. The dress had been
made with the dropped shoulders of the late sixties because even at Fort Leavenworth the frontier Army
managed to stay about a decade behind the current
fashion. Samantha had washed her hair until it shone, then
piled it high and intricately, held in place with a bit of
green ribbon snipped from a skirt bow. The low-cut
bosom of the dress combined with her elaborately upswept hair to make her look excessively bare and the
widow clucked disparagingly.

"You'll take your death of cold, miss. Haven't you a
cloak?"

"No, ma'am," Samantha replied, admiring her image in
the hall mirror.

"I'll lend you a shawl then."

While she went in search of it, Samantha smoothed the
velvet skirt and wondered if she had been too enthusiastic
with her alterations. The fit and cut of the bodice would
have horrified Aunt Bee. The shawl was pretty and she
was delighted to have it. She thanked Mrs. Herscholdt
warmly before broaching the subject of a key.

"I don't really see how I can be back by twelve tonight,
ma'am, and I hate to waken you."

Surprisingly her landlady handed over a key without
comment. As Samantha dropped it into her reticule she
heard below the sounds of her escort's arrival. She waited

until the widow had admitted him before she swept down the hall and into the sitting room.

Lieutenant DeBergh greeted her with openmouthed admiration. He looked grand himself in full dress uniform but for some reason, Mrs. Herscholdt had suddenly turned quite chilly. There was an awkward silence before he led her downstairs to the buggy standing before the door. Some Mexicans stopped to watch entranced as he handed her in and tucked a robe about her against the chill.

The ball was indeed an elegant one. The Officers' Mess had been ingeniously decorated and there was a handsome array of guests. Samantha noted that she seemed the only young woman from Tucson without a chaperone. The Spanish tradition was still strong in the town and no decent girl would dream of attending a dance without an elderly female relative as guardian.

Her arrival created a most satisfactory stir. Henry De-Bergh was right when he pled a shortage of pretty girls and if there were doubts about Samantha they did not extend to the young officers of the post. They flocked about her at once to beg dances and she referred them demurely to her escort, who quickly filled her card. It was a gaily decorated little program with a tasseled cord to loop about her wrist. When DeBergh handed it to her with a flourish she saw he had saved quite a few dances for himself.

"You don't mind?" he whispered and she gave him a smile that set him beaming. She had determined to enjoy this evening and it was beginning so happily she could find fault with nothing.

At the first break in the music, Carp Van Sciver appeared, looking quite dashing himself, and she swept him a low curtsy, not forgetting a blinding smile for the pink-cheeked lieutenant who relinquished her with a stricken look. Carp whirled her the length of the room without a word, threading his way through the circling couples to Ellen, who waited by the punch bowl.

Ellen kissed her and beamed. "Oh, Sam, you're beautiful! I'm so glad you changed your mind and came. Poor Tate will be brokenhearted but it will do him good."

It was a mild reproof but Samantha felt it keenly. "I should have told you. I know I should. It was inexcusable of me, Ellen, but truly I didn't know I would come until three days ago."

Carp eyed the card on her wrist curiously but he was too polite to ask the question that troubled him. Ellen simply exercised a woman's prerogative and opened the little folder to look.

"Oh!" she said flatly and Samantha looked at her in surprise.

"Is something wrong?"

"Oh, no . . . no! Why don't you come home with us after the dance, Sam? It will save you that long ride into town and since you're coming for dinner tomorrow you might as well stay the night . . . or what's left of it when this is over."

There was something wrong. She was speaking too fast and too urgently but before Samantha could question her the music began again and a lieutenant hovering in the background moved in to claim his dance.

"Who is it?" Carp demanded under his breath.

"Henry DeBergh."

"Oh, hell! What possessed the girl to come with him?"

"Lord knows!" Ellen murmured in distress. "He asked me the other day where she had gone and like a fool I told him. I wish I hadn't."

"She's in no position to be keeping company with that rake! Look at that row of harpies twittering about her." He was speaking unkindly of the rank of duennas and chaperones along the wall with a few older officers in dutiful attendance. They were certainly watching Samantha. The glint of red in her high-piled hair was picked out by the candlelight and her bare shoulders gleamed as she whirled through the stately figures of a waltz.

"It's bad enough her coming with DeBergh but what's worse, she's prettier than any girl in the room. They'll never forgive her for that."

"By golly!" Carp agreed. "She is a stunner. I never knew she could look like that. Damned pity that fool Royal isn't here to see her."

"Right now I'd settle for Tate Hulse. I'd feel better if he were here."

The soldier musicians outdid themselves. They were heavy on the brass but that did not matter. The officers saw to it they had plenty of punch and probably a little something stronger too and this, with the praise of the dancers, inspired them. Alternating with ponderous German waltzes were faster dances in which the men and their ladies formed sets to whirl and clap through energetic quadrilles. One of the bandsmen sang out the calls and when it came time to turn partners his voice rose above the music: "Oh, swing those girls, those pretty little girls, those girls you left behind you!" and some of the women were literally whirled off their feet by enthusiastic partners.

Time passed for Samantha in a whirl of delight. She had not danced for many months and the pleasure of eager young men seeking her company was not dampened by an occasional glimpse of Ellen's worried face. She was not so innocent she did not suspect what kind of man her escort was. The way he held her when they danced, the bold way his eyes searched her; these told her much but she did not care. She felt quite able to take care of herself and she was having too much fun to worry about it.

The punch was not strong but the dancing was strenuous and when the young men brought her cups of the cool drink she accepted happily. They sustained her mood of reckless gaiety and she avoided Carp though she knew he was trying to catch her eye. The band swung into the sad, sweet strains of "Auld Lang Syne" long before she was ready to give over dancing and before she knew it DeBergh was bundling her into the buggy and tucking the robe about her again. His hands lingered at the task and she teased him gaily.

"We're going to have champagne and scrambled eggs," he told her as they trotted through the waning moonlight toward Tucson. "That's the only way to end a night like this."

"Where?" she asked, puzzled.

"A friend of mine keeps rooms in town and we often

331

gather there for breakfast after a dance. Please say you will."

"All right. It sounds fun, but I can't stay too late."

"I promise to return you to Mrs. Herscholdt before dawn."

"Oh, Lord! It must be long before that."

The six miles to town passed quickly and before she knew it they were rolling through the silent streets. Henry stopped before a two-story adobe house and a sleepy Mexican lad appeared to hold the horse's head.

"I don't like to leave the rig in the street," he told her. "The boy will put it in back until we're ready to go."

He led the way upstairs to a comfortable sitting room with a fire glowing on the hearth and opened the door to an adjoining room with a bed and a dresser with a mirror at which she could bring some order to her wind-blown hair.

When she returned to the sitting room he had freshened the fire and the crackling flames were welcome. Her taffeta underskirt was icy from the buggy ride and she resisted with difficulty an impulse to turn her back to the fire and lift it to admit the warmth. Henry pulled the cork from a bottle of champagne with a resounding pop but no overflow.

"Good!" he chortled. "Usually it's too warm but no trouble tonight." He brought her a brimming glass and touched his to it in a courtly gesture. The cool wine was delicious and she drank it thirstily, recapturing in its sparkle some of the gaiety of the dance. Before he could take it she held it out for more, feeling wickedly delighted to have forestalled him.

She saw no preparation for breakfast and no other guests had appeared. A persistent suspicion that there were none did not deter her enjoyment of the second glass. She was happy and pleased with herself and quite confident she could keep Henry in bounds. She was also well aware of the effect of firelight and the low-cut, restructured gown on her slender figure. She revolved slowly, pretending to examine the room, just to enjoy that effect in his admiring eyes.

When she faced the fire again he was standing close behind her and she felt him touch her hair gently.

"I never knew," he said wonderingly, "there was so much red in it."

"Ummn," she murmured, "happiness brings it out."

She was only making talk but Henry was encouraged. His arms circled her narrow waist and clasped her to him. He breathed warmly on the back of her neck, bared by the upswept hair. She shook her head and made a small, warning sound but Henry was in a hurry. His fingers traced her corset stays upward beneath the taut velvet and she shivered, alarmed at her pleasurable reaction.

"Oooh!" she gasped as they strayed from the velvet to the soft swell of her breasts above it. She squirmed about in his arms to face him, pushing gently with a forefinger at his chin.

"Henry?"

He kissed the finger. "Yes?"

"There aren't any other guests, are there?"

He made a rueful grimace. "Sometimes they just don't make it. This must be one of those nights."

"And breakfast?"

"Breakfast for two is no trouble." He grinned happily.

His hand stroked the nape of her neck, cupped her head and tipped it back. His mouth came down on hers, hard and demanding and of their own volition her arms crept up to encircle his neck. He bent her back, holding her so tight the looped golden cords of the aiguillettes on his uniform jacket hurt her; remembrance of O'Brien's skillful hands thundered in her head and she returned his fiery kiss with a passion that left her breathless.

With equal swiftness it died. Revulsion drowned her pleasure. It was cheap and tawdry and the knowledge that he had planned this shabby seduction from the moment she accepted his brazen invitation disgusted her. Her body stiffened convulsively. Henry misunderstood her outraged reaction and his hands coaxed the brief sleeves of the gown down her arms. She put two stiff fingers in his midriff and jabbed hard. He grunted, more in surprise than pain.

"No," she said. He was staring reproachfully at the sleeves which had come down to her elbows with no other effect than to hobble her arms.

"You idiot!" she snapped, pushing them up. "They're just window dressing. You couldn't get it off with a crowbar!" He looked so crestfallen she giggled. Poor Henry, all this preparation only to be defeated by a gown ten years out of fashion.

"Please, Samantha."

"No."

"Please don't be angry."

"I'm not angry but I don't want this."

"But . . ."

"No. I know what you thought and I can't blame you for trying but the answer is still no. I'll get my shawl and I want to go home now."

He looked irritated but he was experienced enough to know she meant what she said. He was completely baffled by her response to his kiss but there was no mistaking her determination there would be no more. He sighed.

"I'll get you a coat; that shawl's not enough. It's only a block or two."

"What about the buggy?"

He grinned apologetically. "It's put up and the kid's in bed by now."

"My, you were confident, weren't you? Am I the first to disappoint you?"

He put his own blue cape about her shoulders and did not answer that question. They walked in silence to the bake shop. He expected she would leave him without a word but to his surprise she thanked him gravely for the evening and said nothing of its abortive ending. She even handed him her key in a formal way to open the door for her.

As he did so a light appeared at the head of the stairs and the widow Herscholdt peered down at them grimly, bare feet incongruous beneath a faded robe.

"Good evening, ma'am," Henry said politely.

"Evening! It's five o'clock in the morning, Mister De-Bergh!"

"Well, after all, Mrs. Herscholdt, it is Christmas Eve. The dance . . ."

"The dance has been over for hours, Mister! I know what you've been doing. I know all about you and your rooms over Manuel Ortiz's place. I'd expect no more from you but I'm surprised at you, Miss Allyn!"

Samantha was horrified. "You . . . you're mistaken, Mrs. Herscholdt. I . . ."

"Nonsense!" The widow raised her lamp higher. "Look at you. Wearing his coat and slipping over here without the buggy so I wouldn't hear you come. I'm not a fool, young woman. You have been in his rooms, haven't you?"

The coat could be explained but not the missing buggy. "Yes, I have, but . . ."

"Hah!" snorted the widow.

"Now, see here, madam . . ." DeBergh began but she cut him off at once.

"I'm not obliged to stand here in the cold and listen to the likes of you, Mister DeBergh. I don't believe a word you say and I'll have no back talk from you. I'll thank you to take yourself away from my door as fast as you can before someone thinks I'm a party to your goings-on. As for you, miss; you pack your things and leave just as soon as you can. This is a respectable house and if you intend to keep company with such as him you can't do it here! Do you understand me?"

Samantha understood all too well. Enough to know there was no earthly use in protesting innocence. She shut the door on Henry DeBergh's white face and climbed the stairs wearily.

"I doubt I can leave tomorrow, Mrs. Herscholdt," she told the widow as she passed her on the stair. "It's Christmas. I will be gone on Monday, though."

THIRTY-EIGHT

Christmas Day dawned crisp and clear and the cathedral bells awoke Samantha early. It did not matter whether the stagecoach ran today; Ochoa and DeLong's where Carp had banked her money would not open for business.

She sorted her belongings and packed what she could in a carpetbag. The rest went into the trunk which would have to stay behind. When it was strapped and locked, she faced the problem of a message to the Van Scivers. She hoped it could be a note left with the angry widow, but they might come looking for her when she failed to appear for their Christmas dinner. It was a long, unhappy day and when the bells rang Vespers she was glad, both for its end and that Ellen had not come.

Next morning she had a few chilly words with the widow Herscholdt, told her of the trunk and handed over the note to Ellen and the money owing for her room. She begrudged that bitterly but she would not let it show. She had a hundred and fifty dollars left and by her calculations she could reach San Francisco for a hundred and forty-two. The remainder would buy a few meals if she spent nothing for lodgings. There was small margin for error.

The stage company next day required fifty-five dollars but for this she was assured of a seat to Yuma, or so she believed until she reached Maricopa Wells nine hours later. When she asked the agent how soon she could leave for Yuma he looked at her in surprise.

"Why, ma'am, didn't they tell you there ain't no stage to Yuma from here?"

"What on earth do you mean? They sold me a seat on it!"

"Durn fools! The Gila River has done washed out half th' road frum here t' Yuma. Ain't nuthin' goin' over that road now."

"Oh, no! How long will it take to fix it?"

"Lordy, ma'am, I dunno. Week or two, I reckon."

She clenched small gloved fists on his counter and glared at him. "I've got to get to Yuma. Is there no other way?"

"I reckon you c'ld go up to Wickenburg an' over to th' river. All them Colorado riverboats stop at Ehrenberg goin' down to Yuma."

"All right," she said grimly. "Will the stage company pay my way downriver from Ehrenberg?"

He almost swallowed his tobacco. Plainly he thought her touched in the head.

"Now, ma'am, why in th' world would th' Texas an' California Comp'ny pay your fare on a Colorado riverboat? There ain't no kinda connection between 'em."

"Because I paid them to get me to Yuma, that's why! It's not my fault your road washed out."

"Ain't my road nor th' Comp'ny's neither. Cain't help it if th' durn thing washed out." The strain of this exchange was telling on him but he was determinedly polite.

"Now look here, ma'am. You kin stay here till th' road's fixed an' we'll get you t' Yuma or I'll give you back part o' your fare an' we'll call her quits. How's that?"

"But you said I could get to Ehrenberg by stage!"

"I did, dawgonnit! You can an' it'll cost you . . . lemme see," he figured laboriously with his pencil. "It'll cost you exactly five dollar an' fifty cent on top o' whut you paid at Tucson." He could see the storm coming and he held up his hand.

"Lissen, ma'am . . . lissen a minnit! It's a sight further from Tucson t' Ehrenberg than it is t' Yuma. Th' Comp'ny ain't obliged t' haul you all over th' Territory jest 'cause you done paid fer a seat t' Yuma."

"It's not fair!" she burst out, close to tears of frustration. "Now I'll have to pay for the steamboat too!" The loafers gathered around the stove were watching with interest now.

"You broke, miss?" one of them asked. The hopeful way he said it roused her to their stares and she blushed furiously.

"No!" She dug in her bag for the slender roll of greenbacks.

"Here! Three . . . four . . . five . . . six!" She counted bills onto the counter and held out her hand for change. The agent sighed heavily.

"Now, ma'am . . ." he began cautiously, "I ain't gonna discount them bills like I oughtta seein' you done run into some hard luck, but ain't you got no silver atall? I cain't give out no four-bit piece in change for them things."

She was tempted to swear. She was so furious at having to give up her lone fifty-cent piece she failed to understand his remark about discounting her greenbacks. She rang the coin on the wood and snatched back a bill.

"When does the stage leave?"

"Eight o'clock tomorrer mornin'."

He had thought his troubles were over but when all the hangers-on had drifted away she was still there, sitting stiffly erect by the potbellied wood stove.

"This ain't no fit place for a lady t' stay th' night!"

"You know a better one?"

"Folks what has t' stay th' night mostly goes t' Murphy's crost th' street. He'll give you supper an' a bed."

"No thank you. I'll stay here."

"But after th' Phoenix stage gits here 'round midnight, I'm gonna close up an' go to bed myself."

"I'll be quite all right."

"Hell's bells!" he swore softly. "All right. I'll tell th' greaser kid t' keep th' fire goin' but there won't be no one else aroun' here 'fore daylight 'less one o' them cowpokes takes a notion t' look in on you."

"Can't you lock the door when you go?"

He shook his head in defeat and after a while he brought her a big tin cup of coffee and a blanket. When the Phoenix coach had come and gone she slept fitfully, curled on a bench with the carpetbag under her head.

The eighty miles to Wickenburg were covered next day in less than seven hours and they stopped only long enough to substitute a coach for the celerity wagon to cover the last lap over the desert to Ehrenberg and the Colorado River. Samantha found the violent swaying of the coach unpleasant but there was less dust and eventually she fell asleep from sheer exhaustion.

The coach rolled steadily through the night and dawn exploded from the desolate waste behind them as they pitched into Ehrenberg. She eyed the outlines of the town in the first level rays of the sun and shuddered.

The single street paralleling the river was sandy and neglected, littered with refuse. It was bordered by low adobe houses in varying stages of disrepair. Some boasted a veranda or ramada in front and a few of these had a lattice screen for additional shade, slender ocotillo cactus stalks woven and bound with rawhide. Beyond rolled the Colorado, broad and swift and turbulent, ranging in color from blood-red to a rich chocolate hue.

The stage agent could tell her little about the riverboats.

"Cap'n Polhemus went upriver in th' *Cocopah* couple days ago, ma'am, but I doubt he'll be back fer a week or more. Why don't you ask at Barney's; he does a lotta business with th' Steam Comp'ny."

Barney's proved to be a general store with a broad ramada in front, already occupied by a couple of Indians despite the early hour. They were a far cry from the lean and feral Apaches of her acquaintance, dull-eyed and shabby in their cast-off white man's clothes. Inside, a Mexican boy sprinkled water from a bucket on the earthen floor.

"Mister Barney?" she asked. He nodded toward the back of the store.

"Will you tell him, please, I'd like to speak to him?" She persisted, doubtful of his understanding. He disap-

339

peared, returning in a moment with a paunchy, graying man, well-dressed and obviously surprised to see her. He nodded pleasantly.

"Please, I came to ask about a boat. They said at the stage station you would know."

"A boat, miss? What about a boat?"

"I want to go to Yuma. When will there be a boat going downriver?"

"Ah! I see. Well, the *Cocopah* should be coming back down in a week or two if she doesn't get stranded above Callville. The *Gila* is due here any day now but to tell you the truth, I'll expect her when I see her. Things are pretty messed up at Yuma now."

"What happened?"

"The *Montana* burned at Cape Lucas just before Christmas on her way around from Frisco and that leaves only the *Newbern* to haul everything around the Cape. I suspect they'll hold the *Gila* at Yuma until she gets there."

She contemplated the necessity of finding a place to stay until one of the riverboats appeared. No matter how poor an accommodation, it would cut dangerously into her slender capital.

"How . . . how much does it cost?"

"How much does what cost, miss?"

"A place on the boat."

"To Yuma?"

"Well, actually I'm going to San Francisco."

"You going to take the steamer around the Cape from Yuma or the stage to San Diego?"

"I thought I'd take the stage. I heard the railroad has reached San Diego now."

"Not yet, but it has got to Los Angeles. You can take the cars there." He scratched his chin and thought a moment. "Downriver to Yuma, ten; stage to San Diego, forty-two; steamer to Frisco, forty-five. Make it a hundred, right? You might clip a little off that if you took the cars from San Diego to Frisco but I don't know how much."

She knew to the penny what was in her purse and it

was twelve dollars short of the sum he quoted. The added cost of the riverboat had defeated her.

"That's in coin, of course," he added.

"Why?" she gasped.

"Miss, if the government don't quit foolin' with the currency, greenbacks won't be worth the paper they're printed on. The Steam Company's discounting paper money twenty percent, and that's not bad. Some places on the river it's fifty percent."

"That . . . that makes it cost more in bills, doesn't it?"

"Why, sure! Twenty percent more. Cost you a hundred and twenty in greenbacks."

She closed her eyes and drew a long, ragged breath.

"You all right?" he asked anxiously. "Don't you feel well, miss?"

"I'm . . . all right," she managed. "Could I have a drink of water, please?"

"Sure . . . sure!" He dipped it from an *olla* and it looked like weak tea in the cup. "Don't mind the color. Hasn't had time to settle yet."

She drank it gratefully. It was not twelve dollars she needed but thirty-two and her need made her desperate.

"Mister Barney?" she said softly.

"Yes, miss?"

"Have . . . have you any work I could do?"

"Work? You mean a job?"

"Yes. I have to make some money. I haven't got enough."

His eyebrows climbed. She was well-dressed and she looked like a lady. Talked like one, too. You could never tell, though. A thought occurred to him and he considered it carefully.

He was a decent man. There were only two stores in Ehrenberg and his half of this monopoly was profitable enough to keep his family in San Francisco in great comfort. His wife never came to Ehrenberg. He jacked his prices as high as the traffic would bear and sometimes he discounted a customer's banknotes a little more than the going rate, but he wasn't a crook like some river merchants. Looking at this pretty girl who needed money, he was sorely tempted to step a little over the line. But he temporized.

"You an Army girl? Why don't you ask the clerk at the depot to make you a little loan? Name's Vandervere. Good man. He'll help you out."

"No!"

"You in trouble?"

"No . . . yes, I suppose so. I need money enough to pay my fare to the coast, that's all. Lots of people need money."

"Sure, but they aren't girls like you and they aren't in Ehrenberg."

He studied her again, appreciatively. Slender build but the plain brown dress fitted closely at throat and waist and set it off well. That chip hat on her dusty hair was no cheap thing either. Odd about her hands and face, so deeply tanned. Just didn't look like the kind of girl to be bumming her way down the river. Got to be something funny here.

A pretty girl in a tough spot and who knows how far she'd go to make her fare money? But there were too many clacking tongues quick to pass the word Barney had himself a woman. His wife would hear them. He sighed regretfully.

"I got nothing for you here." He jerked a thumb at the Mexican boy. "You wouldn't work for what I pay my help."

"Where can I go? There must be someone. Are there no families with children?"

"No Americans. Not since Lieutenant Summerhayes' wife went East with her little boy." He wondered about Fisher, who ran the other general store, but Fisher was in the same fix as himself, even more cautious, too. There was only one thing a girl could do in Ehrenberg to make herself some money. He avoided the big gray eyes watching him so hopefully.

"You might try Sam Willard at the Silver Dollar. His girl ran off upriver with a gambling man a while back."

"What is the Silver Dollar?"

"A saloon, girl. What else?"

Samantha's shoulders sagged. What could she expect? She couldn't blame him for what he was thinking. He watched her fumble for the carpetbag.

"Is the law after you, girl?"

"No."

"Where'd you come from?"

Her first impulse was to say Phoenix or Prescott but he would probably ask more questions she couldn't answer.

"Tucson. I came out here with my aunt last year. She was sick and the doctor said she'd be better in Arizona. She wasn't. She died." She hoped Aunt Bee wouldn't hold that fabrication against her. It was simple enough for Barney to accept it.

"I just want to go back home, Mister Barney. I thought I had money enough but I didn't know about this discount thing."

"You ever work in a saloon before?"

"No. But I've got to find work!"

"Oh, hell!" he swore. Tearing a scrap of paper from the roll over the counter he scribbled a note on it.

"Take this to Thad Posey. He's got a restaurant right across the street from Willard's place. I don't promise a thing, mind you, but Thad's been talking about taking on some more help. He might give you a job. If he won't . . . you're that much closer to Willard's anyhow."

"Thank you, Mister Barney." She picked up the bag.

"Haven't you even got a nickel, miss?"

"Whatever for?"

"It's mighty hot out there and that bag's heavy." He indicated the Mexican boy. "Give him a nickel and he'll carry it for you."

She wanted to laugh. Barney's benevolence had limits. So much for the vaunted gallantry of the frontier.

"I expect I'd better get used to it. Thanks again for your help."

Her heels sank deep in the sandy street as she picked her way around the unpleasant litter. The broiling sun dealt kindly with that at any rate. The heads, horns

343

and hooves flung into the street when a sheep or a beef was butchered did not decay in Ehrenberg. The sun baked them until they mummified.

There were more Indians and Mexicans in the street now. The former watched her unsteady progress fixedly; the Mexicans were more circumspect. One adobe building in Ehrenberg looked like the next but Sam Willard's place was easily found. Over the ramada hung a crudely painted copy of a silver dollar as big as a cartwheel.

Posey's restaurant had a whitewashed front bearing the single word "EATS" in black paint. The door was open and Samantha entered, panting and grateful for escape from the sun. A fat Mexican woman, crashing dishes into a pile on the counter, eyed her sourly.

"Finish. No more eat now. Come back noon."

"I don't want to eat, thank you. I'm looking for Mister Posey."

"¡Patrón!" bawled the woman. "¡Venga!" Samantha shuddered at the familiar command. A plump little man with sagging jowls and suspicious eyes appeared at once. He looked at the Mexican woman, then at Samantha, rubbed his bald head and hooked his thumbs in faded Army suspenders supporting worn trousers over a coffee-colored undershirt.

"Somethin' fer you, ma'am?"

She handed him Barney's note and he read it, looked at her, and read it again.

"You wantta work here?" He sounded incredulous.

She looked around her. The restaurant consisted of a single long room with freshly whitewashed walls, a dozen tables with as many chairs as could be crowded around them and a single, immense coal-oil lamp suspended from the middle of the ceiling. There was a serving counter in front of a door to the kitchen. The Mexican woman gathered the pile of dishes in her arms but did not go; her black eyes flickered from her boss to Samantha. Posey shuffled his feet on the earthen floor.

"You cook?" The question was even more incredulous. The woman snorted in disgust.

"I can cook, yes. But you already have a cook, don't you?"

"Sure. So whut kin you do?"

"How do they get the food?" She gestured at the tables. "Do you bring it to them?"

"Nah! They git it off'n th' counter there. How else?"

"Then I can wait table for you. They'd like that, wouldn't they?"

His round, sober face creased in a grin. "I sh'ld reckon they would." He studied her and then the note again.

"Barney sez yer a decent gal. Tell ye flat out, missy, I got no use fer a tramp. Don't mean nuthin' personal but that's a fact. I gotta bunch o' good, sober fellas eats here regular now an' I don't wantta bring in no trash."

So Barney thought her a decent girl. That was a small victory.

"I understand, Mister Posey. I don't know if he told you or not, but I didn't know about the discount on greenbacks and I'm short of money to pay my fare to the coast. I'm trying to go home and I want a job long enough to make what I need. I'm no tramp and I won't make you any trouble."

"Ye didn't read the note?"

"Of course not."

"You in some kinda trouble?"

She wondered if anyone came to Ehrenberg who was not. The question seemed to be obligatory.

"No. My only trouble is lack of money. I want to work for it."

She held out her hands and he examined the small calloused palms in surprise. They did not go with the dress or her speech and they made him feel a little better about her. She was a looker, he had to admit, and if she could stand the work she would draw trade.

"How much ye want to wait table? Three times a day an' help Dolores clean up. Sunday's off."

"How much will you give me?" she countered.

"Dollar a day."

"Is that all?"

"All ye kin eat, free." He squinted at her shrewdly. "Where ye gonna put up?"

"I . . . I haven't looked for a place yet."

"Thought not. Dolores sleeps in back. Ye kin too. That's a dollar a day all found. Cain't pay no more'n that."

Five weeks, she thought. Five weeks and two days. It's better than the saloon. "All right, Mister Posey. When do I begin?"

"Nuthin' like right now! Help Dolores git them dishes cleaned up an' ye can start on dinner. Gotta be ready noon sharp. She'll show ye where to put yer carpetbag an' where ye kin sleep. I'll git ye a bed-sack an' some fresh shucks to stuff it."

Samantha smiled at Dolores, who nodded in return. Her job not threatened, she was prepared to be at least neutral for the moment.

"By the way," demanded Posey, "whut do I call ye?"

"Sally. Sally Allen," she replied. He accepted that without question and she followed Dolores into the kitchen.

THIRTY-NINE

From Glendive to Miles' encampment at the mouth of the Tongue River was six long days of travel up a track cut alongside the Yellowstone. Only because the ground was frozen was it passable for wagons. Until October, when Miles drove Sitting Bull and his band of Sioux from the river, they had harassed every train passing over it, but Tom encountered only a few ragged families of Indians who begged for food.

He reached the Tongue on the last day of December but Miles and most of his regiment were gone. Crazy Horse had settled for the winter and Miles had gone after him. Expecting bad weather and poor communication with his base, Miles had moved south in an unusual formation: supplies first. He sent Major Dickey with an oxtrain to set up an advance depot sixty miles up the Tongue and he left explicit orders for Tom's ammunition to be brought to that depot as soon as it arrived.

The base camp commander reinforced Tom's escort to about company strength—forty men—but the reinforcements were no prize. Stragglers and leftovers from the main column, they represented half a dozen companies of two different regiments and were a hard lot to manage. Tom paused only for a night and then pushed on.

He found the trail up the Tongue River worse than any he had passed over so far. Major Dickey had improved it a little, throwing logs and brush into the worst holes and chopping a by-pass around the impossible gorges, but getting mule-drawn wagons over it was an appalling task. Tom's personal goal lay beyond Dickey's wagon depot; once he had delivered his ammunition, he had to find Miles. That crusty and hard-driving general was the key to the plan he had devised at Glendive and his fear that Samantha would not wait much longer urged him on. He drove his lumbering, crashing wagons as fast as the reluctant teamsters would go. All the first morning the clouds hung just above the bluffs enclosing the Tongue and at noon the snow fell in soft, floating flakes.

For three exhausting days he fought his way upriver, and from the increasing litter along the track he guessed that Miles had pushed his infantrymen equally hard. Snow flurries blew in on the wind from Canada with increasing frequency and it grew colder by the hour. He dreaded the miserable trail when it became snow-covered. Just before dark on the third night, two soldiers from the Twenty-second Infantry walked into his bivouac from the south with welcome news: Dickey's wagons were only a half day's march ahead.

They claimed they were scouts who had lost their way, but Tom suspected they were straggling back to base camp. They told a confused tale of fighting on New Year's Day when Miles' force encountered hostile Sioux somewhere beyond the wagon depot. Tom realized with a shock that 1877 was already three days old.

"Major Dickey, he went with Ginral Miles an' they's a cap'n at th' waggins now. He got wounded when th' ginral whupped them Injuns upriver a piece."

"Ah, that Ginral Miles, he's slyer'n ary ol' fox!" put in the other soldier. "He got hisself a couple howitzers rigged t' look like waggins an' when he sees hos-tiles . . . whap! He whups th' canvas off'n them guns an' purely blows them Injuns away."

Next morning, their fourth on the trail, the wagons were scarcely under way when they heard distant firing. Tom drove his men savagely. Either Miles was falling back before more Sioux than he could handle or a raiding party had struck the wagon depot. In either case his ammunition would be needed. About midmorning there was some volley firing but after that it grew sporadic and at noon he found a corporal and four men huddled around a fire in the middle of the trail. They looked at him dully.

"What's going on up there?" Tom demanded. "What are you doing here?"

The corporal was evasive. "We wuz sent back t' look fer you, Lootenant. They's Injuns been snipin' th' waggins since daybreak an' th' cap'n wuz worrit about you."

"Well, what the hell are you doing, coffee-cooling it in the middle of the road like this? Why didn't you come on as fast as you could?"

The corporal looked pained. "Didn't see no sign o' th' lootenant an' we figgered might be you heered all that shootin' an' forted-up a ways back."

The reply so enraged Tom he choked on his fury. "So you were going to skulk here awhile and then tell the train commander we'd turned back, is that it? Corporal . . ." He lifted a mittened fist and shook it. "If you were in my outfit I'd have you breaking rock for a year!"

He whirled on a knot of his own men who had gathered curiously behind him.

"Move, dammit! Get these wagons moving! You, Corporal Herlie . . . take two men and this pack of stragglers and get to that ox train as fast as you can. Tell the officer in command we're coming and I'd appreciate word from him where he wants these wagons when we get there."

Herlie, who had proved reliable on the march upriver, saluted and hustled his sullen party forward. Tom was still shaking with rage. What he wanted of Miles required that officer's good favor and a report that he had quit and run at the first sound of gunfire would hardly earn it.

Within the hour he could see Dickey's wagons corralled on a flat reaching east from the river. Herlie returned with word from their commander. So far there had been only some sniping by Indians. No one knew what had happened to Miles but the appearance of hostiles in his rear was alarming. Tom was to bring his wagons straight onto the flat and they would open a gap in the circle of their own so he could come in. There was no firing from the wagons now but in the bluffs above a rifle thumped occasionally. Once a bullet howled high overhead and the teamsters whipped up their mules in earnest.

Tom brought his wagons across the rutted and frozen meadow at a jangling trot and found the wounded captain in a rude pit revetted with poles. He was sitting on one ration box with a foot, wrapped in a buffalo robe, propped on another. He peered at Tom from within a knitted shawl wrapped around his head and face like a turban.

It was hard to understand the man because he spoke through the shawl, but he seemed to be welcoming the reinforcement and complaining about their speed at the same time.

"They hit us early this morning," he mumbled. "Came from the south. Don't appear to be many of 'em an' they're all afoot. I sent a sergeant an' all the men I could spare up the bluff to drive 'em off a way but it sounds to me like they bogged down . . . or quit on me." As if to emphasize his point a rifle banged loudly from the heights overlooking the wagons and the captain shifted fretfully on his box.

"I'm damn glad to see you, Mister. We got to get those bluffs cleared an' I don't have another officer. Can't get up there myself."

"I'll go," Tom told him. He looked for Herlie and found him a few yards away. The corporal sighed and sucked beads of ice from his shaggy mustache.

"Herlie, get all our wagons inside and tell the teamsters to unhitch, then pick twenty of our people and bring 'em to me on top. I'll meet you there. Strip off everything except belts and canteens and make sure every man has a full belt of cartridges." He turned back to the captain.

"Have you got anybody who can show me the quickest way up there? I'll take over your men and as soon as mine get there we'll sweep that crest clean."

The captain grunted. He was delighted to have another officer and particularly one so full of fight. "Sergeant Kemper will show you. I sent him up there once this morning and he's back. Kemper! Where is he?"

A beefy, red-faced soldier hugging the fire in the bottom of the pit stirred reluctantly. "Here, Cap'n."

Tom eyed the noncom with distaste. He viewed the whole gaggle of men huddled in the pit with disgust. There was an air of timidity and disorganization about them that made him uncomfortable. He supposed that like his own escort this train guard was made up of castoffs and stragglers from the fighting column. This would be a far cry from going into a fight backed by the tried and familiar noncoms of his own troop.

"Kemper!" called the captain as the sergeant climbed slowly from the pit. "Take that man Smith back up there when you go."

Smith was even more unattractive than the noncom; a young soldier with shifty eyes and a red nose that dripped steadily in spite of the freezing wind and his monotonous snuffling. It seemed he had become separated from the skirmishers on the bluff and had found his way directly to the fire.

Single file, Kemper leading and Smith in the rear, Tom urged his unhappy guides up the steep bluff. Slipping and scrambling, they clawed their way upward, guided by an occasional shot above. As they topped the first crest it began to snow again in heavy gusts of soft, thick flakes.

Here and there Tom spotted a cluster of empty cartridge cases that tinkled on the rocks underfoot and once a smear of blood. He wondered if it was Indian; there had been no mention of casualties among the wagon guards. From the looks of this lot, he thought disgustedly, if one of them had been hit the rest would have trampled each other in their rush to carry him down.

He began to sweat in his buffalo coat, but if he took it off he could not carry it and keep his hands free too. Abruptly the sergeant stopped and Tom collided with him heavily. With remarkable speed for a man so encumbered by coat and mittens, Kemper unslung his rifle.

"What is it?" Tom demanded, panting. He could see nothing but more of the deeply gullied bluffs.

"Injun! Look at th' bastid go! See 'im runnin' up that gully?" He pointed with his rifle and Tom caught a flash of something moving fast through the scrub brush. It was hard to see through the thickening snow.

"By God, there's another!" grunted Kemper. He jerked the rifle to his shoulder and fired, the long gun making a fearful roar. Smith jumped and whimpered, pressing close to Tom. The sergeant flipped open the block of the Springfield to reload and a whiff of evil-smelling smoke blew across Tom's face.

He had his revolver out now, but it was clumsy in his mittened hand and the distance was too great for the Colt. He could see both Indians for a moment, running with phenomenal speed up a steep draw

"Keerist!" swore Kemper. "They're gonna run right into our people!" He snapped a second futile shot at the fleeing pair.

"Come on!" Tom urged. "Let's get up there!" He

351

pushed past Kemper and thrashed upward. The sergeant found a game trail just above him and followed it, keeping abreast of the scrambling officer. Smith blundered and panted along behind Tom.

Private Smith was no recruit; he had been in the Army more than a year and on the Yellowstone since the past summer. But he was a hopeless soldier because he had fallen into a very soft job as soon as he arrived and stayed there as long as he could. He had been assigned to guard duty on the riverboat *Josephine*. The guard changed many times thereafter but Smith stayed on. Somehow the Fifth Infantry lost track of him and he remained on the *Josephine* until falling water drove her out for the winter. His company took him back then with no great affection and he rapidly became a sort of family joke.

It was as if the *Josephine* was the only home he had ever known. He had been comfortable there; the crew was good to him and he had never been shot at. Since he left the riverboat he had been continuously uncomfortable, nobody was good to him and every bush seemed to hide an Indian intent on killing him. He talked so much about his lost home that whenever one of his company saw him, he cupped a hand behind his ear and made a strange noise.

"Whoooo . . . hoo! What's that I hear, Smitty? Th' ol' Dirty Joe blowin' fer ye?"

Dennis Smith cursed his tormentors and dreamed of lost comfort. Sometimes he actually thought he heard the Dirty Joe blowing for a landing. He was soft and incompetent and miserable and his company commander put him on jobs like train guard just to be rid of him. He was terrified of going up this bluff but even more terrified that he might fall behind the sergeant and this strange, bloodthirsty lieutenant. He stumbled and flailed desperately to keep up.

"Smith hold yer gun up!" Kemper yelled at him. "You stick th' muzzle in th' ground an' you'll blow yer head off when you shoot it!"

Smith was so winded he did not hear clearly. He wasn't sure if the sergeant had told him to hold his rifle up or stay closer to the officer. He did both and managed to step heavily on Tom Royal's heel. Tom never noticed but Smith was thrown completely off-balance. His feet shot from under him on the snow-slick dead grass and he measured his length on the ground. His rifle slammed into it beside him. Since it was loaded and fully cocked the impact fired it.

The heavy .45-caliber slug hit Tom Royal squarely in the back of the head and knocked him a dozen feet down the slope where he came to rest face down in a clump of laurel. He never moved thereafter.

"Sweet Jeezus . . . help me!" moaned Smith. Kemper skidded to a stop and stared openmouthed.

"You silly bastid! What have you done?"

Smith stared at the motionless body of the officer and began to sob—great choking sobs that shook his whole body.

"I di'nt mean to! Honest to God, Sarge . . . I dunno how it happened! Oh, God ha' mercy on my soul! Is he dead, Sarge? Is he dead?"

One glance at the lieutenant told Kemper the answer to that. "God damn you to hell, you stoopid, helpless . . ." He broke off in mid-curse and whirled to look up the bluff. A pebble bounced and clicked down the slope toward him.

Scrambling like a cat, the burly soldier threw himself behind a rock and peered around it. Whatever he saw made him relax, lowering his rifle and easing the hammer to half cock. He scowled ferociously at the weeping private.

"Git up here, you witless sunnuvabitch!" Blindly Smith crawled toward him. "Bring yer rifle, stoopid!"

Smith fumbled for the weapon, averting his eyes from the limp body in the laurel bush. He retrieved it and made his way painfully to the sergeant's rock.

"Load it!" Kemper growled.

"No!" wailed Smith. "What I wanta do that for?"

"Load yer goddam rifle like I tell ya!"

Numbly Smith opened the block, ejected the empty cartridge with a shudder and somehow fumbled a loaded

353

one into the breech. Kemper reached over to slam it closed.

"Look! Ya see that? Not over there, dammit . . . here!" He jerked Smith's rifle barrel into line. Not fifteen yards away lay an Indian on his belly, staring woodenly at the two soldiers. From the ashen hue of his face he was badly hurt.

He had probably been hit when the captain's skirmish line first climbed the bluffs and had crawled into the wash to escape notice. When Smith's rifle went off he moved, revealing himself to Kemper. He was unarmed, completely helpless, and he lay there waiting for them to finish him off. Propped on his forearms he faced death expressionless.

"Kill him!" hissed Kemper. Smith made a gagging noise.

"I can't! He's done. Look at th' pore bastid. Shoot him yesself if you wanta!"

"You shoot him, or I'll beat yer goddam head in! Do what I tell ya!"

Shaking violently, Smith brought his Springfield into approximate line with the motionless Indian. The muzzle wavered slackly but with a superhuman effort the miserable soldier managed to jerk the trigger. At that range it was hard to miss but he did. Dirt and snow spouted from the ground by the Indian, who closed his eyes momentarily, then resumed staring at them. The eyes glittered unnaturally in his pale face.

"Goddam, Smith . . . you couldn't tomp sand in a rathole!" Kemper jerked the rifle from the boy's limp hands, reloaded it and thrust it back.

"Now this time hit 'im! Git up an' walk over there if ya hafta, but hit th' bastid!"

Whimpering, Smith shut his eyes and jerked the trigger. By blind luck the bullet slammed into the Indian with an audible thump. He hunched up a little, gave a wheezing groan and went limp.

"Why? Gahdammit . . . Sarge, why'd ya make me do that?" choked Smith, close to hysteria.

Kemper grinned. He was an old soldier and battle-wise. He had served with the Fifth Infantry since 1863. He had a purpose in what he was doing to Smith and it was not idle meanness.

"I'll tell ya inna minnit. Help me find his gun; it's gotta be aroun' here sommers. He didn't come far hit like he was."

"That's what I mean!" blubbered Smith. "He was awready half dead! Why'd I hafta shoot 'im again?"

"Shut up an' look fer th' gun."

The sergeant searched the ground rapidly, poking under the laurel bushes. Smith blundered aimlessly after him. There were two bodies he had to avoid looking at now and in a minute he was going to be sick. Nothing like this had ever happened to him in his worst dreams.

Kemper grunted triumphantly. He had found what he was looking for: a short cavalry carbine, breech open and empty, a dozen spent cartridges scattered nearby. The Indian had used every one he had before he crawled the ten yards to the place where he died. Kemper picked up the carbine and one empty cartridge. He examined the weapon and grunted again in satisfaction.

"Beautiful!" He pointed to the stock. "See there? C Troop, Seventh Cav'ry. That red booger was at th' Custer fight. Ya still sorry ya shot 'im?"

Smith gulped and stared at the carbine.

"Awright!" Kemper snarled. "Now lissen t' me an' lissen good! I ain't gonna tell ya but oncet an' ya ain't never gonna fergit it. Ya unnerstand?" He pointed with the carbine at the dead Indian.

"This is how it happen. That Injun wuz layin' there waitin' fer us. He used his last bullet ta kill th' lootenant." He flipped the empty carbine cartridge accurately into the wash by the Indian's body. "Soon's th' Injun cut loose, ya come back with two shots . . . bam! bam! Hit 'im both times as any fool kin plainly see if he wants ta look." He fixed Smith with a cold eye. "Ya got that straight?"

The private opened and closed his mouth soundlessly twice before he could respond.

"Ya mean . . . ya mean y' ain't gonna tell I shot th' lootenant?" He had already lost his grip on reality and now he doubted his hearing. Kemper swore volubly and obscenely until the familiar oaths convinced the shaken young soldier. An expression of piteous hope dawned on his tear-streaked face.

"Jeezus!" he mumbled. "I thank you, Sergeant!"

Kemper could have shot the Indian himself and saved time and trouble but two years of war and eleven of Indian-fighting had taught him a lot about misfit soldiers like Smith.

"Ya crap-head, don't thank me! I'd as lief see Gen'l Miles drum yer ass outta th' Army an' inta jail fer th' rest o' yer life 'cept he'd sure as hell git me too! Jest ya remember it like I told it ya an' keep tellin' it that way an' ya'll be a goddam hero 'stead o' jailbait. Kin ya do that, Smith?"

"I . . . sure, Sarge! Keerist! Sure I kin!"

Again Kemper grinned. If he had shot the Indian this sweating simpleton would sooner or later have spilled his nightmare to someone. This way, the boy had a profitable lie to tell. He had killed the Indian who shot the officer and by the third time he told that lie he would believe it himself.

"Awright. Now stop callin' me Sarge. I'm pertiklar about who calls me that. When ya talk to me, Smith, ya call me Sergeant, or I'll have yer ass on report ta that cap'n . . if he'll come outta that bomb-proof he's dug hisself long enough ta lissen!" He reached down to brush snow aimlessly from Tom Royal's back.

"Too goddam bad! Shame ta lose that kind."

Smith looked another way, swallowing hard.

"Sling yer rifle, stoopid, an' let's gettim outta here."

The private slid, stiff-legged, down to the laurel brush but when Kemper turned Tom over he was violently and helplessly sick. The sergeant watched him in disgust.

"Here!" he said. "You take the guns an' I'll carry him. Help me gettim up, dammit!"

"What for ya wanta carry that Injun gun, Sarge?" Kemper straightened up and fixed him with a glittering eye.

" 'Cause I damn well said so! Now carry that carbine an' don't call me Sarge again. Ya got that?" The

"C/7" burned into the carbine stock was a valuable asset and Kemper was determined to produce it.

"Uh!" he grunted. "Gimme yer scarf."

"It's cold, Sergeant! Why ya want my scarf?"

"'T' wrap his head in, ya stoopid bastid! I can't carry 'im like this!"

FORTY

Major Compton smoothed the telegram under his fingers and eyed the commander of G Troop sourly.

"Where's his girl?"

"Still at Lowell with the Van Scivers as far as I know."

Compton studied the message again. It began with the usual dire formula, "I regret to inform you . . ." and it was signed "Miles."

"It was relayed to us by Camp Lowell. Someone must have told her by now."

"You'd think so."

"Are you going to send someone over there?"

"What for?"

"Dammit, Tullius, you're his troop commander! What d'ye usually do when this happens? What about his gear; shouldn't she have that?"

"I don't know if she should or his people back East. I don't know if she even wants anything of his. He didn't seem to want her very much when he left here."

"Well, we have to find out. Who's his closest friend here?"

"I'm not sure he had one."

The major fought down rising anger. "Tullius, you're

357

acting like a sorehead. Who was going to be his best man at the wedding?"

"That's young Hulse at Camp Bowie. He and Royal were classmates at the Point and I think Hulse is the only other man in the regiment who knew the girl before she came out here."

"Then Hulse is your man. I'll ask his commander to let us have him for a few days until we get this cleared up."

There were a hundred and five miles between Bowie and Lowell and Tate Hulse covered them in two days. His first horse gave out at the Cienega stage station and he left him there, covering the last lap into Tucson on a team horse begged from the agent. More travel-wise than a cavalry troop horse, this one could not be flogged to a pace that would break his wind and his racking gait completed his rider's exhaustion.

At the Van Scivers' quarters he found no one but the orderly. Wentz said Ellen had taken the buggy to buy chickens from a farm in the Santa Cruz Valley.

"Someding haff schtolen her schickens, Loodenant. Giffs no eckhs now. Missus Van Schkeever haff gone to get anudder schicken so ist eckhs for Loodenant Van Schkeever's—"

"All right . . . all right! I understand. I'll wait."

He stumbled into Carp's study and fell sound asleep in the big leather chair. Only minutes later, it seemed, someone shook him urgently.

"Tate! Tate, wake up!" It was Ellen. "Where did you come from?"

"Bowie." He rubbed his eyes and forced them open. "You know about Tom?"

"Yes. Colonel Oakes told us five days ago when the telegram came." She looked puzzled. "Did you get my letter? Isn't that why you're here?"

"Letter?" He shook his head. "No. Major Compton sent word from Camp Grant he wanted me to see Sam and do what I can to help."

"Oh." She began straightening things on Carp's table, avoiding his eyes. "I sent it by the mail carrier and . . ."

"He hadn't got there when I left. Where's Sam? Ellen, what's the matter?"

"She's gone, Tate. She left the day after Christmas."

His booted heels crashed on the floor as he jerked to his feet. "No!" he exploded. "I want to . . ." He broke off, staring at her in bewilderment. "How could she find out? I thought you said the telegram didn't get here until five days ago?"

"It didn't."

"Then why did she leave? What happened?"

"Don't shout at me, Tate." She looked so unhappy he was instantly ashamed of himself.

"I apologize, Ellen. Forgive me, please. I'm tired and I don't understand what's happened."

"You must be exhausted. Do you want a drink?"

"It would put me out like a candle. Can I have some coffee?"

She made it for him and he sat at the kitchen table waiting until she brought the cup and sat opposite him.

"I don't know all of it, Tate. Like everything else since she came back, we only got little bits and pieces. There . . . there was some gossip about her here on the post before Christmas and she stopped coming at all. I begged her to come just for Christmas Day and she finally agreed but only if I promised there'd be no one else. That's why I didn't let you know. Then suddenly she appeared at the dance here Christmas Eve. We were delighted, of course, and I asked her to stay the night with us, but . . ." She spread her hands helplessly.

"Did she?"

"No. After the dance she . . . just disappeared. It seems she went back into Tucson and Mrs. Herscholdt took offense at something. We waited for her Christmas Day but she didn't come. I should have gone at once but I didn't. I didn't go until the next day and then it was too late. She had left Tucson."

Tate looked more baffled than ever. "But why? What happened with Mrs. Herscholdt?"

"I don't really know but she was still in a state when I saw her. All she would say was something about Sam coming in very late. She said . . . she said she wouldn't have her in her house any more."

"Just because she was late? Who was she with? Who brought her to the dance?"

Ellen gave him a worried look. "Henry DeBergh," she said softly.

Tate's face darkened. "That . . . !" He suppressed what he had started to say with difficulty.

"Now don't you make trouble! What's the use? She's gone and it won't bring her back. She left me a note but it isn't much help. She just said she was going and she was sorry not to see us and would we please send her trunk when she is settled."

"Settled where? Where's she going?"

"She didn't say. I suppose she could go back to Leavenworth but she hasn't anyone there that I know of."

"Did she have enough money to get there?"

"I don't know that either. You know how she was; she never talked about money. She had what Tom sent her and I suppose she saved a little from her salary at the school."

"When did Tom send money? Did he finally write to her?"

"Not since he wrote her when he left Camp Grant as far as I know. He sent the money then."

He squeezed his eyes shut and shook his head as if to clear it. "My God, what a mess! Doesn't that damned DeBergh know where she went?"

"No. Carp asked him. I didn't even want to see him."

"I don't blame you. I think I'll have a word with Henry DeBergh!"

"Why brawl with him? Everyone knows what kind of man he is. Besides . . . people have said wicked things about Sam and if you pick a fight with DeBergh you'll just make it worse."

"Well, DeBergh can wait but I've got to find Sam!"

Booted footsteps sounded in the hall and Carp appeared in the kitchen door. "So!" he said. "I wondered when you'd get here."

"Somebody's got to look for her!"

"Now hold on, Tate! Like I told you before, Sam Allyn's a grown woman and if she wants to leave Arizona I can't stop her. I'm not sure I want to."

Tate stood up abruptly, his face frozen. "What . . .?" Ellen began but Carp cut her off.

"No. I don't believe any slander about Sam and I don't much like your thinking I do. All I meant was she hasn't had much but grief from us and I can't blame her for pulling out."

Tate looked contrite. "You're right and I apologize. This seems to be my day for making a damn fool of myself. I still want to talk to her, though."

"So do we all but no one seems to know where she went. I suppose she'll write to us when she's ready."

"I don't want to wait for that. I'm going to find her. There aren't many ways to get out of Arizona. Do you know if she went east or to the coast?"

"The coast, I'd guess. She took the stage for Maricopa Wells from here, but, man, that was the twenty-sixth of December and this is January. She's been gone for three weeks and she could be east of the Mississippi by now."

Tate pounded his big fist on the table in frustration. "Why didn't you tell me? If I had known sooner . . ."

"Be reasonable, Tate. If she'd wanted to see you she'd have sent word."

"What if she took the steamer around the Cape from Yuma? If she did that she might not even be in San Francisco yet."

"So?"

"I could send a telegram to the Steam Company."

"Then what? Go after her?"

"Why not?"

Carp raised quizzical brows. "You have enough leave coming to do that or are you planning to go over the hill?"

"Don't bait him, Carp!" Ellen said sharply.

"I'm not, but he isn't making much sense."

"But we could at least find out where she's going! A girl like Sam didn't get out of the Territory without somebody noticing her."

"That's true. Someone in Yuma ought to be able to tell you whether she left there by steamer or stage."

"I'll send a telegram to Cy Earnest. He's the provost marshal there and he'll find out if anybody can."

Lieutenant Earnest's reply did not take much time. Wentz brought it while they were at breakfast the following day and Ellen put down her cup with a clatter, waiting for Tate to read it. His face was grim.

"Cy doesn't think she's been there at all. No one saw her leave by stage or steamer and there's no report of her in town." He pushed back his chair and stood up.

"Where are you going?" Ellen demanded.

"To talk to the stage agent in Tucson."

"I've already done that," said Carp. "She bought a ticket for Yuma through Maricopa Wells the day after Christmas."

"There's got to be more than that. If she didn't get to Yuma, where is she? The stage company's the only way to find out."

Ellen looked distressed. "You don't suppose . . ." she began softly and both men looked at her curiously.

"Where would she stay?" Carp asked. The answer occurred to all three of them as quickly as the question. "I think I'll go with you, Tate," he concluded.

Tate shook his head. "I don't for one minute believe she's with DeBergh but if she were, I wouldn't make trouble. Carp's right; she knows her own mind. No, I'm just going to talk to that stage agent again."

He returned that afternoon glummer than ever. "I think Cy Earnest is right. Around Christmas the road from Maricopa Wells to Yuma washed out so bad the stage quit running over it."

"Then she's still in Arizona somewhere?" cried Ellen.

"I doubt it. The agent says the Southern Pacific tracks were into Twin Palms long before Christmas. That's less than a hundred miles the other side of the Colorado River. The contractors are hauling from the railhead to three or four places on the river: La Paz, Ehrenberg . . . even Camp Mojave. All she had to do was get to the river and she could go on to Twin Palms a dozen ways. She could have been in San Francisco two weeks ago."

"What do we do now?"

Tate shrugged. "What can we do? Just wait, like Carp said. Wait for her to write."

Carp put his hand on the younger man's shoulder and shook it gently. "Sooner or later we'll hear from her. I had Wentz get her trunk from that sorehead widow and bring it out here. When she sends for it she has to tell us where she is and I'll let you know."

Tate departed in glum silence to make his report to Major Compton and return to Camp Bowie and there seemed to be an end to the matter for a time but when Carp came home that night he was obviously upset.

"Now what's happened?" demanded Ellen anxiously.

He put a smudged and dog-eared envelope on the table and she snatched it up. "But that isn't from Samantha! That's from Tom!"

"That's right. God knows how long it's been on the way. I suppose he sent it from somewhere up the Yellowstone before he was killed."

She looked at him pleadingly but he shook his head. "No, my dear. It can't possibly have any clue where she's gone. If I thought that I'd have opened it already. No, what's in there is for Sam . . . not for us."

FORTY-ONE

Thad Posey's cook accepted her new assistant very cautiously. Despite her calloused hands this gringo girl simply did not fit Dolores' notion of kitchen help. But she

363

was willing, uncomplaining, and by sheer hard work she won the friendship of the older woman. Not even in the Apache *ranchería* had Samantha worked so hard.

Their day began at dawn when Dolores rolled grunting from her cot to begin breakfast. Samantha followed, pausing long enough to splash water on her face from the barrel by the door. A Mexican boy had already started a fire in the ancient kitchen range and for the rest of the day he was either splitting wood or stuffing it into the stove.

Biscuits by the hundreds had to be baked; dried chipped beef cooked with canned milk into a gluey stew to pour over them; oatmeal set to boil in the big kettle and countless potatoes peeled, sliced and fried in sputtering grease.

As the tables filled, Samantha hustled coffee, biscuits and a bowl of beef stew to each. Bacon and potatoes followed and if a man wanted steak or chops and eggs, they were done to order by Dolores.

Thad Posey's clientele were pleased with the innovation. Now, instead of lining up at the counter, they could sit and call for service. The new girl was very businesslike but a polite greeting earned a man a cheerful smile and even in an ankle-length apron of flour sacking Samantha was an eye-catcher.

Thad's regulars, as he called them, were singled out for special attention; Samantha saw to it they were well cared for. They liked this and in return they were protective if a stranger was moved to brashness by the presence of a pretty waitress.

Breakfast and dinner were no problem in this respect; only at night was there difficulty when the Silver Dollar's customers spilled across the street in search of food. A teamster with a few belts of Sam Willard's vile whiskey in him might rest his hand companionably on Samantha's hip as she bent over his table. She moved out of reach with a chilling look that deterred most and if he were too persistent she begged help from Posey. The pudgy little man could be surprisingly feisty in defense of the respectability he coveted for his restaurant.

By the end of the first week Samantha felt if she did

not have a real bath she would die. She cornered Posey and demanded a tub.

"Tub? Ain't got none. Whut ye gonna do with it?"

"I want to take a bath."

"No place in town t' git a bath 'cept th' barbershop an' you shore cain't go in there. Why'nt ye do like Dolores? Where d'ye wash, Dolores?"

"Een th' reever."

Next morning at break of day she led an apprehensive Samantha to the bank of the Colorado. Joining hands like children they waded knee-deep into the swift current, daring go no farther for they could feel the stones on the bottom grinding together as they were swept by. They sat in the shallow water, splashing and enjoying their chocolate-hued bath. A screen of low mesquite bushes on the bank was protection enough against casual passersby at that hour. Afterward, Dolores took her helper on a round of visits.

Through this Sunday morning ritual Samantha met most of Dolores' numberless relatives in Ehrenberg. Since she avoided contact with Americans outside the restaurant, the hospitable Mexicans were a delight for her. They were miserably poor but because she came with Dolores she was welcomed gladly.

In the yard of each adobe hut there burned a fire between stones with a sheet of iron laid on top. In the morning a pot of coffee brewed there and the family sat with their guests in the ramada to drink this with a biscuit for breakfast. There would be but one more meal in the day and it was begun early. A kettle of *frijoles*, big brown Mexican beans, was put to boil on the fire. After a while, lard and salt were added and the pot left to simmer until after church when the beans were tender and ready to eat in their own thick red gravy.

Then the wife or a daughter of the house mixed a paste of flour, salt and water from which was made the *tortilla*, unleavened native bread. Their making fascinated Samantha. A pretty Mexican girl tossed the wafer-like disc of dough over her arm and pulled or patted it transparently thin. If no male member of the family were

365

present she might hike up her skirt and perform this operation on her thigh, which gave more working surface, then it was tossed on the hot sheet iron to bake. With a heaping spoonful of beans on top it made a delicious meal, occasionally supplemented by dried meat, *carne seca,* pounded and stewed with red or green peppers.

Samantha found the women scrupulously clean and modest. Some Mexicans might have earned the scorn of Americans by their casual ways and indifferent morals, but those she met in Ehrenberg were never like that. Also, if they were puzzled by the American girl who shared a room with Dolores and preferred their company to that of her own people, they never let it show.

Saturday night at the restaurant was generally bad. It had but two relieving features for Samantha; when they closed the door and put out the big lamp Thad Posey paid her for the week, and she could look forward to Sunday. He begrudged the holiday, for he could have kept the restaurant open profitably, but both women insisted on it.

The six paper dollars seemed all too few for the week's hard work but for Samantha there was a small and unforeseen windfall. Now and again a man would leave a coin by his plate; most were trifling: two- and three-cent pieces or an old silver half dime, but sometimes there was one of the new silver twenty-cent pieces. One night a tipsy wagon boss rapped a coin on the table and held it up for her inspection. It was small and dull but unquestionably a five-dollar gold piece.

"For me?" she asked in astonishment.

He grinned and pulled her down to whisper in her ear, trying at the same time to push the coin and his hand into the neck of her dress. She fled to the kitchen, face flaming.

"Five dollars!" she sputtered, almost weeping with rage. "Five dollars gold . . . for that!"

Dolores stared. "*¿Qué pasa?*"

Still stuttering in fury, Samantha told her.

"*¡Pobre niña! ¡Puerco!* Feelthy peeg!"

But her little hoard grew. She was never sure of the

value of the greenbacks for the discount rate fluctuated constantly, but the coins would be worth face value.

One thing about Ehrenberg puzzled her, though. "I haven't seen a dozen soldiers since I've been here, Mister Posey," she said to him one day. "Why is that?"

He looked wistful. "I wisht there wuz more, Sal. Nearest Army post is upriver to Mojave an' they don't git here much. Onliest soljer in town is Lootenant Tassin, th' quartermaster. He runs th' depot an' does Army business with th' Steam Comp'ny. Now an' agin one o' them orf'-cers frum up north comes t' fetch his wife an' kids off'n th' boat er put 'em on it, but they don't make much business fer me."

She noted that bit of information carefully and kept a wary eye for uniforms during her excursions with Dolores. Tom could have returned from Dakota by now and he might even be looking for her, but she doubted that. More likely, if he were back in Arizona, he was relieved to find her gone.

That realistic appraisal fed her bitterness but she had little time for brooding. She had reached the hard conclusion there was no place for her in Arizona. She had made up her mind to leave the Territory and she wanted no encounter with one of Tom's friends to complicate her going.

In February the weather turned bad, business at the restaurant fell off and so did her appetite. That had never happened before, even in the Apache camps, and it worried her. Then a child of one of Dolores' many cousins died and because it was a family in whose home she had been welcome she went with Dolores to the funeral.

The service in the little church with its tawdry paper and tinsel decorations was depressing but the procession to the cemetery was dreadful. Whether through poverty or custom there was no cart; the little body in its white shroud was carried on a rude bier. In front went a man with a homemade cross and next came two musicians— one with guitar, the other with a violin. Their music was indescribably mournful. They were followed by the bier and a knot of weeping women.

There was no wood in Ehrenberg to make coffins for poor people. The little body went into the grave in its shroud. A raw wind blew off the river and across the unenclosed cemetery, which was only a bare sandy spot on the bank, marked by a few stone cairns and a cross or two made of dried cactus stalks. There was not so much as a blade of grass.

Only half listening to the murmuring of the priest, Samantha looked about her and saw the reason for the piles of stones. At her feet was a hole littered with whitened bones. Because there were few coffins, dogs and coyotes dug up the newly buried dead unless the grave were covered with a cairn for protection.

It was Saturday again and that night she was miserable. Her head and throat ached and she could not get the funeral out of her mind. To add to her trouble, the *Gila* had dropped off a string of barges as she passed upriver and the town was full of roistering teamsters loading their wagons.

The Silver Dollar erupted hourly in violence. Men surged into Posey's demanding food and drink. In vain Thad insisted he served no drink and wanted none in his place. They brought it anyway. Dolores, red-eyed and sniffling from the funeral, fell hopelessly behind in the cooking. Making her way, arms full of dishes, to the kitchen, Samantha found her path blocked by a burly teamster.

"Hey! Ye're th' new girl, ain't ye? I heered about ye, girlie; whut's yer name?"

She pushed ineffectually with her elbow. "Let me by, please!"

"Aw, don't be like thet, sweetie! How 'bout a li'l drink, hey?" He thrust a glass under her nose and the smell of raw liquor gagged her.

"No! No, thank you. I want to get by, please."

"Hard-nose, ain't ye? Awright, but it'll cost ye, honey. Cost ye a kiss fer ol' Dan. C'mere to me!"

His arm swept her from her feet and dumped her on his knees, dishes crashing to the floor.

"Mister Posey!" she wailed.

"Haw!" bellowed her captor. "Who th' hell is Mister Posey?" He mouthed the name scornfully and tightened his grip on her waist. "Come on, gal . . . pucker up pretty now!"

"No!" she panted, pushing hard against his chest. "Let me go! Mister Posey!" Her cry for help was lost in the uproar.

"Sah-mahn-ta?"

She twisted violently in the teamster's grasp. His lean, brown face blank with surprise, Severiano stood behind her.

"What you do here, Sah-mahn-ta?"

"Who th' hell is that?" demanded the teamster belligerently. "Is that th' Posey you bin squallin' fer?" He peered over Samantha's shoulder.

"Hell's fahr! Tain't nuthin' but a greaser! Vamoose, kid!" He kicked out a booted foot and Severiano dodged.

"Leave her go," he said woodenly. A second kick caught him in the groin and knocked him sprawling.

"Haw . . . haw!" guffawed the teamster. "Haul ass, greaser, afore I break yer back!"

Severiano was up in a crouch, his face Apache, not Mexican. Something in his glittering eyes roused his tormentor to genuine anger.

"Ow . . . ouch! Stop it!" shrieked Samantha, squirming. His big hands had shifted from her waist to her breasts.

"How yuh like them apples, kid? That whut yew want?"

Severiano's hand came from behind him like a striking snake and the blade of his knife glittered in the lamplight.

"Gawdalmighty . . . he cut me!" Samantha hit the floor with a bump that jarred her teeth and the teamster was up and yelling, holding his hand and staring in amazement at the blood welling through his fingers.

"Thuh li'l sunnuvabitch cut me! Looka there! I'll kill yuh, yuh friggin' greaser!"

Others saw the knife in Severiano's hand and scrambled to give him room.

"Watch yer ass, Dan'l!" someone yelled. Hands pulled at Samantha's shoulders.

"Come on, missy . . . ye'll git hurt down there!"

Through a screen of legs she saw Severiano's face, frozen and deadly.

"Sal? Where are ye?" Posey was calling for her. An enormous, crushing blast exploded over her head and the acrid stink of burned powder seared her nostrils. She clapped her hands over her outraged ears.

"Jeez!" said a hushed voice.

"He hadda knife . . . y'all seen it! Th' sunnuvabitch cut me with it . . . lookit my hand!"

"Yeah, but Jeezus, Dan . . . !"

"Lemme through . . . move, dammit! Are ye all right, Sal?" It was Posey, red-faced and sweating.

"Oooh!" she moaned, holding her head in her hands.

"Whut in hell's goin' on here?" Thad Posey demanded. "Who's got that gun? Y'ain't s'posed to bring no gun in here! Who . . . ?" His voice trailed off in dismay. "Who done this?"

The nearest man was a soldier, staring curiously at Severiano.

"Did you shoot him?" Posey demanded furiously.

"Sure, an' it wasn't me, Mister!" He wore corporal's stripes and his broad Irish face was a study in innocence. "As ye kin plainly see I've got no gun." He spread his hands to show his empty belt. Posey's eyes raked the circle of men and found his answer in the slight shift away from the teamster.

"Dammit, he come at me with a knife! You don't 'spect me t' stand there an' jest lettim cut me, do ye?"

"Git th' marshal!" Posey raged. "Sumbuddy git th' marshal an' Mister, don't you move! Gimme that gun!"

Her ears ringing from the shot, Samantha pushed her way toward Posey and then saw Severiano.

"Oh . . . no!"

He stopped searching for the knife and his glazing eyes changed minutely when he saw her. His breath left him in a rustling gasp and he sat down cross-legged on the floor. Then he slumped over, curling up on his side.

"Oh, my God!" Samantha whimpered.

"Sally, will ye git outta here?"

"He was only trying to help me! Is he going to die?"

"How kin I tell with you in th' way?" Posey snapped at her. "Does anybuddy know where Doc Summers is at?"

"Oh . . . look!" cried Samantha. "Do something, quick!"

Severiano was shuddering convulsively. From beneath his body a trickle of blood crept across the dirt floor. Posey pushed Samantha away and turned the boy over gently. Severiano's face was neither Mexican nor Apache now, only hurt and puzzled.

"Sah-mahn-ta?" he whispered. Before she could answer his face twisted and his mouth gaped soundlessly.

"Oh, please do something!" she wailed. Someone turned her away roughly.

"Come on. You got no business watchin' that."

"Please . . ." She struggled weakly. "I want . . . ooh!" The floor tilted beneath her and she sagged to meet it.

"Yer gal's out like a light, Thad. Whut'll I do with her?"

"Gawd, I dunno! Whur's th' damned doctor? Put 'er in th' kitchen, I reckon."

"Out! Out av here, me bhoy!" muttered the corporal to a younger soldier pressing close behind him. " 'Tis no place fer th' likes av us." They edged out unnoticed just before the doctor and the sheriff arrived together. The doctor knelt by Severiano and shook his head.

"You don't need me for this one. Where's the other?"

Corporal Kelly and his buddy drifted up the street to another saloon in search of beer. They had come upriver on the *Gila* with a load of ammunition for Camp Lowell and Kelly was bound to get his fill of beer before they left the river with the wagons. He drained his glass in three long swallows and peered into it, frowning.

"Beer no good, Corp'l?"

"At four bits a flamin' bottle, lad, cud it be ought else? Nah . . . 'tis not th' beer that troubles me; 'tis that greaser bhoy. I ha' seen th' poor sod sum'ere afore an' fer th' very life av me, I cannot put a name to whur ut was."

"Jeez! That fella like t' blew 'im in half, di'nt he? Whut'll they do to 'im fer that, Corp'l . . . th' fella whut shot 'im?"

"Nought! Those barstids don't gie a tinker's damn fer a greaser kid." He scrubbed his forehead with his knuckles. "Damn me eyes, whur did I see 'im afore?"

Kelly was a dogged Irishman and he worried the problem as a dog worries a bone all the way back to Camp Lowell. Four days later he was acting sergeant of the guard, inspecting posts with Captain Sam Whitside, when the answer came to him.

"Sor?" he said. "Does th' cap'n remember th' breed bhoy we tuk out av th' mountains to ol' Sarn't Rooney's farm arter th' fight wid th' Apaches las' year?"

"The one who brought Mister Royal's girl from the Indian camp?"

"Yiss, sor. Th' very one."

"Why?"

"I saw th' poor lad killed in Ehrenberg a week past. He wuz mouthin' off t' one o' Tully's bully-bhoys abaht a ghurl, an' th' rascal shot 'im."

"Too bad! Mex gal?"

"No, sor. 'Twuz a white ghurl, hustlin' dishes in Thad Posey's rest'runt jist over th' way frum th' Silver Dollar saloon."

"You saw it happen?"

"Yiss, sor. I an' young Kaspar wuz there but I take oath, Cap'n, we'd no part in ut. We ghosted out o' there quick as a wink whin th' shootin' wuz done."

"That's smart, Kelly. Keep your nose clean and you're in line for your third stripe. Sergeant Moore tells me he'll retire when his hitch is up next month."

That night Sam Whitside dined with the Roches and the other guests included the Van Scivers. As the party was breaking up, Sam remembered Kelly's story.

"I forgot . . . I heard something that might interest you, Carp. Remember the breed kid who brought Tom Royal's girl out of the Apache camp last fall?"

"Sure," replied Carp. "I forget his name but I know the one you mean."

"Severiano," said Ellen softly. John Roche, who was holding Ellen's cloak for her, sighed. Instead of putting her arm into it, she had drawn closer to Whitside.

"What did you say, my dear?" Carp asked her.

"A man in my troop told me the kid was killed in Ehrenberg last week," Whitside continued.

"What a shame! How did it happen?"

"Seems he picked a fight with one of Tully's drivers over a girl . . . a white girl at that. All that fuss we made over him must have gone to his head. Ehrenberg's no place for a half-breed to make trouble over a white girl."

"Where in Ehrenberg, Sam?" Ellen asked.

"Lordy, I don't remember. I think Kelly said the Silver Dollar saloon. No! He did not . . . he said it happened in a hash house across the street from that hell hole. Excuse me, Ellen, but that's what it is."

She gave him a forgiving smile and became very gracious to her puzzled host, who was still holding out the cloak.

"Do forgive me, please, John! Here I am listening to Sam when I should be telling you what a lovely evening it has been."

"My dear Ellen, it has been all my pleasure. I'm glad you enjoyed it."

In the buggy she looked at Carp, eyes round and questioning. "How soon can we start?"

"We?"

"Of course!"

"Ellen, that's a rough trip in the buggy."

"We won't take the buggy. We'll have to take a Dougherty wagon so we can bring her back."

"What makes you so sure it's she . . . or that she'll come back?"

She put her arm through his and hugged it close. "There's only one way to find out, isn't there?"

FORTY-TWO

In the first week of March southern Arizona inched toward spring and though a few nights still brought frost there were days when the sun drove the thermometer to eighty. Camp Lowell seemed deserted, most of its garrison having been ordered south to patrol the border.

On the fourth of March, Apaches had struck the San Pedro Valley, sweeping west through Sonoita to the Santa Cruz River, and the Territory rocked with alarm. Government beef was scarce and stringy but free to its wards, and Geronimo had been enjoying this bounty for some weeks at the Ojo Caliente Indian Agency in New Mexico. Free beef was not enough. Reservation life was boring and from that sanctuary he erupted suddenly in a savage raid into Chihuahua and Sonora which proved so fruitless he concluded his rampage with a swing through Arizona.

It was not wholly unexpected. As early as January General Kautz had scented trouble and ordered Camp Bowie reinforced to mount more patrols along the New Mexico boundary. Lieutenant Tony Rucker stripped Bowie of its Indian scouts to comb the old Chiricahua reservation but Captain Worth's Tonto scouts from Camp Apache had to walk to work and it was mid-February before they arrived to thicken the screen. Geronimo slipped past Rucker and when B Troop of the Sixth Cavalry rode south to intercept him along the Santa Cruz River, his band of twenty or thirty warriors simply scattered, having killed or wounded eight farmers and run off eighty-five head of stock in four days of terror.

Governor Safford and his good friend the surveyor general of the Territory, who was also owner of Tucson's leading newspaper, the *Arizona Citizen,* at once joined forces to make political capital of the incident. As a matter of course, General Kautz and the United States Army were their chief culprits.

On the sixth of March the governor sent a message to the legislature, printed in full that same day in the *Citizen,* excoriating Kautz and calling for territorial militia to protect the people. Next day he petitioned Washington to remove Kautz from command. The legislature excitedly voted ten thousand dollars—which it did not have—to raise troops.

With his customary fanfare, John Clum provided soldiers ready-made. Forty-five of his Indian police under command of his assistant agent, Clay Beauford, marched from San Carlos to Tucson. Clum paraded his company before the governor's house and, to the delight of the spectators, put it through some creditable close-order drill ending with a rifle volley in salute. The Apaches were at once sworn into the service of the Territory.

The excitement subsided rather abruptly. Arizonans were growing disenchanted with Safford and the Ring and General Kautz weathered the storm once more. He was stung into giving his side of the case to the newspapers and the War Department twittered nervously but took no action against him. But Kautz, the good soldier, was not distracted by his victory. Quietly he moved two troops of cavalry to the border, where they set up a temporary camp in the foothills of the Huachuca Mountains.

Department headquarters created a temporary command to manage the effort, called the Tucson Military District, and Carp Van Sciver was assigned to it as Acting Assistant Adjutant General. It was popularly supposed that following Geronimo's raid a major operation would be mounted against him and the new District would be its base. Tate Hulse went with his troop to the camp in the Huachucas but there was constant communication between the camp and regimental headquarters at Camp Lowell and he found frequent opportunity to return there.

Ellen's hunch had led her to Samantha in Ehrenberg, though by the time she arrived there Dolores had removed her helper to the home of a relative. It was just as well that Ellen never saw the little room behind Thad Posey's kitchen. She was distressed enough by what she found. The big gray eyes in the thin face had not known her and it was obvious Samantha was very ill.

"Why didn't you go to the American officer at the depot?" Ellen stormed at Dolores.

"She don' like soljers!"

"Nonsense! Lieutenant Tassin would at least have brought a doctor."

"Doc Summers seen her," objected Thad Posey. "He said she done got remittent fever."

Ellen threw up her hands in despair. There had been an Army surgeon at Yuma but Tassin thought he was probably on the border with the troops now so Carp deemed it wiser to start at once for Camp Lowell rather than wait to find out. Dolores wept and Posey was vastly relieved. He considered himself fortunate Samantha was off his hands and his conscience before she died. He brought the carpetbag and a small, worn purse; heavy and clinking.

"It's all there, ma'am, ever nickel of it, an' I'd jest as lief ye count it if'n ye will."

"What in the world . . .?" Ellen gasped when she saw the coins. She wept when he explained.

Assistant Surgeon Girard, who had once examined an egg-sized lump on Samantha's head, peered into her throat and muttered about catarrh but when he learned where she had been living and how, he declared she had nothing more than violent dysentery compounded by influenza. Ellen fought them both with fresh eggs, beef broth and love and the color crept slowly back to Samantha's cheeks.

One evening just as the bugle sounded retreat and the guard took down the garrison flag there was a cheerful pounding at the Van Scivers' door and Ellen sighed. "Small wonder we can't keep Geronimo across the border when we can't even keep Tate Hulse down there to watch him. Did you know he was coming?"

Samantha shook her head and frowned. "How did you know?"

"Who else could it be? How many times has he been here since you came back?"

"I don't know. I wish . . ." Her voice trailed off and she caught her lower lip in her teeth.

"Sam?"

"Yes?"

"Look at me." Ellen touched the younger girl's cheek fondly. "Do you want to see Tate?"

"Why . . . I . . . yes, of course. I must."

"No. Not if you don't want to. It's time you stopped being so grateful to everyone and started thinking about yourself, you know."

Samantha dropped her eyes and her cheeks flamed but she said nothing. When Ellen opened the door, Tate greeted her happily but his eyes searched the hall beyond her.

"Are you absent without leave or have you found a fresh excuse to be here?" Ellen demanded of him.

"Madam, I am the bearer of diplomatic dispatches! Governor Pesquiera is worried about American troops so close to the Sonora border and has sent a note to General Kautz. I brought it."

"I'm surprised Tom Rafferty hasn't confined you to camp."

"Look." He held out a massive hammered silver bracelet with a lump of turquoise set crudely on the top.

"For me?" she teased him. "It's much too big. I'd have to wear it on my ankle."

"Now, Ellen, I can get it cut down for her. Where's Carp?"

"In Tucson, pretending to run the war. I expect him when I see him these days. I take it you're here for the night?"

"I have a room. Hanna said I could use his in the bachelor officers' quarters."

"Good. Listen, Tate . . ."

377

"Yes?"

"She said this morning that she wants to go back to Leavenworth. She asked Carp to find out if the railroad has crossed into Arizona yet."

His grin faded and he dropped his saddlebags in a corner of the hall. Ellen gestured toward the kitchen.

Samantha was stirring something in a bowl and she gave him a smile but did not stop. He dipped a finger and tasted it curiously.

"What is it?"

"Spoon bread for Carp and I'll thank you to keep your fingers out, sir!"

"Ellen didn't seem sure he's coming. You're getting to be quite a cook, aren't you?"

"I already was. You should taste my wood rat."

"Your what?"

"Wood rat. Catle loved it."

"Who in the devil is Catle?"

She shrugged. "An Apache I used to know."

She made a wry face as she said it but Tate was pleased that she could speak of her captivity thus. Ehrenberg had made her tougher in several ways, one of which had startled Ellen not many days before.

She had put off telling Samantha of Tom's death as long as she dared but as Samantha recovered it was inevitable someone would speak to her about it and Ellen did not want it to come that way. With considerable trepidation she had brought the telegram and the worn letter and to her lasting surprise, Samantha accepted both with no visible sign of emotion.

In fact, she did not speak of Tom or the letter again and the Van Scivers concluded it was not a subject for discussion. Carp broke this rule only once to mention that Tom's belongings were still at Camp Grant because Major Compton was unsure where to send them.

"His family should have them, of course," Samantha said quietly.

The days passed and they lost count of the excuses Tate Hulse found to come to Lowell. He never failed to see Samantha when he came. Ellen was puzzled. There was about him the air of a young man in love but if that were so, she wished he would voice it. Perhaps Samantha's renewed determination to leave Arizona would move him to it and that thought was in her mind when she warned him and sent him to the kitchen with his Navajo bracelet.

"I brought you a present, Sam."

"Oh, Tate, isn't it pretty! Let me wipe my hands, I want to look at it." She studied the heavy bracelet admiringly.

"I know it's too big. Ellen says you'll have to wear it on your ankle like a Cocopah girl."

"I knew a Cocopah girl once. Her name was Suzy."

"Funny name for a Cocopah. You'll have to tell me about her someday."

"You wouldn't like it."

"Then don't tell me. Sam . . .?"

"Yes?"

"Ellen says you're thinking of going back East."

"Of course." She put the bracelet carefully on the table and looked up at him. "Did you think I was not?"

"I guess I didn't think. I guess . . ." He scrubbed his chin roughly with his hand. "I don't want you to go, Sam."

"But that's . . . impossible, Tate."

He took her shoulders gently in his big hands. "No, it's not. You know what I want, don't you?"

She looked into his eyes gravely. There was no reason to pretend she did not know. She took his hands from her shoulders and held them together in her own. "Yes, I think I do." She frowned. "Tate, you've been very good to me. I don't want to hurt you."

"There's only one way you can hurt me, Sam, and that's to refuse me."

"Oh, Tate, don't . . . it can't be. Tom . . ."

"I'm not Tom!" he interrupted.

"I know that. But Tom thought . . ."

"I don't care what he thought," he interrupted again. "The longer I knew him the less I understood him and at the end I didn't understand him at all."

She sighed. "Did you know he wrote to me before he was killed?"

"Yes. Ellen told me there was a letter for you."

"He said he had written before but I never got it. Perhaps it was with the mail carrier you told me the Indians killed."

"Would it have made a difference . . . if you had got it?"

"How could I know? Perhaps if I had heard from him while I was still in Tucson a lot of things would have been different. What does it matter now?"

"It doesn't. I shouldn't have asked. You don't ever have to explain that to me. What happened to you and Tom doesn't concern me."

She must have looked unbelieving for he leaned across the table until it creaked under his weight. His usually cheerful face was so serious she was startled.

"I mean that, Sam. It's important. You've got to believe me."

She considered him gravely, aware that his seriousness demanded a careful response from her. It was possible, she conceded. Everything in her experience of him told her that. But could she accept it?

"All right. I believe you, Tate. But that's only part of it."

"You mean DeBergh? Forget it! I had a talk with Henry."

She had not meant DeBergh at all and her eyes flashed. What right had he to question DeBergh about her? "But isn't that digging up the past?"

"Not at all. I was only trying to find out where you'd gone. I didn't ask him why. He told me but I didn't ask him. You know, Henry thinks a lot of you, Sam."

That took her completely aback until she realized he couldn't mean it the way it struck her. Then she giggled.

"I hope he's broadened his outlook a little!"

Tate grinned in response. "I'd say so. Henry's not a bad soul and we agree completely on one thing anyway."

"And what, pray tell, is that?"

"Our taste in women."

"That's indecent!"

He was grinning broadly now. "When you marry me

we'll have Henry and the widow Herscholdt to the wedding."

"I can't marry you, Tate!"

"Can't or won't? There's a big difference."

"Look . . ." She put her hands in his again. "Look what I did to Tom. I can't do that to you and I won't."

"Listen to me, Sam! You didn't do anything to Tom. What happened to him wasn't your fault. What on earth makes you think you could 'do something' to me? I know how *I* feel and nothing can change that."

She shook her head. "Maybe so, Tate. But what about me? I'm responsible for his death."

"No! Whatever Tom Royal was running from would have caught up with him somewhere else if it hadn't found him on the Yellowstone."

"But he wasn't running from me any more. He was trying to get back to me. He said so in his last letter. He was looking for a general named Miles and he was going to transfer to Miles' regiment and then come back for me. He must have been looking for him when he was killed."

"He was never running from you! It was something else. Do you honestly think he'd have been happy if he had to transfer to another regiment somewhere in Montana before he could marry you?"

He was cornering her; breaking down her defenses with awful logic. She had refused to face that question honestly so she had no answer for it. She would not accept it from Tate.

"Stop it!" she whispered, evading his eyes. "You're only tormenting yourself and me. Why are you so different? What makes you think you can live with something Tom couldn't?"

He would not accept defeat. "Because it's a simple fact and I'm going to make you see it. I don't know what happened to you up there in those mountains and I don't care . . . no, look at me, Sam!" He turned her face with a gentle, insistent finger.

"I think you're alive now because of what you did then and that's all I need to know . . . all I want to know. Will you believe that?"

She could only look at him helplessly. Then the front door slammed distantly and she ducked away from his finger on her chin. "Carp's home," she said in a muffled voice. "He'll want his supper."

"All right." His eyes twinkled. "I can wait. But promise me something, Sam?"

"Ummn?"

"Don't run away again without giving me an answer. I can't stay here to watch you and I don't want to chase you all the way to Leavenworth."

"I . . . I promise." She was stirring the spoon bread again and he could hardly hear her. His arms circled her waist, turning and lifting her close against him. The spoon dripped unheeded on his shoulder. He left her no room for escape and she sought none. She gave him her lips and the gentle hunger of his kiss left her aching and unsteady.

"What did you say, Sam?"

"I said, I promise. Let me go now!" The sureness in his eyes, the glad assurance, made her heart beat suffocatingly.

"Thank the Lord for small favors," Carp grumbled when Tate appeared in the front hall. "I take it there is hope for supper?"

"You bet! Spoon bread . . . just for you."

"I can see that. You've got it all over you. Why don't you clean up and we'll have a drink. To celebrate supper."

CURRENT BESTSELLERS
from POPULAR LIBRARY

The Legends of the Old West
Live On in Fawcett Westerns

☐	LITTLE BIG MAN by Thomas Berger	23854	$2.95
☐	HONDO by Louis L'Amour	14255	$1.75
☐	HE RODE ALONE by Steve Frazee	14103	$1.75
☐	NOW HE IS LEGEND by Gordon D. Shirreffs	14233	$1.50
☐	SWEENY'S HONOR by Brian Garfield	24330	$1.95
☐	THE TALL STRANGER by Louis L'Amour	14218	$1.95
☐	RETURN TO ARAPAHOE by Charles N. Heckelmann	04590	$1.75
☐	CROSSFIRE TRAIL by Louis L'Amour	14276	$1.75